CHURCHILL'S HOUR

CHURCHILL'S HOUR

MICHAEL DOBBS

'One of the most misleading factors in history
is the practice of historians to build a story exclusively
out of the records which have come down to them.'
WINSTON CHURCHILL

HarperCollins*Publishers*

This is a work of fiction.
Apart from well-known historical figures and events,
the names, characters and incidents portrayed in
it are the work of the author's imagination.
Any resemblance to actual persons, living or dead,
events or localities is entirely coincidental.

HarperCollins*Publishers*
77–85 Fulham Palace Road,
Hammersmith, London W6 8JB

www.harpercollins.co.uk

Published by HarperCollins*Publishers* 2004
1 3 5 7 9 8 6 4 2

A catalogue record for this book
is available from the British Library

ISBN 0 00 718304 6
ISBN 0 00 719401 3 (trade pbk)

Typeset in Meridien by Palimpsest Book Production Limited,
Polmont, Stirlingshire

Printed and bound in Great Britain by
Clays Limited, St Ives plc

TO WILL.
TO MIKEY.
TO ALEX.
TO HARRY.
MY FOUR MUSKETEERS.

'We shall go on to the end. We shall fight in France, we shall fight on the seas and oceans, we shall fight with growing confidence and growing strength in the air. We shall defend our island, whatever the cost may be. We shall fight on the beaches, we shall fight on the landing grounds, we shall fight in the fields and in the streets, we shall fight in the hills. We shall never surrender.

'And even if, which I do not for a moment believe, this island or a large part of it were subjugated and starving, then our Empire beyond the seas, armed and guarded by the British Fleet, would carry on the struggle, until, in God's good time, the new world, with all its power and might, steps forth to the rescue and the liberation of the old.'

WINSTON CHURCHILL, June 1940

'I have said this before, but I shall say it again and again and again. Your boys are not going to be sent into any foreign wars.'

FRANKLIN D. ROOSEVELT, October 1940

ONE

Christmas Day, 1940.

Winston Churchill sat propped up against the pillows of his bed. The room was cold, a sullen December sky rattling at the mullioned window, but the old man didn't complain. The foul weather had kept the bombers at bay last night. Peace on earth, at least until tomorrow.

A servant entered the room carrying a pair of freshly ironed trousers on one arm and a silver tray on the other. Frank Sawyers was short, hairless, with piercing blue eyes and two missing teeth. He was no more than forty years in age yet his attitude was timeless.

'Did you knock?' Churchill's brow was split by a crease of irritation.

'As always, zur,' Sawyers said, a trifle wearily and with a pronounced lisp and Cumbrian burr.

'And what's that disgusting green stuff?' The Prime Minister took off his reading glasses and used them to indicate the jar on the silver tray. 'No medicine, do you hear me? I'll have none of your quackery. I'm not ill.'

'Chutney. Home-made. By way of me Christmas present to yer, like. With season's greetings.'

Churchill stared at the jar, his blue eyes alert as though suspecting some plot. Sawyers had a knack of producing exotic and unexpected gifts, even through the constraints of wartime, and Churchill knew that no matter how alarming the sour green pickle might appear, it would taste delicious. He didn't have the knack himself; he'd given only books for presents, and mostly his own books at that.

As he approached the bed, the servant glared at Nelson, the patch-eyed cat who lay sprawled across the eiderdown at Churchill's feet. Nelson possessed a foul temper that had grown ever more unreliable from spending too many nights in Downing Street during the air raids, and Sawyers' loathing for the cat had grown with the number of scratch marks left on the back of his hands. He gave the beast a wide berth as he placed the tray on the bedside table and dealt with the refreshed trousers. Then he took down a vivid red silk bathrobe that was hanging on the back of the door.

'Not yet,' Churchill said, 'I've not finished my papers.'

'You'll be late,' the other man insisted. 'Family's already gathered round fire, and if you're not down there soon, Mr Oliver will be on serenading us all with his piano music.'

'Bloody racket.'

'Exactly,' Sawyers agreed, holding up the bathrobe in the manner of a matador tempting a bull.

'Not now, not now,' Churchill said, shaking the paper in his hand. 'D'you know there's a Nazi battleship on the loose in the southern Atlantic?'

'I dare say it'll still be there after luncheon.' The servant stood resolute. 'You can sink it then.'

Churchill was contemplating the next phase of this battle for domestic supremacy when, in some distant part of the old house, notes began to cascade from a piano and a baby started to cry. Instantly Nelson sprang from his warming place at the old man's feet, arching his back in displeasure before strutting from their view. Churchill had been deserted by his last remaining ally. Sawyers barely stirred. Only the rustle of the silk robe and the elevation of the left eyebrow suggested he was claiming victory.

Churchill cursed. His concentration was broken and nothing more would be achieved that morning. He had lost the battle of the bathrobe. He heaved himself from his bed, scattering papers in his wake, and, ignoring his servant, stomped off in the direction of the bathroom.

It was known as Chequers Court, an age-mellowed manor house constructed of red brick and surrounded by parklands and beech woods in the Chiltern hills, some forty miles to the north-west of London. It was graced by ambitious chimneys, loose windows and a system of heating that, in deference to the ancient timbers, remained totally inadequate. Chequers had once belonged to Mr and Mrs Arthur Lee, who had no children and therefore no lasting use for the property, so in 1921 they had handed it over to the nation complete with all its furniture and fine paintings as a country retreat for whoever was Prime Minister of the day. A year earlier the occupant had been Neville Chamberlain, a proud but inadequate man who remained mercifully unaware that the dogs of misfortune were already on his trail and would soon tear him apart. Calamity had got him first, then cancer, and only six weeks ago they had buried him. Dust to dust. So the keys had been passed to Winston Churchill, who had summoned three generations of his family to spend Christmas with him in his new retreat. It was to be a special occasion, one that everyone present would remember, although, in hindsight, not for all the most comforting reasons.

Sawyers had risen before six that morning to make sure that everything was in proper festive order. The fire in the

Great Hall had been lit, the boilers stoked, the baths run, breakfast served in the bedrooms, the great dinner prepared on a scale that was prodigious. Hitler's U-boat campaign in the Atlantic was supposed to be starving the country into submission, but the German Fuehrer had apparently failed to take into consideration the legendary Mrs Landemare, who was in charge of the Chequers kitchen. She was short, exceedingly stout, and married to a renowned French chef, but her prime loyalty was directed towards the Prime Minister, whose gastronomic demands were notorious. Breakfast was taken in bed and often consisted of chops as well as bacon and a glass of something red, while what followed throughout the day would have left the regulators at the Ministry of Food reeling in horror. There wasn't supposed to be much food around, but Churchill had a lot of good friends, and so did Mrs Landemare. As a consequence the huge bleached wooden table that ran down the centre of the kitchen was now piled high like that of a medieval court. The first course – an entire smoked salmon, half a dozen lobsters and several pots of duck terrine – had been provided by parliamentary colleagues, all anxious to display their loyalty and show off the extent of their country estates. The dessert that sat at the end of the table was a thick-crusted pie filled with apples from the orchards at Churt, the home of a previous Prime Minister, David Lloyd George. Churchill's own family home at Chartwell had been the source of most of the fresh vegetables, sent up by train, while as usual Mrs Landemare had made up any shortfall from the contacts she maintained below the stairs of several other country estates. But the pride of place in this year of famine was occupied by the turkey – an enormous beast, sent on the instructions of the dying Viscount Rothermere as one of his last mortal acts, perhaps in repentance for the appalling things his newspapers had often written about Churchill. It had been plucked, stuffed, basted, and was now roasting under the watchful eye and moist brow of the blessed Mrs Landemare.

'Unusual large, cook,' Sawyers had said as he'd watched her thrusting chestnut stuffing deep inside the bird.

Mrs Landemare had given a defiant twirl of her white cap to keep the perspiration from dripping into her eyes. 'What were you expecting me to give him for his Christmas dinner? Toast? Anyhows, Mr S, we might find there's even a couple of mouthfuls left over for the likes of us.'

'Wouldn't want it to go wasting, cook,' he'd said. 'I might even be able to find a bottle of something to go with it, like.'

'You are a man after my own heart, Mr Sawyers, so you are,' she had exclaimed, smiling. She didn't mean it, of course. Sawyers was unmarried and always would be – 'a gentleman's gentleman, one of those who lisps to port,' as she would explain it to friends, 'but there's nobody else on God's earth who can deal with Mr Winston the way that he can.'

And so long as Mr Winston was happy, he wouldn't miss an occasional bottle. Ah, but as for Mr Randolph, the son, he was altogether another matter . . .

Randolph Churchill, the sole, much-excused and overindulged son of the Prime Minister had been expected to arrive at Chequers the previous evening, Christmas Eve, but a hurried phone call had offered some vague excuse about pressing duties – easy enough to concoct, given his status as an officer in No. 8 Commando and a newly elected Member of Parliament. But Sawyers was sceptical. The younger Churchill hardly ever passed through his constituency and his regiment was notorious for its careless habits; the only landmark Randolph and his fellow officers could be relied upon to hit while on exercise was the officers' mess. That, in Sawyers' eye, was not enough to condemn him – it seemed little more than aristocratic excess, the pampering of the privileged class – but there were other reasons why Sawyers reserved for 'his master's little echo' the contempt that only servants can manage to keep out of sight of others. The first was the man's spitefulness. It wasn't for Sawyers to moralize if Randolph decided to spend the night his son was born in the arms of another man's wife, but to make it so blatantly obvious was unnecessarily cruel. Like burning beetles. And there was a more personal reason. Even after all the years Sawyers had served his father, after the many times he'd been forced to help the son to his bed, take off his soiled clothes, clean up after his excesses, he knew that Randolph didn't even know his first name. Didn't care. Wasn't important. For the younger Churchill, Sawyers was as insignificant and expendable as old orange peel.

He arrived that morning, shortly before his father came down and while the rest of the family including his young wife Pamela was gathered round the log fire, singing carols. He appeared, dark-eyed, dishevelled, and told them he had spent the night on some railway station platform waiting for his train. That was possible, as a matter of fact, but doubtful as a matter of habit. Hardship wasn't Randolph's style. But Sawyers would find out where he'd been sleeping, given a few days. The network that operated below the stairs of all fashionable homes – the same one that made up for any short-ages in Mrs Landemare's kitchen – would also make up for any shortcomings in Randolph's explanation. The man simply didn't realize that the servants knew. Could tell whether a bed had been slept in, by how many and to what purpose. The telltale signs on a freshly laundered sheet were as clear to a chambermaid's eye as an elephant's rump, and if the chambermaid knew, the news would get round the scullery faster than a mouse.

Yet, for the moment, there was harmony. Sawyers stood guard as the family sang their carols, led by the old man, who had a voice that sounded as if it had been broken on a capstan. It was as close as Churchill got nowadays to his son-in-law, Vic Oliver, who was playing the piano. Oliver had never truly been part of the Churchill family scene; he was a music-hall comedian who had been born an Austrian and who was now a naturalized American citizen. It was difficult to count the number of reasons why Churchill held reservations about him: he was brash, he was so much older than Churchill's daughter, Sarah, he had been married twice before. He also preferred to crack jokes for a living when in Churchill's view he should have been cracking German skulls. Oliver used words like 'cute' and 'Britisher'. In retribution, Churchill had given him a copy of Fowler's *Dictionary of Modern English Usage*. But mostly Churchill's antipathy was because of the effect Oliver had on Sarah. She had always been a perfectionist, desperate for applause and approval – it was one of the reasons why she had become an actress – yet she could never persuade herself that she merited any measure of her success. She had rushed into marriage, but it had only caused her sense of inadequacy to grow worse. She was beautiful but fragile, while Oliver was domineering. It had left her limping like a butterfly with a broken wing.

The eldest daughter was Diana. She had the same blue eyes and auburn hair of Sarah, inherited from their father, yet Diana was as reticent as her father was extrovert, as sensitive as he was bullish. When the Churchill family was at play, to most outsiders it seemed as though they were at war, and at such moments Diana would withdraw to the sidelines and wait to tend the casualties. Her husband, Duncan Sandys, was constructed of sterner stuff. He was a Member of Parliament and a colonel on active duty, and she clearly

7

adored him, but marriage was never an easy option in the Churchill family.

Only Mary, the youngest, seemed completely at ease, more down to earth than any of them, her family path beaten flat by the struggles of those who had gone before. As they exchanged presents, they fussed over Pamela's baby, Churchill's first grandchild, still only ten weeks old, and when it was time for the King's radio broadcast they stood for the National Anthem, then sat on the edge of their seats as they waited for one of his terrible stutters to tangle his words – all except Randolph, who relaxed in the folds of his armchair with a whisky. But His Majesty didn't falter, announcing that his countrymen could look forward to the New Year with sober confidence. Well, some of them, at least.

When the King had finished they were at last released to the dining room. 'Pour the wine, Sawyers!' the old man instructed. As the first dribble of golden liquid fell into his glass, he grabbed the bottle, trying to decipher the label. 'Where are my reading glasses, Sawyers? What have you done with them?'

'I suspect you'll find 'em in yer top pocket.'

'Dammit,' Churchill said, fumbling for his elusive glasses, 'so what is this you're trying to poison us with?'

'An excellent hock. A gift to yer from Mrs Chamberlain. From the late Prime Minister's personal cellar.'

'German, is it?'

'That's right. Given him by an admirer.'

'Ah, one of von Ribbon-top's bottles, I'll be bound.'

'I'll throw it away, then.'

'Steady on, it's a pre-Nazi vintage, I'll say that much for it,' Churchill said, peering at the label. 'A shame to get rid of it before we've had a chance to taste it. So damn the Fuehrer and pour, Sawyers. What are you waiting for, man?'

'Damn the Fuehrer, zur.' The servant moved along the table, filling glasses and condemning the Fuehrer at every turn, ignoring the scowls of Clementine who, even after so many years of enduring blasphemy at her table, still insisted on showing her displeasure.

'And God save us from the bloody Bolsheviks,' Churchill added, pulling apart a lobster.

A considerable quantity of Mr Chamberlain's hock had been tested by the time Sawyers brought in the turkey, laid out upon a huge wooden carving dish.

'A fine specimen, Sawyers,' Churchill pronounced, nodding at the bird.

'Indeed, zur.' The servant sharpened the carving knife as Mrs Landemare and a maid carried in dishes of vegetables.

Randolph took the opportunity to raise his glass in mock salute. '*Meleagris gallopavo*. The turkey. About the only useful thing the Americans ever sent us. That and tobacco.' He swallowed deep. 'Such a fundamentally useless nation.'

'Randolph!' his mother snapped in reproach. 'You forget. Your grandmother was American.'

'And we shouldn't attack those who extend the hand of friendship,' his father warned, more softly, but the son swirled the green liquid in his glass as though to excite the argument. The rest of them knew what to expect. Sawyers stared in warning at Mrs Landemare and the maid, who vanished like ghosts at dawn.

'It seems to me a strange sort of friendship, Papa, that ends up with our pockets being picked and our Empire held to ransom.'

'That is a wholly reprehensible remark.'

'And holy fact. You know it is. They've bled us dry. Filched every last penny from our pockets until we're practically bankrupt.'

9

'Please don't argue with your father, not today,' Clementine said, knowing her words would prove entirely useless.

'Mama, we are penniless. Quite literally. Not a bean.'

'You always exaggerate, Randolph.'

'Papa, please tell Mama what happened when you wrote to Roosevelt the other week to tell him our reserves were exhausted.'

Churchill looked in despair at the turkey.

'Papa, please . . .' Randolph insisted.

'Shall I carve, zur?' Sawyers said, forcing his way into the conversation. 'A bit o' leg, Mr Randolph, or do you prefer breast?'

But the younger Churchill was not to be diverted.

'Mama, we told the President we had next to nothing left, down to our last fifty million in gold. So what did he do, this so-called friend of ours? He sent one of his own destroyers to South Africa to collect the entire bloody lot. He thinks Papa is Santa Claus!'

'We owed him the money for war matériel. He was in a most difficult position,' Churchill began defensively. But already Randolph was rushing past him.

'No, Papa. *We* are in the difficult position. And he takes advantage of us.'

'He is a great friend.'

'Gossip on the circuit is he doesn't even like you.'

'You may deal in gossip, Randolph, but I must deal in hard facts!' Churchill responded irritably.

'And the fact is, Papa, that we've paid him every last shekel, and he sends us nothing but junk.'

'Destroyers. He sends us destroyers,' Clemmie intervened.

'Junk!' Randolph spat. 'The only ships he sends us are rust buckets from the last war which are so old they're already obsolete. Do you know, Mama, that before we get them they have to be officially certified by the US Navy as being useless? And they bloody are.'

'The President has to operate within the laws of his country and under the eye of a sceptical Congress,' Churchill responded. 'His hands are tied.'

'Papa, Papa.' The son raised his own hands in operatic despair. 'The time for excuses is gone. That might have washed while he was running for re-election, but now he's won. Back in the White House for another four years. Roosevelt is tied by nothing but his own timidity.'

'His people do not want war.'

'Our own people don't want war!' Randolph banged the table in anger. 'We seem to have got it nonetheless.'

Churchill chewed on his unlit cigar. As so often, buried in the midst of his son's excess lay an unwholesome chunk of truth, like gristle running through meat. Roosevelt had promised his people peace, had told the mothers of America again and again – and then again – that their boys were not going to be sent to any foreign war. It was politics, of course, democracy at its most base, the lowest common denominator, but there came a point where you judged a man not simply by his words but by his habits. And it worried Churchill more deeply than he cared to admit how the US President had fallen into the habit of ignoring his messages. His silences could no longer be explained away as electoral distraction, that was now gone, the barrier surmounted, yet since the election a few weeks earlier there had been a remarkable chill in the wind that had blown from Washington. Roosevelt hadn't even replied to Churchill's telegram of congratulation, and his debt-collecting methods had come to resemble those of an Irish landlord rather than a Christian friend. And that was the point, for Churchill clung to his view that he was fighting not just for the narrow interests of Britain but on

11

behalf of a shared cultural tradition that crossed the Atlantic and stretched back two thousand years and more. Yet Roosevelt would have none of it. It seemed America wanted only to be paid.

'Carve the bloody turkey, Sawyers,' Churchill said. 'And let's pretend it's Christmas.'

Arguments over lunch were nothing new and Christmas still had many hours to go in the Churchill household, yet it was never fully to recover its spirit. Indeed, the day was eventually to founder completely, ruined by events that had taken place some weeks beforehand and in another part of the world.

The SS *Automedon* had set sail from Liverpool on 24 September 1940, bound for Singapore and Shanghai with a beggar's muddle of a cargo consisting of crated aircraft, motor cars, machine parts, cigarettes and many cases of whisky. It seemed likely to be an unexceptional voyage.

She wasn't a ship of much note in anybody's logbook, a twenty-year-old ocean workhorse with a tall funnel, a single screw and a crew of English officers helped out by mostly Chinese deckhands. By mid-November the *Automedon* was some two hundred and fifty miles off the coast of Sumatra when, late one night, her radio operator picked up a distress call from a Norwegian merchant vessel. The signal said that she was being followed by an unknown ship; a little later the Norwegian reported that she had been stopped, after which – nothing. Total silence. It was a strange incident, but these were strange times and the affair caused more curiosity than concern to the *Automedon*'s Captain Ewan. However, it was enough to ensure that when an unidentified ship appeared at first light some distance off the port bow, Ewan spent a considerable time peering through his binoculars at the vessel. The stranger was flying a Dutch flag, innocent enough, and Ewan could see what looked like women hanging out washing on lines stretched across the foredeck. She was drawing slowly closer. McEwan concluded that the vessel was a friendly merchantman, much like dozens of others the *Automedon* had passed since leaving Liverpool.

They were on parallel courses and only a couple of thousand yards apart when the new vessel suddenly increased speed and identified herself as the German raider *Atlantis*. At the same moment, she fired a warning shot across Ewan's bow. He had been duped. He immediately ordered his radio operator to send a distress signal, so the *Atlantis* began to pour round after round into the *Automedon* in a desperate attempt to prevent the signal being completed and her location discovered. The German assault was totally successful. After being hit twenty-eight times in less than three minutes, the *Automedon* lay listing and defenceless, her radio silenced, her captain killed on his bridge and her fate entirely unknown to the wider world. The Kriegsmarine had claimed one more victim.

The *Automedon* was a small ship, little more than seven thousand tons, yet in time her loss was to change the course of the war. Indeed, in time, it would change the world.

None of this was known to the Churchills when, around midnight, they gathered in the Long Gallery, a room filled with the smell of smoke and old books that stretched along the north front of Chequers to form its library. That night, behind its blackout curtains, it had been transformed into a makeshift cinema.

'You shall sit beside me, Pamela,' Churchill said to his daughter-in-law, patting the seat next to him on the sofa while the others searched around to find themselves comfortable perches, all except for Clemmie, a most reluctant participant in any of her husband's late-night frolics, who had long since bidden them farewell and departed for her bed.

'A special treat for Christmas,' Churchill told Pamela, as Sawyers erected the screen and fussed over the projector. 'There is a friend of mine, Mr Alexander Korda, a Hungarian who makes very fine films. He and I are much alike. He loves cigars. He is often broke. And he is always impeccably dressed.'

Pamela wanted to giggle. She doubted if Mr Korda had gravy stains running down the lapels of his jacket.

'He has sent me his most recent work,' her father-in-law continued. 'It's not yet been released to the public. It's about Horatio Nelson. I've even given Mr Korda some advice on the matter – oh, just a few words here and there to place in the admiral's mouth.' He waved his brandy glass in a simulation of modesty, and began to address her as though she were a public audience. 'You know, at the opening of the last century when Napoleon's armies dominated the continent, the people in these islands of ours fought on alone for many years. At times it seemed impossible that they should prevail, until Nelson rallied them to the cause. Now it seems that history wishes to repeat its great cycle, and once more we search for our Nelson.'

'Some of us think we've already found him,' she replied, smiling and taking his soft hand.

His eyes began to mist. 'You know, my dear, you are a most unusual pearl. I shall never know how Randolph found you, let alone persuaded you to marry him.'

Perhaps it was better that the old man never knew. The truth was that Randolph had picked Pamela up on a blind date and proposed to her the following night. Married six weeks later, just as war had broken out. It was only afterwards that she discovered she was the eighth woman he'd pursued with the prospect of marriage in less than a month. Oh, it was one of those things that happened in wartime. For young soldiers such as Randolph, war had a brutal simplicity. They expected to die, so every long night, every available woman, was taken as their last. They didn't so much embrace the moment as grab it in both hands, and in the rush the common standards and decencies were often thrown to one side. But the British were ridiculously inept at the soldierly traditions of rape and pillage, so instead they hurried to churches and register offices, hoping to find in their marriage beds something that was worth fighting and dying for.

But Randolph hadn't died. He was there in an armchair, picking his nose and demanding another drink from the ubiquitous Sawyers. Yet for all his shortcomings he had introduced her to a new world that took her breath away. Eighteen months ago Pamela had been an unsophisticated teenager from rural Dorset with nothing more on her mind than flower arranging and the occasional midnight fumble with a taxi tiger; now she found herself at the epicentre of a war. When she had first met Randolph, his father had been an outsider, distrusted by his colleagues and despised by many, yet now he was the Prime Minister, and that made everyone in the family a target. He'd warned them all. If the Germans invaded, he had told them, they should fight to the very end. 'With bullets, with bayonets,' he had declared.

'But, Papa,' she had said, 'I don't know how to use a gun.'

'Then go to the kitchen and find a carving knife! You know how to use a carving knife, don't you, woman?'

He could be such a little boy at times. Perhaps that was why they got on so well. They could both still enjoy the enthusiasms of being children, she because she hadn't yet grown up, and he because in some ways he never would.

'Enough time-wasting, Sawyers,' he now told the valet. 'Out with the bottle and on with the show!'

'It's on table beside yer.'

'What is?'

'Yer brandy.'

'Ah, what a charming coincidence. Then what are you waiting for?'

Lights were switched off until there was nothing but the glow of the wood-stoked fire and the flickering of the film. Soon they were immersed in the tale of Nelson and his mistress, Emma Hamilton, a dancer and woman of questionable virtue who came to captivate the warrior's heart. The actress was Vivien Leigh.

'She is extraordinarily beautiful,' Churchill whispered in Pamela's ear. 'So very much like you.'

Beside her on the sofa, Pamela felt the old man melt as England was shown friendless, alone, its armed forces denied supplies, with nothing to eat, a country fighting for its survival and little other than one man's determination to keep it from succumbing. Yet, as Emma pointed out, England seemed so insignificant, 'just a tiny little bit' on the globe compared with the might of the enemy that had spread so far across the map of Europe. Her eyes lit up with wonder as she was told in reply: '. . . there are always men who, for the sake of their insane ambition, want to destroy what other people have built. And therefore this "tiny little bit" has to send out its ships again and again to fight those who want to dictate their will to others.'

Pamela felt her hand being squeezed with almost painful force as the words showered from the screen upon Churchill. She knew they were the words that he had written.

So the images flickered and the ships went out once more to confront the European tyrant, willing to be blown to bits in the hope that the enemy would be pulverized to even smaller pieces. England expected it of them. Then Nelson, mortally wounded at the moment of his supreme triumph, paid the price that freedom so often demands.

'Thank God I have done my duty,' he gasped, his words melting into the strains of 'Rule Britannia' and shouts of victory from those Englishmen who had survived.

In the glow of the firelight, Pamela could see tears streaming down the old man's face. They were still there when the last foot of film had passed through the gate and was clattering around its reel.

'That is how I should like to die,' Churchill whispered. 'Such a fine ending.'

She knew he was being completely sincere.

He disappeared into the folds of a huge silk handkerchief. Pamela decided it would be ungracious to point out that he'd noticed only the Boy's-Own bits of the film and that the final moments had concerned themselves not with the glories of Nelson's death but with the demise many years later of Emma as an ageing alcoholic sprawled piteously on the wet cobbles of some foreign port. It wasn't just the men who paid a price in war.

The clocks had long since chimed two. Sawyers damped down the fire. The filmgoers were stretching their legs and preparing to depart for bed when, from somewhere in the distance, the sound of a motor-car engine carried on the frozen night air. Churchill suddenly grew still. A change came over him, like a dog sensing danger that he couldn't yet identify. But a motor car meant a new message, and on this day and at this time of night, the message could mean only one thing.

Disaster.

*   *   *

'Couldn't it wait?' the old man enquired, his voice beginning to rasp with fatigue and anxiety. But he already knew the answer. Sir Stewart Menzies, known simply as 'C' in the corridors of power, was the head of Churchill's Secret Intelligence Service. It made him one of the most powerful men in the country; he hadn't dropped by at two in the morning simply for the large whisky and cold grate that greeted him in the Hawtrey Room.

'I'm sorry, Prime Minister.' Churchill's spymaster unlocked a briefcase and extracted a slim manila folder, which he placed on the table and smoothed open. 'You won't have heard of the *Automedon*, I suspect. No reason why you should. But it's been sunk by the Nazis.'

Churchill glared defiantly, waiting for the bullet to strike him.

'It happened last month, on her way to Singapore. Small cargo of car bits, cigarettes, whisky, that sort of thing.'

'I suspect the distilleries will be able to resupply them,' Churchill responded slowly, hoping words might quell the sense of unease that was rising up his gullet.

'She was boarded before she was sunk, several of her crew killed, including the captain, and the rest captured and taken to the Japanese port of Kobe. They were disembarked in Kobe while waiting to be loaded onto another German ship. That's when one of our agents managed to speak briefly to members of the crew. We've been able to confirm their identity and . . .' – he paused, steadying himself – 'we have no reason to disbelieve their story.'

'Which is?'

'While the German boarding party was on board the *Automedon*, they discovered the ship's safe in the strong room. They blew it open. Got everything inside it. Decoding tables, maps of harbour defences, minefields, intelligence reports, the lot.'

18

'Such material is the currency of war. This surely amounts to little more than loose change.'

But Menzies was shaking his head. 'That's not it, I'm afraid. While they were making their tour of the ship, they also found the body of an Admiralty courier. Beside him was one of our security bags. It seems he was in the process of throwing it overboard when . . . Well, he didn't make it. Neither did the bag.'

Churchill knew of these bags. Green canvas, with brass eyelets to allow the water in and lead weights sewn inside to ensure that the bag and its contents sank quickly to the bottom of the ocean. The couriers were instructed to defend these bags with their lives. The courier on the *Automedon* appeared to have done precisely that.

'It seems,' Menzies said slowly, as if every word had suddenly become a burden, 'that inside the pouch was a letter addressed to Brooke-Popham.' The name needed no elaboration. Air Chief Marshal Sir Robert Brooke-Popham was the British Commander-in-Chief, Far East, based in Singapore. His was one of the most sensitive and difficult commands anywhere in the Empire.

'Usual routine for top secret material,' Menzies continued. 'Instructions that it be opened by no other hand et cetera et cetera.' He sipped at his whisky, but appeared to find no enjoyment in it. His lips were tightly pursed. 'When the German ship reached Japan, the letter apparently found its way to the German Ambassador in Tokyo – we have that from intercepts – and he in turn handed it on to Kondo.'

'Kondo?'

'The Vice Chairman of the Japanese Imperial Naval General Staff.'

Churchill stared into the cold, empty hearth. 'And what did the letter contain?'

'It was ... dear God, I think you'll remember it, Prime Minister.' Menzies sighed, his shoulders falling in discouragement. 'A copy of the analysis drawn up by our Chiefs of Staff on our ability to defend ourselves in the Far East in the event that the Japanese declare war on us.'

Churchill froze. He did not stir for many moments, but the glass in his hand tilted as his fingers seemed to lose all sensation. The only sound in the room was the slow dripping of whisky onto the carpet.

Eventually a tremor came to his lips. 'What on earth was it doing on a tramp steamer like the *Automedon*?'

'It's a tangled little tale,' Menzies said, finding comfort now that he would be able to offload the burden – and, with it, much of the blame – onto other shoulders. 'Apparently the War Office didn't want the paper to get to Singapore too quickly – not in the middle of the difficult negotiations with the Australians – you know what's been happening. They've been pestering us with demands for more and more British reinforcements to be sent to the Far East, while we've been insisting that there is no real need. So apparently it was felt that the paper would only ... How can I put it?'

'Complicate the situation.'

'Precisely.'

'They decided to cover their arses,' Churchill growled. 'They would send it, but so slowly that by the time it arrived it might be buried in obsolescence. Of no use to – and no blame upon – anyone.'

'I think that's a reasonably accurate summary, yes. They also wanted to get it to Singapore in a manner that would arouse no suspicion. So they ...'

'Put it on a rust bucket.'

'That seems to be about the measure of it, Prime Minister. I'm so very sorry.'

But Churchill was no longer listening. His face was flushed with both anger and anguish as his mind cast back to the contents of the paper that he himself had commissioned. It ran to seventy-eight closely argued paragraphs and came to one damning conclusion – a conclusion so devastating that he had refused to allow it to be discussed even by his War Cabinet.

Churchill leant forward, as though wanting to spring at the other man, fixing him in the eye. 'The Japanese have it? You are sure?'

His stare was returned.

'On the basis of what we know, it seems all but certain.'

'Then may God preserve us.'

The Chiefs of Staff had concluded that the British couldn't beat the Japanese. Not a chance, not on their own. Hong Kong, Malaya, Singapore, all the territories and possessions of the British in the Far East, the jewels of their Empire, were virtually defenceless. Waiting to be plundered.

And the Japanese knew it.

A little later, as Churchill climbed the stairs to bed, he found himself accompanied by an unfamiliar and deeply troubling sensation. Only in the middle of the night, when he was still struggling to sleep, did he finally recognize the ruffian.

It was fear.

TWO

Anthony Eden, the Foreign Secretary, was a man of both power and charm; some even said that he would be the next Prime Minister. Yet beneath his suave and immaculately groomed exterior there were occasions when he betrayed the inner tension that left him thin and always anxious.

'Try hanging it on the other wall, will you?' he instructed tersely.

The two workmen cast a disdainful eye at the politician. 'Not the only thing that could do with a little hanging,' one of them muttered darkly, but out of earshot. 'This wall, that wall, whichever wall he wants, it's still only a ruddy painting.'

Eden turned from his examination of the panelling. 'You have a problem?'

'Not really.'

'Speak up, man. Better in than out.'

'Well, sir, I don't understand why we have to move the blessed thing at all. Been there long enough. Why do we have to move it just 'cos some Americans are coming?'

'Because it's George the Third.'

The explanation was met with a blank stare.

'He was mad,' Eden continued.

'But still a king,' the workman countered doggedly. '*Our* king.'

'I take your point. But kings aren't particularly popular with Americans. Particularly this one.'

The towering portrait of George III with its ornate gilt frame had dominated the meeting room of the Foreign Office since, well, ever since anyone could remember, but now it was to be moved. Eden had instructed that all appropriate arrangements were to be made for welcoming the forthcoming American delegation and had clearly come to the conclusion that a portrait of the mad king who had helped ignite the American Revolution would cast an inappropriate shadow over proceedings. It had to be moved somewhere less prominent.

'Let's try it on the other wall,' he suggested, waving an elegant cuff but without much sign of conviction.

The workman and his partner didn't move a muscle.

'What?'

'Not going to work. Not there. Not anywhere,' the workman said.

'Why on earth not?' Eden enquired, stuffing his thumbs deep into the pockets of his waistcoat.

'Look at it, sir.' The workman took a step forward. 'It's just too big. Turn his face to the wall and you're still going to see his ermine slippers sticking out underneath. It's enormous.' Then, less loudly: 'And we should know. Been moving it all morning.'

Eden cast a dark eye at the workman. He had thought him a monarchist, but now he suspected him of being simply a troublemaker. 'Are you a Communist?'

'What?'

'Oh, never mind.'

The Foreign Secretary went back to examining his dilemma while the workman picked at the fragment of his cigarette with a broken orange fingernail. 'Why the hell we have to be so nice to the bloody Yanks is beyond me,' he said, turning to his colleague. 'Late for the last war, they was. Run away from this war. Doing nothing but sitting on their backsides in Wall Street and soaking us dry.'

Suddenly Eden turned, furious. He'd heard. 'We need them because right now we have no one else.' He strode up to the man who he was now certain was a Bolshevik. 'Where else do you think we'll get the destroyers and other weapons we need to win this war?'

But the workman was not to be cowed. He was no revolutionary, but in his eyes it was Eden and his kind who had got them into this bloody war in the first place. If he was to be asked for his opinion, he was going to give it.

'I hear we can't afford it. Can't afford the Americans as friends.'

Eden snorted in exasperation. That was the difficulty with men such as this who wandered into every corner and crevice of the Foreign Office. They heard too much, yet understood so little. 'Of course we can't afford it, but that's no longer the point. The Americans have suggested they lend us the matériel instead, for the duration of the war. We borrow everything – the bombers, fighters, ships, guns, tanks, vehicles – then afterwards give them back. It's called Lend-Lease.'

'But not fighting . . .'

'Not fighting, exactly. But assisting. Making it possible for us to win the war. A partnership.' He clapped his hands. 'But that's it!' he cried. 'We could get another picture. Put it alongside. Something . . . well . . . American. Don't we have something down in the basement?'

'We've got a George Washington somewhere,' the workman's colleague began.

'Splendid! Fetch it up. Put it alongside. It'll balance the whole thing out.'

The workman was less enthused. 'Stupid pillock,' he said softly and very slowly to his colleague. 'We'll be shifting pictures all ruddy afternoon.'

Which is precisely what happened. They hauled and sweated their way up from the basement with the new portrait, a remnant from the State Visit of President Woodrow Wilson in 1918. The basement was three floors down. Which meant three floors back up. But no matter how much they shifted the paintings around the room, still it would not work. The portrait of the first American President was only a fraction the size of the umpteenth English king, and in whatever position they were tried, the result looked more like deliberate insult than diplomatic master stroke. Eden eventually threw up his hands in despair.

'You'll have to take them *both* down to the basement,' he said.

'What? Take down the King?' the workman asked in bewilderment. 'To the basement?'

'We can't afford to offend the Americans. There's no other way,' the Foreign Secretary announced before examining his pocket watch and rushing from the room. He left the workman squatting on his haunches, trying to manufacture another spindly cigarette.

'Take down the King? To the basement?' he kept saying over and over, as if through repetition he would come to understanding. 'Makes you wonder, don't it?'

'What's that?' his colleague asked.

'Who the bloody hell's in charge here.'

The bathroom was small, narrow and hopelessly impractical. It had no windows and only the most rudimentary of ventilation systems, and was buried behind several feet of concrete. The planners who had built the fortified Annexe around the corner from Downing Street had wanted to ensure that, whatever else happened to him, Churchill wasn't going – in his own words – 'to be blown out of his own bloody bath'. It was no idle threat; bath time was one of his set rituals. He would throw himself into the water, submerging completely, then surface once more, blowing like a whale. In between dives he would reflect, dictate, compose and shout orders, all the while cheating outrageously on the maximum level of bath water recommended by his own scrimping Government.

A flustered assistant came stumbling from the room, brow beaded in sweat, his glasses steamed, his notebook crumpled, the ink running down the page, nearly knocking into Randolph as he fled. Another male secretary was hovering, waiting his turn to go in, and Sawyers was fussing away near at hand, but both of them drew back as the Prime Minister's son appeared, clad in the service dress of a captain, No. 8 Commando.

'Papa?' Randolph said, standing in the doorway. He took a step forward and was immediately enveloped in a fog of condensation, through which the outline of his father began to emerge, pink, perspiring, standing in front of the sink, shaving, completely naked.

'Don't shut that door,' Winston snapped, wiping away at the mirror. 'Not unless you want me to cut my own damned throat.'

'Why don't you bathe in St James's Park,' Randolph said. 'It could scarcely be more public.'

'Whaddya mean?'

'You think Hitler wanders around the Reichs Chancellery waving his baubles about? It's so bloody undignified.'

They couldn't help arguing. Always had. For them it was

like breath, and love, and light – as natural as the dew following the night.

'I blame myself,' Churchill began testily, 'for sending you to the wrong type of school. Private showers and all that nonsense. It's unhealthy. Encourages misconduct when you're behind locked doors. And lack of candour when you're not.' He resumed scraping away the soap on his chin with a large open-bladed razor. 'At Harrow, we used to be naked all the time, in the swimming pool, in the showers. That's when I first met the men who now occupy some of the highest positions in the land – men of the cloth and of the law, even some in my own Cabinet. That's why they all trust me. They know I have nothing to hide.' He threw the blade into the sink and began groping for a towel. 'Nakedness teaches you to look another man directly in the eye.'

'Better still, not to trust him behind your back.'

Churchill turned. 'Let's not argue, Randolph. Not on your last day. Not before you leave for the warrior's life in the desert.'

'Cairo is scarcely the desert, Papa. Must you romanticize everything?'

'There will be nothing romantic in what is about to take place in the Middle East. Where you are going could yet prove to be the fulcrum of the whole war.'

'Is that why we've been sent by those weevils in the War Office to train amongst the ice floes of the Clyde? So we can serve in the Middle East?'

'From what I've heard, the officers of your regiment appear to have undertaken most of their training in the bar rooms and fleshpots of Glasgow.'

'What else is there to do on a winter's night in such a God-awful place?'

They were at it again. Bristling. Born to fight. And Randolph carried with him the appalling burden for a fighting man of being the son of a Prime Minister. No one took him seriously. He wanted to be part of this war and was desperate to be sent overseas in search of action, for whatever else they might say about him, he was no coward. He'd joined his father's old regiment, the 4th Hussars, in the hope it would get him sent to a battlefront, but they made it no further than Hull – held back, it was said, because he was his father's son. So he had transferred to a commando unit – surely there would be action there. But only brawls on the street with Scotsmen. So the bathroom became a battleground, too.

Suddenly the moment was broken by a familiar voice.

'If you'll excuse me, Mr Randolph.'

Sawyers, damn the man. When he issued a request it carried all the authority of high command, even with his lisp. Reluctantly Randolph made way as the valet placed a set of carefully laundered silk underwear over the wooden towel rail, but his real purpose was to scold them both, reminding them that this might prove to be their last moment together on earth and they might never have the opportunity of forgiving or forgetting what was said between them. The servant managed to convey all this with no more than a raised eyebrow.

Churchill took his valet's cue. 'My darling boy,' he said, and instantly a truce was declared. 'You are about to embark upon the greatest adventure of your lifetime, and I know that whatever it is you are about to do will be done with honour and with formidable distinction.'

He finished climbing into his underwear and dressing gown, and was decent once again. 'You know, Randolph, nine months ago when I became Prime Minister, I promised the people victory. Victory whatever the cost; that's what I told

29

them. They have borne the terrible cost yet seen precious little of the victory. So I beg you – be brave, fight boldly. The Middle East may not be the place where the final triumph is decided, but let it at least be where it is begun.'

'I'll do my best, Papa.'

'Brighter days lie ahead, of that I am certain. So in everything you do, be a Churchill!'

And they embraced.

'But how shall we win, Papa – finally?'

'Not alone. With others.'

'What others?'

'The Americans, of course.'

'The Americans?'

'They have already taken the first step. President Roosevelt has declared that his country will become the great arsenal of democracy.'

'Hah! He got that almost right,' Randolph said, his tone mocking.

'He's agreed to lease and lend us all the materials we need,' his father responded forcefully.

'So that we can scrabble around as her mercenaries?'

'It is an act of unprecedented generosity.'

'Or unprincipled calculation! The Americans sit back and make their profits while we fight their war. The only time they ever come into a war is when it's all but bloody over. Then they'll crawl out from their bunkers in time to pick the pockets of the wounded.'

'The Americans will join us! Not just as supporters and suppliers but as combatants, too. They *will* join with us. That I promise you.'

'Papa, what strange world are you living in? You know what Roosevelt has said, time and again. Fight to the last Briton!'

30

'Oh, but you are cruel. The President has had to act cautiously.'

'What? You mean he's had to keep his clothes on! He won't step into the showers with us and he daren't look the American voters in the eye.'

Their voices were rising once again.

'Statesmen practise the art of the possible, Randolph.'

'Roosevelt has the moral compass of a piece of driftwood!'

'Such things take time.'

'And precisely how much time do you think we have, Papa?'

'That may well depend upon what you and your brother officers achieve in the Middle East.'

'Then I'd better get out there,' Randolph snapped, turning away, carried along relentlessly by his addiction to argument.

'My boy!' Winston called, despairing. 'Not – like this. Not to war.' Tears began to puddle in his eyes. 'You know I love you.'

The words stopped Randolph in mid-stride. Slowly he turned back, and his father rushed to embrace him.

'I'm sorry, Papa,' Randolph sighed. 'I fear I'm not good company at the moment. Been trying to sort out my affairs before I go, but . . . You know these things. So silly when you set them against war and what's happening.'

'You have troubles?'

He shrugged. 'A few bills I'd completely forgotten about.'

Ah, that again. 'How much?' the old man asked jadedly.

'Just a couple of hundred.' He was unable to return his father's steady gaze. 'Not going to happen again, I promise you – promised Pam – I've given up gambling. Washed my hands of it. Mug's game. No bloody good at it, anyway.' He tried to make light of it – just as he had done last time.

'I shall write you another cheque.'

'That . . . would be splendid, Papa. For Pam. Mean a lot to her. And allow me to go off with a clear conscience.'

'I shall hold you to your promise.'

But Randolph was already brighter, his confidence returning. 'And I shall hold you to yours. Drag America into this war, and I swear – on my life as a soldier, Papa – I'll never gamble another brass farthing.'

Churchill's blue eyes were fixed on his son, trying to tie him to the spot, not wanting him to leave, knowing this moment might be their last. 'May God give me enough time,' he said softly. 'Little by little, step by step, they will be drawn to the fight. They must. Otherwise all this suffering, all the sacrifice, the lives that have been given up . . .' – he faltered slightly – 'and those that are yet to be given up will have been in vain.'

'I must go, Papa. I have a job to do.'

'And so have I.'

'We have an understanding?'

'I give you my word.'

Once more Randolph threw himself into his father's arms, then he was gone, with his father's tears fresh upon his cheeks.

Churchill watched him go. For a long time he stood on the spot, reaching out after his son's shadow, clinging to the echo of his words, wondering if they would ever see each other again. Then he whispered.

'Not today, Randolph, not tomorrow perhaps, but they will come. Before it is too late. I promise you.'

The rocket was one of Churchill's 'little toys'. He was fond of his toys. He had set up a specialist group of boffins and pyromaniacs to produce them – 'any new weapon, tool or war-thing that might assist us in the task of smashing the enemy to smithereens,' as he had put it. The official designation of the group was MD1, but to most it was known simply as the 'Singed Eyebrow Squad'.

This morning they were testing a small rocket, no more than three feet in height. What the precise purpose of the weapon was to be, no one was entirely sure; the purpose would come later, after the principle had been proven. Churchill had gathered an unusually large group for the weekend; not only family and personal aides, but two Americans and an assortment of braid from all three services, with a couple of Ministers thrown in for ballast. After breakfast they had gathered on Beacon Hill overlooking Chequers, wrapped in overcoats and scarves against the chill February air, the low sun casting long shadows while an inspection party of crows flew languidly overhead. Those responsible for the day's matinée scurried like grave-snatchers through the mist in the pasture below, while Sawyers weaved his way through the entourage on the hilltop dispensing coffee and shots of whisky.

'Faster, man,' Churchill encouraged, 'or we'll all freeze.'

'If we're going to invite a three-ring circus every weekend, we'll be needing more hands to help.'

'What? Are you saying you can't cope?'

'I can. Boiler can't.'

'What the hell's the boiler got to do with winning the war?'

'Do yer know where Mr Hopkins goes to read his papers?'

Churchill began to growl, his breath condensing in the slow-warming air and giving him the impression of an elderly dragon. It was bluff, and Sawyers knew it.

'He goes to the bathroom,' the servant continued.

'I often read my papers in the bath.'

'He's not in the bath but in his overcoat. Only place in the whole house that's kepping warm. So he tekks his work into the bathroom and disappears, like, for a couple of hour. Inconvenient fer other guests, so it is.'

Hopkins was frail, American and of huge importance. Churchill thrust out his small tumbler for another shot of warming whisky.

'So what are you suggesting?'

'Like I say, we need help. More hands. Two more maids.'

'Two?' Churchill protested.

'Two, if we're to kepp a fire in every room and clean sheets on beds. And help poor Mrs Landemare. She's not getting any younger.'

Oh, but he was playing the game, and with consummate skill. Sawyers understood his master as well as any man, his foibles, his vanities, his indulgences. His meanness and his dislike of new faces, too.

'We don't need two, dammit. This is a war headquarters, not a holiday resort.'

'I'm sure Mr Willkie don't mind sleeping in a British general's sheets, but what wi' boiler being in such poor shape, I'm afraid there weren't time to launder 'em, like, before he arrived.'

Churchill snorted in alarm. Upsetting Mrs Landemare would have consequences creeping close to the point of disaster; upsetting the Americans might take them far beyond. Hopkins was a close friend of Roosevelt, while Willkie had been his opponent in the last presidential election. They had arrived as the President's personal emissaries – 'to check up on me', as Churchill had grumbled in exasperation. And to check up on Britain. Roosevelt had announced the principle of Lend-Lease but now he needed to decide how much to send and to lend. Some of his advisers had been whispering in his ear that he wouldn't be getting much of it back, that most of it might soon be falling into the clutches of the German High Command.

So he had sent Hopkins and Willkie to test the temper of both the country and its wayward leader: as the President had put it to Hopkins, 'we need to know whether the Brits will carry on fighting – and whether Churchill will ever stop.'

Churchill knew all this, knew that his American guests had been sent to spy, and he had responded by trying to seduce and suborn them. Their conclusions – and therefore their comforts – were of immense importance. It was the opportunity Sawyers had been waiting for.

'A ship lost for ha'p'orth of tar,' he mused, 'and a war for an unlaundered sheet.' He shook his head in mock resignation.

'One!' Churchill proclaimed defiantly, but knowing he had lost. 'One extra maid. That's as far as we go.' He glared at Sawyers. 'And you'd better make sure she's up to the job.'

Oh, but she was. Sawyers had already made sure of that. A niece of Mrs Landemare's husband. French, but almost one of the family.

'I'll do me best,' the servant sighed, turning away to tend to the guests, and to smile.

In the valley below, the huddle of technicians had broken and a man was waving his arm furiously. From on top of the viewing hill, an officer of the Royal Artillery returned the signal and came hurrying across to Churchill.

'Permission to proceed, Prime Minister?'

'Unless you'd prefer us all to freeze first.'

And there was more waving, and scurrying to a safe distance in the valley below, followed by several tense moments of – nothing. While Churchill stamped his foot in impatience, the Americans turned and smiled graciously. The moments stretched. The senior officers seemed grim and the Ministers embarrassed. Yet suddenly, beneath them, the mists parted like a biblical sea and they saw the rocket beginning to climb into the air. It was hesitant at first, as though uncertain of its direction, the steam and smoke from its motor bursting forth in fits and starts, until it had climbed to perhaps fifty feet in height. Then the engine coughed. The rocket seemed to lose faith. It pitched over.

It was at this point, as all seemed lost, that the machine found its life once more and roared into action. It headed straight for the group on top of the hill, leaving a trail of angry, swirling vapours behind it. The circling crows cried in alarm as everyone on the ground scattered like mice, their sticks flying, hats tumbling, all dignity gone, until with one final bullying roar the weapon embedded itself not twenty feet from where they had been standing.

Sawyers alone had not moved. As the smoke and panic finally dissolved, the others collected their wits and fallen headgear, and rose to find him still holding a tray brimming with glasses. Not a drop had been spilled.

Churchill was panting; he had shown surprising agility for a man of his years. As the others gathered round he waved in the direction of the still-smouldering rocket. 'Needs a little tweaking, don't you think?'

'Winston,' Hopkins said, reaching for a drink, 'if it does that to us, think what it might do to the damned Germans. You might yet win the war. Terrorize them into surrender.'

'Yes, somehow cannonballs seem so much more logical. In celebration of which I think perhaps we shall watch the Nelson film tonight,' Churchill announced.

'Lucky man, was the admiral,' Sawyers muttered as he gathered up the remaining glasses.

'What are you grumbling about, man?'

'A pot o' powder and a bit o' breeze, that's all he ever asked. Like a personal valet, he was. Only thing he ever wanted was tools to finish the job. One extra maid. How are we supposed to manage wi' just one extra maid?'

'The tools to finish the job?' Suddenly Churchill let out a roar of merriment and clapped the servant on the shoulder. 'Sawyers, at times you can be brilliant. You are simply too stupid to realize the fact. Ah, but you are fortunate to serve a man like me, someone who is able to pick the diamonds out from the slag heap of your mind.'

Sawyers stared back blankly.

'Hurry up, man,' Churchill barked. 'We'll be wanting luncheon in a little while.' And with that he strode happily down the hill.

The broadcast he made the following evening from Chequers was his first in five months. It was still being written right up to the moment of delivery. It bore no resemblance to any earlier draft, for Sawyers' moment of insight had unleashed a flood of fresh thoughts.

Churchill sat at his working table surrounded by the books and oil paintings that filled the walls of the Hawtrey Room, his back to the fire, his script lit by nothing more than a single bulb beneath a green shade, the atmosphere dense and theatrical, almost conspiratorial. He was still scribbling fresh thoughts in the margin of his typed script even as the sound engineer, standing in the doorway, indicated it was time. A growl grew in his throat, a little like the sound of a torpedo about to burst from its tube, and he had begun.

He welcomed them, reassured them, drew them in, recounted to them what they already knew, but gave them fresh heart in the retelling.

After the heavy defeats of the German Air Force by our fighters in August and September, Herr Hitler did not dare attempt the invasion of this island, although he had every need to do so and had made vast preparations. Baffled in this mighty project, he sought to break the spirit of the British nation by the bombing, first of London and afterwards of our great cities.

He made it seem like times past. Oh, if only they were . . .

It has now been proved, to the admiration of the world, and of our friends in the United States, that this form of blackmail by murder and terrorism, so far from weakening the spirit of the British nation, has only roused it to a more intense and universal flame than was ever seen before!

Through the words of defiance they could hear him sipping his whisky, wetting his lips for what was to come.

All through these dark winter months the enemy has had the power to drop three or four tons of bombs upon us for every ton we could send to Germany in return.

If he seemed to falter a little, it was only for dramatic emphasis, to lead them on.

We are arranging so that presently this will be rather the other way around . . .

Defiance – and mockery. The universal sign that the British were not yet completely buggered.

Meanwhile, London and our big cities have had to stand their pounding. They remind me of the British squares at Waterloo. They are not squares of soldiers. They do not wear scarlet coats. They are just ordinary English, Scottish and Welsh folk – men,

women and children – standing steadfastly together. But their
spirit is the same, their glory is the same, and in the end their
victory will be greater than far-famed Waterloo!

In every corner of the country, in places of work, of rest,
of relaxation, even in places of suffering, chins came up and
the blood flowed a little faster. But this was not to be a message
simply for British ears. Thanks to Sawyers, Churchill's words
were to find both a new focus and a new audience. His
words were weapons in this war, and now he aimed them
directly at Americans.

While this has been happening, a mighty tide of sympathy, of
good will and of effective aid has begun to flow across the
Atlantic in support of the world cause which is at stake.
Distinguished Americans have come over to see things here at
the front and to find out how the United States can help us best
and soonest. In Mr Hopkins, who has been my frequent
companion during these last few weeks, we have the envoy of
the President, a President who has been newly re-elected to his
august office. In Mr Wendell Willkie we have welcomed the cham-
pion of the great Republican Party. We may be sure that they
will both tell the truth about what they have seen over here,
and more than that we do not ask. The rest we leave with good
confidence to the judgement of the President, the Congress and
the people of the United States.

He said these words, but he did not believe them. Churchill
had never met the President and had grave doubts about his
judgement. He didn't trust the Congress and he knew that
the last thing on earth the American people desired was to
get involved in Churchill's bloody war.

It now seems certain that the Government and people of the United States intend to supply us with all that is necessary for victory.

All that is necessary for victory – short of actual help. They'd sent those ancient destroyers, of course, but demanded their thirty pieces of silver in return. Many of those much-vaunted destroyers had been useless, little more than rusting barges with clapped-out engines and rotting hulls – although someone had taken the trouble to ensure that the wash-rooms were equipped with towels and fresh soap. When would the Americans learn? You couldn't fight a war with clean hands.

In the last war the United States sent two million men across the Atlantic. But this is not a war of vast armies firing immense masses of shells at one another. We do not need the gallant armies which are forming throughout the American union. We do not need them this year, nor next year, nor any year that I can foresee.

He swallowed his shame, telescope to unseeing eye, even as he uttered these profound deceits. He had no choice. Step by step, as he had explained to Randolph. He had to pretend to be at one with Roosevelt, to be alongside him, joined to him at the hip – otherwise he would never be able to lead him astray.

In order to win the war, Hitler must destroy Great Britain. He may carry havoc into the Balkan States. He may tear great provinces out of Russia . . .

Yes, an attack on Russia, that would happen some time, of that Churchill was certain. It was the nature of the Nazi

40

beast, couldn't restrain itself. But when? Would it be in time to save Britain?

He may march to the Caspian; he may march to the gates of India. All this will avail him nothing. It may spread his curse more widely throughout Europe and Asia, but it will not avert his doom. With every month that passes the many proud and once happy countries he is now holding down by brute force and vile intrigue are learning to hate the Prussian yoke and the Nazi name as nothing has ever been hated so fiercely and so widely among men before. And all the time, masters of the sea and air, the British Empire – nay, in a certain sense the whole English-speaking world – will be on his track, bearing with them the swords of justice.

'In a certain sense the whole English-speaking world'? In what sense, pray? Roosevelt and his Americans might pretend they were up to wielding the sword of justice, but the last place they intended to bury it was deep inside the guts of the German war machine.

The other day President Roosevelt gave his opponent in the late presidential election a letter of introduction to me, and in it he wrote out a verse in his own handwriting from Longfellow, which he said applies to you people as it does to us. Here is the verse:

> *Sail on, O Ship of State!*
> *Sail on, O Union, strong and great!*
> *Humanity with all its fears,*
> *With all the hopes of future years,*
> *Is hanging breathless on thy fate!*

Roosevelt was sending poetry and bars of soap when what Churchill wanted was guns, more guns and bloody shells!

41

But he must turn it, use the cascade of words to excite the passions and dull their wits, to avert their gaze so that he could launch his monstrous deception . . .

What is the answer that I shall give, in your name, to this great man, the thrice-chosen head of a nation of a hundred and thirty millions? Here is the answer I shall give to President Roosevelt.

Put your confidence in us. Give us your faith and your blessing and, under Providence, all will be well. We shall not fail or falter. We shall not weaken or tire. Neither the sudden shock of battle nor the long-drawn trials of vigilance and exertion will wear us down.

He paused for the briefest moment. His voice lifted.

Give us the tools – and we will finish the job!

Oh, it was true Churchillian splendour, rhetoric that rang around the world. Yet he meant not a word. It was a promise he never had the smallest intention of keeping. Like blossom before the frost, it would vanish before the day was done. The bombardment of words was intended for one purpose only, to encourage the Americans to move forward an inch upon a slippery slope. After that, he would drag them the other three thousand miles.

THREE

The blue waters of the Mediterranean had been turned into a shooting range, one in which the enemy had many more guns than the British, so the troopship conveying Randolph's unit was required to take the long and laborious route to Egypt – round the tip of Africa and up through the Red Sea. The *Glenroy* was desperately overcrowded, and matters were made worse by the constant bickering that took place between the naval and army elements on board. In the view of No. 8 Commando, the captain was incompetent and soon was being referred to as 'the bugger on the bridge'. The ship's crew, in turn, regarded Randolph's unit as 'long-haired nancies'. It was partly a clash of class. The seamen were rough-handed workers – social underdogs, often from the slums – while many of those who formed No. 8 Commando had joined up straight from the bar of White's Club in St James's. Amongst these ill-mixed men who were crowded onto the ship, Randolph stood out most prominently of all, for no one could forget that he was somehow different, and if the point managed to slip anyone's attention Randolph was always on hand to remind them. He and his closest friends were impossible, articulate, extravagant, impertinent, and took great pleasure in being gratuitously bloody rude. Long before the voyage was over, one of the crew had daubed a slogan on the lower deck: 'Never in the history of humankind have so many been buggered about by so few.'

Randolph loved his father, and perhaps too much, almost to the point of destruction. He had been brought up at his father's table and encouraged to be his own man, yet by insisting so stridently on his uniqueness Randolph turned himself into no more than a pale shadow. He would bicker and abuse, ignoring all criticism, just as he had learnt from Winston, but he had failed to capture the essential counterbalance, that elusive quality of grace. In any event, what can be intriguing from an old man is inexcusable from the young; what was seen as drive and determination in the father appeared as little more than bloody-mindedness in the son. And Randolph, like Winston, would never, never, never give in.

He'd promised he would stop gambling but it was a long voyage – three weeks – cooped up on the *Glenroy* in the growing heat and with little else for distraction, apart from alcohol. Just like White's Club. There was poker, roulette, chemin-de-fer every night – and for very high stakes – hell, they were probably going to die, so what did it matter? They would gamble on anything: the number of empty bottles in a barrel or the number of peas on a plate, double or nothing.

In spite of being his father's son, Randolph was a rotten gambler and a worse drunk. And when he was drunk he never knew when the time had come to walk away.

In three weeks at sea, Randolph lost three thousand pounds. Enough to pay the rent on the family home until the baby was well into old age. A small fortune, even for someone who wasn't already broke.

Up until the baby had been born, Pamela had spent much of her time at Downing Street with Randolph's parents.

During air raids she had slept in the wine cellar, in a bunk below Winston – 'one Churchill inside me, and one Churchill above,' as she told it. It was a relationship that drew her close to her father-in-law and at times even made Randolph's sisters envious, for while their lives seemed always to be touched by chaos, Pamela grew fat with her child and became almost a good-luck charm for the old man as he fought to keep the bombers at bay and the invasion unlaunched. 'You are what this war is all about,' he once told her, placing his hand on her protruding stomach.

The previous September, at the most crucial hour in the Battle of Britain, Churchill had driven with Pamela and Clemmie from Chequers to the RAF's headquarters at Uxbridge in order to see for themselves the progress of the extraordinary conflict that was taking place above southern England. They had watched in the operations room as, one after one, squadrons of Spitfires and Hurricanes had been thrown into the sky against the onrushing enemy. There came a moment during that afternoon when not a single aircraft was left in reserve, when it would have taken just one more wave of bombers to have swept Britain aside. But it hadn't come.

Afterwards, as they had driven back towards Chequers, Churchill had seemed buried deep within his own thoughts, exhausted, his chin sunk low upon his chest. After a while he had stirred and turned to Pamela.

'Do you keep a diary?'

'No,' she had replied, startled.

'You should. These are moments that, if we survive, we should allow no one to forget.' Then he had fallen back into silence for several minutes, until the chin came up once more. 'Anyway, if you don't have a diary, what the hell will you live on when you get tired of Randolph?'

'I shan't get tired of Randolph.'

'Everyone gets tired of Randolph,' he had told her.

But she hadn't. Randolph was a handful, of course, garrulous, bibulous, fond of reading the histories of Macaulay to her in bed. When she had visited him at his commando training headquarters in Scotland, she'd been alarmed to discover that he had run up a hotel bill of gargantuan size, but he was unabashed. *'Morituris bibendum,'* he had hollered, which he loosely translated as: 'Those who are about to die deserve a bloody drink.'

Anyway, he told her they could afford the occasional drink, and a little light gambling, too. It was only amongst his close friends, he explained, and he won more than he ever lost. After the baby had been born he'd found them an old rectory in Hertfordshire, rented for a pittance with the help of his father's name. It was their first home; Pamela loved it, and him. When he was there the walls echoed with excitement, and when he was away she felt nothing but draughts and missed him with a power that at times astonished her. During the day she would wander around the house in one of his old uniform jackets, smelling him, touching him, trying to imagine him beside her, and at night she would turn off the gas fire and go to bed early under a pile of blankets and with a copy of Macaulay beneath the pillow.

She missed him all the more when she discovered she was probably pregnant again. Christmas at Chequers.

She was young, not yet twenty-one, lacking in experience of things, but she wanted so much to show him that he had found the best wife, mother and housekeeper he ever could.

Then his letter arrived. It offered an apology, of course, and a renewed vow of eternal self-denial which this time, he told her, he meant. But the self-denial Randolph required was, in truth, all on Pamela's part. He sent her detailed instructions that she was to pay off his gambling debts by instalments of perhaps ten pounds a month, to a list of names that seemed endless. He didn't suggest any way in which this sum might be raised. It was to be her problem – and exclusively her problem, for he forbade her to breathe a word of this to his father. He made it sound as though somehow it were all her fault.

Three days after the letter arrived, the bleeding started, accompanied by excruciating pain that left her bent in two and crying for mercy. It was only with the greatest difficulty that she made it to the bathroom, bleeding profusely.

She had been pregnant; she was no longer. And would never be again.

Yet another American had appeared on Churchill's doorstep. In the last few weeks the Prime Minister seemed to have done little but charge up and down the stairs of Downing Street to the tune of 'Yankee Doodle', but he didn't complain. It was far better than being marched up and down Whitehall to the sound of a glockenspiel.

John 'Gil' Winant had been sent to replace the excruciating Joe Kennedy as Ambassador to the Court of St James's. Kennedy had been as crooked as a fish hook, but the new man was of altogether finer construction, the sort you could invite to dinner without having to count the spoons. He was a tall, brooding figure, painted with an expression of profound earnestness. Some thought he looked a lot like Abraham Lincoln, but whereas Lincoln was a wordsmith as glorious as any his country had produced, London had just discovered that Winant was a lamentable public speaker. He had delivered his first address in Britain, to a luncheon of the Pilgrims' Club, an Anglo-American friendship society. The members of the audience assumed the sentiments in the speech were excellent, but no one could tell, for it had been impossible to make out a word he had said. They had hoped for someone of a different cut to the mean-mouthed outpourings of Kennedy, but this was going to the other extreme. Was America's new voice to be no more than a whimper?

Churchill had attended the lunch. As they were leaving the Savoy Hotel, he decided to take matters into his own hands and grabbed Winant's arm.

'Your Excellency, a fine speech.'

'Did you truly think so?'

'Worthy of many plaudits – and a little celebration. Do you have time for several whiskies?' And before the ambassador could muster an audible answer, he was being led towards the Prime Minister's car.

'That is on two conditions, of course,' Churchill continued. 'The first is that we become the greatest of friends. As you know, I am half American, on my mother's side. A Jerome from New York. I even lay claim to a little Iroquois Indian blood, at least an armful, I'd say.'

'Half American. But I suspect entirely English,' Winant returned, smiling. He had a most attractive smile, his dark, deep-set eyes glowing with sincerity. His hair was unkempt, a little like a distracted schoolboy, while his suit was crumpled and sat awkwardly on his gaunt frame – as did his marriage, so rumour had it. Clearly he lacked a woman's touch.

'The second condition I insist upon is that you call me Winston, and I be permitted to call you Gil. No formality between us, no barriers. We are brothers. I want to like you very much indeed.'

That, as Churchill knew, might be no easy undertaking. Winant had a long career as a liberal activist and labour organizer that seemed to pit him against so many of the interests Churchill's life had embraced. 'Doesn't matter,' Churchill had growled, 'so long as he hates Hitler.'

They drove to the rear entrance of Downing Street, which nestled against the parade ground of Horse Guards. There were many signs of recent bomb damage – hurriedly filled holes, empty windows, scarred buildings, blasted trees in the park. A long section of the garden wall at the back of Downing Street had been toppled, leaving bricks lying in forlorn piles. A gang of workmen was carrying out repairs. As soon as his car had stopped, Churchill sprang from his seat and began clambering over broken bricks and through piles of sand until he was in the midst of the workers. He seemed not to notice that he was standing in a puddle of cement.

'My dear Gil, let me introduce you to the men who are the backbone of the British Empire. The bricklayers!' He thrust his stick at one of the men in exchange for a trowel, and then began loading cement and bricks upon the new wall, eyeing their line, tapping them to a level, and all the while puffing great clouds of smoke from his cigar as he chatted in great animation to the workers. They gathered closely around him, laughing at his jests, shouting their encouragement, and taking care to keep him supplied with fresh bricks.

'You see, Gil, I, too, am a bricklayer, a member of the Amalgamated Union of Building Trade Workers. And proud as punch of it. Lady Astor, one of your American compatriots, a woman with a notoriously sharp tongue, once told me that I was as common as muck. I was able to tell her that she was entirely wrong, that I was not as common as muck – but as common as brick. And I had a trade union membership card to prove it.'

He was playing them like an audience at a music hall.

'Ah, I am forgetting my manners,' he said when at last he

stepped back. 'I must introduce you men to my very great friend, Mr Gil Winant. He is the new American Ambassador, which makes him your great friend, too.'

'Last one wasn't, was he?' a voice sounded from the back of the huddle.

'On the contrary, I was very much attached to him,' Churchill said, smiling. 'Like my appendix.'

'But you 'ad that cut out years ago,' the voice came back, to general laughter.

'And you, sir, will get me into a great deal of hot water making baseless accusations like that,' Churchill replied, grinning broadly.

They cheered him as he stepped into his garden through the hole in the wall. He turned to wave his stick at them. 'Londoners – are we downhearted?'

'No!' they cried as one.

It was a piece of theatre, typical Churchill, the sort of thing he'd made sure his other visitors like Hopkins and Willkie had witnessed. Reality wasn't as simple as that, of course. For every Londoner who could still summon up the spirit of defiance, there were those who were gradually weakening, being ground down by yet another winter of war. In his heart, Churchill knew they would not go on – couldn't go on – through another winter unless somehow he could find new hope to sustain them. But he couldn't even feed them properly. The shipping losses in the Atlantic were enormous and the prospect of starvation still hovered over every meal. He had to give them hope, some taste of victory, not an endless diet of setback and evacuation.

Every week brought a new nightmare and another battlefield. So far the Balkans had remained undisturbed, but it was about to be turned into a slaughterhouse. Hundreds of thousands of German troops were massing to swallow up Yugoslavia and Greece, taking advantage of feuding local leaders who, rather than taking on the Wehrmacht, seemed more intent on fighting each other – 'Cvetkovic, Markovic, Simovic, Subotic and every other damned sonofabitch,' as Churchill had complained in frustration. Meanwhile a new commander had arrived to breathe fresh life into the German campaign in the North African deserts. Someone called Rommel.

And the Japanese, that unfathomable, unknowable race on the far side of the world – what in damnation were they planning?

His concerns pursued him everywhere, through his days, through his dreams, no matter what he pretended to the bricklayers. By the time he had crossed the garden and reached the back door of Downing Street, they were weighing heavily on his heart once more. He threw open the door and kicked off his shoes.

'Sawyers! Where are you, man?' he shouted. 'Stop hiding and help. Some idiot has poured cement all over my shoes.'

They sat in a small sitting room that was cold and bleak. The curtains were dusty, the windows taped over, some of them cracked, but Churchill still preferred to spend his daylight hours here in 10 Downing Street than entombed in the underground bunker at the nearby Annexe. It was a small reminder of how things used to be.

The American was beginning to warm up and Sawyers hovered attentively, ready to refill his glass. Shy and uncertain as Winant sometimes looked, he was no fool. He had a long and distinguished public career behind him, much of it in New Hampshire, where he had been elected governor three times. They called it the Granite State; evidently they liked the quiet touch.

'I welcome you to London, Gil, with all my heart. It's a pity that the medical condition of the President makes it so difficult for him to travel, but that makes your position here of even greater significance. I don't think it an exaggeration to say that a whole world might depend upon it. It's one of my great sorrows that I have not yet met Mr Roosevelt, but, in you, I know I have a friend who will bring us together in thought as well as deed. You must be my mirror into his mind.'

The words struck Winant as strange because, of course, Churchill *had* met Roosevelt, many years before. The old man seemed to have forgotten, but Roosevelt hadn't. It had been 1918, at an official dinner in London. The occasion hadn't been an unqualified success; Churchill had been both voluble and a little vulgar, and when Roosevelt returned from the dinner he told his colleagues that Churchill was nothing less than 'a stinker'. It was a story that Joe Kennedy had paddled all around Washington, and so keenly that Winant was surprised the old man hadn't been reminded of it. But then, given the nature of the story, it was perhaps no surprise at all.

'I have very clear instructions, Prime Minister – forgive me: Winston,' the ambassador said as the valet poured more whisky. 'The President has instructed me to tell you that we shall do everything within our power to help you win this war.'

'That is more than I had dared hope –'

'Short of declaring war ourselves, of course.'

'Ah.' Churchill thrust his own glass towards Sawyers.

'The Lend-Lease Bill will be through Congress in a few days; you know the President's set to sign it. Soon we'll be able to send you all those tools you asked for to finish the job.'

The ambassador had intended the words as encouragement, but for a moment Churchill's expression suggested he'd just smashed his finger with a hammer.

'You know, Winston, your broadcast came as a profound relief to many Americans. Ridiculous, I know, but there are still those who suspect you of wanting to find some means of getting us involved in another European shooting match.'

A gentle warning shot across the bow. There were many in the United States who still gave kitchen space to tittle-tattle that Churchill was bent on repeating the history of the last war, when a reluctant America had been dragged into the conflict three years after it had started as a result of the sinking of a number of ships by U-boats. The most notable loss had been the passenger ship *Lusitania*. More than a thousand souls had gone down with her, many of them American, and hundreds of thousands were to follow. Some blamed Churchill personally for this, suggesting he'd as good as arranged the U-boat attack in order to shame the United States out of its isolation. Many Americans still sat round their fires talking of the untrustworthy English.

Churchill stirred uneasily, eager to move on. 'What of the Far East, Gil? It has been occupying my mind. We cannot rest content while Japan conducts a campaign of slaughter and genocide that is every bit the equal in savagery to Hitler's.'

'But in China.'

'Such savagery never knows its bounds. It will not confine itself to China. Where will it turn to next? To French Indo-China? To the Dutch East Indies? To our own colonies of Hong Kong and Singapore, even India? There are vast riches waiting for them there.'

'Which is why, presumably, they are already colonies. And why the European powers would fight once more to retain them.' Winant seemed so much more composed face to face than in front of an audience. And he knew his master's mind. Churchill decided he would be a most effective ambassador, and was not a man he should underestimate.

'I must tell you, Gil, in all seriousness, what I have written to the President.' Churchill turned to his glass, sipping, swirling, as though trying to wash away some foul taste, before staring at the American. 'I told Mr Roosevelt that if the Japanese were to attack our Far Eastern possessions, we would not have the military capability to resist them. No matter what I might be forced to say in public to shore up the general morale, you and your President must be under no illusion. On our own, we could not win such a war.'

On their own, the British could not win . . . Little wonder, Winant thought, that the old man was driven to drink.

'That's why I have asked the President if he will send some part of the US Pacific Fleet to Singapore,' Churchill continued. 'As a sign that an attack on British possessions will not be tolerated. No words, no great declaration, no threats, just a symbolic gesture that even the Japanese will understand. A few American ships in Singapore could prevent the outbreak of the most terrifying tempest across the whole of the Far East.'

'I'm afraid the President can't agree to that, Winston,' Winant said quietly, as though the softness of his voice might in some way diminish the force he knew his words would have on Churchill.

'But . . .' For the briefest of moments Churchill paused, buried beneath the weight of his disappointment. 'My dear Gil, I'm not talking of a vast armada, only a few ships, even a couple of rust buckets would do, so long as they fly the Stars and Stripes . . .'

'I'm sorry.'

'It could prevent catastrophe –'

'Our commitment is to Britain, not to its colonies. I think Mr Roosevelt would argue – and with considerable force – that it's not the job of the United States to steam around the world shoring up other people's empires. We don't like empire, no matter whose flag it flies.'

That was Roosevelt speaking. The President came from a long line of radicals and revolutionaries; he loathed all empires and the British Empire as much as any – a kingdom of pigsticking and polo, he'd been heard to call it. There was no way he was going to shed American blood for that.

Churchill couldn't afford to be diverted. 'But if the Japanese were to control the whole of the Far East they would become the most mighty power in the Pacific. Surely America could not tolerate that?'

'The Pacific is even wider than the Atlantic, Winston – and one hell of a long way from the Hudson.'

'In his State of the Union Address only a few weeks ago your President spoke of his ambition to lead the world from fear.'

'And you know what he also said to me, Winston? That the most terrifying thing in the world is to be a leader who looks over his shoulder and finds no one there.' Winant leant forward from his armchair, as though trying to close the distance between them. 'He hears you, Winston. But he also has to listen to the American people who are suspicious of everything to do with this war. You know, all the while Congress has been debating Lend-Lease, women have been marching outside carrying banners accusing the President of wanting to murder their sons. That hurt him, down deep. They even hanged his effigy. There's a lot of steam behind the no-war protests, Winston, they don't want any more American boys to die in Europe or anywhere else. Their voices are powerful. And Mr Roosevelt has had to listen.'

'Public opinion can be a most demanding mistress.' He did not mean it kindly.

And so they continued, the Englishman and the American, confronting each other, testing each other's ideas, trying to find common ground but discovering their ambitions were as far apart as the continents from which they came. Churchill rose to his feet, his passion too great to remain seated, and he stood by the pale light of the window, his hand on his brow. It was what he had feared. Roosevelt wouldn't move, not even an inch. He looked through the window and saw only disaster. If war broke out in the Far East, Britain would lose it, and the shockwaves of defeat would quite overturn Britain's little boat. It would be the end, but he dare not admit it.

'What will you do?' Winant asked.

'KBO, I suppose,' Churchill muttered, his jaw jutting forward. 'Just KBO.'

Winant was taken aback, not knowing what to do or say and having no idea what the old man was talking about.

The moment was broken by the arrival in the room of a young woman. It was Sarah, Churchill's daughter, who had been visiting her mother. Winant rose, looking strangely like a schoolboy once more, the composure of recent moments vanished as Churchill made the introduction. She was tall, elegant, with a broad, open forehead and Churchill's blue eyes.

'Forgive the interruption, Papa,' she said, kissing his cheek, 'I've come to say goodbye. May I see you at the weekend?'

'You shall!' he said, dragging himself back from his broken dreams. 'And Mr Winant here, too.' He turned to the American. 'Gil, you will be our guest at Chequers. You are one of the family now.'

Winant stumbled in reply, wondering if he were being asked

merely out of politeness and not wishing to intrude. Sarah rescued him, reaching out to touch his sleeve. 'Papa won't take no for an answer,' she told him. 'He never does.'

To Winant she seemed delicate, a little fragile, and desperately appealing. And then she was gone.

Sawyers was hovering at the door. Behind him a pair of generals and an air vice-marshal were impatiently waiting their turn. 'Time for me to go, too,' Winant said. 'You've work to do. A war to wage.'

Churchill stood and extended his hand. 'I'm grateful for your candour, Gil. I know that's what the President wants, it's also what I want. No barriers between us, to hell with the diplomatic niceties. I pray we shall always be as straight with each other as brothers.'

Sawyers escorted the ambassador out. On the way to the door he gave the American a potted history of the old house. He also pointed to some of the features that had been added more recently – reception rooms that were badly damaged, windows broken and blocked up, great holes in the ancient plaster on the ceiling.

'In all honesty, Your Excellency, Number Ten's not exactly what yer might call a substantial house. George Downing was a bit of a bad 'un, like. Built the street wi'out foundations.'

'What happened to him?'

'I believe he went to America, zur,' the valet replied, leading him through the hallway.

As the great black door opened, it revealed a day growing dark and starting to spit with rain. Sawyers produced the American's coat and hat, both of which had been given a stiff brushing.

'Tell me, Sawyers, what does "KBO" mean?' the ambassador asked as Sawyers helped him shrug into his coat.

'Begging your pardon?'

'"KBO." He kept muttering it.'

'Ah, it's a military phrase, zur. From trenches in last war.'

'Meaning?'

'"Keep Buggering On."'

'Yes, of course it does,' the American said, smiling. 'You must find your job fascinating, Sawyers.'

'I do find it has its moments, zur.'

'An important job, too.'

'Nowt special.'

'But you are with him from morning to night. You see everyone and everything, on the way in and on the way out. I guess that makes you more important than the Lord Chief Justice and the Minister of War put together. And much better informed.'

'Sadly not.'

'Oh, and why is that?'

''Cos I'm by way of being too pig ignorant to understand or remember owt that's said, zur.'

Winant looked nonplussed.

'I'm quoting Mr Churchill, Your Excellence. Word fer word.'

Winant's eyes danced with amusement.

'We're looking forward to seeing you at Chequers at weekend, zur,' the valet continued as the ambassador stood on the doorstep, inspecting the weather. 'But you'll find it very English. Might I suggest that you put aside a particularly warm pair o' pyjamas for the occasion? The central heating in't up to what most American gentlemen seem to expect. I'm sure if Mr Roosevelt sends us any more American guests, we'll have to ask him to send a new boiler along wi' 'em.'

The rain was growing heavier. The American pulled up his collar and scoured the sky. 'Well, Sawyers, we'll see what we can do. Tanks, battleships, bombers – and one new boiler. Lend-Lease at your service. Which reminds me, you will be getting another American soon, the man who's coming to run the whole Lend-Lease show. Harriman. Averell Harriman's his name. '

'We look forward to meeting the gentleman. I'm sure he'll be given a right warm welcome by Mr Churchill and the entire family. Night, Your Excellence.'

As the door closed behind him the ambassador, hat clamped firmly to his head, disappeared into the rapidly fading light. As he hurried through the drizzle, he wondered if Hitler knew that Downing Street appeared to be defended by nothing more than one unarmed policeman and an uppity servant.

She found him seated in an armchair by the fire in the Hawtrey Room, with Nelson asleep on his lap. It was late, almost midnight.

She hadn't wanted to disturb him, but she knew of no one else who might understand, no one else who knew Randolph well enough – his recklessness, his passions, his appetites and ego, his moments as a little boy lost, all of which she had been able to tolerate and even welcome, until they had ended up smothering her in debt and left her bleeding on a bathroom floor.

He never turned her away, not like he did so many of the others. She seemed to occupy a special part in his world – so did Randolph, of course, but Pamela didn't shout at him. And while his own elder daughters seemed to have inherited the 'Black Dog' of darkness that so often pursued him, Pamela was fun. Uninhibited. Almost a talisman. It wasn't simply marriage and the baby, but a link that stretched back through the mists of time. Pamela had been born in the manor house at Minterne Magna in Dorset, which three centuries earlier had belonged to the Churchill family. The first Sir Winston Churchill had been born and was buried there. Links that bound them together from long ago.

He was studying the contents of a buff-coloured box. It was his box of secrets, in which Menzies and his intelligence men sent him their most sensitive items – his 'golden eggs', as he called them. She saw it and her heart sank. The papers came first. This was the wrong moment.

He looked up. She could see the rime of exhaustion clinging to his eyes before he returned to staring into the fire.

'This morning, we shot a German spy,' he said, very softly. 'Parachuted in. Fell badly. The constabulary picked him up in less than three hours. And in less than three months we sat him in a chair, bound his arms and then his eyes, and proceeded to snuff out his life.'

She was surprised to see tears glinting in the firelight.

'He was born in the same year as Randolph.'

'He was a spy, Papa.'

'He was a brave young man.'

'A German. An enemy.'

'And shall we shoot them all?' He began stroking Nelson, staring into the fire. 'When will it cease, Pamela? When shall we be able to return to the lives we once knew?'

'Only when we have won.'

'And, I fear, not even then.' He seemed to be in pain. For many moments he sat silently, hurting, his mind elsewhere, seeking comfort from the cat.

'Every night, before I fall asleep, I place myself before a court martial,' he began again. 'I force myself to stand trial, accuse myself of neglect. Have I done my duty? Have I done enough? Did all those men who died that day at my order give up their lives for sufficient reason, or did they die for nothing more than vanity?'

'You know no man could do more.'

Churchill tapped the buff-coloured box. 'Goebbels made a speech the other week. About me. I've just been reading it. Ever since Gallipoli, he said, Winston Churchill has spent a life wading through streams of English blood, defending a lifestyle that has outlived its time.'

'He's a liar. The blood has been spilled by Germans, not by you.'

'But perhaps he has a point, you see.' He held out his hand, summoning her close. She knelt at his feet.

'The world in which I grew up and through which I have travelled all my life has outlived its time. My world is a world of Empire and Union Jacks, where the scarlet coat of the British soldier has stood proud and firm in every corner of the globe. Yet now . . . No matter what the outcome of this war, Pamela, that world is lost. The days of an atlas splashed in red, of emperors and adventure, of natives and majestic nabobs, they are all gone. Of another time.'

'I don't understand, Papa.'

'After this war is over, whoever holds the reins of authority, it will not be Britain. We are too small, too content, perhaps even too kind. You need an edge of ruthlessness to rule. So whose creed shall we find in the ascendant? Hitler and his fascism? Commissar Stalin and his Bolshevist crusade? Or America, perhaps, which worships before the altar of Mammon? Which would you choose, Pamela?'

'Why, America,' she said uncertainly.

'Better America, a thousand times better. Even though at times they totter around like blind men, especially when they set foot in other parts of the world. They don't understand that all men are not as they are. And even when they stumble over the truth, they pick themselves up and carry on as if nothing has happened.'

'But you have praised their generosity . . .'

'Sometimes they are like gangsters.'

'They have given us destroyers, Lend-Lease . . .'

'In return for which they have taken all our gold and dollar reserves, demanded we give them military bases in every corner of the globe, and now their negotiators have started talking about handing over our art treasures and ancient manuscripts.' His chin fell to his chest. 'The bonfire of glories that once was the British Empire belongs to an age that has passed. That wretched man Goebbels was right. And so, in his way, was Randolph.'

'Randolph?'

'When Mr Roosevelt announced Lend-Lease, he likened it to lending a neighbour a hose pipe when his house catches on fire. You don't quibble about its cost, so long as it's returned. But Randolph says it's more like offering a piece of used chewing gum, never expecting it to be returned.'

'You act so warmly towards all the Americans . . .'

'They are the New World, the young world. And I trust them as much as I would any seven-year-old. So we will douse them in flattery and humbuggery, and never give up hope that our American friends will find within themselves the will to fight the right war. But we can no longer rely on that.'

'So what will you do?'

'Do?' For a moment he seemed to be searching for an answer in the flames. 'I shall do whatever it takes. I gave Randolph my word. So tonight, and every night, as I stand before my court martial, I shall have to show that I have done something to ensure that Mr Roosevelt has pitched his tent a little nearer the sound of gunfire.'

She stroked his balding head, trying to bring him comfort, as though he were a young child. 'What can I do, Papa?'

His eyes found her. 'Do what only you can do, Pamela. Give me grandchildren. Give our family and our world a future. Make this all worthwhile.' He kissed her hand. 'What more can an old man ask?'

She had been right. This was not the time. She screamed, but only inside. He couldn't know, didn't deserve to be showered in the wretchedness that was welling up inside her. That would come later, when she was in bed, alone. He had so many other lives to care for; she would have to look after her own.

She left him staring into the embers of the dying fire.

FOUR

Spring. New life. Daffodils. Crocus. Blossom. Warmer days. Death.

The bombers were back. The intermittent raids of winter had given way to a renewed onslaught that pounded London night after night.

Queues. Britain's way to win the war. Line after line of women waiting patiently for whatever was left. Hour after hour, without knowing what might be there when at last they came to the head of the queue, ration book in hand, coins in purse or pocket. The Ministry of Food had just announced five exhilarating new ways of serving potato – wartime 'champ', hot potato salad, potato pastry, potato suet crust. 'And save those orange rinds,' the official advertisement insisted. 'Grate your orange peel and mix a little with mashed potatoes. The potatoes will turn an exciting pink colour!'

But would still be mashed potatoes.

Yet not everyone dined on pink mash. It was a foodstuff entirely unknown to Lady Emerald St John. In truth, her name was not Emerald – she had been born a Maud, but she thought it common. She was not a 'proper' lady, inasmuch as she was American and had married into the title, although she had parted from her husband many years previously, relieving him of not only his marital obligations but also a substantial chunk of his fortune. And, above all, Emerald was no saint. It was why people flocked to her dinner parties, always assured of entertainment, excitement, intrigue – and a little wickedness. Not sexual wickedness, Emerald had worn herself out on three husbands and was past most of that, but as the folds about her face had fallen to wrinkles, she compensated with a tongue that had developed the snagging capacity of a billhook. Sitting at one of her tables was like playing roulette with one's reputation. Someone would always walk away a little poorer.

Pamela arrived late, just as the others were preparing to sit down. The introductions were hurried and she wasn't concentrating; she'd squeezed in a couple of drinks on the way. But there was a Japanese gentleman, whom people addressed as 'Your Excellency', identifying him as the ambassador, Mamoru Shigemitsu. He seemed lost in conversation with his American counterpart, Winant, whom she recognized, and another man whom she did not, American by the cut of his clothes, tall, middle-aged, yet still athletic in build. The party was completed by two parliamentarians and their wives, a Free French naval officer and two young French women, but all eyes seemed to be on Shigemitsu.

The Japanese was small in physique and most earnest in his expression, polite, but persistent, and very defensive. That was no surprise. He had arrived at the Court of St James's three years earlier, and with every passing season his task had grown more difficult. Japan was at war with China. It was not a popular war. The newspapers were filled with countless headlines about Japanese brutality, accompanied by disgracefully provocative photographs. Not that the British could tell the difference between a Chinese or Japanese, of course. They even delighted in their ignorance.

As much as Shigemitsu tried to reassure his audiences that Japan had no intention of attacking British possessions, not a soul believed him. Yet still he did his best.

'Japanese believe in Hakko-Ichiu,' he said.

'How fascinating, Your Excellency,' the diminutive Lady St John purred across a forkful of fish. 'What exactly does it mean?'

'It means "all the world one family". At peace.'

'How beautiful. It's a religious idea, is it? That when we've all finished being beastly to each other on this earth, we go to the same heaven?'

'No, no,' Shigemitsu protested. 'Peace on this earth. All one family. On this earth.'

'Oh, I see. I'm so relieved. There are so many rumours that Japan wants to attack us in the Far East. Tell me, Your Excellency, that's not going to happen, is it?'

'Japanese wish British people nothing but harmony,' the Japanese responded, picking over his words as though he had a mouthful of bones.

'And the Chinese?'

Shigemitsu swallowed his trout unchewed. He examined his plate, not wishing to catch Lady St John's eye for fear of betraying his annoyance. Her bluntness was ill-mannered; was she female and stupid, or simply Western and therefore incorrigibly rude?

'Our only wish is to create what we call a Greater East Asia Co-Prosperity Sphere.'

'Ah, so that's what you are doing in China. Trying to make them all prosperous. Now I understand.'

The ambassador laid down his knife and fork. Of course she didn't understand, and the silly woman was probably incapable of doing so, but it was his duty to try to bring her to some form of awareness.

'The European powers – French, Dutch, British – have many colonies in Asia. Control all oil and other raw materials. We consider the position . . . unbalanced.' He gave a little bow, as if to indicate that he was entirely satisfied with his selection of the word. 'Japan wants only similar influence in our own continent. Access to raw materials in Asia like Britain – even America.'

He made it sound so reasonable, but he had unwittingly opened up a new flank. The unknown American took it as an invitation to join in.

'And you make war in order to get them,' he stated.

The ambassador's colour darkened. 'We do not want war. War would not continue if Britain and America did not keep sending weapons to China along the Burma Road. My government believes that is very unfriendly act.'

'More than ten million dead Chinese since the war started four years ago, most of them civilians. Three hundred thousand killed in Nanking in a single winter. If you want to talk about unfriendly acts, maybe we should start with that.'

'Perhaps, sir, and begging your pardon' – he gave another little bow – 'you are not aware of the full facts of war.'

'I guess you're right, Mr Ambassador. I don't know enough about war. But since I arrived in London a few days ago, I'm beginning to catch on fast.'

'Perhaps, sir, you will permit me to suggest that you discuss the matter with your European friends, who have been fighting colonial wars for hundreds of years. They might be able to hasten your understanding.'

There was another little bob, like a karate chop.

'Mr Ambassador,' the American said, refusing to use the honorific title of 'Excellency', 'Americans hate all colonial wars. Which is why we insist on the right to continue sending supplies to China.'

'You will forgive me, sir, if I see American history in a slightly different colour. I believe – I ask you to correct me if this is not true – that your country purchased the entire territory of Louisiana from the French.'

'Not the same thing at all. Louisiana isn't a colony, it was a natural extension of the United States.'

'A very understandable argument, sir. And it was certainly closer to the United States than Alaska, which I believe you purchased later.'

'The territory of Alaska was practically empty. Full of nothing but fish and ice. I think there were maybe four hundred Russians living there.'

'Unlike the islands of the Philippines, which you fought for. Forty years ago. You will please forgive me if that is an inconvenient or inaccurate fact. Or the islands of Hawaii. I believe the United States annexed them at about the same time.'

Damn, but he was good. Lady St John beamed. She hadn't had this much fun since she had plied the then-German Ambassador, von Ribbentrop, with his own champagne and asked him to expound upon his feelings about Jews.

'I will grant you, Mr Ambassador, that history has a stubborn streak,' the American responded. 'It doesn't form itself into convenient straight lines. And the United States, like all nations, has a history that allows for questioning and criticism.' The American seemed to be conceding, perhaps aware that the Japanese was preparing to chase him fully around the globe via Guam, Puerto Rico, Cuba and several other colonial contradictions. 'But I am not concerned with history, sir. I am talking about today. And tomorrow. And the slaughter of tens of millions of innocent civilians. Whatever the cause, whatever the grievance, whatever the injustice for which redemption is sought, nothing can support such a cost.'

69

'It is most unfortunate that today warfare carries with it such a terrible price.'

'Which is why the United States has declared it will never become a combatant in this one.'

'It is a most happy situation for your United States,' the ambassador said with a smile of steel, 'that, unlike every other nation represented around this table, you have not become involved in war. For my part, I pray most earnestly that your good fortune will continue, and that you will remain free from the curse of war.'

'Hell, we don't pick fights, Mr Ambassador. We finish 'em.'

It was, in Lady St John's view, a most glorious cockfight, but it had gone far enough, for the moment. There were three other courses to get through; something had to be kept in reserve.

'Would you like some more, Your Excellency? Or have you had enough?'

'More than enough. Thank you, Lady St John.' He bowed, which allowed him to break eye contact with the American.

'I don't know much about English manners, Lady St John, but if it's not being impolite, I'd love some more,' the American said, without waiting to be asked. He'd be damned before he followed Shigemitsu. 'It's what the workers on my railroad would call "damned fine chow".' He paused only momentarily. 'I guess that's the Chinese influence, eh?'

And suddenly the table was alight with a multitude of different conversations. Pamela, who had been as transfixed as Emerald at the outpouring of male hormones, was seated between the American and his ambassador. They were both tall and dark, middle-aged, with fine eyes, but there the resemblance finished. Winant was uncombed, uncertain and largely inaudible at such occasions, whereas the other man

70

most evidently was not. And he seemed to own a railway. She placed a hand gently on his sleeve.

'Forgive me, but I didn't catch your name.'

'It's Averell Harriman.' He smiled, a little stiffly. He gazed down at her; she knew he was struggling to keep his eyes steady. It was her dress. She'd lost almost all the weight she had gained while pregnant, but a couple of additional inches had clung to her breasts and, in this dress, they showed.

'I'm Pamela Churchill.'

'I know you are. I've already met your father-in-law. He says we must all become good friends.'

'I hope you're going to do everything he tells you.'

Harriman laughed. 'That's pretty much my job description. I've been put in charge of the Lend-Lease operation. The President has told me to come over here and give you everything you want.'

'Like Santa Claus.'

'Something like that.'

'In which case, I can promise you, we shall become very good friends indeed.'

And suddenly there was laughter around the table, except from Shigemitsu.

Later, he was the first to leave. Lady St John led him to the door.

'Your Excellency, it's been such a pleasure having you with us. And particularly for me. May I let you in on a little secret? It's wonderful to be with guests of – how shall I put this? – of a similar stature. We little people should stick together, don't you think?'

He gave a stiff bow, and left. He did not think he would ever return.

*   *   *

71

In reasonably rapid succession, the hallways of Chequers echoed to the sound of bath waters parting, heavy male footsteps, a female scream and the crashing of a tray laden with crockery.

'Who the hell are you?' Churchill said, making puddles on the hallway carpet and trying to rearrange his towel with more discretion.

'Héloise. I am Héloise,' the young woman responded in a heavy accent, her eyes filled with horror.

'And what the hell are you?'

'I am the new maid.' She was struggling to avert her eyes.

'New maid. What new bloody maid?'

'The new maid we agreed on, Mr Churchill.' It was Sawyers, who had appeared as if on wings in response to the sounds of mayhem.

'I told you we didn't need one. Look at the mess she's made.'

'Well, if it's to be a race to see who can ruin rug first, I suspect you're in wi' a pretty good chance yerself, zur,' the valet replied, indicating the sodden carpet. 'Suppose I'd better do introductions. This is Héloise. Cousin to Mrs Landemare's husband. From Marseilles,' – his accent and lisp made a mockery of the name – 'before joining us here. And a very dangerous escape it were, too, so cook's been telling me.'

The girl gave a nervous bob.

'And this,' Sawyers added, turning and raising his eyebrow as though in disbelief, 'is the Prime Minister.'

'*Je suis* Churchill,' the Prime Minister growled in his execrable accent. 'I don't like new faces. And I don't like people who go round dropping trays and making a racket. If you're going to make a habit of it, you'd better stay out of my way downstairs.'

Héloise promptly burst into tears and fled. Churchill was left feeling very damp and a trifle silly.

'And tell her I prefer my eggs scrambled,' he said, stepping round the mess on the floor.

It was the twentieth of March. Pamela's twenty-first birthday.

She spent it without any form of communication from Randolph.

She sat in the rented rectory that had meant so much to her, yet which now stared back at her like a stranger. Once it had seemed to catch every shaft of sunlight, but now it collected only draughts and dust. She thought of the many nights she had burrowed beneath the blankets, hugging a favourite bear and pretending it was Randy creeping into the bedroom rather than several degrees of frost, but those days were gone. She was twenty-one. Her first day as a legal adult. Old enough to vote. And utterly miserable.

She ate her dinner alone in the kitchen, growing a little drunk as she dismantled one of Randolph's prize bottles of vintage champagne. It was part of a consignment he'd been given as a wedding present by one of his chums from White's. As she drank from a glass of the finest crystal, his photograph stared at her in reproach from its ornate silver frame – another present. She was surrounded by luxury in a house where even the mice could no longer afford to eat.

She was by upbringing a straightforward country girl, not simple, but not sophisticated either, and when Randolph had introduced her to a new life she hadn't at first entirely understood its rules. Only now was she beginning to realize that Randolph didn't understand them, either. Idiot. He was still staring from his silver frame. Defiantly she raised her glass to him and uttered something very rude.

She spent another night shivering beneath her blankets, banging her head on bloody Macauley, before she made up her mind. They had a mountain of wedding presents – crystal decanters, a canteen of exquisite cutlery, an antique carriage clock, fine wines, Lalique figurines, modern pearls and pieces of ancient porcelain, every kind of indulgent trinket that had been given to them by their rich friends – or, more accurately, the rich friends of Randolph's father. She put everything up for auction. Within two weeks they were gone, every last bit and bauble, including her jewellery and his watches. A month later, so was the rectory, rented out for three times the amount they were paying for it. Arrangements were made for the baby, who was provided with a nursery and nanny at Cherkley, the country home of his wealthy godfather, Lord Beaverbrook, which in turn gave Pamela the freedom to 'do her bit' and take a job in the Ministry of Supply. It also enabled her to take a top-floor room at the Dorchester Hotel.

Now the Dorchester, at first sight, might have seemed an unconventional choice for a woman trying desperately to save herself from financial delinquency, but it had some surprising advantages. Many of the most powerful people in London had moved into the hotel for the duration, and Pamela knew that while she was there she would never have to pay for another meal. It also happened to be one of the safest locations in London – reinforced with steel and with a deep basement. Above all else, it was close to her father-in-law. Pamela was, after all, a Churchill, and there were benefits to be had from being related to the most powerful man in the land. One of these benefits was the substantial discount that the Dorchester offered her on their standard charges.

As she told her incredulous friends, she was so hard up she couldn't possibly afford to live anywhere else.

*   *   *

There were many visitors that Easter weekend – not just family but generals, aides, the Australian Prime Minister, the Americans. It was not a season of peace.

The strain had been growing for weeks. Cold winds blew from every corner of the globe and Churchill, as always impatient, interfered in everything. He grew impatient with others, showed anger at delays and was left shouting vainly at the gods who seemed to have turned their back on him.

Every day he would examine the charts that displayed the progress of the convoys as they fought their way across the Atlantic, hurling questions at his Admiralty staff, demanding instant answers, grasping at hope. He followed not only the fate of the convoys but even individual cargoes, insisting that the machine guns, aircraft engines and fourteen million cartridges being carried from America by the *City of Calcutta* be unloaded on the west coast. 'Why in blazes do they insist on running the additional risk of taking them round to the east coast?' he demanded. 'Are they incompetent, or simply mad?'

Everywhere the news was bad. Bulgaria had joined the Axis, there were fears that Spain would follow. Yugoslavia stood defiant, but it would not be for long. Germany fell upon her and two days of bombing killed more than seventeen thousand civilians in the capital city, Belgrade. Everyone knew that Greece would be next. Churchill ordered British troops to be moved from Egypt to help in the defence of Greece, much to the open displeasure of his generals, but Churchill insisted. Yet even as the troops prepared to move, Rommel began a new advance in North Africa and threw the plans into chaos. The British began to retreat, but they couldn't even manage that properly. The new trucks and tanks that had been sent to the desert kept breaking down in the sand. Churchill once again lost his temper, demanding to know whether the War Office wanted him to go and fix the bloody machines himself. 'The Germans move forward and discover our men playing at sandcastles!' he spat contemptuously. 'They've taken two thousand British prisoners. We'll just have to find comfort in the fact that they've taken three of our bloody generals as well.'

Further east, Britain's supply problems grew with a pro-Nazi coup in oil-rich Iraq. 'It is just as happened in the last war,' Churchill sighed. 'We liberate them, then they turn on us.'

'Ungrateful Arab swine,' one aide said, but Churchill turned on him. 'Only a fool expects gratitude in the desert!'

Not for one moment did the light of battle leave his eyes, but it seemed to be devouring him, burning him out. At every point on the map there were new wounds. Britain was bleeding to death.

He saw it for himself. On Good Friday he had left for a tour of the West Country in the company of the American Ambassador. They arrived in Bristol not long after the Luftwaffe had left. Churchill had walked through streets that were no longer recognizable, had watched as inhabitants with bewildered faces emerged from their hidey-holes to find their world destroyed, had spent all morning outside without once seeing the sun through the clouds of swirling smoke. The Mayor of Bristol, soot streaked upon his face, had likened his city to ancient Rome. And so it was. Ruins.

In one corner of the city they stumbled across the remnants of a wall that had once been a row of houses. On it someone had scribbled: 'There Will Always Be An England!' but the message had been all but obliterated by scorch marks from the flames. From somewhere Winant found a piece of chalk and, kneeling in the dust, carefully restored the message to its original form.

Later that day, the old man returned to Chequers deeply affected, his jaw locked in uncharacteristic silence. He seemed unable to settle. He paced relentlessly, then instructed the Coldstream Guards who were stationed in the grounds of the house to set up a firing range a little way from the house. A few sandbags, a couple of makeshift wooden targets. He wanted to do something violent. Most of the men joined him – not Vic Oliver, he hadn't been invited – and they stood around in a light drizzle, although none seemed keen to join him as he took aim and emptied the magazine of his pistol, a Colt .45, into the target. A bullet for every fresh catastrophe of the last few days. The Atlantic, the Balkans, the deserts, the West Country. Bullet after bullet smacked home, sending splinters spitting across the lawn, and still he continued firing. A bullet for the pain of his son-in-law, Duncan Sandys, who had just been terribly injured in a car crash. Another for Sarah, who had arrived at Chequers to tell him that her marriage to Vic Oliver was falling apart.

And the very last bullet he saved for those thoughts of failure that had begun to intrude upon him at night. He was a man who throughout his life had taken pride in his ability to sleep soundly and wake refreshed, but now devils pursued him through his dreams as well as his waking hours. A whispering campaign had begun in the darker corners of the House of Commons; mutterings about 'midnight follies', 'cigar stump diplomacy', 'too much meddling and too many yes-men'. Things were all going hell-ward. And suddenly his aim failed and the bullet sped wide.

'Anyone gonna join me?' he demanded, his voice taut as a bowstring. No one stepped forward. They all knew better than to get within snapping distance of the Black Dog. So he thrust his empty weapon at his detective, Thompson, and began striding back towards the house, his hands deep in the pockets and head bent low. Only Winant seemed willing to fall in step beside him, bending his tall frame to get nearer to the old man's words, causing his unkempt hair to fall across his face.

'So tell me, Gil, my Intelligence people suggests the *Herrenvolk* are lengthening the runways on many of their airfields in Poland. You heard anything about that?'

'Can't say I have,' the American said. It made Churchill feel a little happier. It seemed he was ahead in one game, at least.

'What the hell do you think they're up to?'

'I've no idea. Not for our benefit, I guess.'

'Our' benefit. Churchill liked that. He was beginning to warm to this diffident, angular American. His shirts were habitually crumpled and his blue overcoat a diplomatic disgrace, but the man had heart.

'And it's not for the benefit of bloody Lufthansa, either,' the old man continued. 'It can only be for the bombers.'

'What bombers?'

'The bombers they will use when they fall upon Russia.'

'But Russia and Germany have a friendship pact . . .'

'So did Cain and Abel.'

'What do you think it means?'

'It means the Germans are looking east, in search of bigger game. Perhaps our tiny British islands have become an irrelevance in Hitler's eyes, a sideshow – perhaps he thinks that Winston Churchill is no longer worth the bother.'

'You make it sound personal.'

'Of course it's bloody personal! He's leaving us to die from starvation, imprisoned in our own impotence. But there might be salvation in the insult, Gil. If Germany attacked Russia, they would not dare invade these islands until they were done. It gives us time – time which we both must use.' He stopped abruptly and grabbed the ambassador's sleeves. 'Don't you see? It will change the whole nature of the war. Make it stretch around the world. Surely America must realize that it could never stay out of such a conflagration.'

The blue eyes were staring up at the taller Winant, boiling with emotion, willing the ambassador and all his countrymen to draw alongside. But it was a passion that Winant knew was so often misdirected. For the best part of a year Churchill had been bombarding Roosevelt with messages that over-flowed with obsession and excess. In the old man's eyes, every hour was the moment of destiny, the hour when civilization would collapse unless Roosevelt sent more destroyers, offered more credits, built more planes, declared war. The bombardment had been conducted without respite and it had reached the point where Roosevelt often didn't respond to Churchill's telegrams, simply ducked them, left the moment to grow cold. Not every hour could be Churchill's hour. The American President had his own battles to fight – against the isolationists who didn't want to touch the war, against the leaders of organized labour who didn't want to touch it either, not unless they got paid a whole lot more, and against Congress where good will was flowing about as slowly as treacle on a frosty day. So Roosevelt had taken to ignoring Churchill's incessant words of doom. 'I close my eyes,' the President said, 'and wake up in the morning to discover that, somehow, the world has survived.'

Winant, too, hoped for a brighter outcome. 'If Hitler attacks Russia, so might the Japs,' he suggested. 'Turn north. Into Siberia. Away from your colonies to the south.'

'No. I fear not. Siberia has no oil, no rubber, no resources. Nothing for the Japanese war machine to feast upon.'

'You mustn't always look on the dark side, Winston,' Winant said in gentle warning. 'The American people are optimists. It unsettles them if they can see no light in the gloom.'

'And what if there is no light? Do you simply sit back and pray you will find your way through the darkness? Or do you pick up a box of matches and start a bloody good fire?'

'And burn your house down in the process?'

'Perhaps you are right,' he muttered, unconvinced. 'But the Japanese Foreign Minister Matsuoka is prowling through the corridors of the Kremlin even as we speak. What the hell's he up to? Lost his way in the dark, has he?'

'He's just come from Berlin. Our intelligence suggests it's possible he's in Moscow preparing the ground.'

'For what?'

'For a declaration of war.'

'Against whom?'

'Why . . . Russia, I mean.'

'Then let it be war! War! War!' he shouted histrionically, to the alarm of the following group. Then he shook his head. 'But once again your optimistic American intelligence has got it utterly wrong'

'How can you be certain?'

'Because intelligence needs to be dipped in a bucket of common sense before it's laid on the table. And common sense suggests the Japanese haven't gone to Moscow with bunches of flowers in their hands in order to declare war, any more than they arrived in China with fixed bayonets for the purpose of setting up a wood-whittling business.'

'You don't think much of American Intelligence, then?'

'They got it half right. There will be war. And not all the optimists in America will be able to stop it,' the old man growled, before stomping off in the direction of the house.

*   *   *

Sawyers sat with Héloise at the long central table in the kitchen polishing silver, while Mrs Landemare prepared lunch.

'But I do not understand,' Héloise protested.

'Yer too young to understand such things,' Sawyers responded.

'Oh, you don't 'alf talk a lot of tommy-rot at times, Mr Sawyers,' Mrs Landemare said, peering into a bubbling pot.

'How so?'

'The girl needs to know these things, otherwise she's going to be dropping breakfast trays from here until the gates of Heaven.'

'Well, she's your relative . . .'

'My hubby's relative.'

'Your responsibility, then,' Sawyers said, reaching for a fresh buffing rag.

Mrs Landemare's face came up from the pot, her ruddy cheeks and remarkably broad forehead covered in little droplets of steam. Sawyers was opting out. Typical man.

'It's war what does it mostly,' Mrs Landemare began, turning to Héloise, 'although it goes on just as much when there ain't any war, I suppose.' Her awkwardness was stretching almost to the point of contradiction. 'It's just that . . . Well, you haven't got no mother and father, poor thing, so it's not surprising this is all a bit new. So, how can I put it?' She sipped from a ladle, then threw a little more salt in the pot. 'Great country houses are like little worlds all of their own. The ladies and gentlemen get dropped at the door, and for the time that they're here the rules of the outside world get put to one side. So Mr C wanders around without a towel at times. Don't mean nothing by it, it's just his way. So you make a bit of noise when you get near his bathroom, just so he knows you're coming.'

'Not too much noise, mark you,' Sawyers added, polishing

furiously. 'Hates too much noise, he does. And make sure he never finds you whistling.'

'He has his breakfast in bed and gets up late, he has his liking for cigars and the brandy,' Mrs L continued. 'Loses his temper a lot. Well, he's got so much on his plate.'

'Yes, I see,' Héloise whispered.

'No, no, I mean he has a lot on his mind. So he don't stick by ordinary rules all the time. And neither do his guests.'

'But what does that have to do with breakfast?' Héloise pressed.

'Well, often times his guests – all very important gentlemen, as you know – can't bring their wives. Don't *want* to bring their wives. In fact, truth be told, sometimes they have very little to do with their wives, not only here but when they're at home. You get my drift?'

Héloise wasn't sure.

'The guests are all rich folk, important people, well-to-do. They don't live like the rest of us. They may have . . .' – she stretched hesitantly for the appropriate phrase – 'arrangements. Understandings. Now they're all decent and respectable folk, mind, every one of them, but sometimes . . . well, you French understand these things. Life gets complicated. Particularly during times of war. The men think they've not got long to live, the womenfolk get swept up in the passion of the times, never knowing what tomorrow will bring, and so they . . . live a little for the moment. After lights out. No harm done, so long as no one knows and none tell.'

'You mean, while the lady guests are in their rooms . . .'

'. . . the gentlemen visit.'

'The Walk o' Many Wonders,' Sawyers said, mostly to himself.

'Don't surprise you, do it? You being French, an' all.'

'And Mr Churchill, he knows what is going on?'

'Mr C? Good Lord, no. He's as blind as ruddy old Nelson, he is. Don't know – and I suspect don't much care, either. He's got far more important things on his plate – er, mind. So, if two guests have what we might call an understanding, we make sure their rooms are suitable. Close by. Rules of the English country house.'

'But how do you know this? About strangers?'

'Bless me, they're not strangers. We know their servants. There ain't no secrets below stairs.'

Suddenly Héloise began to laugh. 'So that is why Mr Sawyers goes through the guest wing banging the breakfast gong so very early in the morning. It is not for breakfast at all. It is . . .'

''Cos gentlemen need to know when time's come to be back in their own beds,' Sawyers said, completing the thought.

Héloise began to giggle into her polishing cloth.

'Now don't you go telling me this don't happen in France,' Sawyers said, determined to defend English honour.

''Course it does,' the cook responded softly, gazing once more into the steaming pot. 'And not just above stairs. How d'you think I got my hubby?'

'Cook!' Sawyers protested.

'Well, in them days, of course, you could rely on a Frenchman to do the honourable thing,' she said, wiping her hands on her apron and smiling.

The impressive thing about Churchill's Black Dog of depression was not simply how savagely it would attack him but also how suddenly it would stop. One moment it was there, the next it had fled, run away into the darkness. When he joined his guests for drinks in the Great Hall before dinner that evening, his spirits seemed to have been entirely restored.

He walked in with cigar ash tumbling down the front of his dinner jacket and Nelson the cat in his free hand, demanding that something loud be played on the gramophone. He chose Noel Coward, tripping round the room from guest to guest, singing along with the music in a voice that was loud and out of tune, but word-perfect. *'In a jungle town where the sun beats down to the rage of man and beast the English garb of the English sahib merely gets a bit more creased. In Bangkok at twelve o'clock they foam at the mouth and run, but mad dogs and Englishmen go out in the midday sun . . .'*

'Mr Coward is a close personal friend,' he told the Americans. This seemed to startle them since they assumed Coward was, as Harriman put it, 'one of those actors who never knew which way round to button his trousers.'

'He is a great Englishman,' Churchill responded, which scarcely seemed to answer the Americans' doubts. 'When the war started he asked me what he should do. I told him to get on a warship and go to sing where the guns are blazing. Cheer 'em up!'

He waved his cigar in the manner of a conductor's baton, causing a fresh avalanche of ash to fall down his front and onto Nelson.

'Coward told me that the composition came to him during a two-thousand-mile car journey from the city of Hanoi to the borders of Thailand,' Churchill continued. 'Funny thing was, he said he didn't see a single Englishman on the trip. Nothing but Frenchies!' The admission of this patent fraud seemed to upset Nelson, who dug his claws deep into Churchill's sleeve and leapt for his freedom. 'Ungrateful beast. Brought him here to keep him away from the Blitz. Think I'll ship him off to Randolph in the bloody desert.'

In the wings, Sawyers rubbed his latest scar and growled his approval.

It was as though Churchill hadn't a care in the world. He serenaded, he smiled, he kept them all entertained. But Sawyers, circulating with the whisky and soda, watched him carefully. He knew the signs. The old man never truly relaxed. He was always on the foredeck, cutlass in hand, scanning the horizon for bad weather or enemy sails. He wasn't simply ready for action but insistent on it, straining at every seam and with the echoes of every past battle from Borodino to Blenheim ringing in his ears.

'Something of an actor, your Prime Minister,' Harriman said, accepting another tumbler of whisky.

'No, zur, not really,' Sawyers responded. 'Not much of an actor by any stretch. Particular when he's pretending to be happy.' The servant passed on.

Just as Sawyers had expected, the mood changed. By the time the music had finished, Churchill had corralled his senior military men against the piano.

'A splendid way to celebrate Easter, Prime Minister,' a general began, seeking to open the campaign on favourable terms. His hopes were immediately dashed.

'Celebrate? What the hell are we supposed to be celebrating? Just the latest defeat, or is there some new disaster I haven't heard about?'

The level of conversation dropped in every corner of the room.

'What the hell's going on in the desert, General?' Churchill continued. 'You sweep aside the Italians and advance all the way into Libya, then at the first sign of real resistance turn around and run.'

'As I think you know, Prime Minister, that is something of an oversimplification –'

'I prefer simplification to obfuscation. All I've been getting is excuses as to why we seem unable to stand and fight. One

85

bloody German arrives, General Rommel, and the whole applecart goes tumbling.'

'Not just one German, Prime Minister. Rommel did bring thirty thousand other Germans with him.'

'We have more! Yet we practise only the manoeuvres of retreat! Can't you understand what a devastating message such failure sends around the world? The British Army can whip a few damned ice-creamers, but as soon as they set against any Huns they turn and run!'

'I must protest –'

'I'm the one who's doing the bloody protesting, General! We are on our knees imploring the Greeks and Yugoslavs to stand up to the Germans, we ask the Turks to come in, too, yet we can't even do the simplest job ourselves. We ran from them in Norway, we ran from them in France, now we can't even manage a little rough and tumble in the desert.'

The general was beginning to wilt before the repeated broadsides, but found no means of retreat. The grand piano was digging into his back. 'The fact of the matter is, Prime Minister, that the Germans have better-equipped divisions. Better aircraft, better tanks, better guns –'

'And better generals, perhaps. Ever thought of that? If this were any other army we'd be organizing a firing squad for a couple of 'em.'

'Sir, really!'

'D'you know what's happened?' Churchill was jabbing at him with a finger. 'D'you know the cost of your failure in the desert? Almost overnight we've not only undermined our position in North Africa but in the Balkans, too – and in Washington. Every day I have to go cap in hand to the Americans to beg for more aid, but how hard are they going to listen if they think that everything they send is going to end up disappearing down a sand hole – or worse, being turned over to the Afrika Korps?'

'The terrain is very difficult, Prime Minster, flat and dry. Nowhere to establish a good defensive position.'

'You fall back on your supplies, while Rommel's getting ever farther away from his. Why can't you just turn and chop him off?' Churchill's hand came down with considerable violence, again and again. The general sighed. Churchill still seemed to assume that warfare was conducted with bows and arrows; he had no idea about the complexity of modern mechanical warfare.

'We need to draw everything together, make preparations before we can mount a counter-attack.'

'Make sure all the tunics are buttoned properly, eh?'

The general bristled with indignation, but Churchill paid no heed. His fists were clenched, his head bent forward like a battering ram, as though he wanted to fight the campaign in the desert himself across the rugs and wooden floor of Chequers.

'General, let me offer you another simplification. Two weeks ago, I was told that we'd won a great victory in the desert and that our position was secure. Today the road to Cairo and Suez lies wide open awaiting the German boot. Once again we are in disarray and I have nothing to report to the people but failure. I promised them victory, I was told we had it – and now this! Everything we have invested in the North African campaign is in danger of being swept into the sea. You send me charts and statistics and requests for more supplies, but I've sent my own son there and thousands more like him. British soldiers, the best we have, ready and keen to fight. Yet they can't fight if those in command won't ask them to. One victory, one victory against the Germans, that's all I look for. Is that too much to ask? If it is, tell me, then either we can find a new Prime Minister who is content to run up the flag of surrender – or I shall find new generals who understand what England expects!'

The overflowing emotion was partly for show, of course – but only partly.

'An old man in a hurry,' Winant whispered to Harriman in a far corner of the room. 'But what a magnificent sight.'

'What was that?' a voice demanded. They were no longer alone. Fingers plucked at their sleeves and their nostrils filled with a fresh, unmasculine fragrance.

'Are you two gentlemen conspiring?' the voice continued. It was Sarah; Pamela was at her side.

'Not at all,' Winant protested.

'Then you are being remarkably unsociable, sticking to yourselves in the corner like this. Almost everyone else here is so dull and military. You're not allowed to hide away.' Sarah forced her way between them, almost flirtatiously.

'We were simply remarking on how much energy your father has,' Harriman offered in defence, smiling down at her.

'He's instructed us to make sure you feel at home. Part of the family. Overwhelm you with admiration and alcohol; weren't those his precise words, Pam?'

Sarah raised her own glass and drank, a little too eagerly. The mistiness in her eyes suggested she hadn't the same tolerance for the stuff as her father. Winant looked around the room, but her husband was nowhere to be seen; he hadn't made an appearance all evening.

'We are diplomats, madam,' Harriman said, amused. 'We are above temptation.'

'Mr Harriman –'

'Averell. Please call me Averell.'

'Averell, I'm going to let you in on a little secret,' Sarah replied in a stage whisper that encouraged him to draw closer still. 'Diplomats are like women. Only ever to be trusted when they're on their own.'

Their laughter was interrupted by Sawyers, who had reappeared with a gong. He gave it a gentle rap and announced that dinner was served.

'What will it be tonight, I wonder? Rissoles? Or Blitz Broth?'

'What on earth . . . ?'

'Rissoles. An English delicacy. Sausage skin stuffed with vegetables. They're all the rage, apparently. And Blitz Broth is something the Government has just suggested is the answer to all our problems. God knows what's in it. Bones, mostly. No wonder Pam's been able to lose so much weight since the baby.'

Harriman turned to the other woman. 'I'm distressed to hear that you're suffering so much, Pamela. As the coordinator of the Lend-Lease programme, I guess it's my duty to do something about it. Will you let me invite you to dinner sometime? I think the President would insist.'

Pamela's smile of encouragement was nudged aside by an overstated sigh that escaped from Sarah. Her eyes had fixed upon her husband, who had appeared in response to the summons of the gong. 'Enjoy your dinner, gentlemen,' she said. A cloak of unhappiness seemed to descend on her shoulders as she detached herself from their company. They watched her go.

'She is a most elegant woman,' Winant said softly, almost to himself.

'And married,' Harriman added.

'Of course. No offence intended,' he said, turning in apology to Pamela. 'I'll have to content myself with admiring her from afar.'

'What a completely rotten waste of time,' Pamela

responded, taking both their arms and leading them into dinner.

The instinct that Churchill had expressed to Winant on the firing range had been right. Yosuke Matsuoka, the bespectacled, bushy-browed Japanese Foreign Minister and a Cavalier of the Order of the Sacred Treasure, First Class, had not gone to Moscow with the intention of declaring war. He was fêted and fussed over by Stalin, plied with praise and considerable quantities of vodka and caviar, and on Easter Day they did a deal.

It had happened before. Less than two years earlier Stalin had signed a Non-Aggression Pact with Germany. They were ideological enemies of the most implacable kind, of course, filled with mutual loathing, but necessity brings together the strangest partners on the diplomatic dance floor. The pact had set aside their differences, at least for a while. Hitler would not attack Stalin, leaving them both free to pursue their other interests. Within days, Hitler had begun his war, taking his conquests right up to the Soviet border, but not an inch beyond. While Poland was crushed and Britain and France were reduced to wringing their hands in despair, Stalin's neat diplomatic sidestep had kept his country out of the war and free from attack in the West.

Now he staged a repeat performance, signing a five-year peace treaty with the Japanese that recognized their conquests in China and saved himself from attack in the east.

'It is everything I feared,' Churchill said softly, replacing the telephone in its cradle. It was long after midnight; Harriman and Winant were seated beside him in his study.

'Bad news, Winston?'

'Of the worst kind. Peace has broken out across all the Russias.'

'I'm confused,' Harriman responded. 'How can peace be bad news?'

He turned to his guests. 'Peace is not a natural state of affairs in Russia. It is not a condition that endures. When Stalin declared to the world that he had made peace with Germany, war erupted before the echo had died. Now he declares peace with Japan.' He disappeared for a moment inside a haze of blue cigar smoke. 'The forces of Imperial Nippon can no more be held from aggression than wind can be persuaded not to blow. If they do not turn north, then it must be south. Trying to build the Japanese Empire on the ruins of our own.'

He turned to stare at both of them, his heavy brow creased, the jaw set firm.

'Soon, gentlemen, Japan will be at war with Britain. But before that day comes, they will find themselves at war with Winston bloody Churchill!'

FIVE

The bombers came early that evening. The warning sirens heralded a night of relentless torment, unusual even by the standards of Londoners. Winant was with Churchill in the Cabinet Room of Number Ten. Both men tried to ignore the growing signs of advancing chaos, but eventually a great sigh escaped from Churchill.

'We must go. If I stay, others must stay. And I have promised Mrs Churchill.'

They both placed helmets on their heads and made their way out of the front door of the soot-streaked building, through the cobbled quadrangle of the India Office, past tangles of barbed wire and sandbag pillboxes, until they came to the doorway that led to the underground complex of the Cabinet War Rooms. Here, buried beneath a three-foot thick concrete slab that had been reinforced with steel rods and tram tracks, the outside world ceased to exist. The air tasted of oil, the artificial light lent skin a pale and corpse-like hue, the noise of the ventilation system was constant and in the corner of the eye there always seemed to be the scurrying of rats. The only indication of the world above them was a sign in the corridor, like a railway signal, that indicated the weather conditions outside, and which was always posted to 'Windy' during a bombing raid. A small joke, a gesture of

English defiance, but entirely unnecessary. Even down this deep they could hear the bombs beginning to fall.

'You will forgive me, Gil,' Churchill said as he entered a small, windowless room. It was desperately claustrophobic, with room for little more than a cot and a washstand, and a small fan for ventilation. Churchill sat on the bed. 'Forgive me, Gil, but I am forced to involve you in a childish deception. In order to calm her, I was forced to promise Mrs Churchill that I would retire here as soon as the bombing started. I have done so. The bargain is honoured, my word is redeemed.' He forced himself to his feet. 'And now we can go upstairs.'

Restless. Winant had never seen him in any other guise. Always on the move, unless he slept. Now they began to climb again, Churchill leading the way in his one-piece siren suit, his shoes pounding on concrete steps, up ladders, along a long circular stairway that led them ever higher until they came to a small manhole. They emerged onto the roof of the Air Ministry. An observation post had been built out of sandbags and here they took shelter, gazing in awe at the power of the events unfolding around them.

Great pillars of fire stretched up from the searchlights, punching holes in the roof of the night sky, while every moment new stars blazed into life, then died, as the guns went about their business. In the distance a single glowing ball was trailing smoke across the horizon, like a comet come to earth. Winant barely had time to wonder whether the crew had made it out before his eye was dragged away by the sights of other men dying out there, and women and children, too. He had never known flame in so many forms – amber, burning like a cruel sun; deep indigoes; purples; malevolent greens; crimson, like blood. And the purest mocking white where the magnesium flares fell and the fires were most fierce. It made him think of the Day of Judgement, and it also made him afraid.

People were being buried, and burnt, beneath it all. He could hear them screaming, but only in his imagination, for in his ears there was room only for the pounding of the guns and the dull crunching of the bombs, the droning of the planes overhead and the desperate ringing of the bells of the fire engines below. His nostrils filled with the acrid stench of a city being reduced to ash; it was a memory that clung to him every day for the rest for his life.

Winant couldn't know it at the time, but the Germans dropped more than a hundred thousand bombs that night, the majority of them incendiaries. They devoured St Peter's in Belgravia and the Old Church in Chelsea, they reduced Jermyn Street to cinders and ruined much of the rest of Mayfair, tore great gashes across the heart of London. In the morning, those who were left would emerge from their shelters and their hiding holes, crawl out from beneath their tables and stairs and from the dark underground places where they had made their beds, and they would try to reassemble the pieces that had been left behind. They would pick amongst the rubble, digging out their neighbours who were still alive, burying those who were not. Then they would begin the search for food, and for what was left of their lives.

The American was watching London being tortured to death. And he knew this had happened most nights for months.

Churchill said something, but Winant couldn't hear; he moved closer. He could see tears trickling down his cheeks. Then he made out the words.

'When will it all end?'

For a moment, the old man's strength seemed to fail him and he slumped onto the chimneystack that stood nearby.

Winant waited, his eyes smarting from the heat of the tormented wind that came from the fires.

Slowly Churchill's chin came up and he began reciting a favourite poem. '"And not by eastern windows only/ When daylight comes, comes in the light/ In front the sun climbs slow, how slowly!/ But westward – look! – the land is bright."' He turned to the ambassador. 'Always a favourite verse of mine. Never more apt.' He indicated that Winant should sit on the stack beside him. 'My dear Gil, we owe you so much.'

'But I have been able to give so little.'

'I shall never find words that will properly express my gratitude for what you have just done with the convoys.'

'It was the President, not I,' Winant began. Roosevelt had decided that the US Navy would accept responsibility for security in the whole of the western half of the Atlantic. It meant that for two thousand miles of their perilous journey back home, the British convoys might have some hope of safe passage.

'But I know you supported it, encouraged it. I have watched you as the weeks have passed. You came knowing so little of our land, and you have become its great friend.' Churchill reached out to squeeze the other man's hand. 'But I must ask for more. Must have more! You see about you what is happening. We shall carry on the fight, of course, if necessary until there is nothing left but cinders, yet by then it will be too late.'

'What are you saying, Winston?'

'America must join this war. Not simply through its words and the output of its factories but with its men-at-arms and its entire might. Together the British Empire and the United States have more wealth, more aircraft, more steel, more technical resources, than the whole of the rest of the world. We can put an end to this incineration of our dreams. The President must declare war.'

'You know he cannot do that. Only Congress can declare war. And it is the President's view that they will not do so – not yet at least. And for what it's worth, I agree with him.'

Churchill thrust an arm at the red sky that glowed like an Egyptian dawn, his voice filled with reproach. 'What more will it take to convince them?'

'Winston, for every American who shouts in your support, there's another who says it's not his war, that Britain may yet be defeated, that there is no point.'

'And we shall be defeated if you will not join us! Will you inherit a world filled with nothing but suffering and slaves?'

'There are those in Washington who would do anything to help you. You must be patient. The job will be done.'

'There is no patience to war,' Churchill exclaimed heatedly, 'except in the grave.'

'If it were up to me, with all my heart I would throw our lot in with yours. But it is not up to me. Nor is it up to the President. It is up to the Congress. And they will not.'

'No! No more procrastination. No more delay. I shall telegraph the President. I shall demand – or beg, if that's what it takes. America must join us in this war.'

'You know as much about the American Constitution as any man. You know it was drawn up with the specific intention of avoiding foreign entanglements.'

'Oh, and how well it has stood the test of time!' Churchill did nothing to hide his contempt.

'Winston,' the ambassador replied, embarrassed by the confrontation, 'the President cannot.'

'He'll never know if he doesn't try.'

'He's doing everything he can.'

'Waging war to the last Briton!'

They sat, two friends divided by adversity and neither man daring to say more.

The moment was broken by a shout from the manhole that led to the roof. It was a Fire Guard. 'What the bloody hell do you think you two are up to?' he shouted, half choking.

They turned, silhouettes against the burning sky.

'I said what the . . .' His words died on his lips as he saw the glow of a cigar in the night.

'You have a point to make?' a familiar voice growled.

'I didn't recognize . . . Couldn't see . . . It's just that . . . I'm sorry, sir, but you're sitting on the chimney. Blocking it. We've had to evacuate everyone from the floor below. Thought you were a ruddy German incendiary. Didn't realize you were . . . Oh, hell.' He disappeared like a rabbit down his hole.

The two men clasped each other, struggling to control their laughter.

'It seems I am ever at fault,' Churchill said, growing serious once more. 'I hope that you will forgive me, my friend. Both my temper and my tongue were misplaced. Nevertheless, I shall send my telegram to the President. And you will understand, I hope, if I ask you to strain every sinew to ensure there is a reply. Mr Roosevelt is a busy man. Sometimes I know he finds my communications difficult to deal with. But this is not a message that can be allowed to die of neglect.'

'I shall do my utmost.'

'I know it.'

Then: more shrieks and tearing explosions, the rattle of shrapnel falling on rooftops near at hand. Winant was pointing. 'Look, Winston, they've hit the Admiralty.'

As the smoke cleared, they could see the cupola above the clock tower had gone, and much of the rest of the building's superstructure.

The Prime Minister stared intently. 'The Admiralty. My old offices.'

'What a pity.'

'Not entirely. It opens up a new line of sight. Now I shall be able to see Nelson on his Column more clearly.'

The bombers had been elsewhere. Liverpool, Swansea, Southampton, Bristol, Coventry. Harriman had gone to see for himself the effect the raids had had. He found tears. Defiance. Death. When he returned to his suite in the Dorchester after two days without sleep, his shoes were ripped and his clothes were sour with smoke. He kicked open the door to his rooms and sighed as he saw the accumulation of clutter that had been pushed beneath it: letters, telegrams, bills, invitations. On a single sheet of crested notepaper he discovered a long list of messages. The receptionist had tried to assemble them in what she thought was an appropriate order of priority. Downing Street had called; the Prime Minister wanted to see him that afternoon. The Foreign Secretary also requested a meeting, as did the Minister of Supply. He needed to contact his embassy, his daughter, his broker. A message from his shirt maker, regretting that the new shirts he had been expecting to collect from the shop in Jermyn Street were no longer there, and neither was the shop.

And a note from Mrs Pamela Churchill, just to let him know she was still hungry.

The Prime Minister didn't get his answer. The President wasn't ready, and the last thing the American President intended was to be pushed around by an ageing imperialist. He still had many doubts about Churchill. At the start of the war he had reluctantly come to the conclusion that Churchill was the best man Britain had for the job, even if he was drunk half the time. Little had happened to change his mind. According to the reports reaching Roosevelt, Churchill was still drinking, but was still the best man for the job.

Half drunk. And wholly ungrateful. Roosevelt had done everything he could. He'd stretched the Constitution to its breaking point, had sold battleships to the British, had twisted the Neutrality Acts beyond recognition, and was about to send across so much weaponry under Lend-Lease that if it all arrived at once the British islands might sink beneath their own seas. And still the bloody man demanded more.

"Mr President, I am sure that you will not misunderstand me if I speak to you exactly what is in my mind. The one decisive counterweight I can see to balance the growing pessimism," Churchill had written, "would be if the United States were immediately to range herself with us as a belligerent power."

A belligerent power? Declare war? Madness. Roosevelt had grown accustomed to ignoring the messages that overflowed with alcohol and emotion and that called for all sorts of impossibilities – even though he had learnt never entirely to dismiss impossibilities. It was a lesson picked up the hard way. Roosevelt had been paralysed by polio in middle age, couldn't walk, had lost the use of his legs, might've died. He was a cripple in a wheelchair – and, yet, he was the most powerful man in the world. The only impossibilities lay in the limitations of a man's mind, and Roosevelt was coming to learn that Winston Churchill had very few limits. He might yet get those things he demanded.

But not today. The Englishman would get no response to his call, no matter how hard he pushed. Roosevelt wasn't going to sacrifice his career and reputation as Wilson had twenty years earlier by getting dragged too deep into the troubles of Europe. Anyway, the Congress was split, the American public at odds, the country not even close to the degree of unity needed to pursue a war. Lindbergh, the star of the America First movement and the arch-proponent of appeasement with Germany, had just spoken at a rally in New York City. Thirty-five thousand people had jammed the streets to hear him. That was one hell of a political hand to play.

And there was the depressing but inescapable possibility that the Brits were about to get their butts whipped. They might be kicked out of the Middle East, and then out of the entire war. So what would be the point of joining them?

No, he'd gone about as far as he could. The arguments would go on, he would listen to them, then he'd ignore them – just as he had ignored those advisers who wanted most of the US Pacific Fleet to sail to the Atlantic, and the others who'd argued that is should sail to Singapore. If ever they could get their acts together, he'd pay heed, but in the meantime the Pacific Fleet could stay just where it was, in Hawaii, at the port of Pearl Harbor.

And that old English imperialist could be left to swing in the wind a little longer.

After their dinner he had taken her for champagne at the Four Hundred Club, but neither of them was much in the mood.

'It's changed,' Pamela said.

'What has?' Harriman asked.

'London. It's a different place, somehow sadder. More drab. Last year we would have sat here surrounded by laughter and with all the women parading in their finest frocks. But now . . .'

Even a middle-aged man like Harriman could feel it. Everything seemed subdued – the conversations, the colours, the humour of the waiters, the teasing gaiety of the girls. Even the champagne seemed flat. In that distant first year of war the party-goers had taken delight in thumbing their noses at Hitler by partying with abandon and usually to excess, but the mood had changed, ground down by the bombing. Death wasn't playing on some distant battlefield any more. Some of the couples were even carrying their gas masks.

'You look tired,' she said, touching the back of his hand. 'Do you want to go home?'

He shook his head. 'I wouldn't sleep.' Anyway he was enjoying the sensation of being examined closely by young blue eyes.

'I was in Plymouth two days ago. It was still burning. Little but ruins, places where the day before there had been whole terraces of homes. And in the Naval barracks –' Suddenly he caught himself. 'I apologize, Pamela. I'm being a bore. This conversation is not suitable for a young woman.'

'I am not just a young woman,' she reprimanded gently. 'I'm a Churchill. You can't shock or surprise me. And telling me will probably help you.' Her hand was back on his. He squeezed it.

'They'd hit the barracks,' he began once again. 'Lots of damage, many dead. Just young kids, most of them. They'd turned the gymnasium into a temporary casualty station, with all the wounded laid out in their beds. At the end of the gymnasium there was a low curtain, and from behind this curtain came a terrific banging. Hammering. I noticed all the young kids glancing that way, so I went to see what was up.' Harriman was nearly thirty years older than Pamela, his

102

features worn with experience, carrying so much more emotion and pain than younger men, she thought.

'They were nailing the dead in their coffins,' he added, his voice snagging on the memory. He reached quickly for his glass. 'I never had any idea what you people would put up with in order to win this war.'

'You still don't.'

'Meaning?' He stared into her eyes. She could see pain, doubt, exhaustion swirling within him, and the smudge of defeat.

'The champagne's flat,' she said. 'Let's go.'

As he gathered their coats, he thought it was the end of their evening, but instead she linked her arm through his and began guiding him through the streets of London by the half-light of the moon. Low clouds were being driven by a cold wind, enough to keep the bombers away that night, and beneath their feet the white-painted edges of the pavement peered dimly through the night. The streets through which they passed gave off only faint details, hiding behind their blackout curtains, and he soon lost his bearings. There was no colour, no light, nothing but different shades of darkness. He sensed more than he saw. Dead streets, abandoned buildings, hollowed eyes where once there had been windows and life. And everywhere the smell of ancient dust and old coffins.

He asked no questions, content to be led as she held his arm ever tighter, feeling revived by her youth and determination. They had been walking for a considerable time when he thought he could hear signs of life up ahead. The noises of a railway line, whistling steam, the clatter of trains straining slowly through the night.

And suddenly people, loitering outside the entrance to a railway arch that had been concealed with what even in the dark was a makeshift construction of timber and canvas sheeting. The stench that hit him as she led him inside was enough to make him want to turn and run. Hundreds of people, men, women, children, had crowded beneath the arch, sleeping on rough cots, wooden boards, in old boxes. Many had nothing but blankets on the cold concrete floor. There was no evidence of facilities for washing, and the toilets by the front entrance were nothing more than buckets screened by canvas covers. As he looked, to his disgust, Harriman saw that the buckets were overflowing and effluent was swimming beneath the covers towards those sleeping nearby. Condensation crept down the vast brick walls, winking malevolently in the light of a few hurricane lamps and candles. The scene was almost medieval.

Near to the latrines, two women in ragged skirts and old woollens huddled around a coke brazier, roasting an onion in the embers, trying to ward off the foul smell of the sulphur.

'Why did you bring me here?' he whispered.

'This is the front line,' she replied. 'The homeless. The people who have lost everything in the bombing.'

'But why here?' He gazed around in disgust, struggling to resist the temptation to put a handkerchief to his face.

'Railway arches, factory cellars, church crypts – there are dozens of these places.'

'But why don't you rehouse them, feed them, find some-where better?'

'I rather think that's become your job.'

He looked at her in confusion.

'Averell, the war isn't going to be won just on the battle-fields. It will have to be won right here, too, amongst the people. They have to be given the hope that one day they will have something better than this, or otherwise . . .'

'How can they put up with this, even for a day?'

'Ask them.'

Cautiously he crossed to where the women were huddled around the brazier. A filthy mongrel lay curled at their feet. They eyed his tailored overcoat and gloves with suspicion.

'Come to gawp, 'ave we?' one said, pulling a filthy woollen shawl around exhausted breasts.

'Not to gawp. To help.'

'One of those Yanks, are you?' the other said, the distrust replaced by curiosity. 'Wouldn't have no cigarettes in those expensive pockets of yours, would you, love?'

He fumbled around and offered up an entire pack. Her eyes grew large with desire.

'Take them,' he said.

'What, all of 'em?'

'A little Lend-Lease.'

'You mean we 'ave to give 'em back?'

He shook his head and smiled. 'Compliments of President Roosevelt and Mr Churchill.'

'Well, if they're good enough for Winnie,' the first said, snatching the pack. 'Likes a good smoke, does ol' Winnie. Came 'ere last week, 'e did. With 'is missus.'

'He came here?'

'That's what I said. Looked at us all and said it was disgraceful. Said 'e was sorry.'

'Did he tell you what he was going to do about it?'

''Course 'e did. Said he was going to get you Yanks into the war, whip bloody old Hitler and light 'is cigars on the ruins of Berlin.'

The evident sincerity of the woman's faith astonished Harriman. She stood in filth yet talked of victory.

'Do you think you will win the war?' he asked.

''Course we will.'

'Why are you so certain?'

'We got to win. Otherwise the 'ole country's going to be like this. Like one of those camps in Germany.'

'Camps?'

'The camps he's built. Thousands of people go in, and none of 'em ever seem to come out. Priests, politicians. Jews, of course. All forgotten.'

'Prisoners of the Reich.'

The woman shook her head slowly. 'No, not prisoners, love. You Yanks got a lot to learn.'

She turned her attention away from him and towards the pack of cigarettes, which she began to share carefully with her friend. After the division of the spoils, one cigarette remained. With rough fingers she nipped it in two, compared their lengths, settled one half behind her ear and handed the other across to her friend. When Pamela looked up at Harriman, she found his eyes filling with a mixture of awe and pride. A pack of cigarettes. His first contribution to winning the war.

As they left, they could hear the woman breaking into a soft lullaby of delight in a voice as cracked as a paving stone. *'It's the same the 'ole world over. It's the poor what gets the blame. It's the rich what gets the pleasure. Ain't it all a bloody shame . . .'*

It was likely to be a difficult anniversary. It was a year to the day since the great parliamentary convulsion that had overwhelmed the Government of Neville Chamberlain and left him bleeding on the steps of the Capitol, and a few were intent on doing the same with his successor. Mutterings about Churchill's high-handedness had begun during the long nights of winter and had taken vigorous root beneath the spring Blitz. Members of Parliament were feeling excluded, fed up with hearing more about what was going on from the barmen at their clubs than they ever did from the Government, so they had demanded a debate, a chance to put their points, to make the Government listen. Churchill had responded by turning it into a vote of confidence. This meant that Members would be forced to take sides, to vote for either Churchill or Hitler, so it became inevitable that he would win and win overwhelmingly. Yet this tactic itself smacked of an overly thin skin and – well, even more high-handedness. He would win the vote, but it would make it more difficult for him to win the argument. It was a risk he had decided to take. Some would grasp the opportunity to throw logs beneath his wheels – but, surely, only a few?

Anthony Eden, the Foreign Secretary, had opened the debate for the Government, standing tall at the Despatch Box, as over-groomed as ever. Before the war he had led a group that became known as 'the Glamour Boys', yet somehow his fastidious appearance no longer struck the right note in a city under desperate siege. His speech seemed to struggle, too, so nit-picking that it entirely missed the point.

Then came the turn of the log-throwers.

The House was crowded, febrile, with many Members wanting to make their point yet knowing they would have precious little time to do so. It encouraged an intensity of feeling and expression that soon became remorseless.

One accused the Government of fighting the war 'with kid gloves', others said the strategy was wrong, the intelligence lacking, the propaganda misplaced, the Foreign Office outma-noeuvred. They were like abandoned housewives queuing up to complain over the garden fence. The Speaker looked to the right and left of him, calling Member after Member, but none seemed to have much good to say for the Government, even the West Country backbencher who rose to profess that he was an ardent supporter of the Prime

Minister, but – that little word that could explode in their midst with the ferocity of a hand grenade – but 'what we want is a panzer and not a pansy Government!'

It was far from uplifting rhetoric, but it hit home, and it hurt.

These were armchair generals who fought over every theatre of war, from the furthest reaches of the Atlantic to the deserts and oilfields of the Middle East. 'How was it that our Intelligence was apparently taken by surprise by the events in Iraq?' one demanded to know. 'Our Secret Service is obviously not comparable with that of the last war . . .'

Then the Speaker called John McGovern. He was from the Clydeside, his accent was broad, his vowels long, his anger totally unquenchable. 'The country is being led to disaster,' he told the House. 'The people o' this country ha' been misled and lied to, in the most brazen manner.' He gazed around the packed benches, his eyes burning with fury. 'There is a growing antagonism to the war. The people themselves canna see light in this war. They canna see the great victories that ha' been promised to them.'

Yet these log-throwers had produced mere twigs compared with what was about to follow.

Leslie Hore-Belisha was a deeply disgruntled man. He was short and portly, a man of few social graces but soaring ambition who had once thought he should be Prime Minister, and let everyone know it. The Bore-Belisha, or Horeb-Elisha, as Churchill referred to him. He had once been the Secretary of State for War, a Cabinet colleague of Churchill's, a vital and reforming figure, but ultimately always an outsider in the corridors of power, and not solely because he was a Jew. He had never been a team player and as a result had paid the price; now he wore his resentment on his sleeve and had become one of Churchill's most prominent critics.

From his first breath, denunciation dripped from his lips. Ministers were misguided. Dangerous. Self-deceiving. Acting on wrong information, and wrongly interpreting it. They had failed to bomb Italy, failed to send enough troops to Greece, failed to build enough tanks, failed, failed, failed! And in his travels across the disasters of recent months, he stumbled across not a single word of support for Churchill, whom he described as 'almost the only man who can lose the war in an afternoon.' The Prime Minister had brushed aside Parliament and bemused the press, he said, and had used America as a crutch, leading Britain astray about what help might be expected from across the Atlantic. ' We ought to thank God for President Roosevelt every day, but it is unfair to him and to his country to overstate what is possible.'

Churchill squirmed, but only inside. He tried to give the impression that he was enjoying the moment, chin up, even smiling. But he would not look at Hore-Belisha.

Others did. Even cheered the bastard on.

Then, oh, then, David Lloyd George rose to his feet. The man was a legend, a speaker of spellbinding powers, a Welsh wizard who had been Prime Minister during the last war, who had taken a devastated nation and led it to victory. He was a man of humour, of grace, of deep mischief, who had befriended Churchill early in his career, guided him, even given him a post in his Cabinet. He was now seventy-eight years of age and well beyond his prime, but even past his best he was still better than most, and fashioned to a far finer quality than Hore-Belisha. Lloyd George knew when to smile, when to applaud, knew how to kill with a quip and to consume an opponent with a word of kindness. He liked Churchill, admired him, you could see the affection twinkling in the old eyes as he looked across the floor of the House at his former protégé, yet he made no attempt to hide his belief that the Prime Minister had got the war hopelessly wrong.

He didn't want this motion of no confidence in the Government, he stated immediately. The last thing he wanted was to get rid of the Prime Minister; what he wanted was to get rid of the Prime Minister's bad habits. And that wasn't going to happen if Churchill continued to ignore the House of Commons. Growls of support erupted from all sides. He threw scorn at Churchill's arguments, and his statistics. 'The Prime Minister has said that Germany has seventy million "malignant Germans".' He shook his head. 'No. There are eighty million Germans. You do not kill ten million Germans with a word, however potent it may be.' He mocked, and others mocked with him.

'The war is passing through one of its most difficult and discouraging phases,' he continued in lilting Welsh tones that were drenched in sorrow. 'We must have an end of the kind of blunders which have discredited and weakened us.' And although his voice was no longer strong, they heard every biting word. 'We have to cross a very dark chasm. But there is, of course, America.' Ah, America, to which Churchill looked at every turn. Lloyd George nodded towards the Prime Minister, as though in agreement with him. 'Now, I am not disparaging America. We have to hold out until America is ready with her equipment . . .'

'Tools!' someone shouted.

The aged warrior was still staring directly at Churchill, his blue eyes piercing through the long silver-stranded forelocks that fell across his face. 'But it is most important not to exaggerate what we are going to get, or how quickly we are going to get it.' He was taking Churchill head-on, using his own words as a lance to prick him. 'I warn my fellow countrymen not to be impatient, and to see to it that we *ourselves* do the job, until America is ready – and to do it more thoroughly than we are doing it now!'

It was crushing stuff coming from a man who had so much experience, who had earned so much respect, and who had once been so close to Churchill. Yet there was more to come, one specific change that he sought. He thought the Government was too much of a one-man show – Churchill's show. And one man couldn't – and shouldn't – try to do it all himself.

'The Prime Minister must have a real War Council. He has not got it. Now, the Prime Minister is a man with a very brilliant mind, one of the most remarkable men who have graced this House. There is no doubt about his brilliant qualities' – he looked around him, smiling wickedly as the claim was greeted with much laughter and cheering from all sides, not all of it meant kindly – 'but for that very reason he wants a few more *ordinary* persons to look after him.'

'He's got some already!' one wag called out, pointing at Eden and the row of Ministers beside him. A collective shuffle of discomfort spread along the Government front bench. Hurl bombs and bullets, they could withstand them all, but the Welshman's wit was far more piercing.

'The Prime Minister wants men against whom he can check his ideas,' Lloyd George continued, 'who are independent, who will stand up to him and tell him exactly what they think.' They all knew what that implied: he was accusing Churchill of bullying, of riding roughshod over others. 'But it's no use their doing so if they know nothing about it. Now I'm not disparaging the men – at least some of the men – whom the Prime Minister has in his Cabinet' – fingers were being pointed at the Ministers beside Churchill, and the laughter had once more tipped into gentle mockery – '*but*,' he said, in a tone that implied he was letting them all in on a wicked secret, 'I have seen one or two of them at work.'

Belatedly, the Ministers themselves began to join in the laughter. If they were to be accused of incompetence, they at least needed to show they had a sense of humour. Yet it was biting, hurtful stuff. This was a Government of one man and a bunch of coconuts and, in Lloyd George's view, that simply wasn't good enough.

The House had grown agitated, restless like a nervous colt, in danger of bolting in the wrong direction. When Churchill rose to his feet, he knew he had to bring them back under control. His notes lay before him on the Despatch Box; they contained copious squiggles and amendments in the margins. He hadn't come prepared for such a battering, but he was a masterful horseman. He reached for his whip.

First he had to ride to the rescue of his Foreign Secretary, Eden. It was a pity that he needed rescuing, but he was a refined man with a sensitive nature, not well fitted for the bear pit, better suited to taking tea. That's why he was in the Foreign Office. Churchill accused Eden's opponents, baldly and unashamedly, of helping the enemy.

'I did not think the speech of Mr Lloyd George was particularly helpful at a period of what he himself calls' – he checked his notes – 'discouragement and disheartenment.' He looked up directly at his old colleague, seated only a few feet away, and his voice grew sad. 'It wasn't the sort of speech which one would have expected from the great war leader of former days, who was accustomed to brush aside despondency and alarm and push on irresistibly towards the final goal.'

There was respect and deep affection interwoven with the admonition. They were two old warriors who for so long had ridden together towards the same enemy.

'I am not one – and I should be the last – unduly to resent

unfair criticism,' Churchill told them, 'or even fair criticism, which is so much more searching. But there is a kind of criticism which is a little *irritating*. It is like that of a bystander who, when he sees a team of horses dragging a heavy wagon painfully up a hill, cuts a switch from the fence and belabours them lustily.' His faithful supporters shouted at Lloyd George across the floor; Churchill held up his hand for them to cease. 'He may well be animated by a benevolent purpose – and who shall say the horses may not benefit from his efforts, and the wagon get quicker to the top of the hill? Still, I think that it would be a pity if this important and critical debate consisted wholly of critical and condemnatory speeches.'

Yet he had no desire to slash too deeply at Lloyd George; the man was too much of an icon, too much of a friend. The same could not be said of Hore-Belisha.

'He and some others have spoken of the importance in war of full and accurate intelligence of the movements and intentions of the enemy.' Churchill raised his whip, and brought it thrashing down. 'That is one of the glimpses of the obvious and of the obsolete with which his powerful speech abounded.' Churchill's men laughed and jeered. 'He is so far-seeing, now that we have lost his services, this man who told us at the end of November 1939 that we were comfortably winning the war!'

The anger was spilling over, but he needed to draw back just a little, and remind them who the real enemy was.

'This vast German war machine, which was so improvidently allowed to build itself up during the last eight years' – he looked around, searching for the guilty men who had fallen asleep on their watch – and wasn't Hore-Belisha one of them? – 'has now spread from the Arctic to the Aegean, and from the Atlantic Ocean to the Black Sea. Yet that is no source of strength . . .' He banged his fist upon the Despatch

113

Box. 'The German name and the German race have become and are becoming more universally and more intensely hated among all the people in all the lands, than any name or any race of which history bears record.'

From all sides they growled their approval; he had led them away from the swamp and back onto firmer ground of his own choosing.

'We are no small island gathered in the northern mists, but around us, gathered in proud array, are all the free nations of the British Empire.' He spread his arms wide in imperial pride, and they shouted their support. 'And from across the Atlantic there is the mighty Republic of the United States which proclaims itself on our side,' – he glanced at Lloyd George, 'or at our side, or at any rate, near our side.' And they cheered that, too.

He stood before them, defiant, his hands clasping the Despatch Box, that beloved piece of wood and brass where fifty years earlier his father had stood, and as he gave them facts and figures and mixed insult with idealism, his eyes searched around this place with its ornate wood carvings, its soaring roof, its intimate leather benches with their musty smell of powerful men. It had been twelve months since they had summoned him here to be Prime Minister, and although he had not yet found them victory he had at least enabled them to survive. That was his achievement, more than any other man's, which was why he so resented what they had done in dragging him here to search for loose threads in the tapestry of his war.

'It is a year almost to the day since, in the crash of the disastrous Battle of France, His Majesty's present Administration was formed. Men of all parties joined hands together to fight this business to the end. That was a dark hour, and little did we know what storms and perils lay before us –

and little did Herr Hitler know when, in June 1940, he received the total capitulation of France, and when he expected to be master of Europe in a few weeks and the whole world in a few years, that today he would be appealing to the much-tried German people to prepare themselves for the war of 1942!'

They were with him now, almost all of them – but for how long?

'When I look back on the perils which have been overcome, upon the great mountain waves through which the gallant ship has driven, when I remember all that has gone wrong, and remember also all that has gone right, I feel sure we have no need to fear the tempest. Let it roar, and let it rage!' he cried, his voice rising with it. 'We shall come through!'

They cheered and stretched to clap him on the back. Even Lloyd George smiled and nodded his appreciation. It had not been one of Churchill's finest, but it had been enough.

In the end, only three Members voted against the Government. It was an overwhelming victory, on paper.

Yet it was the last victory Churchill was ever to have in this chamber. He didn't know it, but as they applauded him out, it was to be the last time he would ever set foot inside this hallowed place, or stand at his beloved Despatch Box, or hear his voice ringing back from these rafters.

'Gimme a cigar,' Churchill snapped, striding into the room and slamming the door behind him as a warning to all those who hovered outside.

'How was the debate, zur?' Sawyers asked, holding out a box of small brown torpedoes.

The Prime Minster threw his formal black jacket at his

valet and slumped into a chair by the fire. Soon he was stabbing at the end of a cigar with a toothpick. 'I never thought – never thought it possible – to hear an Englishman utter such words as I have heard used against me in the House today.'

'Mr Lloyd George is Welsh,' Sawyers corrected, 'and though I've never met him I strongly suspect Mr McGovern of belonging to some sort of Scottish sect. As for Mr Hore-Belisha . . .'

'Don't mention that bloody Hebrew's name to me! I had him here for lunch.'

'Served him meself.'

'Explained everything to him.'

'Seem to remember yer even hinted he might get a job, like, back in Government.'

'And he turns on me like a gypsy!' Churchill said bitterly, stabbing through the end of the cigar as though it were his opponent's heart. Sawyers held out a lighted candle. 'I should have the bastard conscripted into the RAF and dropped somewhere over Germany.'

Churchill's tirade was brought to a halt as he struggled to persuade his cigar to ignite, but the respite was only temporary.

'To listen to the man you'd think that the German military machine was all but invincible – doesn't he realize that if Hitler wins the bloody war it will be my head on the block first, then Hore-Belisha's and all his kind?'

'Well, yer won vote.'

'Won't stop the rats scurrying around in the bilges gnawing at everything in their path.'

'Suppose we all have our days as rats,' Sawyers said, blowing out the candle.

Churchill looked at Sawyers warily. Was the man trying to mock? Churchill was, in his own words, the arch ratter and re-ratter, a man who had jumped ship from one party to another, then swum back again. Was his insolent bloody valet trying to make a comparison?

'Nowt wrong wi' a bit o' debate. A triumph, really,' Sawyers continued.

'What the hell are you talking about?' Churchill enquired, drawing impatiently on the cigar. It was not cooperating.

'I were jest wondering, like, if any other place in the whole o' Europe would let 'em get away wi' that sort o' criticism.'

'Mcaning?'

'You'd not get that sort o' nonsense in Germany, now, would you? Not in France, not Spain or Italy, Russia, not – anywheres, really. 'Cept right here, in Britain. Thought that's what we was fighting fer. To kepp our Parliament, like, so as grown men can stand up and make fools of the'selves.'

'Lloyd George made a fool of himself,' Churchill muttered, still struggling with the cigar. 'He said I was a bully. But I'm not a bloody bully, am I, Sawyers?'

'You need a fresh light, zur.'

'Who can I trust, Sawyers? Not anyone.' He suddenly sounded tired, the zest and energy gone, all given up in the House. 'I am surrounded by generals whose only expertise lies in the art of evacuation, and politicians who have no higher ambition than to hurl abuse at me.'

'In his own way, mebbe Mr Lloyd George were right. You can't go doing it all by yerself.'

'But I have to,' Churchill said, sounding petulant. 'I can rely on no one.' He was falling into the pit of corrosive self-pity that was one of his least endearing qualities. Then he glanced at his cigar. It was as cold and dead as could be.

'Bugger!' he exclaimed, hurling it into the hearth. 'For God's sake, Sawyers, why do you bring me such rubbish? Can't I be allowed a decent smoke once in a while?'

Sawyers said nothing. The reason the old man didn't always get the cigars he wanted was because he never paid for them, relying almost entirely on supplies sent to him by well-wishers and supplicants.

'What about those Havanas – you know, man, the cabinet full of 'em that came through the other week? You remember. Had a little brass plaque: "A tribute of admiration from the President and People of Cuba."'

'Gone away, they have. Like pheasants in firing line.'

'What? I want a cigar, not a bloody riddle.'

'Your security service was concerned they might've been interfered with, like. Poisoned, mebbe. So they've took 'em away fer testing.'

'What in Hell's name do they think they're doing?' Churchill shouted, jumping to his feet, all lethargy forgotten.

'Mebbe they're thinking along same lines as Lloyd George.'

'What?'

'That you can't go doing the whole lot by yerself.' He stared directly at his master, daring him to contradict. 'But wi'out yer, job simply won't get done.'

Sawyers closed the door behind him. Even before he reached the end of the corridor, he could hear Churchill back on form, energies restored, bellowing for his staff.

10 May 1941. The night of the full moon. In brilliant moon-light, they tried to bomb the heart out of London. They almost succeeded.

More than 1,400 Londoners were killed that night, including the mayors of Westminster and Bermondsey. Five thousand houses were destroyed and twelve thousand Londoners made homeless. It was the worst single night of the Blitz. The Luftwaffe's bombers made nearly six hundred sorties, using the shimmering waters of the Thames as their unmistakable route to the heart of the city. Only fourteen German bombers failed to return.

It was to change the face of London. St Paul's Cathedral and Westminster Abbey were hit, as were many other churches. Whole swathes of Westminster were flattened, and across the bridge St Thomas' Hospital was left burning, along with the British Museum, Bond Street, five docks and more than thirty factories.

The Parliament building was hit, too. A bomb passed clean through the structure of Big Ben, although the clock continued to strike. Incendiaries fell on the debating chambers of both the Commons and the Lords, and also upon the towering medieval oak-beamed roof of Westminster Hall that stood beside them. Fires broke out and grew in every corner; it was a hopeless task for the volunteer firefighters. Soon it became clear that if they were to save anything, they would have to make a choice. They could save the home of the politicians, or they could save the royal hall, but not both. The chamber of the Commons was a modern construction, less than a hundred years old, while Westminster Hall had stood for almost a thousand. It was a place where crowds had cheered King Henry playing tennis and mocked as King Charles faced the axe; it was a place that had survived riot and revolution, and had struggled through every kind of iniquity concocted in the chamber next door. So, for Englishmen, it turned out to be not much of a choice at all.

They hacked through the locks on the vast oak doors of the Hall and began playing their hoses upon the timbers of the roof. Soon the tenders and water pipes had run dry, so while the bombs were still falling around them they manhandled a trailer pump down the steps of Westminster Pier to draw water from the river. In the flagstoned belly of the hall they found themselves up to their waists in water, even as smouldering chunks of the roof fell about them, making the water seem as if it would boil. But, in the end, they won. The Great Hall was saved.

While this was happening, the chamber of the House of Commons, the home of the politicians, was left to burn to the ground.

It was the night that would change everything.

A little earlier on the evening of the tenth of May, the main dining room of the Dorchester Hotel was thronged with guests. Pamela sat at one of the best tables in a quiet corner with Harriman, wondering at this strange man who had come all the way across the Atlantic to become a warrior. He was a most unlikely man of war. It seemed he had everything: a railway, many houses, the ear of the President, two doting daughters – although only the most passing mention of a wife – and even a ski resort in Idaho. He seemed to want for nothing, and yet he had an air of sadness about him that made his eyes unnaturally dark. As she listened more closely to his patrician mid-Atlantic accent, she thought she could detect the hint of a childhood stammer.

They were well into the first bottle of wine before he started to relax, the creases around his eyes slowly dissolving and reforming at the corners of his mouth. He talked about his father, excessively – were there ghosts? – and about his parent's ability to make both money and enemies. A rigid upbringing, she guessed, that had left something unbending in him.

As he talked, she began comparing him with her own father, who was dull where Harriman was dynamic, whose vision stretched no further than the gates of his estate while this man had flown across an ocean to help build something new. Harriman was also older than her father, yet was centuries more youthful.

It was as though he could read her mind, for suddenly he was asking about her family.

'My father? Oh, just another country lord. Horses, foxhunting, cold bedrooms and crumbling plaster. Usual thing. My family are all either black sheep or desperately boring.'

'Black sheep?'

'One tried to blow up the King and the whole of Parliament in the Gunpowder Plot.'

'What happened to him?'

'A traditional little ceremony we call hanging, drawing and quartering.'

'Christ,' he said, almost choking on his beef. She had his attention now. 'A real villain, eh?'

'A real Digby. Insisted on having the last word. Apparently, as they plucked out his still-beating heart and held it up to the howling mob, his lips moved and he said: *"Veniam, vincam."* Which loosely translated means "Next time I win."'

'Seriously?'

She smiled. Americans were so wonderfully gullible.

The moment passed as the wine waiter returned to pour the last of their wine.

'Another bottle, Pam?'

Before she could respond, the wine waiter interrupted. 'Sir, it's such a splendid choice, but I'm sorry to tell you we've only got one more bottle in the cellar. It may be the only bottle left in the entire country,' he added mournfully. 'Heaven knows when we'll get more. The Germans are drinking it all now.'

'Then we'd better have the last bottle before they get here,' Harriman said.

121

The waiter stiffened. The moment froze. 'Being an American, sir, perhaps you don't understand.'

'Understand what?'

'Even if, as you say, the Germans do get here, I can assure you that we shall hold out.'

Harriman went pale with humiliation. 'Yes. Of course. I'm so sorry,' he muttered as the waiter withdrew.

'Please forgive me, Pam. Foolish of me. I meant nothing by it,' he continued.

'Averell, you still have a lot to learn about the war.'

'And, it seems, about British waiters. And wicked relatives. Teach me?'

At around the same time as Pamela and her dinner companion were finishing their dessert, operators in the radar station at Ottercops Moss on the Northumberland coast began arguing amongst themselves about the nature of a signal they had been tracking for the best part of an hour. It didn't make much sense. A single unidentified blip on their scanners had been spotted flying westward out of the North Sea. There was so much other action in the skies that a solitary plane didn't raise many eyebrows, but as it drew closer to the coast, two Spitfires from RAF Acklington were ordered to intercept. It was a night filled with confusion; the Spitfires failed to make contact with the intruder, and at one point were even instructed to intercept each other.

Fighter Command Headquarters in Middlesex were also plotting the action on their map table, but they responded with nothing more than a shrug of their shoulders. Those bumpkins in the radar station at Ottercops Moss had a reputation for false alarms. Anyway, the solitary marker was one amongst literally hundreds that were flooding across their maps; it would have to take its place in the RAF's long queue of concerns.

The signal continued to advance, and crossed the north-east coast of England at 22.12 hours. Then it altered direction, swinging north towards the Scottish border, which it crossed some twenty minutes later, before resuming a westerly course and heading in the direction of Glasgow. It had the characteristic speed of a Messerschmitt 110, a twin-engine long-range fighter, but this tentative identification was treated with derision. The track of the aircraft was way beyond the range of an Me-110; it could never make it back to base.

What they didn't know was that the pilot had no intention of returning to his base.

Shortly after eleven o'clock, the signal disappeared from radar screens, and an explosion was seen near Floors Farm on Bonnyton Moor, south of Glasgow. An underwhelmed newspaper reporter later wrote that the crash had resulted in one casualty, a young hare.

But the pilot was not killed. He had already baled out.

When the sirens kicked in, Pamela and Harriman were halfway through the second bottle of wine and the life of Jane Digby, sister of the ninth Baron Digby and Pamela's ancestor. Another black sheep.

Averell watched as Pamela counted off her forebear's conquests on the elegant fingers of both hands. Jane had been the daughter of a Digby admiral who had fought with Nelson at Trafalgar. She seemed to have inherited much of her father's adventurous outlook. She married in turn an English lord, a Bavarian baron, a Greek count and a Bedouin sheikh, and between times became the lover of princes and at least two kings. Pamela was running out of fingers.

123

'Quite a girl,' Harriman observed, uncertain whether it was appropriate to applaud or condemn.

'Caused a terrible scandal, of course.' Pamela smiled. 'England expects every man, but not their womenfolk, too.'

'Wickedness is everywhere,' Harriman concluded as the wailing of the sirens forced its way between them. The waiter was back, bowing and offering to show them the way to the shelter. Pamela's face froze in disappointment.

'The bloody shelters,' she whispered. 'How I hate them.'

'We could take the bottle. Go back to my room,' Harriman suggested. 'Much more comfortable.'

'If a little more adventurous,' she added primly, 'with all these bombs about.'

'What would Jane have done?'

'For half a bottle of wine?' Pamela shrugged. 'Almost anything.'

'I never know when you are teasing me, Pam.'

'You and that incomplete education of yours.' She swept up the bottle from the table and rose. 'You lead. I follow. Isn't that the way you stuffy old men are supposed to like things?'

By the time they had reached his suite of rooms on the first floor, the bombs were already falling. His hand went to the light switch but she pulled it gently away.

'I can't sit and talk with all that going on outside,' she said, 'and Jane would never have tried. Let's watch for a while.'

So the curtains were pulled back and they gazed out upon the opening scenes of a great dance of death. The fires and flashes of light grew quickly in intensity, drawing Pamela like a moth ever closer to the window until she was pressing up against it, crying gently as fresh explosions from guns and bombs began to rattle at the panes. Harriman was behind her, peering over her shoulder at the splendours and the horror that lay outside, until he was standing very close with his arms cast protectively around her.

'Is this safe?' he enquired. 'So close to the window?'

She wondered if it was her turn to be teased, until she remembered he was American.

And suddenly their world was thrown upside down. Afterwards, Pamela couldn't remember which sensation came first – the brilliant flash, the overwhelming roar, the ripping at her eardrums. There must have been some sort of warning, for even as the bomb exploded outside Harriman had picked her up and thrown her away from the window. As the force of the blast hit the building, the room was instantly filled with dust; all the windowpanes cracked – they were taped and didn't completely shatter – but small shards of glass were sent flying around them. One of the thick curtains was pulled half off its rail, and the room somehow seemed to have too much air in it, then almost none at all. Pamela struggled for breath. The echo of the blast seemed to rumble on for ever, and when at last it faded all she could hear was the gentle gurgling of an upturned bottle of wine and the pounding of her heart.

She found that she was under a table. The American had thrown himself on top of her. Her dress had been torn from her shoulder. It had allowed her breast to tumble free, a fact made all the more obvious by the heaving of her chest as she struggled to control her fright.

They lay together, breathless. Bombs were still falling outside, but they seemed to come from a world that had suddenly grown more distant. For a moment she thought she might have been injured, for needles of heat were spreading remorselessly up the insides of her legs until they began to feed the smouldering fire that had taken hold at the top of her thighs.

125

He was struggling to speak; she could feel the brushstrokes of his breath on her cheek, her neck, on her unconstrained breast, every fresh gasp like bellows upon a fire.

'Damn near miss, Pam.'

'No,' she whispered. 'I don't think so.'

A ploughman heard the aircraft passing low overhead, followed seconds later by a huge explosion. He rushed outside to see a parachute falling from the night sky and, armed with nothing more than a hayfork, soon captured the airman. The pilot of the Me-110 offered no resistance, not least because he had badly damaged his ankle on landing.

The Scotsman helped the injured pilot back to his cottage, where his mother offered her unexpected guest a mug of tea. In excellent but accented English, the pilot asked instead for a glass of water. He seemed to be particular about every-thing. He was at pains to emphasize that he was not armed and that his plane had carried neither ammunition nor bombs. He announced that his name was Alfred Horn. He said he had flown from Munich and had come to see the Duke of Hamilton. He showed no signs of hostility.

Soon soldiers from the Home Guard began to arrive. They came in a collection of vehicles and had little idea of what to do, so after much confusion they took the prisoner to their headquarters in a nearby scout hut. From there he was passed up the chain of military command much like a fire bucket until, in the early hours of the following morning, he ended up in the hospital wing of Maryhill Barracks in Glasgow, where his ankle was treated. Throughout the night he continued to repeat his name, and also his request that they should summon the Duke of Hamilton. He seemed to know that the Duke's home was nearby.

126

The prisoner was a man of striking appearance. He had prominent brows, eyes that were exceptionally deep-set and a chin so square it seemed to have been fashioned from the end of an anvil. He also had the demeanour of a man used to issuing orders rather than being questioned by the likes of ploughmen and Home Guard privates. He showed no signs of submissiveness, and began to grow irritable when the Duke of Hamilton failed to appear. He was unlike any other prisoner they had encountered, and he quickly became an item of considerable interest, with many people arriving to peer around the door of the hospital barracks at this strange arrival.

It was one of these inquisitive visitors, a squadron leader in the Royal Observer Corps, who was the first to begin unravelling the mystery.

'Who's that?' he asked the guard on duty.

'Horn, sir. He's called Alfred Horn.'

The squadron leader was about to say something else, but shook it from his mind and went away, looking troubled. He was back a few minutes later.

'Who did you say he was?'

'Name of Alfred Horn, sir.'

The squadron leader stared at the patient with the intensity of a hunting cheetah, then retreated into the corridor, looking grim.

'That's no flaming Alfred Horn,' he snapped.

'No?'

'It seems scarcely credible, but I think I recognize him from his photograph.'

'Who is he, then, sir?'

'Damn it if that man's not Rudolf Hess.'

'What?'

'Hess. Adolf Hitler's deputy!'

127

SIX

There was awkwardness the following morning as they walked through the fresh ruins of London. The sights they saw made their tumbling through the hours of the previous night seem not only indulgent but also selfishly irrelevant. Although the bombers had long gone, the fires still burned ferociously, filling the air with smoke. The sky glowed red.

Great gaps had been torn through the buildings of London. Homes had been ripped open to show their pathetic guts; half-rooms with pictures set at crazy angles and furniture peering over the abyss, and ducks still flying across the wallpaper. Broken rooms, broken lives.

The rubble stank – of ash, cinder, tar, burnt hopes. Families clawed at the still-smoking embers, scrabbling for clothes, blankets, sheets, dolls, past lives. Tarpaulins covered the gashes, turning entire streets into tented encampments. Women with exhausted faces boiled water in kitchens that had neither walls nor windows, while children sat around in shabby, worn clothes, their eyes empty, their soot-covered faces streaked with tears. Shreds of burnt paper fell all around like autumn leaves, and dark brown tea spilled from cracked mugs.

They passed a double-decker bus. It was resting at a jaunty angle, its face buried in the roof of a building more than a hundred yards from where it had been travelling. There was blood streaked across its windows. Firemen and volunteers worked tirelessly to damp the flames, but many buildings were left to burn themselves out and die alone. The bells of the ambulances and other emergency vehicles tolled ceaselessly. The casualties were horrendous.

They felt ashamed.

'Pam, about last night.'

'Yes?'

'I guess . . . What I mean . . .' His embarrassment was momentarily covered by shouts of alarm as a roof collapsed nearby, sending an angry fist of smoke and dust punching into the sky.

'Hell, Pam, you're married, I'm married, I've got a daughter your age. It doesn't make a lot of sense, does it?'

She looked around her. 'Nothing makes a lot of sense right now.'

'It can't continue.'

'The war?'

'Us.'

'Oh, I see.'

They walked a little further, their shoes crunching on a carpet of broken glass.

'We should regard last night as a one-off,' she said, her tone leaving it up to him to decide whether it was proposition or question.

'I guess so,' he replied, after a long pause and with evident reluctance.

'I had a good time.'

'So did I!'

'A little Lend-Lease, then.'

'You're a hell of a girl, Pam. I hope we can still be . . .'

'Friends?'

A broken main was spilling water down the gutter. Nearby a grocer, his shop destroyed and still smoking behind him, had set up a stall on tea chests and was selling oranges, potatoes and eggs, which was all he had left, to a line of dark-eyed women. Beside the stall a young boy was ladling milk from a churn into empty bottles. The women glanced suspiciously at the state of his hands.

A girl no more than seven years old approached Pamela. Her smock was torn and she was clutching a rag doll under one arm. 'Have you seen my mummy?' she asked. 'Daddy says we've lost her. She's got hair the same colour as yours. Do you know where she is?'

A gaunt-eyed man came running after her and muttered something in her ear before leading her gently away.

Pamela, surrounded by a flood of so many sorrows, burst into tears. She sobbed on Harriman's shoulder as they stood surrounded by the wreckage of people's lives.

'Surely this can't go on,' he whispered.

'Of course it can,' she said, shaking herself out of her grief. 'War isn't a bloody one-night stand, Averell. Or is that the only thing you Americans are any good at?'

Héloise, the new French maid, was also in London. She had asked for permission to spend a day shopping and sightseeing, and Mrs Landemare had thought it an excellent idea to show her around the other end of operations, in Downing Street and the Annexe. She deserved her day off, for she was proving to be a willing worker. Churchill usually spent three nights of the week at Chequers, arriving on Friday and not leaving until the following Monday morning. He was always accompanied by an endless retinue of guests, some who stayed for only one night, others for only one meal, and as soon as they had left, their place was taken by new arrivals. This imposed a huge burden upon the staff, whose task was made all the more difficult as the Prime Minister's demands bounced between the extravagant and the outrageous. Yet somehow they coped. He arrived with secretaries tumbling in his wake and left with assistants rushing to ensure everyone had their place in the cars, but even when Churchill was no longer there the pace of activity at the old house grew only slightly less frantic. There was cleaning and clearing to be done, laundry to be ironed, larders to be stocked, and the pressing knowledge that, in a few days, he would be back.

So Héloise had earned her day in town. It was a pity that London was still in a state of chaos, but it was a warm day, she had on a fine spring dress and even in the confusion there were still many young men who had the time to spare her a smile. She seemed not to mind as the bus she was on made painfully slow progress through the streets of the West End. Héloise sat on the upper deck, which gave her a good view of the English capital, and she made no objection when a well-dressed young Japanese man chose the seat next to her, in spite of the fact that the upper deck was far from crowded. Indeed, she seemed almost to welcome his company, for within a few moments she had dropped deep into conversation with him.

Churchill's return to London was accompanied by even more commotion than usual. It wasn't every day that the Deputy Fuehrer dropped in. As soon as his car had stopped outside the door of Downing Street the Prime Minister leapt from his seat, scattering papers to every side, rushing across the threshold, barking instructions, summoning colleagues, stirring the blood of everyone around, but as he headed for the Cabinet Room he found that two men were ahead of him, waiting by the door.

'Prime Minister.' Sir Stewart Menzies nodded in greeting as he struggled with a bulging file.

Max Beaverbrook was puffing at a cigar that was even larger than the Prime Minister's own. 'Winston,' he growled. 'Bloody thing, this Hess business.'

'How does Max do it?' Churchill asked himself, awe mingling with suspicion as he strode inside the Cabinet Room. Menzies had the intelligence services under his command and was in a position to know, but Max . . . Max was one of his oldest friends, and in the same breath one of his greatest rivals, a Canadian entrepreneur who had left behind a murky past to seek better times in Britain. And how well he had succeeded. His lists of achievements were legendary – politician, peer, press magnate, Cabinet Minister along with Churchill during the last war, and now Ministerial colleagues once again in this. He was a man who treated his friends with extraordinary generosity and ran his newspapers with outstanding ruthlessness. In short, a man too powerful, too rich and too graced by good fortune ever to be completely trusted. Now it seemed he also had an intelligence service that was every inch as effective as Menzies'.

'Max, not a bloody word in your newspapers,' Churchill began as they settled themselves around the Cabinet table. 'Not a bloody word, do you hear me? Not until we figure out whose arse Hess has come here to kick.'

Later, Churchill was to record that from the start he had never regarded the Hess affair as one of serious importance. This was what he usually claimed when he had lost the argument.

And the argument was fierce. Was it really Hess?

Beaverbrook said it was, for he knew Hess well from before the war and had already identified him from photographs wired down from Scotland, but Churchill insisted that Menzies send one of his intelligence officers to Glasgow to confirm the matter.

'This could be the greatest propaganda coup of the war,' Churchill told them, 'and we don't want to bugger it up before we start.'

Yet confirmation of the Deputy Fuehrer's identity proved to be only the start of the debate. It came to a head later that night as they met around the table in the Cabinet War Rooms that were buried in the basement beneath the Annexe – Churchill, Menzies, Beaverbrook, Eden the Foreign Secretary, Margesson the War Secretary, and several others. No one felt comfortable here; the ceilings were too low, the reinforced beams too red and bright, the atmosphere too much like that of a tramp steamer's engine room, but after the terrible pounding that London had taken in recent nights it would have been folly for so many powerful men to have gathered together in the same place above ground.

'So, it's confirmed,' Churchill began. 'The man is Hess. And he wants to stop the war.' He nodded at Menzies, who began reciting a brief outline of the facts, so far as they had been put together. Hess had come alone, unarmed, wanting to meet with the Duke of Hamilton whom he had met briefly before the war and whom he believed to be a friend of the King.

'Knows you too, doesn't he, Max?' Churchill prodded.

'I know all sorts of scoundrels, Prime Minister,' the Canadian offered in reply, returning Churchill's stare.

'Have we come to any conclusion about his mental state?' Eden enquired.

'No indication that he's mad, if that's what you mean, Foreign Secretary,' Menzies replied.

'And thank heavens for that,' Churchill said. 'Spoil all the fun if he were frothing at the mouth.'

'Fun, Prime Minster?' Eden asked, perplexed.

'I propose to make a statement,' Churchill began, 'to the effect that Hess has fled to Britain in the name of humanity – and where else in the whole of Europe would any humanitarian flee other than to this country? Hess hopes to bring an end to the war. It is a sure sign that a collapse of morale is under way in Berlin and that the Nazi hierarchy is split. If his Deputy chooses to flee, how long will it be before the rest of Germany deserts Hitler? They know they can no longer win this war.'

'If only that were true.'

'What?'

Beaverbrook's gnome-like head came up from drawing doodles on his paperwork. His colonial accent was strong, his words typically blunt. 'You can't say that. It's all wrong.'

'What on earth do you mean?'

'You go round suggesting Hess is a peacemonger and that there are many more like him back home, and you'll blow a hole in the entire war effort.'

'Explain.'

'How do you think this will play on Pennsylvania Avenue?' Beaverbrook replied. 'The only way Roosevelt and his men are going to get involved in the war is if they think every German is a rabid maniac who's thirsting to get his hands on their first-born. You tell them that they're all really kind and cuddly, and America goes back to sleep.'

Churchill was silent for a moment, disappearing behind a cloud of cigar smoke.

'It's certainly a point to be considered,' Eden offered cautiously.

'And I take the point,' Churchill said, a little grudgingly.

'It would perhaps be best to avoid a discussion of his motives, be they humanitarian or otherwise. We shall instead concentrate on his plea for peace.'

But Beaverbrook was shaking his head.

'That also troubles you, Max?'

'Not me. But I think it may trouble many others. You know what it's like out there, on the streets – or what's left of them. You start telling them that there's some sort of peace deal on offer and many of them won't stop to ask questions, they'll simply grab hold of it and begin their street parties. Sure, they've been offered peace with honour before and it didn't work out last time either, but when you've just lost your home, your neighbourhood, your hope, it's exactly the kind of tune they might dance to.'

Churchill looked around the room. He could see in their faces that they thought Max was right. And now that Churchill himself had been given a chance to pause and reflect, he, too, thought Max was right. But he did so resent having to acknowledge the fact in public.

'I've always made it clear that any so-called peace which leaves Hitler dominant in Europe would not be worthy of the name.'

'And I agree,' Beaverbrook added, trying to be helpful.

'It seems, therefore, that the most important point to emphasize in this extraordinary matter is the light that it throws upon the divided leadership in Berlin.' Churchill was trying to sum up, to move on, but . . .

'You still have problems, Max?'

'If Hess's arrival says anything to the outside world – well, it may be about splits in Berlin, sure. But it also talks about splits right here in Britain.'

A blue haze of silence hung across the room.

'He didn't come here to talk to you, Winston – not to me,

either,' Beaverbrook continued, his voice softer. 'Looks like he wanted to do a deal with others. Those who think the war's not going too well. You know the whispering that's going on. You remember the debate we had in the House the other day.'

The silence continued.

'From what I gather, Hess still loves his Fuehrer, thinks Germany is going to win. He's come as a salesman, not to surrender.'

Menzies was nodding his head gently.

'We can't afford to make a public spectacle of Hess,' Beaverbrook said, looking directly at the Prime Minister. 'You said we had to figure out whose arse Hess had come to kick. Well, I guess it's ours.'

It had seemed like the greatest propaganda coup of all time, but suddenly no one was so sure.

'What, then, are you suggesting we say?'

They were still arguing about that when news of the German communiqué came in. Berlin had beaten them to it. According to German radio, Hess had been under suspicion for some time. He had disobeyed orders, stolen a plane. Was ill, had a mental disorder, had been suffering from hallucinations for years.

For Hitler, it seemed, the matter was quite simple.

Hess was raving mad.

The following morning Churchill went to the spot he loved most on the earth.

It was gone.

Where his debating chamber had stood, there was nothing but twisted girders and empty spaces. This had been his shrine of liberty, his fortress, his Parliament, but not a trace remained. The walls were blackened and scarred, the ashes that lay beneath his feet were still warm. Churchill stood amidst the rubble and closed his eyes, wanting to hide these sights from view, and to remember. A year ago he had stood in this place and promised the people victory, and they had given him their trust. Yet there was no victory. He had found nothing but disaster.

The skies that morning were blue and cold, more like February than spring, with the barrage balloons pointing north into an Arctic wind, their tail fins twisting behind them, buffeting through the smoke like salmon through the current. On the opposite bank of the river St Thomas' Hospital was still ablaze, and there were fires all the way from Lambeth Palace to St Paul's.

The girders that had once supported the roof of this beloved place now lay around him like some abandoned children's toy. The tower of Big Ben stood scarred and drenched in soot. Oh, in many ways the Parliament was a ridiculous institution, inefficient, impractical, built on marshlands of confusion, but it was this little place that represented the crucial difference between them and the way things were in Germany. The people of these islands knew about compromise, about the moments when plans were washed away and there was nothing left but to bugger on and muddle through, while the Germans made a religion of efficiency and authority. They couldn't tolerate disappointment, couldn't bend with a changing wind. That, in the end, would bring them low.

But when would that be? He no longer knew. What he did know was that at their present rate of destructiveness the Germans would sink four and a half million tons of shipping over the next year – and the Americans and British could just about replace those losses with new-built ships.

The mathematics were simple, their conclusion irresistible. In a year's time the war would still be raging and no nearer its end. Yet, as he looked around the blackened ruins, he knew that within that terrible year London would be dead. It would all have been for nothing. Victory was slipping through his fingers.

That was why Hess had come. That was why he thought there were those who were ready to talk peace. The Nazis thought that Britain had had enough, and would do a deal. Hess wasn't a rat deserting a sinking ship but a cat that had come a-hunting, and there were many who might yet fall prey.

Churchill stood, a lonely silhouette amidst the destruction, his head bowed, like a crusader returned home to find nothing but damnation. Above his head, Big Ben chimed the hour, the sound echoing in the emptiness around him with exceptional force. He raised his eyes. The smoke was gradually beginning to thin and shafts of sunlight were burning their way through the gloom.

He gazed around the bare and broken walls, almost as if he expected to find the enemy lurking there, then raised his walking cane and pointed violently towards Big Ben. 'You see that?' he shouted. 'The blessed clock still works. It still works!' He gave a cry of hope. 'So you, Herr Hess, can carry on spouting like a wounded whale about the benefits of your German peace. But Mr Churchill is going to stick to the policy he knows best. KBO!' he bellowed. 'KBO!'

Then, more softly: 'After all, he doesn't have much bloody choice.'

HMS *Hood*. To utter the name was to summon up two centuries of supremacy that the British had enjoyed upon the seas. She was the most famous battleship in the world, a 42,100-ton killing machine, and ever since the day she had been launched her exceptionally sleek lines had made her an object of both beauty and awe.

She had been named after Lord Samuel Hood. The Hoods were an outstanding naval family that spawned many princes of the sea, and Sam was one of its best. He had commanded Nelson and was also his close friend, although unlike Nelson, he died in bed at a great age.

Death was never far from the vessel named after him. On the very day her keel had been laid at the height of World War I, three British battle cruisers blew up under German fire at the Battle of Jutland. It was one of the worst days in British naval history. For some, it was the sort of injustice that the *Hood* was intended to redeem, yet for others in the superstitious community of seamen, it seemed more like an omen.

For two decades she had been the largest warship in the world. She had been the British flagship at the battle of Mers-el-Kébir – not that it was much of a battle. It had been less than a year ago, and had been fought between the British and the French. Ten days beforehand the French had been allies, but they had capitulated to the Germans and Churchill was desperate to ensure that the fleet didn't end up in Hitler's hands. So he had taken the only step that could guarantee it. He ordered the fleet to be sunk while it lay at anchor. More than 1,250 French sailors were killed, mostly beneath the guns of the *Hood*. Drowned like rats. One British officer and a rating had been slightly injured.

Churchill had wept when he had announced the events to the House of Commons. It was as nothing to the weeping around many hearths in France.

Churchill had reason for his concern. War is a game of

fluctuating tides, and seven weeks after the French fleet had been snatched from the grasp of the Germans, the Kriegsmarine brought into service the latest of their own battleships. She was named *Bismarck*. She was almost as big and just as fast as the *Hood* and carried the same number of huge fifteen-inch guns, but there was one crucial difference. *Hood* had already been the mistress of the seas for a generation. It was too long.

A few days after Churchill had stumbled through the ruins of his beloved Parliament building, he began to receive reports that the Germans were increasing their aerial reconnaissance around the Denmark Strait that ran between Greenland and Iceland. They were checking the ice pack. It was a signal; it seemed likely that some of their ships were preparing to break out from their home ports and into the Atlantic.

Then the *Bismarck* was spotted speeding up the coast of Norway alongside a heavy cruiser, the *Prinz Eugen*. From here they could launch themselves into the Arctic Ocean and loop around Iceland through the Denmark Strait. Once past this point they would be in amongst the precious convoys. At this time of year the ice pack kept the Strait navigable for only thirty to forty miles of its width; it was the narrow gateway that led to the endless Atlantic further south. If the *Bismarck* were to be stopped, it must be here – and she must be stopped, for the convoys were all that was keeping Britain from the grip of starvation. So the Admiralty in Whitehall responded with the best it had. It ordered the *Hood* to the waters off Iceland, along with the very latest battleship in the British fleet, the *Prince of Wales*.

The Royal Navy threw ships into the Strait. They took with them the latest radar equipment and aerial patrols, but it wasn't until a frozen lookout armed with nothing more than a pair of old-fashioned binoculars had shouted the alarm that the British knew where the *Bismarck* was. She was only seven miles away. It was the evening of 23 May.

All hands in the British task force were ordered to prepare for battle. They changed into life jackets, flash gear, gas masks – and clean underwear, to help ward off infection in case they were wounded. They also clambered into cold-weather gear. It was bitterly cold. Anyone ending up in the waters off Greenland at that time of year had only minutes to live.

Yet even as the *Hood* and the *Prince of Wales* prepared to give battle, the *Bismarck* slipped away, losing herself in the drifting banks of snow and encroaching darkness. She didn't want to fight – not here, at least. Her mission was to take on convoys of fat, sluggish merchantmen, not capital ships, so she ran and hid. It wasn't until the early hours of the following morning that the British found her again. When they did, they immediately opened fire.

They had been firing on the German ship for two minutes before the captain of the *Bismarck* reluctantly gave the order to use her own guns. He would much prefer to have run, but he couldn't afford to have his ship shot out from underneath him, not on her first mission. So, although he had hadn't been hit, he came head to head with the greatest ship on the ocean. It was shortly before six in the morning.

Whether it was luck or skill would be left to the historians, but with one of her first shots the *Bismarck* hit the *Hood* near the base of her main mast. It wasn't a fatal blow – an ammunition locker caught fire, but the fire gradually died down, the moment passed. Yet all those on board knew what it meant. Not a single British shell had yet found its target, while the Germans already had their range.

Almost immediately, the *Hood* was struck once again. The consequences this time were extraordinary.

Barely a second or two after she was hit, a huge geyser

of fire erupted from her deck, blasting into the cold Arctic air. It was so bright that it temporarily blinded some of those watching from other ships. The aft magazines had blown up. The explosion ripped the heart out of the great warship. The *Hood* came to a complete stop, smothered in yellow cordite smoke, and straight away began to list. Already the bow was up, rearing out of the water as though desperate to escape, like the involuntary kicking of an executed man. No order was given to abandon ship; there was neither time nor any point. The stern sank first, vertically, then the bow, the forward guns firing one final salvo even as they pointed towards the sky. It was if they were trying to batter down the doors of Heaven.

And she was gone.

The *Hood* was the most famous ship afloat. It took her less than three minutes to sink. She left behind nothing but a mire of floating wreckage and an oil slick four inches deep.

She had a crew of 1,418 men. Only three survived.

It took only minutes for the screams of dying men to reach as far as Chequers that morning. Churchill was working in bed when he heard the terrible news. He did not take it well.

He ran from his room, wearing nothing but his pyjamas, and onto the gallery behind the Great Hall. 'Stop that infernal racket!' he shouted to those down below.

'Why, it's only a bit of Beethoven,' Vic Oliver replied nonchalantly from the keyboard of the piano.

'It's the Funeral March!'

'No way. That's entirely different. Like this.' And the son-in-law struck more sombre chords.

'No more! I know the bloody Funeral March. And I won't have it in this house!'

He was in one of those moods that brooked no argument, but the Great Hall was crowded and Oliver saw no reason why he should tolerate being abused like a backward child.

'No,' he insisted. 'Even a dog that's been dead for a week could hear the difference. Listen, everyone.' He turned to embroil all the guests and started up again.

'You mock the dead and I will not have it!'

Oliver banged the lid of the piano down to cover the keys. 'I was not mocking the dead. I resent that, Winston. I was maybe mocking you just a little. Not the same thing, in my book at least.'

'Not in this house, *at least*, sir.'

'Which reminds me. Time to get back to London and entertain the troops. Thanks for your hospitality, Winston, but I really gotta go.'

Oliver worked on a personal creed that he should always be the one to walk out first – on a dying show, on a decaying marriage and, if necessary, on Winston. He was growing more than a little tired of the histrionics of the Churchill family, and never a day went by without him being reminded that they, too, were growing more than a little tired of him. It was time to leave.

Churchill watched him go, his fists balled in fury and eyes swollen with unrestrained temper. He knew he had made a fool of himself but didn't know how to apologize to his other guests. Sawyers came to his rescue.

'I'm sorry to have to tell you all, ladies and gentlemen, that His Majesty's ship the *Hood* has been sunk.'

The gasps of alarm and sorrow that erupted gave Churchill his cover. He retreated to his room.

As discussion of the latest disaster began to ripple around the Great Hall, Winant moved to the fireplace where Sarah was languishing elegantly and a little tragically. He couldn't fail to notice that, during the entire iniquitous attack by her father upon her husband, she had done nothing to intervene.

'Sorry,' Winant said, offering her a cigarette. 'Anything I can do to help?'

'Not any more,' she sighed. When she lifted her head to accept a light from the tall, gangling figure of Winant, he could see there were tears around her eyes. 'That poor ship. Those poor men,' she whispered. 'Makes our troubles seem almost indecent.'

'Come on. I'm taking you for a walk in the garden. Let's get away from all this.'

She smiled forlornly, and took his arm. It was a tiny gesture that somehow, for him, meant so much, and he had to struggle not to be childishly jealous when, minutes later as they arrived at the mellow brick gateway to the Rose Garden, he found Harriman and Pamela had beaten them to it. So they went elsewhere, not talking much, just walking slowly, holding on to each other, content in each other's company.

He brought Sarah back in time for lunch. He was soon to wish – desperately – that he hadn't, for when her father reappeared, he was dragging his Black Dog behind him. Winant later thought that he seemed a little like Lear, lashing out almost blindly, incapable of restraint. It was so unlike him – not that the old man should have a temper, but that he should have no control of it.

Churchill remained sullen throughout the Brown Windsor soup, head down, while others struggled to maintain a conversation without him. Then, over the mutton, the head lifted as though he had received an electric shock.

'Nearly two thousand brave British seamen died in an instant this morning,' he said.

There was a momentary silence before Winant took it

upon himself to respond. 'My country offers you its heart-felt condolences.'

'Don't want your condolences, Gil,' he responded petulantly. 'I want your country at our side waging bloody war.'

Winant bit his lip in frustration. 'You know, Winston, that Congress –'

'How is it that the Congress doesn't hang its head in shame?'

'Prime Minister,' Winant said, slipping into official mode to defend himself against the insult, 'only recently you suggested that the aid my country is providing amounts to one of the most unselfish acts in the whole of Christendom. You know we are behind you.'

'You glower from the other side of the globe as if a sour look or a harsh word will be sufficient to deter men like Hitler. They will not. My country is dying in order to preserve liberty and civilization, not just for ourselves but for your people, too. Yet you leave us to die alone. You call that Christian? Then pray forgive me if I seem to have read a different Bible.'

'We've been through this before. The President has to work within his constitutional responsibilities and the limits of public opinion,' Winant replied softly, hoping the other man might yet grow calm. He did not.

'Ah! I hear so much about following in the footsteps of public opinion, yet so little about leadership. And I tell you, there is no leadership in permitting an entire world to be enslaved for fear of taking a few casualties.'

'Winston, please. I know you're upset about the loss of so many lives on the *Hood* – we all are. It was tragic.'

Churchill was pointing his knife belligerently. 'Tragic, indeed. But the lives we lost this morning were no more than those we lose in a single night of bombing in our towns and cities. Tens of thousands of innocent civilians are being murdered in their own homes, and your countrymen refuse to lift a finger to restrain the brutal arm of the aggressors.' He had grown breathless with the force of his emotion. 'Are we to believe, then, that in this fight for freedom, one American life is to be valued more highly than any number of Englishmen?'

'My own life I would gladly give, Winston. You know that. You also know that I cannot speak for others.'

'No, they speak for themselves. Hess arrives in this country spouting his humbug about peace, and what happens in America? Why, they make a grab for their money and run! Wall Street tumbles. Your investors take to the hills because they fear that the slaughter in Europe might stop and they'll lose their profits.'

'I agree with you, Winston. Freedom has its excesses, and the response of Wall Street was a disgrace. It so often is. But it's partly your fault. You've said so very little about why Hess flew here. It's scarcely surprising that rumours flourish. How can you expect Americans to jump into a war if they think there's a chance it might be about to end?'

'But the war will not come to an end until they do jump in!' Churchill snapped, pounding the table in frustration and causing the cutlery to jump. 'When will your countrymen realize that? Without your fighting men, this war will go on and on until there is nothing left to fight for. Every freedom will have been torn down and the whole of our civilization will lie rotting at our feet.'

He thrust himself back in his chair, breathing like a wounded bull. Winant thought he could see fear flecking his eye; he had never known that in Churchill. And Winant himself was a little afraid, of what more might still be said. Their friendship was on the brink.

Then Sawyers was at the old man's side, deliberately distracting, holding open a box of cigars.

147

'Thought you might like one of these, zur,' he said, thrusting the box almost insistently at Churchill. 'The ones from Cuba.'

'What the hell are you doing, Sawyers? Are you trying to kill me?'

'They're good 'uns. Been checked.'

'By the security services?'

'No. By me.'

'You?'

'Well, zur, the security gentlemen set up a committee, like. To decide what to do about your cigars. Had two meetings, they have, but they still can't make up minds how best to test 'em.'

'So you . . . ?'

'That's right. Last night. Tested 'em meself.'

'How?'

'By fire, o' course. How else?'

Churchill stared ferociously at his valet, then into the box while his guests waited for another outburst. But suddenly Sarah was giggling, and the others joined in. Slowly the old man's shoulders relaxed and he reached for a cigar.

'Well, I dare say they can stand a little more testing, Sawyers. And give one to the Ambassador.' It was about as close as Churchill was capable of coming to an apology.

Still he was restless, couldn't settle. After dinner, they had all gathered in the Long Gallery to watch a new American film, *Citizen Kane*, but the old man seemed distracted and he walked out halfway through. Even after Sawyers had put him to bed, he couldn't sleep. Every time he closed his eyes the darkness fell upon him and he imagined he was drowning. Like the men on the *Hood*.

He lay there, sleepless, motionless, tears dropping onto his pillow.

It was a little while after he had turned out his light that he heard noises from down the corridor. His bedroom was off the gallery that ran behind the Great Hall; it was also where most of the guest bedrooms were located. Normally Churchill would have been exasperated at a disturbance so late at night, but he suspected it might be Winant, restless, like him. Churchill knew he had been foul to a man whom he had come to regard as a friend. Perhaps, he decided, he should settle the matter, with a little grace, and allow them both to rest.

He was at the door of his bedroom when the noises beyond became more distinct. A door had been opened, then closed. Now he could hear cautious footsteps in the hallway, followed by the scrape of a different door opening and, very gently, being pulled to.

A thousand suppositions crossed his mind. They all came to one conclusion. He had been right, it was Winant. He suspected the American was now in Sarah's room, beside her, in the place of her husband, as he had been during dinner and throughout much of the day. Churchill was no great moralist – he couldn't be and still respect the memory of his wayward mother – yet what he had heard disturbed him profoundly. He had watched his mother trying to swamp her unhappiness in repeated infidelities; he knew that it rarely worked. And now Sarah. As he stood in the darkness, for the moment all his other cares were pushed aside in sorrow for his daughter.

Then he heard another sound. It was indistinct, but somehow surreptitious. Very slowly, he opened his door just enough to be able to peer into the hallway.

There, framed against a distant window, he saw the silhouette of Héloise creeping back up the stairs.

*　　　*　　　*

When Sawyers came in the following morning, the old man was sitting up in bed, wrapped in his silk pyjamas, looking like a freshly scrubbed pig.

'Sawyers,' Churchill began, examining the other man carefully through the smoke of the first cigar of the day, 'you know most things that are going on around here, don't you?'

'What sort o' things?'

'I'm not certain, of course, but I get the impression,' Churchill continued, in a manner that was uncharacteristically opaque, 'that one of our guests is – how can I put this? – growing a little too close to my own family.'

'Meaning?'

'Come on, man! Help me out here.'

'Where is here, exactly?'

'In bed. That's what I mean. In bloody bed. Don't be so obtuse. Did all of our guests spend the night in their own beds? Or was one of them . . . resting elsewhere?'

The servant ignored him, busying himself instead with the laying out of Churchill's clothes.

'Sawyers?'

The servant placed a pair of freshly pressed trousers on a clothes stand, taking meticulous care to preserve the creases as if it were a job that might occupy him for an entire day. Only then did he turn towards the bed.

'Mr Churchill. They're *your* family. And I'm not any sort o' domestic Gestapo.'

'I could have you shot for insubordination.'

'And you could get yer own breakfast, zur. But I don't think that's likely, do you?'

'You can be bloody rude.'

'I do me best.'

Churchill wondered whether to lose his temper, but there was no point, not with this extraordinary man. He was so

150

much more than a servant; he was counsellor, a guide, a shield and, on occasions, his judge. In any event, his reaction had already told Churchill all he wanted to know. Sawyers was never insolent without a reason, so there was a reason.

'Then let me ask you something that *is* your business. The French girl. Mrs Landemare's kin. What do we know about her?'

Suddenly the audacity was gone, like a jacket slipped from his shoulder. This was indisputably his territory. 'Can I ask why yer wanting to know?'

Churchill drew on his cigar. 'Not at the moment.'

'Very well. She does her job, does as she's told. Quiet sort o' thing. Learns quick. From Mer-sails – think I told yer that. A naval family. Parents long dead, I'm sure o' that, but she's got an older brother. Think he helped bring her up, like, after parents died.'

'Problems?'

He shook his head. 'Always ready to help, she is. Don't think she's ever complained, no' the once.'

'Then we must be thankful for such small mercies. But keep an eye on her, will you?'

'For what?'

'I'm not sure. But if you see anything, be sure to tell no one but me.'

SEVEN

The saga of the sinking ships had yet to reach its conclusion. The battle in the Demark Strait had not been entirely one-sided. The *Hood*'s sister ship, the *Prince of Wales*, had managed to hit the *Bismarck* with three shells – a seemingly miserable consolation for the loss of an entire battleship. But two of the shells had caused a serious fuel leak, enough to force the *Bismarck*'s captain to reconsider his plans. Instead of rushing towards the hunting grounds of the Atlantic, he turned the ship and headed for repairs towards occupied France, where she would soon come under the protective screen of U-boats and the Luftwaffe's fighters.

The British pursued her, launching Swordfish biplanes armed with torpedoes. Yet the Atlantic is vast, the conditions were inclement, and they had great difficulty finding her. When at last the outline of the *Bismarck* appeared through the low cloud and swirling storms, the British planes went in to attack, only for their torpedoes to fail. They had been fitted with the wrong type of detonators. Yet in one of those cruel ironies with which war is littered, it turned out to be a miracle of deliverance, for it was later discovered that the Swordfish had found not the *Bismarck* but the *Sheffield*. The British had been trying to blow up one of their own ships.

They changed the detonators and tried again. This time a

single torpedo found its target, striking the German ship in its stern. There was no danger of the *Bismarck* sinking from the blow, but when the confusion of the explosion had receded it was discovered that one of her rudders had jammed. All attempts to loosen it failed. So, as her pursuers closed in, the newest and most powerful ship in the German Navy was left sailing round in circles. It could lead to only one conclusion.

As the pale light of dawn began to break, every eye on the *Bismarck* turned to the horizon. Some men touched crucifixes or twisted wedding bands, others stared at photographs of children and loved ones, or reread letters from those they had left behind. Many prayed quietly at their battle stations, some joked, others said nothing at all. Every man had his own way of waiting to die.

All this and much more was on Churchill's mind when he rose to address Members of Parliament, sitting in their temporary home of Church House. Churchill did not like this place. It was strange, alien, far too modern. The seating was arranged in a circle, and he felt surrounded. He had come to deliver more bad news. The situation in Crete, where the British had retreated after the German occupation of Greece, was looking ever more grave. And the Battle of the Denmark Strait was still a disaster, no matter how nobly he tried to wrap it up. Although they had pursued and bombed the *Bismarck*, still she would not sink. He told them that even as he spoke, British ships were firing on the *Bismarck*, but the shells seemed to be having no effect, so they were going to try torpedoes. She was surrounded, crippled, she would not escape, he told them, but they grew restless. There was something innately unsporting in the tale. The stag must die, but many who listened wished desperately that it could be put out of its misery rather than hear that its legs were being broken one by one.

He moved on, to Northern Ireland. More difficult news.

He announced that there was to be no conscription in the province, it was to be treated differently from the rest of the country. They all knew this was a grievous personal defeat for Churchill, who had argued that this should not be, that the province was not different and therefore could not be treated differently, but even he had not been able to carry the day. The Americans had objected, most vociferously. Roosevelt himself had intervened. He would not have Irish Catholics being conscripted to fight for Britain any more than he would have Americans. It left Churchill furious, but helpless. Another battle lost. It left a sour taste.

As he was talking, he became aware of a whispered but animated discussion taking place in the official gallery. A folded piece of paper was being handed down to one of the Members, who passed it along the line, hand to hand, leaving a trail of agitation in its wake. It was like watching a torpedo weaving its way towards him. Then the note was thrust into his hand, which trembled very slightly. He took a moment to glance at it.

'I do not know whether I might venture, with great respect, to intervene for one moment, Mr Speaker,' he announced, folding the paper in two. He looked at the expectant faces around him, holding them, playing with them a little. 'I have just received news . . . that the *Bismarck* is sunk!'

A wave of jubilation burst forth across the men around him.

The *Bismarck* was gone, taking almost every member of its crew with it, more than two thousand men, who now lay alongside those from the *Hood*.

The cheering continued. For a while, the news had wiped away the doubts and restlessness, but Churchill knew they would soon be back. Not even he could sail around in circles forever.

*   *   *

Pamela and Harriman stood on the dockside wrapped up against a cold wind, watching as the ships were unloaded. The first Lend-Lease convoy had arrived, laden with food.

'There, in those crates. Our secret weapon.' The American pointed as a crane lowered the first cargo onto the dockside.

'Am I allowed to know what it is?' she asked.

'It's called Spam.'

'Never heard of it.'

'It's powerful stuff. Comes in cans. May even take the place of rissoles one day.'

'You pig!'

'And the other boats are filled with American delicacies like powdered egg and soya flour.'

'You dragged me all the way here to show me boats full of shrivelled eggs and Spam?' Laughter trickled in between her words and she grabbed his sleeve, but he stared straight ahead, unbending, leaning into the wind.

'No. I brought you here to tell you we have to stop this.'

Her good humour died and she felt the wind between them. 'We should never have started again.'

'No.'

'Oh, but it was fun.' She squeezed his arm tightly. They stood silently for a moment, pretending to be looking at the activity on the docks.

'Do you think Winston knows?' Harriman asked eventually.

'Of course not. Why do you think that?'

'He's asked me to go to the Middle East.'

'Why? When?'

'To see what's needed for the battle in the desert. He wants me to go straight away.'

A long, sad pause.

'And he's written to Randolph. Wants him to take care of me while I'm there. Show me around.'

'What?'

'Ironic, isn't it? That's why I wondered if he knew.'

'No, Papa isn't cruel. Fact is, he's not very good at dealing with that sort of thing. He would never interfere.' Silence. 'So . . . what do we do?'

'Say goodbye, I guess.'

'War is so beastly, Averell.'

'It makes. It breaks.'

'How long . . . ?'

'Weeks. Maybe a couple of months.'

The first hint of tears.

'Pamela, when I get back . . .'

'You mustn't see me, not at all. You won't see me.'

'Not sure I can accept that.'

'You'll have to. I won't be around any more.'

'Meaning?'

'I'm leaving London, too. I can't afford to stay, not at the Dorchester. You know, Randy's gambling debts . . .'

He was still staring straight ahead, his features stiff, frozen in the wind. 'Where will you go?'

'No idea. To the country. Somewhere very cheap.'

'That's not fair.'

'As you said, war makes, war breaks.'

'Look, Pam . . .' At last he turned to look at her. The wind had caused tears to collect at the corner of his own eyes. 'I like you so very much. You're – hell, you're everything I'm not. I'm a different person with you, a better person. I wish there was some way we could just stick with today and forget about tomorrow, but . . .'

'I know.'

'You mean a very great deal to me. I can't have you simply walking out of my life. Anyhow, I'd like to help. Look, let me take care of your bill at the Dorchester. It would be so easy, just put it onto my tab. No one need ever know. You just carry on as you are.'

'No, Averell. That's so sweet but I couldn't.'

'Of course you can.'

'Then what I mean is I shouldn't.'

'Shouldn't? As in – you shouldn't have let me into your bed again the other night. Do you regret that?'

'Of course not, silly goat. It was wonderful.' She sighed, a long, strained sound that carried memories of the nights they had stolen from the world.

'Then let me do this for you. Please. For Winston. He needs to have you nearby, not stuck away in the country.'

She hesitated.

'It's almost your duty,' he persisted. 'Anyway, it's either that or powdered egg.'

'For Winston, then.'

'To hell with June,' Churchill had announced. He was desperately tired. Nothing worked, not even the weather. It had been the longest and dreariest spring in memory, so he had declared his intention of spending a few days recuperating in his own country home at Chartwell. Clemmie and Pamela went with him.

The main house overlooking the sweeping vale of Kent was closed for the duration, with most of its rooms cocooned in white shrouds, so they had settled in a cottage lower down the hill, one of those he had built with his own hands. He hadn't spoken much, content to wander around the grounds on his own, calling to the black swans and ducks, searching for the hiding places of the butterflies, encouraging the yellow cat, who seemed to have forgotten all about him. Eventually Pamela went searching for him. She found him sitting on the bench by the goldfish pond, wrapped in an old overcoat he used for bricklaying, dribbling biscuit crumbs to the goldfish. The yellow cat was staring at him suspiciously from a tuft of reeds.

He produced a cigar from his pocket and began to prepare it. Pamela reached across. 'Let me,' she offered. He smiled in appreciation. She had a rare talent for taking care of an old man's comforts.

'Do you like Chartwell, Pamela?'

'I love your home, Papa,' she replied with enthusiasm. It was a lie, gently offered, so as not to upset him. In truth she found the house cumbersome, its details complicated and over-worked. Better to have bulldozed and started from scratch.

'It was my enduring sorrow that my mother never saw Chartwell,' he said. 'But it will be yours one day. Yours and Randolph's.'

For the first time she realized she had never, not even for a moment, contemplated the prospect of a blissful old age sitting around the fire with Randolph, not at Chartwell nor anywhere else. Their marriage had been so impetuous, yet, as Averell had said, war makes, war breaks, and somehow the war would sort it out. Otherwise . . . bulldoze and start again from scratch, perhaps.

She sought to move the conversation towards firmer terri-tory. 'Your mother, Papa, she . . .'

'Died a little while before I first saw the house. She would have found pleasure, I think, sitting on the lawn beneath a parasol, looking out over the lakes with one of Mrs Landemare's cakes crumbling in her hand. Ah, but perhaps it was never more than a dream. She was always so busy, had so little time . . .'

'Oh, Papa,' she sighed, nestling beside him and tracing her finger across his brow, trying to wipe away the creases of

159

concern. He closed his eyes like a small boy. The cat moved closer, cautiously, then, much to Churchill's delight, sprang onto his lap.

'You know, I never had much of a family,' he said. 'We seemed always to be on the move from one house to the next, from one crisis to another, my father absent more than he was at home, my mother . . . Oh, my darling mother. She used to shine for me like the evening star, so brilliantly, but at a great distance. That's why I built this place, built so much of Chartwell with my own hands. As a proper home. For our family.' At last he looked at her, his pale blue eyes almost beseeching. 'When this bloody war is done with, shall we go back to being the same?'

She held his hand, but said nothing.

'Of course not,' he declared softly. 'Nothing will ever be the same. Not us. Not England. Nothing lasts for ever.'

She wondered whether he knew, was making a point. 'We can never live in the past, Papa.'

'No, of course not. But when I try to peer into the future, I see nothing but mists of doubt. I weep for what is to come.' He held her hand as if he never wanted to let go.

'Papa, what's wrong?'

'I think Sarah is having an affair with Gil Winant.'

It took a moment for his words to strike home. Pinpricks of alarm began to spread from her stomach across her chest.

'What do you feel about that, Papa?' she asked, not looking up, pretending to focus on stroking the cat, shivering inside.

'How is a father supposed to feel? I want nothing more than her happiness, but . . .' The cat was now rubbing her face up against his sleeve. With great tenderness he began to wipe her eyes with the corners of his handkerchief. A relationship reborn. 'I think perhaps I should send Sarah away,' he continued.

160

'Whatever for?'

'I cannot let it continue, not under my own roof. They will say she is wanton and wicked.'

'Oh, Papa,' she said scornfully, 'what century are we living in? Even in your mother's day such matters were little more than organized deceits, and I don't seem to remember you talking about her in that way.'

He turned on her, as though his cheeks had been slapped.

'You never knew her!' His tone was sharp.

'I know that men were important to her – in fact, the focus of her life. Not just one man but many. And under the family roof.'

Bewilderment began to flood his eyes. No one had ever dared talk like that about his mother, a woman three times married and courted many times more, but throughout it all she had still been his mother, the distant, elusive, untouchable evening star that had shone brilliantly yet so intermittently upon his early life. He had been thirteen when he came down to breakfast to find her sharing the table with a stranger, and a couple of years older before he had begun to understand what it implied. Now he choked on the memories. He stiffened. The cat scurried away in alarm.

'You have no right to judge my mother!'

'I don't. If I had known her I think I would have loved your mother as much as anyone could. But I love Sarah, too.'

'No more than I!'

'Then why punish her, send her away?'

'How can a father rest, knowing what is going on?'

'But you don't suggest sending Gil away. You could, you know, with a single word. Get him recalled, just like that.' She snapped her fingers.

'Because . . .'

161

'Because, Papa, he is a man. Because he is too valuable to you. And because you love the idea of having an important American like him under your thumb. Isn't that it? Do I smell just the faintest whiff of double standards here?'

She had to push the matter to its limit; it was her own funeral they were discussing.

'That is ridiculous –'

'Then tell me, Papa. One simple question. What would your mother have done?'

He sat panting for breath as, deep inside him, war was waged.

'What will you have me be, a bishop or a bloody Borgia? I don't know what to do, Pamela. Does that make you feel better? All I know is that it is a circumstance that will end up breaking my heart. But why, Pamela, why do you set about me so?'

'Because, Papa,' she whispered, 'whatever you decide to do with Gil and Sarah, you will have to do with Averell. And with me.'

The husband had been the ghost at all their feasts, and now he was there, made flesh, his hand outstretched in greeting.

'Mr Harriman.'

'Please – call me Averell.'

They were standing beneath the awning of Shepheard's Hotel, where Randolph stayed when he was in Cairo. The heat was searing. Every piece of brickwork radiated heat and even the palm trees seemed to wilt. The air was full of flies and dust, and the pavements wriggled with dirty boys. From the road came the noise and stench of complaining donkeys.

Randolph was sweating. Harriman had seen photographs of him at Chequers, but they were clearly several years old, for they had shown a young face that burned with energy and, yes, even beauty. But the man before him was greying, overweight and with an expression that had become glazed with indulgence. The American reached out, taking the proffered hand warily. He searched Randolph's eyes for any trace of animosity or understanding, but found only a puddle of gin.

'My father speaks very highly of you, Averell. Says I should take care of you. Be a pleasure. Come inside to the bar; I'd rather be buggered than stand outside any longer in this heat.'

And so they started, the husband and the lover . . .

Soon they were occupying Randolph's favourite corner in the bar, where the breeze and the gin were at their most cooling. Harriman had been told that the younger Churchill was a lieutenant, but he wore the uniform of a major and carried the air of feudal chieftain. As they sat, the entire Egyptian world seemed to pass by his table, and he greeted them variously with cries of welcome, curses or complete indifference.

The man was not a fool, Harriman quickly came to realize that. But he was the son of perhaps the most famous man in the world, which meant that his life would never be his own. Above all, he was not allowed to go to war. Harriman doubted if the Prime Minister himself had forbidden it, but he didn't need to, the System would take care of that for him. So while Randolph had trained to be a commando and was as eager as his father had ever been to prove himself, he hadn't seen a single day of combat. Almost all his friends and colleagues had been to war, many of them thrown into the disastrous campaign to save Crete, but while they had fought and some very close to him had already died, Randolph ended up in the corner of this fetid colonial hotel having to do battle with nothing more threatening than flies and his bar bills.

In place of medals, he wore his frustrations. Every fighting man who passed the table had his arm grabbed, every senior officer had his ear bent – and every attractive woman had her body silently propositioned. None of them seemed to mind too much; it was that sort of place and, after all, it was that sort of world. As for the rest of humanity that passed by, they provided an audience for Randolph's tireless stream of complaints about how the war in the Middle East was being run and largely lost.

An officer in the uniform of the Scots Guards approached with a companion on his arm and, spotting Randolph, tried too late to avoid eye contact.

'Averell, may I introduce Colonel John Marriott?' Randolph said.

'Churchill,' the senior officer muttered, not struggling to hide the impression of impatience. 'And Mr Harriman. I've heard of you. Welcome.'

'Thank you.'

'Allow me to introduce my wife. Momo, say hello to Mr Harriman.'

An elegant arm with exceptionally long red fingernails was extended. 'Hello, Mr Harriman.' Her voice was American, her jewellery expensive and her hand lingered just a fraction too long in his.

'But you'll excuse us,' her husband added. 'Must be on our way. A war to fight,' he said, casting a caustic eye in the direction of Randolph.

As the couple withdrew, Harriman couldn't help but notice the swing of her hips. He assumed it was intentional. This was not a subtle city. It was a place where the perfume was too heavy, the servants too ingratiating, the streets too loud, the liquor too cheap, with everything corrupted by its imperial idleness and military intrigues. Cairo gave the impression that nothing would last and everything was on offer, a bit like a New York fire sale.

Over lunch in the magnificent dining room, Randolph poured out more of his frustrations about the incompetence with which the war was being run, and Harriman took careful note. After all, what with his father and his friends, Churchill was probably the best-informed man in Cairo. They ate magnificently while Randolph gossiped. And when the bill was presented, they indulged in a squabble about who was to pay. Randolph was an habitual bill-grabber – he would always dine expensively, in company, and reach for the bill, regardless of the fact that he was broke. Pamela had complained of that. But Harriman had longer arms; his fingers – and his guilt – got there first.

'Averell,' Randolph declared, conceding defeat, 'you are a fully paid-up, first-class swine. I think we shall become great friends.'

Harriman blanched. Then the question he had been dreading most, and for which in spite of repeated practice he still had not properly prepared.

'Tell me, when you were in London, did you see anything of that wife of mine . . . ?'

A thousand miles away, the wind continued to blow achingly cold. Churchill abandoned his stay at Chartwell and decided to return early to London. His car was the last to leave; when he clambered into the back seat, he found Pamela already there. He said not a word, wrapped himself in a car rug and stared out of the window.

Their convoy hurried past the base at Biggin Hill. The

airfield was quieter than it had been for many months. The bombing raid that had gutted the House of Commons had proved to be a final spasm of destruction, at least for the moment. But it was only a matter of time before they would be back.

The bell on the police car ahead of them rang out as it passed around the wrong side of a traffic island and pushed its way through red traffic lights. Churchill enjoyed being driven fast. Usually he thrilled to its sense of speed, of power – his power. But today his mood was sombre and distracted. He remained silent. Pamela assumed it was her fault.

But Churchill could never tolerate silence for long. Eventually he began to mutter, still staring out of the window. 'That wretched man Hess. Tried to kill himself.'

'How?'

'Rushed past the guard and threw himself over the banisters. Know how he feels.'

'Oh, Papa.'

'But he's going to be all right. Just a broken leg. Ridiculous fellow. Couldn't even get that right.'

'Won't there be questions? What will you say about it?'

'Why, nothing, I suppose. Ever since he arrived people have been demanding that I say something about the man, but in all honesty I have no idea what to say. Sometimes it seems better just to shut up.'

And that was it. He slumped back into his seat. He still had not looked at her. That was why she had stolen into his car, in order to break through the silence that had fallen upon him ever since she had made her confession. His silences were corrosive; she couldn't allow it to continue. That gave her the idea.

'I think what you have done about Hess is exactly right,' she began again.

'But I have done nothing. That satisfies no one. So the entire world resorts to rumour and speculation. Silly minds do so hate a vacuum.'

'Precisely.'

'What's your point?' he asked, at last turning to look at her.

'Silence can be a weapon.'

'What are you talking about?'

'You remember you once told me that a few years ago Mama went on a sea voyage to India for several months. You knew she had become friendly with one of the other guests on board, a single man. You told me how every day you waited for the postman to arrive in order to ransack the letters, hoping to find one from her. And every day that you had none, you died a little.'

'I never stopped loving her. I never lost faith,' he insisted, pounding his chest and looking at her in accusation.

'If only I had married a man like you, Papa,' she said coolly, refusing to match his emotion. He continued to stare at her with suspicion.

'But you know how it hurt, Papa,' she continued, moving him on. 'You know the suspicions that passed across your mind.'

'Like crows tearing at my carcass.'

'So what must they be thinking in Germany? Whether Hess came with Hitler's blessing or not doesn't really matter – but surely they were expecting something, even if only an outburst or an accusation. Yet they have nothing. And you remember what that was like.'

'Every day that went by without hearing from her, I felt the most terrible sense of loss. My suspicions grew, dark thoughts formed in my mind. Waiting for the postman and his letters became an obsession.'

167

'Every day since Hess arrived here, Berlin must have been growing more anxious about what has happened – and what is going to happen.'

'I don't understand. What *is* going to happen?'

'I've no idea. It seems to me that's up to you. You control what Hess says, and when he says it, Papa. So you can control what Hitler thinks. You are rather like the postman.'

He slumped back into his seat and was staring out of the window again, but lost this time in thought rather than animosity.

'So what will you do, Papa?' she asked eventually.

'I'm not yet sure – except to keep that bloody man Hitler guessing. Stick a few pins in his rump. Start by sending a Minister along to see Hess, perhaps, but say nothing about what they discuss. Make it seem like . . .' He suddenly grew awkward.

'A lovers' tryst?'

'That'll do for a start,' he said roughly, but would say no more.

He was still angry and uncomfortable with her, but she took comfort from the fact that least they were travelling in the same direction once again.

Randolph proved to be an enthusiastic host. For several days he took Harriman on a tour of military installations, making introductions, pointing out weaknesses, proposing remedies, and once the heat of the day had subsided he introduced the American to the lighter side of Cairo's nightlife – first at the Mohamed Ali Club, where the more refined womenfolk waited to find escorts, and later at the Kit Kat Club and Madame Badia's, where the women seemed altogether less fussy. All the while Harriman made careful notes. Then one evening they sailed up the Nile on a dhow, and beneath the stars Randolph began to speak of Pamela. He spoke very fondly. He had no idea. So Harriman got drunk. He couldn't decide whether the other man's ignorance was because Pamela was so skilled at subterfuge, or because he was the sort of Englishman who would always underestimate a woman. In either case, it was uncomfortable territory, so he pursued Randolph into a state of inebriation until he had little recollection of what was being said and none of how he made it back to the British Embassy, where he was staying. He woke up the next morning feeling dreadful. He got up late, very late, which was most unlike him. Breakfast almost became lunch, and as soon as he had finished it he hurried around to Shepheard's Hotel.

He thought he would have to wake Randolph. They could talk while he was dressing, make up for time already lost that morning. Harriman knocked quietly at the door of Randolph's room, and entered.

Judging by the number of sleeping bags that lay stretched out on the backs of chairs or thrown casually into corners, this was a room accustomed to a fair amount of passing military traffic. Shared room, shared costs. Not the sort of thing Harriman was used to. The fan was spinning noisily, which is perhaps why Randolph hadn't heard the knock at the door, or he simply didn't care, for he was lying naked on his bed. Sitting on top of him was a woman with long, red fingernails. It was Momo Marriott, the wife of the colonel in the Scots Guards. A bead of sweat was trickling down her backbone. She didn't appear to mind the intrusion, or it might have been that she was simply too focused on other things to notice. Randolph, too, seemed unfazed.

'Sorry, old chap,' he spluttered, gasping for each breath. 'Bit busy at the moment. See you in the bar in ten?'

Harriman fled. He hadn't felt so discomfited and out of place since – well, since the previous night, when Randolph had begun gushing about Pamela. But by the time he reached the bar his mood had changed. Throughout his life he had never found comfort in the idea of making another man a cuckold. Now, in Randolph's case, it didn't matter a damn.

EIGHT

Sunday, the twenty-second day of June. It was the shortest night of the year. Four million men stood hidden along a front that stretched from the Black Sea to Finland. They squashed mosquitoes, read the Bible, wrote to loved ones, checked their equipment, ate, drank, prayed, and prepared for death – some other man's death, they hoped.

Fourteen minutes past three in the morning. A lightness in the eastern sky. But still Russia slept.

A minute later, they began to move, backed by three and a half thousand tanks, seven thousand field guns and more than two thousand aircraft. They swarmed from their hiding places in the birch groves and fir forests and began to cross the rivers, the bridges and the crude wooden barriers that marked the frontier. The German invasion of Russia had begun.

It was to result in the greatest slaughter in the history of the human race.

Churchill had taken to his bed the previous evening in an unsettled mood, like a salmon sensing a changing tide. He had woken in the middle of the night and sat bolt upright, waiting, and that was how they had found him when they came to give him the news.

'The first act is over, now the second begins,' he had whispered. 'The curtain rises, the scenery has changed, the greatest story of our lifetime moves on.'

So intense had been his excitement that morning that he had cut himself while shaving.

'Here, better let me do it,' Sawyers had remarked.

'I can manage,' the old man snapped, impatient to get on with the day.

'You're dripping blood on me floor.'

'But don't you see, I was right, Sawyers. I was right!'

'About what, zur?' the valet asked calmly, sitting him down and taking the razor that was being waved like a fly swat.

'About those wretched runways in Poland. They were extending them. For bombers. And that's why their bombers have deserted London. Flown east.'

The words came more fitfully as Sawyers stretched his neck to scrape patiently at the lather beneath his chin.

'I had an inescapable instinct, Sawyers. That it would be today. Sunday. He always invades on a Sunday.'

'Catch everyone on his knees, like.'

'Hah! He won't catch that devil-worshipper Stalin on his knees. But I hope to God he doesn't catch him asleep in bed, either.'

But he probably would. Churchill had been sending the Russian leader warnings for weeks, but the Great Commissar had turned a deaf ear to them all. He would neither forgive nor forget that it was Churchill who had been the foremost abuser of all things Soviet, who had tried to strangle the Bolshevik Revolution at birth, who had on more than one occasion tried to bury Russia in arms and violent abuse. Stalin would never trust the word of Churchill, but he was about to get plenty more of them to consider.

That evening, Churchill broadcast to the world from his desk in the Hawtrey Room. He had spent the day in a state of growing agitation, working and reworking in his mind what he would say. He called what was taking place in Russia 'a climacteric', and he hurled the English language into the fray.

He described Hitler as 'a monster of wickedness'. He said he had 'an insatiable lust for blood and plunder'. He accused him of planning 'slaughter, pillage and devastation'. Then he called him a 'bloodthirsty guttersnipe'. And that was simply by way of introduction.

Not content with having all Europe under his heel or else terror-ized into various forms of abject submission, he must now carry his work of butchery and desolation among the vast multitudes of Russia and of Asia. The terrible military machine which we and the rest of the civilized world so foolishly, so supinely, so insensately allowed the Nazi gangsters to build up year by year from almost nothing – this machine cannot stand idle, lest it rust or fall to pieces. It must be in continual motion, grinding up human lives and trampling down the homes and the rights of hundreds of millions of men!

After he had been shaved that morning, he had begun to burst with excitement once more. 'Don't you see, Sawyers? In a single night, everything has changed,' he had said, furiously wiping steam from the mirror. 'Yesterday, we were alone. Solitary warriors. Yet this morning we stand along-side Stalin and the multitudes of Russia.'

'You – and Stalin?' Sawyers had enquired, struggling to hide his incredulity. 'You mean "that devil-worshipping Stalin"? The same one?'

'You understand nothing!' Churchill had barked, throwing

cologne around himself. 'If Hitler invaded Hell I think I could find it in myself to make a favourable reference to the Devil.'

But his valet understood things well enough. Sawyers was right. As the day wore on Churchill had realized that to persuade anyone that there was now common cause with the birthplace of Bolshevism would require a somersault of such prodigious proportions that it would leave many breathless with mirth. It would require him to turn away from a course he had followed with monastic fervour for almost half his life. He would need cover, and the only cover he knew was words. A hurricane of them.

No one has been a more consistent opponent of Communism than I have for the last twenty-five years. I will unsay no word that I have spoken about it. But all this fades away before the spectacle which is now unfolding. The past, with its crimes, its follies and its tragedies, flashes away. I see the Russian soldiers standing on the threshold of their native land, guarding the fields which their fathers have tilled from time immemorial. I see them guarding their homes where mothers and wives pray – ah yes, for there are times when all pray – for the safety of their loved ones, the return of the breadwinner, of their champion, of their protector.

He loved the English language, loved it almost too much. There were times when he would drive it like a gun horse until it all but dropped. As he spoke he beat time with his hand, as though he were driving the horse to the limits of its endurance.

I see the ten thousand villages of Russia, where the means of existence is wrung so hardly from the soil, but where there are still primordial human joys, where maidens laugh and children play. I see advancing upon all this in hideous onslaught the Nazi war

machine, with its clanking, heel-clicking, dandified Prussian offi-
cers, its crafty expert agents fresh from the cowing and tying down
of a dozen countries. I see also the dull, drilled, docile, brutish
masses of the Hun soldiery plodding on like a swarm of crawling
locusts.

That, at least, was something he and Stalin might agree
upon.

We have but one aim and one single, irrevocable purpose. We are
resolved to destroy Hitler and every vestige of the Nazi regime.
From this nothing will turn us. Nothing!

His voice rose until it was pounding with emotion.

We will never parley. We will never negotiate with Hitler or any
of his gang. We shall fight him by land, we shall fight him by
sea, we shall fight him in the air, until, with God's help, we have
rid the earth of his shadow and liberated its peoples from his
yoke!

His mouth had gone dry; he sipped his whisky, ready for
the climax – the Pauline conversion, the climb-down, the
turn-around, or whatever others might call it. But it had to
be done.

Any man or state who fights on against Nazidom will have our
aid. Any man or State who marches with Hitler is our foe. It
follows, therefore, that we shall give whatever help we can to
Russia and the Russian people. We shall appeal to all our friends
and allies in every part of the world to take the same course and
pursue it, as we shall, faithfully and steadfastly – to the end!

The world had changed. It was spinning them all around, and by the time Churchill made his way upstairs to bed that evening, he was exhausted. It had been a gruelling rite of passage.

Sawyers helped him off with his jacket. 'Strange old world. Who'd've thought it? Old Uncle Joe Stalin our ally.'

'Our ally – certainly. But our friend?' The old man shook his head. 'They are barbarians. Not even the slenderest of threads connects Communism to any form of civilization. Which is why the battle that is about to take place upon the soil of Russia will be as terrible as any fought in history. Whoever wins it will dominate Europe from the steppes to the distant sea.' His tone grew darker. 'They will dominate these islands, too – unless, somehow, America becomes part of it.'

He fell back on the bed as Sawyers began to untie his shoes. He reached for the whisky on his bedside table. Alongside the glass stood a framed photograph of his family, taken the previous Christmas. Sarah, Vic Oliver, Randolph, Pamela, all smiling . . .

'Everything in my life comes back to bloody Americans,' he sighed, as his head hit the pillow.

The weather had changed. Everything had changed.

The gales of the endless spring had vanished and summer had at last arrived, determined to make up for lost time. The sun seemed to drag slowly across the sky and, deep inside their blacked-out and shuttered buildings, the British stifled.

And the Russians suffered. They were being driven back on all fronts. Within nine hours of the start of the invasion, the Luftwaffe had destroyed one thousand two hundred Soviet planes. Within five days the Wehrmacht had advanced halfway towards Leningrad. Within three weeks the Red Army had lost two million men. *Rassenkampf* – race war – had taken on a new meaning. The doors of village houses were opened with hand grenades, children were questioned with bayonets, young women were reduced to a level lower than beasts.

The brutality was far from one-sided. As the Red Army fell back, they slaughtered all political prisoners, and wasted the lives of their own soldiers on a prodigious scale. Yet still the Germans kept coming.

And in Paris, in Prague, in Poland, too, Hitler's men were beginning to round up Jews. Thousands of them.

Churchill summoned his military chiefs and advisers to the Map Room in the Annexe. They found him staring at the huge map of Eastern Europe. A front had been marked on it that seemed to stretch for ever.

'It takes the breath away,' Churchill said, his words tinged with awe.

'The Wehrmacht don't seem to have lost much breath,' one of his Chiefs of Staff observed drily. 'They haven't stopped for days.'

'They must, eventually. But where? When?'

For a while, no one spoke as they contemplated one of the most extraordinary military adventures of all time. Then, slowly, it came.

'A few weeks, Prime Minister. I can't see how the Russians can sustain things longer than that. Losing too many men, too much territory. A few weeks, that's all. Then they're out of this war.'

'I agree, Prime Minister. They'll do just what they did in the last war and sue for peace. Couple of months at most.'

'Stalin's wretched purges have sliced through any chance they had of putting up effective resistance,' a third joined in.

He pointed at the front. 'Look – Leningrad, Smolensk, Kiev, the Crimea – even Moscow's under threat.'

'Two months,' Churchill muttered. 'Anyone here think they can hold out for longer than two months?'

No one did.

'Then, by September, by the time the leaves begin to turn, Russia will be under their heel and they will fall once again upon us.'

Please, God, not again. Not another winter under the hammer, waiting for the invasion barges and the bombers to come back. They couldn't take that again . . .

The atmosphere grew oppressive. Even when the room had been empty the ventilation system had struggled to cope with the sultry weather, but beneath the crush of bodies in the Map Room it failed completely. The air seemed thick enough to chew.

Yet suddenly Churchill had snapped back to life. 'We must act! There is no time to lose!' he said. 'We can take advantage of them. While their attentions are elsewhere. Let's kick a few German rumps. Make hell while the sun shines!'

The Chiefs of Staff began exchanging anxious glances. 'What, precisely, do you have in mind, Prime Minister?'

'A large raid across the Channel,' Churchill began, the blood rushing once more. 'Twenty-five – thirty thousand men. Use the commandos, some of the Canadians, too. A target in occupied France that'll set the French spirit ablaze once more.' He was back at the maps. 'One of the ports. Dieppe, perhaps. And let us stay there a while,' he insisted, stabbing his finger at the French coastline.

'Too soon, I fear, Prime Minister. Too much chance that we'll end up in the same fix as we did at Dunkirk.'

'But it will split their attentions, don't you see? The Hun

won't know whether to turn east or west. It gives us profound tactical advantages.'

His words were met with silence.

'Then Norway,' he suggested irritably, turning to another map. 'We know enough about the bloody territory.'

'Norway *again*, Prime Minister?'

'A bridgehead in the north that will enable us to join hands with the Russians. Show that our alliance isn't simply one of minds but of men and of muscle. It would be a hugely symbolic gesture.'

'And a highly risky one, if you don't mind me saying so, Prime Minister. We'll examine it, of course, but after the recent problems in Greece and Crete we're desperately short of air cover. And we all remember what happened last time.'

It was a cruel blow but, in the eyes of the Chiefs of Staff, entirely necessary. It was Churchill who had pushed the British Army into Norway without adequate air cover in 1940. It had been a disaster. Another of Winston's follies.

'Then what the hell do you propose to do?' Churchill shouted, glaring around at them. 'Or are we to do absolutely bloody nothing and wait until next week before we do it?' His chest was heaving with frustration.

'I think what we should do is examine everything you've proposed, Prime Minister,' one said. 'Test them. Come back with a reasoned proposal.'

'You've already had a reasoned proposal,' Churchill spat.

'I didn't mean to imply –' But the look in Churchill's eye cut him short.

'Not enough commandos. Not enough air cover,' he growled in contempt. 'Well, we have bombers, don't we? We can at least bomb the bastards!' With that he stormed out.

He left London a few hours later. The heat had become insufferable and even at Chequers it remained endlessly oppressive. He felt claustrophobic, as though the walls were closing in on him. He fled, silently and alone, towards Beacon Hill, dragging his fears behind him.

The shimmering eye of the sun had just touched the top of the beech wood when, from behind him, he heard a peculiar squeaking noise. He turned in annoyance, and found Sawyers approaching. His cheeks were red and he was carrying a galvanized bucket, which was the cause of both the squeak and the sweat that prickled on his brow.

'Do you have to make such an infernal racket?'

'Only bucket to be found. Thought yer might be needing it.'

'And why in God's name would I need a bloody bucket?'

Almost as he had finished complaining, he saw that the bucket was filled with ice, and in the middle of the ice sat a bottle of Pol Roger.

Churchill snorted like a pricked bull; it was all he could find as an expression of gratitude. 'You expect me to drink it out of the bottle?'

From his jacket pocket Sawyers produced a glass, wrapped in a tea towel, which he proceeded to polish with meticulous care.

Churchill studied the valet, who had a suspicious bulge on the other side of his jacket. 'You brought another glass?'

'Just in case you didn't want to be drinking on yer own, zur.'

'My God, but you have your moments, Sawyers.'

Churchill settled down on the stump of an old moss-covered tree. The bucket was placed beside it, and Sawyers began administering the last rites to the champagne. As the shadows lengthened, the scent of early summer travelled easily on the air and the wings of dancing insects glistened in the last rays of sunlight. From the beech wood came the sounds of courting pigeons. It should have been idyllic. For a moment, Sawyers let him pretend.

'Next weekend, zur,' he asked eventually. 'Who shall we expect?'

'The entire bloody world and his uncle,' Churchill complained into his glass. Then, more softly: 'And the family, of course. I want to see the family.'

'Mr Oliver?'

'No. I don't think he will be coming back.'

Sawyers paused to show that he understood.

'Sarah will come, I hope,' Churchill continued. 'Mary, too, if she's available.'

'And Miss Pamela?' Sawyers asked, affecting nonchalance, studying his glass as though a fly had fallen in. 'And wha' about our Mr Harriman? I believe he's due back in a few days from that trip o' his to foreign parts.'

Churchill's eyes flashed at his valet. Just how much did the wretched man know? Everything, of course, that was his job.

Conflicting loyalties twisted inside Churchill like old ivy. A letter had recently arrived from Randolph. 'I have been tremendously impressed by Harriman,' Randolph had written, 'and can well understand the regard which you have for him. In ten very full and active days he has definitely become my favourite American.'

Oh, Randolph, most darling and deceived of sons . . .

'I have become very intimate with him,' the letter concluded.

Churchill's head sagged. 'What do I do?' he whispered. And again: 'What do I do?'

About Randolph, about Pamela, about Harriman, Sarah and the rest. About the fact that in two months' time the bombers and the invasion barges could be back. About his buff-coloured box, from which he had just learnt that the Japanese were on the point of marching their armies into Indo-China, moving remorselessly south, ever closer to the British Empire. Soon they would have air and sea bases in Saigon, just six hundred miles from Singapore. And about the Americans, whom he could never persuade to fight.

He was no longer in control. He was reduced to sitting like an old man on his stool and watching as the world strutted by.

He looked up. Sawyers was standing there, his eyebrow raised, waiting for his answer. Pamela. Harriman. Under his roof? His heart ached. Yet he needed America, needed Harriman. Slowly, bleakly, the words came.

'Let them come.'

He drained his glass and handed it back to Sawyers, who wiped it as carefully as if it were a chalice.

'Even the Almighty had to watch his only son suffer. Nowt to be done. You jest have to have a belief that it'll all come out right in the end.'

It took Churchill many moments before he was able to compose himself. His lips struggled as they found the words. 'I shall be unwise and let you into a state secret. You are a good man, Sawyers.'

'State secret, you say? Then I think I should forget you ever said that.'

'Yes. I already have.'

And suddenly the fire had been rekindled. He thrust his walking stick in the ground and hoisted himself to his feet, setting off towards the house. He left Sawyers struggling with the bucket in his wake.

As they drew near to Chequers they could see the Prime Minister's detective and private secretary scurrying back and forth in search of their lost charge. It was a game Churchill

182

liked to play, slipping his shadows, a game he was able occasionally to win.

'Beat 'em,' he declared with an air of satisfaction. 'And we may yet beat 'em all, Sawyers.'

'Let's hope so,' the servant panted, trailing behind, clutching the bucket to his chest.

'Oh, and what about your maid?' Churchill continued, coming to an abrupt halt as though tripping over a new thought.

'Héloise?' Gratefully the valet caught his breath. 'Jest what I told yer last. 'Cept for her brother.'

'What about her brother?'

'You remember, the one in navy? Mrs Landemare reckons he's dead. Earlier in war. On active service, she thinks.'

Churchill's head was up, like a hare sniffing the breeze and sensing danger.

'I know nowt else,' Sawyers concluded.

'Oh, but I think I do,' Churchill replied, as the last fractions of the sun slipped beyond the horizon. 'It's God's great bloody plan, you see. To make us all suffer for our sins. And it's my past. I believe it's catching up with me.'

Mers-el-Kébir, near Oran in French Algeria. 3 July 1940. Less than two weeks after the armistice with the Germans.

The French fleet lay at anchor behind the harbour wall, in the shadow of the steep cliffs that ran along this section of the North African coast. As dawn broke, a British naval destroyer appeared on the horizon. She was under full steam. As she drew nearer, she signalled to the French: 'A British Fleet is at sea off Oran waiting to welcome you.'

It proved to be a most imposing welcome. The fleet consisted of the battleships *Valiant* and *Resolution*, the aircraft carrier *Ark Royal*, two cruisers, eleven destroyers – and HMS *Hood*.

They knew each other, the French and the British. The *Hood* and the French flagship *Dunkerque* had sailed together as allies against the German fleet, and the British commander sent a message to his French counterpart, Admiral Gensoul, suggesting that they should continue to do so. He proposed that the French fleet should sail to a British port and continue the fight, or if that were not acceptable, the fleet should be handed over to the British so that they could continue the fight alone. Failing that, the British suggested, the fleet should be put out of commission so that it was unable to fight for anyone. But if none of these options were acceptable, the French were told, their fleet would be sunk.

The British fleet steamed to and fro across the bay, waiting for a reply. But it was several hours before Gensoul at last agreed to talk. A British officer arrived by motor boat, yet as he drew near the fleet he could see that tugs were standing by and control positions were being manned. The French were preparing to sail.

At 4.15 in the afternoon, the British officer, Captain Holland, was at last allowed on board the *Dunkerque* to meet with Gensoul. The French admiral explained, formally, coldly, that he took orders only from the French Government. Holland replied that the terms his own Government had offered were not negotiable.

All these events had been followed by Churchill from the Cabinet Room. He reached the conclusion that Gensoul was interested only in delay, and that French submarines and air reinforcements were on their way. He gave orders that the matter was to be settled quickly.

At 5.15, while Gensoul was still talking with Holland, the British commander on HMS *Hood* sent a new signal to the

French. He said that unless his terms were accepted within fifteen minutes, their fleet would be sunk.

Holland quit the *Dunkerque* five minutes before the deadline expired. He later wrote that Gensoul had bidden him a most courteous farewell, and that as he sailed past the battleship *Bretagne*, the officer of the watch had come to attention and honoured him with a stylish salute.

At 5.29, a minute before the deadline, Gensoul signalled that he could not accept the British terms. However, he declared he would be willing to sail his fleet to the USA. He must have known it was a hopeless gesture.

Twenty-three minutes later, the British fleet opened fire. The first salvo fell short, the second hit the harbour wall where some of the French ships were moored, scattering them with a fusillade of concrete that killed several crewmen. At the third attempt, the British shells found their mark. Direct hits. Within moments, the *Bretagne* disappeared in a sheet of flame.

The action lasted less than ten minutes. By the time the order was given to cease fire, the French fleet lay in substantial ruins. The *Bretagne* was gone, the *Dunkerque* run aground, other ships broken and beached. The casualty list was enormous; more than a thousand French sailors died on the *Bretagne* alone.

One of them was the brother of Héloise.

It was his normal practice to leave them waiting. 'We shall depart at three,' he would declare, then get distracted, which meant he wouldn't rush through the garden of Downing Street to his waiting car until several hours later. Yet today was not as normal. He couldn't wait to leave.

'Now, now! We're off!' he cried, grabbing his hat and stick

and diving for the door, leaving his servants and assistants clutching frantically for coats, papers, luggage and all the other paraphernalia required of a weekend at Chequers. The heat remained blistering, yet they knew they wouldn't be given a moment to relax.

Their route led them up through Notting Hill and past White City as they headed west. He wasted no time; beside him sat a secretary, notebook balanced precariously on her knee, scribbling hard, clutching the case for his reading glasses in her spare hand, her foot perched on his precious box to keep it from slamming shut as the car sped round every corner. All the while the bell of the police escort rang out, demanding more haste.

The convoy did not proceed directly to Chequers but swung into the entrance of the airfield at Northolt. The ensign hung limply from the flagpole yet everything else seemed as crisp as starched linen – so different from three weeks earlier when Churchill had arrived unannounced. It had been a shambles. 'We weren't expecting you, sir,' the hapless station commander had wailed. 'You didn't tell us you were coming.'

'Neither will Hitler!'

It seemed to have had its effect. Today the security barrier was down, the cars forced to halt, the sentry demanding sight of the Prime Minister. Even the grass verges were freshly trimmed. A plume of blue cigar smoke swirled into the afternoon air as Churchill wound down his window. The guard bent low to peer inside.

'Welcome back, sir,' he said, snapping to attention. 'And good luck.'

'With what, Corporal?'

'Bloody everything, sir.'

'You and I, we'll beat the buggers yet, eh?' he cried, waving as the car sped on.

His mood was irrepressible. The last few weeks had brought him little but dejection, yet it was his special gift that from somewhere deep inside he always seemed able to find the spark to re-ignite his energies. Some said it was simple stubbornness, others overweening ambition, friends said it derived from a sense of destiny, and certainly there was more than a touch of arrogance; he often left behind him the impression that he was the only man in the room – and perhaps the entire kingdom – who was fighting this war. His reactions were predictable only in the fact that no one could ever take him for granted. Forty minutes later, when Harriman's plane landed on the tarmac, the Prime Minister was nowhere to be seen.

They found him in the sergeants' mess, surrounded by eager faces and fragments of Messerschmitt, drinking coffee laced with whisky and telling a vulgar joke.

When he saw Harriman he bounced immediately to his feet. 'Gentlemen,' he said, 'this is my friend, Mr Harriman. He is American. He has just returned from a mission to the Middle East – the first of many of his countrymen who will soon be at the sharp end of our war.'

''Bout bloomin' time, too,' a voice spoke up from the pack.

'You might well say that, sergeant. And I shall let you into a little secret,' Churchill declared, banging the table with the palm of his hand. 'Your views entirely coincide with my own.'

They stamped on the floor as he left, shouting out their approval until the whole hut shook. He turned as he reached the door, and there were tears in his eyes.

'Gentlemen, when I think of what we have achieved over the last year – and what, alongside our American allies, we shall achieve in the next – I know that we shall win. We're going to beat the bastards, the whole bloody lot of 'em!' he told them, waving his stick. And he could still hear their cheers when he was many yards away.

'You're in spirited form, Winston,' Harriman said.

'Never better.' He took the other man's arm as they walked, heads bent, almost conspiratorially, towards the waiting cars. 'I have news, Averell, most profound news. The President has invited me to meet with him. I sail in two weeks' time. I hope you will accompany me.'

'That's fantastic. Face to face. Things'll move so much more quickly.'

'We few, we happy few, we band of brothers!'

'But what's all that about Americans being at the sharp end?'

'Joined in battle. One cause, one crusade!'

Harriman was silent for a moment. 'Things must've moved fast while I was away.'

'Germany has hurled itself upon Russia, and the dogs of Japan snarl ever more savagely, creeping behind our backs. Half of all mankind is now engaged in this struggle, Averell, and the President knows that America cannot stand aside.'

'No one would be happier than I about that, but . . . War? You seriously think he intends to declare war?'

'Why else would he invite me to travel so far?'

Harriman knew Roosevelt. He knew the President had an extraordinary ability to leave all those in his company with the impression that he was entirely at one with them and that their cause had his full enthusiasm. But Roosevelt was not a man of enthusiasms. He was a man who played his cards so close to his chest that he had trouble changing his shirt, yet now he was offering a summit meeting. Churchill might have to travel a great distance, but if it implied war, then the President had already travelled much further.

'Hell, things *have* moved fast,' Harriman repeated. Over

their heads thundered a Flying Fortress – a B-17, fresh from the factories of Boeing in North America, its four radial piston engines straining and making the ground shudder beneath their feet. To one side stood several brand new Liberators – B-24s. They looked ungainly without their camouflage, but soon they would be painted up, and thirty thousand feet above Berlin. At last, it seemed, things were on the move.

'There's so much to do, so little time to do it, Averell. I'll need every moment of your time if we are to maximize the benefits of my meeting with the President.' From the inside pocket of his jacket the Prime Minister withdrew an envelope. It wasn't sealed. 'I dictated a memorandum for you this morning about the summit. It's entirely current and, of course, in the highest degree confidential. We shall discuss it this weekend at Chequers.' He stopped as they reached the door of their car and took the American by the sleeve. 'Averell, you'll forgive a little pedantry, I trust, but I must ask you to take the greatest care of such personal notes. Before you return to London, destroy it. By fire.'

'It'll go straight into my case, Winston. I never leave it unlocked.' He tapped the stiff leather bag that swung at his side.

'And – forgive me – the key?'

'On a chain – and on my belt.' Harriman produced a small bunch of keys from his pocket. 'Don't worry, Winston, they'd have to rip my clothes from my body before they could get to it.'

'Then I am deeply reassured.' He ushered his guest into the back of the car. 'Come. Chequers calls. As does the family. They are all gathered, waiting to kill the fatted calf in your honour . . .'

*   *   *

'You didn't write,' she whispered.

'I thought we were . . . going to let things cool off. Anyway, I was with your husband. It didn't seem right.'

'It feels so very strange, you being with Randolph.'

'I kept worrying that I would get drunk and say something.'

'Did you?'

'No. I let him do most of the drinking – and talking. I don't think he suspects.'

'He wrote to me. About you.'

'What?'

'Sang your praises. Said you were charming, that you spoke delightfully of me.'

'You have no idea how miserable that makes me feel.'

'He even said he thought he had a serious rival in you.'

'He knows . . . ?'

'Nothing. I think he genuinely likes you.'

'Damn. That doesn't make for a simple life.'

'I genuinely like you, too.'

'Which makes life about as unsimple as it gets.'

For a moment she wondered whether she should tell him about her conversation with Winston, but the idea quickly evaporated. He was having enough difficulty with his scruples; if he had to face Winston in a state of anything other than blithe ignorance it would only make his conscience toll all the louder.

'What should we do?' she asked.

'Do?'

'Yes, do.'

'What do you think, Pam?'

She considered the options for a while. The night was dark, sultry. An owl called from somewhere in the distance. In another part of the house the hinges of an ancient window complained as it was closed. A clock chimed three.

190

'Averell, it took a lot of gentle persuasion for Sawyers to put me in this room.'

'Why did you want to change?'

'I told him I preferred the view. Truth is, this bed makes so much less noise.'

'Ah.'

'So, you silly goose,' she whispered in his ear, 'I'll let you decide.'

The old house creaked as it settled down for the night. It gave the maid a little cover. For the rest, she would have to rely on the lateness of the hour and the alcohol they had all consumed on their way to bed. She crept in stockinged feet down the corridor, avoiding floorboards she knew to be loose, until she had come to the room assigned to Harriman. She paused outside the room, listening carefully for many moments before she pulled at the handle. The door gave way silently on hinges that she had recently and most meticulously oiled.

She was gone some time. When at last she reappeared, she retraced her footsteps and vanished up the staircase that led to the servants' quarters on the floor above. She was as silent as a moonbeam, offering nothing more than the briefest passing shadow.

At the far end of the corridor, from behind a door that had been no more than an inch ajar, there crept the subdued glow of a cigar. Then, with the gentle click of the latch, it was gone.

NINE

In late July the Japanese moved south, just as Churchill had feared. Unopposed, they marched into Saigon, the capital of French Indo-China. They were now a thousand miles nearer the heart of Britain's Far Eastern Empire.

There were still those who thought the Japanese might turn and declare war on Russia, but with every pace the armies of Nippon took down the spine of Indo-China, that possibility grew more feeble.

There was another factor compelling them south. Roosevelt had wanted to punish the Japanese for moving their troops into Indo-China and warn them to advance no further. So he had decided to freeze all Japanese assets in the United States. Churchill, ever eager to encourage the American President, did the same. It seemed an initiative that was tough, unambiguous and above all united, bringing the two English-speaking nations together.

Yet it was a policy that contained a terrible sting in its tail. 'Do as we demand.' It was in effect a claim to racial superiority and Anglo-Saxon ascendancy, a point which Churchill knew would not be lost on refined Japanese sensibilities. It would throw them into a fury. It would also cut them off from the materials they required to wage war – most importantly oil. It would force them to decide.

Either she could back off, withdraw from Indo-China, lose face, renounce her own claim to empire and humiliate herself before the white man. Or she would have to assert herself and grab the resources she needed – in other words, make more war.

No one knew what they would do – the Japanese didn't seem to know themselves, and Roosevelt thought this uncertainty was an excellent sign. It suggested that the Japanese were being forced to think again, to find another way. But if they didn't, it threatened disaster. The armies of the Rising Sun stationed in Indo-China formed a great claw around the kingdom of Thailand. It would be their next target. And once they were in Thailand, they only had to fall out of bed and they would land upon the British territories of Malaya, Burma and Singapore – territories which, Churchill knew, he could not defend, not alone. The United States had to come into the war, whether they liked it or not.

When she found him he was looking at the North Star, like a lone traveller trying to find his bearings. Churchill had been avoiding her – not ignoring her completely, but always finding someone else to talk with and something else to concentrate on whenever she came near. It wasn't difficult for him to find an excuse – the summit occupied all their minds and waking moments.

'Papa.'

He stirred, but did not look round. The scent of jasmine and sweet Havana hung between them.

'We must talk, Papa.'

She came closer, her footsteps gliding across the weathered York-stone paving. Still he did not move, a silhouette against the night sky. When at last he spoke, it was with reluctance.

'I can never understand why young people find marriage such a problem,' he began. 'In my day, all you needed was champagne, a box of chocolates and a double bed. You got on with it and sorted things out.'

'I wish I could have been as happy as you and Mama.'

'Happiness – now there's the problem. Everybody rushing around like March hares looking for happiness. But marriage isn't about being happy. It's about rubbing along. Why, if Clemmie had demanded happiness she'd have upped and left me years ago. Anyway, how on earth could you have expected to be happy with Randolph? Even I don't like him at times.'

'Averell says he likes him.'

'Is that what he said? But what else would he say? He's a diplomat.'

She was at his elbow. She put her hand on it; he didn't object.

'Something else he said, Papa.'

Still he looked at the star and not at her.

'He said he thought you were expecting too much from Roosevelt. That the President is the sort of man who prefers making conversation to making war.'

'Don't we all?'

'Averell wants America in this war, Papa. Even if San Francisco has to be bombed to make it happen.'

'Now that is *not* very diplomatic of him,' Churchill said testily, still scoring points.

'But he's afraid. He thinks that the summit won't reach nearly high enough for you.'

'Why are you telling me this?' he asked, his voice soaked with unease.

195

'Because I thought you needed to know. My problems with Randolph don't change my loyalties towards you.'

'Loyal to the father, but not to the son. It's an awkward balance to attempt.'

'Loyalty is a two-way affair, Papa, particularly between husband and wife.' Her tone was sharper.

'Are you suggesting that Randolph is not loyal to you?'

'Oh, in his way,' she replied, unable to hide an edge of contempt. 'But Randy has an unfortunate habit of banging his brothel doors ever so loud. I find the noise keeps me awake at night.'

'It would seem that is not the only thing that keeps you awake at night!' he snapped in retaliation.

'Oh, Papa, don't let's argue. I'm only trying to help.'

'Help? Somehow I suspect that history will be churlish and not smile upon your affair with Averell as being motivated by a desire to help the war effort.'

It was a cruel, unfair jibe, but he was torn inside about her affair with Harriman. He felt soaked in guilt every time he thought of it. So he was taking it out on Pamela.

'Oh, Pamela, why must you be so headstrong?' he asked, trying to evade his own complicity. 'Why can't you wait until Randolph gets home, be more patient?'

She drew back, affronted. 'Why can't I be patient? Perhaps it's because I've spent so much time in the Churchill family that I have become like them.'

She was angry, and turned to go. The night had suddenly become chilly, the heavy scent of honeysuckle and cigar overpowering.

'I was only trying to help you, Papa,' she repeated, her voice full of hurt.

He said nothing – didn't know what to say.

'Goodnight, Papa.'

Only then did he turn.

'Pamela!'

But already she was gone.

'The Presence', as he was sometimes known to his staff, had many manifestations: sombre, triumphant, emotional, abusive, always argumentative, sometimes vulgar. He was mercurial and melodramatic, and rarely restrained. While he waited for Operation Riviera – his meeting with Roosevelt – Churchill grew ever more unpredictable.

He paced the lawns, ate for England, bellowed from his bath, worked his staff to exhaustion. 'I shall need two women tonight!' he would roar as he prepared to dictate memoranda and instructions until the first light of dawn had begun to creep into the sky. The relentlessness never flagged, even at Chequers. In the evenings he would skip around the Great Hall, cat in hand, twirling to the music of the gramophone, barking out instructions to a servant or secretary, pausing at the fireplace to test whether some overpitched phrase might take wing and fly, then dance another lap. He drove himself – and others – on and on. And, in his desire to push history around, he also grew more arrogant.

He continued to be acerbic towards the military, and to their face. He demanded initiatives and victories, while they seemed always to argue for delay. He never took time to understand why the tanks he sent them got stuck up to their axles in the sand or why the new American bombers spent more time on training flights than bombing runs. He always insisted there was a better way – his way.

He could be pitiless. He attacked the dead and defenceless Chamberlain, calling him 'the narrowest, most ignorant, most ungenerous of men', even as he finished off the last drops

197

of the man's hock. He denounced the French through mouthfuls of champagne. He reserved the worst of his temper for the Russians, but not to their face. He listened patiently to the demands of their ambassador, Maisky, and sent his new ally away laden with praise and promises, yet once the door had closed the prime ministerial expletives reached a pitch that would have done justice to a Liverpool docker. Diplomacy was, of necessity, a game of two hands.

Only the Americans escaped his venom.

The maelstrom of his emotions threatened to overwhelm him. Late one evening at Chequers he decided that he wanted to watch his film about Nelson and Emma Hamilton once more. For Churchill, their story of deliverance had become a creed, a well of inspiration and reassurance from which he drank ever more greedily. Yet the crew with the projector equipment had already left. When this was discovered, he lost all sense of proportion. He became like a child deprived of a favourite toy, stamping, wild-eyed, shorn of all reason. He demanded that the police set up a roadblock on the route to London so that the crew could be stopped and turned around. When still they did not arrive, his temper was volcanic.

To those who knew him best and loved him, such behaviour was untypical; to many others, it seemed more like a hardening of Churchill's emotional arteries. One of these was Beatrice, the wife of the Foreign Secretary, Anthony Eden.

'Damn the man!' she muttered as the bedside telephone clattered into life. 'Is he drunk again?'

With a sigh, her husband switched on the bedside light and rubbed his eyes.

'It's almost three o'clock,' she complained.

'There is a war on, my dear,' Eden replied, rubbing his eyes.

'Even the Germans have to sleep!'

Eden was an elegant man, handsome, well educated, much experienced, a man of considerable personal and political courage. He had fought the first war, foreseen the second war, and had resigned as Neville Chamberlain's Foreign Secretary in protest at the lack of preparation. It was inevitable that he should have been recalled by Churchill, and many saw him as Churchill's natural successor. He was a man of exceptional talents yet also of considerable inner turbulence. In spite of an exceptional war record, some saw the uncertainty as a lack of fibre; his wife was one.

Eden reached for the phone, but it did not still his wife.

'Isn't it enough that we have to put up with his interminable speechifying – without this?'

'I suspect it's about the Roosevelt thing.'

'Hah! His moment in the limelight. And I notice he intends to grab it all for himself and leave you behind, Anthony. All the others, too, except for Beaverbrook. Why is Max going to the meet the President and not you? You're the Foreign Secretary, for pity's sake. You should insist.'

But already he wasn't listening, his attentions concentrated on the telephone. It did nothing to deter her.

'He treats you like a naughty schoolchild. Bellows at you constantly. Never trusts you an inch. You're not a Foreign Secretary, Anthony, you're nothing but an errand boy.'

Eden turned, covering the mouthpiece. 'He told me the other day he regarded me as his son,' he whispered, trying to deflect the scorn.

'His son? But he's loathsome!'

He went back to the telephone while she proceeded to beat her pillow with frustration. When he finally put the phone down, she turned on him, as she had done so many times during their marriage.

'I've supported you throughout your political career, Anthony. I've been a loyal and devoted wife.' They both knew that hadn't been the case, but for the moment it wasn't the issue. 'I will not stand by and watch you publicly humiliated.'

'I don't see it that way.'

'No? Then there are many others who do. There are mutterings everywhere about Winston, about his follies, his rudeness. His refusal to listen to anyone else. Least of all to you.'

Eden couldn't argue the point. It was no longer possible to open a newspaper without finding complaints – not outright attacks, but an incessant dribble of grumbles and grievances of a kind that would never have appeared a year ago. There were even gentle hints that Churchill should be thinking about the right time to make way for a younger successor – and the name that kept coming to the fore was that of Anthony Eden. Was that why he had been excluded from the list of those asked to attend the summit? Perhaps his wife had a point.

'So what did he have to say?' she asked.

'It wasn't Winston. It was one of the aides.'

'He doesn't even have the decency to do his own dirty work?'

'They're sending round a paper. Apparently it requires immediate attention.'

'So you will get up from our bed and answer the door in the middle of the night to do his bidding. As you always damned well do.'

'He is the Prime Minister, Beatrice.'

'Yes. As once I had hoped you might be.' Her words were drenched with personal disappointment and spite.

She rose from the bed.

'I am going to the guest room, Anthony. I don't propose

to be disturbed again tonight. Or any night. Not by Winston Churchill.'

She left the bedroom. And such was the state of their marriage that she never returned.

When finally he left, on Sunday the third of August aboard a special train, he did so with a retinue fit for a medieval king – generals, admirals, air chief marshals, diplomats and doctors, press men, policemen, secretaries, servants, and, of course, the ubiquitous Sawyers. But no ministers, not even Max Beaverbrook, who was travelling separately.

The train took them to Scotland, pausing in Inverness to pick up twelve brace of grouse, and so laden they proceeded by lifeboat and destroyer to Scapa Flow where, riding on a fretful sea, they found the ship that would take them to their rendezvous. The *Prince of Wales*. The ship that had fought with the *Hood*, watched her die, fired the shells that had struck and fatally slowed the *Bismarck*, and which still bore the scars of the encounter. She was one of the finest warriors afloat. The British wanted to make an impression.

It was early on the first full day of their voyage, a day of gales and grey turbulence, that they received a message marked Most Urgent. The Germans had found out. Transozean Wireless, the mouthpiece of the Propaganda Ministry in Berlin, was already broadcasting the news that that Churchill and Roosevelt were to meet. Somehow, the security surrounding the summit had been blown to pieces.

The message caused consternation on board, and the captain ordered an immediate change of course, just in case. Yet Churchill remained remarkably unaffected. He lay upon his bed in the Admiral's quarters above the propellers and chewed at an unlit cigar.

'It would seem that some rascal has opened up a direct line of communication with the enemy,' he suggested to Sawyers.

Then, curiously, he smiled. For a moment, and for the first time in weeks, he seemed almost content.

It was while they were on the voyage that Churchill at last got to see his film. Every evening after dinner the projection equipment would be set up in the wardroom and they would watch a film of his choice. Inevitably, one night was spent with Emma and her Nelson.

Once more he watched as the sailor's life unfolded in flickering scenes that he knew so well: defying the threats of his superiors to banish him to the wilderness; rising through the jeers of a hostile Parliament to warn against those who would appease Bonaparte; shining a light that would lead England through its darkest times. Nelson had been the embodiment of everything that England needed but he had been ignored, reviled, and rediscovered only in the nick of time.

Just as Churchill had been.

Yet, as the *Prince of Wales* forced its way through heavy seas towards her destination, Churchill began to see the story through different eyes. There was more to it than Nelson and his half-blind love of England. There was also Emma.

She was adulterous and despised, and they mocked her: 'the oldest story in the world, the most sordid and the most contemptible. Find a public hero and there you'll find as sure as fate a woman parasite.' Yet as much as they abhorred her she was devoted to him, and her passion that had ignited in the heat of battle grew to last a lifetime.

Without Emma, the story of the admiral couldn't have been told, his victories never won.

And how much she looked like Pamela.

If Pamela made a mockery of her marriage, she mocked no more cheaply than had Emma, or, indeed, Churchill's own mother.

Suddenly he was no longer involved in a story of duty and honour but of sorrows and ruination. He was watching a once-beautiful woman lying old and neglected on the cobbles of a French gutter, having knowingly sold her life's happiness for a few moments with the man she loved in order to give him both the courage and the cause to do what needed to be done.

Wars weren't won simply through fighting and dying, but by holding fast to something that made sense of it all. Nelson and Emma had found that, in England, and in each other.

'They told us of your victories, but not the price you had paid,' Emma whispered to her beloved sailor. Emma had won her own victory, but the price she had paid, in living long and alone, seemed so much greater than the price paid by Nelson in dying.

As he sat in the semi-light of the wardroom, tears flowed freely down his face and he did nothing either to stem or to hide them. He knew now that he had wronged her. In his confusion, he had been too harsh, but he would stand by Pamela. He would not cast stones. Sometimes it took more courage to seduce and to deceive than to spend all one's nights sleeping in the tents of the righteous. He would remember that, and he hoped others would, too, when the time came for them to judge him.

TEN

Dawn, six days after they had left London. The *Prince of Wales* had slackened her speed. Her passengers woke to find low, churning clouds off the starboard bow, through which they could see the outlines of peaks and dense forests. The beam of a lighthouse reached out to greet them, and overhead they could hear the sound of circling aircraft.

Placentia Bay, Newfoundland. The point where the North American land mass stretched east as far as it could reach until it toppled into the grey ocean. A place of mists and old mariners' tales – and of muddle, for it was discovered that the Americans were operating on a different time zone to the British, and the *Prince of Wales* had arrived too soon. She was forced to turn around and sail away to eat up an unexpected hour. But when, finally, she dropped anchor, she did so amidst the vastest fleet the bay had ever seen: the American cruisers *Augusta* and *Tuscaloosa*, the old battleship *Arkansas*, the destroyer *McDougal*, the Canadian warships *Restigouche* and *Assiniboine*, the *Hood*'s own escort, HMS *Ripley*, and many others. Every ship seemed to overflow with cheering seamen and the air rippled with the music of marine bands. As the sun burned away the mists, a small figure could be seen waving from the deck of the *Augusta*. It was the President.

Churchill stepped into the admiral's barge and, accompanied

205

by his military chiefs, crossed to the *Augusta*. He was dressed in his uniform as the Warden of the Cinque Ports, all blue serge and brass buttons with a plain peaked cap. Strangely for the extrovert Churchill, it seemed remarkably restrained amidst the gold braid and naval gloss that surrounded him. In his pocket he carried a letter of introduction from the King.

Roosevelt waited in his light and loose-fitting civilian suit. It hid the braces and leg irons that encased his crippled body, while a broad smile hid the pain that came with standing so long to greet his guest. They met on deck, political leaders of great nations that shared a common language, a religious faith and an extraordinary history. Only time would tell to what extent they might also share the future.

Churchill bounded eagerly up the walkway like an impatient suitor. For days he had fretted, asking repeatedly: 'Do you think he will like me?' Now the moment had come when the veils and mysteries would be lifted and they could face each other as men.

'Mr President, I am so very glad to have this opportunity to meet with you at last.'

Roosevelt flinched. 'Why, Mr Prime Minister, we have met before. Don't you remember?'

They came from different worlds, and from different directions. They dined, they drank, they discussed, they prayed together and grew to know each other better. Yet Churchill came panting for war, while at their first meeting Roosevelt started to talk about peace. He wanted a document drawn up, a joint declaration of principles about the sort of world in which they hoped to live. A Foreign Office official concocted a draft over a breakfast of bacon and eggs.

It contained eight clauses of high principles about the right of all people to choose the Government under which they live, about equal access to trade and raw materials, about collaboration and cooperation, about freedom from fear and want, about free access to the high seas and the abandonment of the use of force.

It was to prove the most concrete result of the leaders' historic meeting and became known as the Atlantic Charter. It made headlines all around the world.

The symbolic importance of the Charter was immense, but from Churchill's point of view it was still inadequate. It talked vaguely about the final destruction of the Nazi tyranny; it talked about Japan not at all. Churchill was later to mutter that the civil servant who drafted the document should have ordered another egg; it might have given him the chance to finish it.

After three days and nights, they parted. In the afternoon sun, Churchill stood on deck and waved his cap at every American ship as they passed, and continued to wave until they were almost out of sight. He continued to look west until the sun had finally fallen on his day. No lover ever wept more unashamedly than did he.

On the journey home they came upon an Allied convoy, seventy-two ships, sailing in twelve columns, the grubby, plodding workhorses of the Atlantic, laden with their Lend-Lease dowry and heading home. The *Prince of Wales* made two runs through the convoy, raising flags to signal 'Good Voyage', and signing it simply: 'Churchill'. The crews of the freighters cheered wildly. They could see a small figure returning their wave from the bridge of the battleship, and they sensed rather than saw the two fingers raised aloft in the special salute that was beginning to become his signature: 'Victory'.

The *Prince of Wales* stopped briefly at the Icelandic capital of Reykjavik. Churchill saw the country's leaders, the crew saw naked bathers relaxing in the sun. Then the weather changed. That evening as they set sail once more, they ran into the jaws of a piercing storm, but nothing could dampen his spirits.

'A little champagne to celebrate, sir?' the steward enquired that evening in the wardroom.

'I never drink a little champagne,' Churchill said. 'It is not a drink to trifle with. You should never suggest taking short measures of champagne, any more than you suggest a man should take short puffs of oxygen. Why, I've drunk half a bottle every night of my life since I was twenty-five. Forty-two years.' He stared at those around him, his blue eyes flashing mischievously. 'I reckon I could fill this entire wardroom with all the champagne I've drunk in my life.'

His claim prompted a heated debate. Measurements were taken, volumes calculated, figures scribbled, voices raised, until an admiral who had taken responsibility for the good name of the ship declared that the Prime Minister was wrong, that the champagne he had consumed would fill only half the room. Churchill looked astonished. He gazed around the wardroom in wonder, as though it were a temple.

'Bugger,' he said. 'Hell of a lot to do before I'm seventy!'

It was in similar mood that he eventually arrived back in London, more than two weeks after he had departed. Huge crowds had gathered at King's Cross to greet his train, with policemen hard-pushed to restrain their enthusiasm. Young boys shinned up lamp-posts for a better view, women porters climbed on top of their trunks, newsreel photographers stood on the roofs of their cars. A large official welcoming party had collected on the platform, including Clemmie and Churchill's brother, Jack, but as the train pulled in with triumphal whistles and much venting of steam, the driver couldn't see what was happening and in the confusion he stopped the train well short. Politicians, officials and photographers began to stampede up the platform in a race to be the first to greet him, but after a few moments of shouting and good-natured shoving their British reserve took control and they fell back to allow Clemmie through. The old man leant from the carriage window, still in his nautical uniform and cap, cigar in his hand, a wide beam on his face, waving until he was certain that the photographers had all they wanted. Then a bright hop from the carriage, a kiss on Clemmie's cheek, a Victory-salute, a round of handshaking and a progress through the cheering crowd that was as enthusiastic as any he could remember since . . .

Since Munich. Since they had gathered at the airfield in Heston to embrace Neville Chamberlain after he came back from his meeting with Hitler, clutching his little piece of paper and promising peace in our time. Less than three years ago.

For a moment he felt as though a ghost were whispering warnings in his ear, but he ushered it quickly away. He wasn't coming home with empty words of appeasement, he was pledging war! Together, side by side, in the air, on the battlegrounds, beneath the waters, upon the oceans and in every corner of the globe. Roosevelt had as good as guaranteed it. Churchill placed his cap on top of his cane and held it aloft like the laurels of victory. He'd gone with doubts, of course, like any nervous suitor, but he had wooed, and had won, hadn't he? Now, surely, it was only a matter of time.

Rarely had they seen their Prime Minister so bullish. He beamed, he bubbled, he ordered that photographs of the summit should be distributed as widely as possible: 'Let the whole world see the President and the Prime Minister joined as one, Christian soldiers marching as to war!' He had gone with the objective of bringing the Americans into the war, and he reported to the Cabinet that he had all but succeeded. The President would become more and more provocative; he sought only the proper excuse to ask Congress for a formal declaration of war. 'Everything will be done to force an incident,' Churchill told his Cabinet.

Yet distance and the passage of days dimmed the dream. Like a wayward lover returning to his legitimate spouse, Roosevelt fell back into line once he was tucked up in Washington. At his first press conference, he was asked if the United States was any closer to war. He flatly denied it. War? What war?

Many Americans drifted into greater isolation. 'Because they have not fired a shot or dropped a bomb, the vast majority of them cling to the delusion that they are at peace,' *The Times* reported. 'Many persons in all parts of the country are tempted to believe that, as Hitler had turned east, the war was withdrawing from the west and from the Atlantic and that their own security was assured.'

The same issue of the newspaper carried a map of Russia. It showed the German Army advancing on Leningrad, Kiev, Kharkov, Moscow, beyond Minsk, surrounding Odessa . . . Stalin had his balls on a butcher's block, so Americans rejoiced – and relaxed. The Bill to extend military service stumbled through the US Senate by a single vote.

In Paris, ten thousand Jews were arrested and sent to concentration camps. Elsewhere in France, the leaders of a peaceful anti-German march were executed.

In London, as though to sum up the futility of it all, the Food Education Society announced that 'half a dozen young nasturtium leaves placed between two slices of bread and margarine make a tasty sandwich, especially for those who find margarine unpalatable.'

All this took place within four days of Churchill's triumphal return.

Pamela had come in response to a strange message from Sawyers.

'He needs yer, Miss Pamela.'

'I doubt that, Sawyers.'

'He's not himself. Could do wi' a friendly face around.'

'I'm not sure I fall into that category. Has he asked for me?'

'Not exactly, but . . . very out o' sorts, he is. I think you should come.'

So, not knowing what to expect, she had set out for Chequers on a late-night train. It immediately seemed to be a bad idea. The train was packed, nothing but standing room, and the air stiff with cigarette smoke and the stench of stale bodies. The other passengers were mostly soldiers starting their weekend leave; as they squeezed past, several deliberately barged her with their gas masks, taking the opportunity while apologizing to examine her all too closely. One of them, an officer, waited for the train to sway then fell provocatively against her, his breath soaked in Craven A and beer, his hand resting on her breast. From beneath an overtrimmed moustache, he suggested bluntly that they might have sex in the lavatory.

'I don't think so, thank you,' she replied, removing his hand. 'Looking at you, I think there are already enough bastards in this world.'

'Not to worry, little girl. I can wait till you grow up. Plenty of others,' he sneered, shuffling on.

The train's progress was frustratingly slow, with much blowing of steam and the frequent application of brakes. Timetables meant nothing in war. Outside Chalfont St Peter it came to a complete stop for almost two hours. The atmosphere had grown desperately heavy, lit by nothing more than dark-blue blackout lamps and the glow of a hundred cigarettes. She began to think she might faint. The officer was shambling back towards her, more drunk than ever; she took her hatpin and held it prominently in front of her breasts. He wasn't going to fondle her again without a fight. He turned away.

But he didn't disappear for long. As soon as their train rattled into the darkness of Wendover station, he was there at the door, a leer on his face, forcing her to squeeze past his body.

'Excuse me, please.'

He didn't move.

She stepped forward. With a flick of her wrist the top corner of her suitcase caught him directly in the groin. It folded him like a concertina.

'You just can't rely on women nowadays,' she whispered, stepping past.

The station platform was in complete darkness, the night air filled with steam and coal smoke that tasted of sulphur. A beam of torchlight was weaving its way towards her, and behind the beam she made out the bald head of Sawyers.

'Am I glad to see you,' she said, handing him the suitcase.

'Entirely mutual, miss,' he responded. He led her towards an army staff car with a Guardsman at the wheel.

'Courtesy o' Coldstreams, miss. No taxis after midnight. We thought you'd best be having a lift.'

'It's gone two in the morning. You must be exhausted,' she said, looking into his bleary eyes as he opened the rear door. 'But won't you be missed?'

'I put him to bed early. He didn't sleep at all last night. Not like him.'

'What's wrong?'

'I don't know and he won't tell. That's why I was thinking yer might be able to help. You two seem to have an uncommon relationship, like.'

'Why do you say that?'

'He don't shout at you.'

'Sawyers, I'm very much afraid he's not even talking to me.'

'He don't hold grudges, miss, you know that. 'Cept on Hitler.'

Soon they were driving up the long tree-lined avenue that led to the house. The War Office had wanted to have all the trees felled, fearing that on a clear night they gave the Luftwaffe a straight run at Chequers, but Churchill had refused. 'I plan to knock a few trees down in Berlin first,' he told them.

The front door closed quietly behind them. 'You go on ahead, Sawyers,' she said. 'You'll have to be up again in a few hours.'

'Thank you, miss. I'll just put yer case in yer room. Goodnight.' He climbed the stairs and made his way along the bedroom corridor. His progress was entirely silent; he seemed to know which floorboards creaked. She wished Averell had such skill.

She followed him slowly up the stairs, passing Winston's bedroom. A light was shining from beneath the door. She hesitated, then knocked gently. She found him sitting up in his four-poster bed, clad in white silk pyjamas, staring at nothing. Papers lay strewn around him but gave the impression of being untouched. A cold cigar was in his hand. His whisky glass was empty.

'Papa?'

His eyes flickered briefly in her direction, but he said nothing. Perhaps she was still an outcast in his camp.

'Papa?' she said once more. 'Is there anything I can get you?'

Stiffly he shook his head.

She couldn't decide whether to withdraw or to stay. He looked hostile, wanting to be alone, the lower jaw jutting forward, but some instinct – and Sawyers' warning – forced her to make one last effort.

'How did it go, Papa? With the President?'

His words came slowly. 'I am no longer sure,' he mumbled, almost inaudibly.

'Did you like him?'

'I thought it went well. Thought he liked me. There was a bond, it seemed, a coming together. But I was stupid, had forgotten we'd met before. I think that might have hurt him. First impressions, so important.' At last his eyes came up to meet her. 'I failed.'

'Why do you think that?' She stepped forward and nestled on the end of his bed.

'We dined together, discussed together, drank together. Even prayed together. Oh, but I gave him such a mighty service on the deck of the *Prince of Wales*. Chose the hymns myself. Two mighty flags draped from the bridge, the fighting men of both our nations joined in prayer and in song.'

'I've seen the photographs. I think the whole world has.'

'I was so sure I couldn't fail. Onward Christian soldiers! Churchill and Roosevelt, centre stage, with God himself waiting to walk on from the wings. But . . .' He shook his head in sorrow. 'I was wrong. I saw the President as a mighty buffalo, stamping with impatience and ready to charge forth across the plains of duty.' His voice grew firmer. 'Turns out

214

he's not a buffalo but a jack rabbit. Never know which bloody hole he's going to pop out of next.'

'I'm not sure I understand.'

Suddenly red anger was burning through the exhaustion in his eyes. 'I went there for war, Pamela. Sailed halfway round the globe so I could hear him say that he would take up arms until all our enemies are swept to the darkest corners of Hell. But instead . . .' He waved his cold cigar in scorn. 'At our very first meeting he suggests we talk about the terms for peace. His wretched Atlantic Charter.'

'But I thought . . .'

Suddenly the dead cigar went flying across the room. 'I didn't go there for peace, Pamela. I went for war!'

'The Charter talks about those things we are fighting for.'

'But he's not bloody fighting, is he? And have you read that piece of paper? Do you understand it? I've read it a hundred times, but I don't. Pious nonsense about peace and love and affirming the right of all peoples' – he spat out the words – 'to choose the form of Government under which they will live.'

'Not an excellent idea?' she enquired cautiously.

'What? We're fighting this war to save the British Empire, not to have it torn limb from limb, woman! Give democracy to natives who still worship witchdoctors? You might as well feed them gin.'

'But you agreed, you signed.'

His hands had become fists, shaking with frustration above the blanket, wanting to lash out but unable to find a target. Then the strings that held his fury together were cut, and he slumped back helpless on his pillow.

'I had to sign it, Pamela, had to. We need him. But he hates the Empire. And I think he may hate me.'

'Averell says not. In his letter he says the President is

intrigued by you, likes you enormously. Thinks you're wonderfully crusty and cutely old-fashioned.'

'Ah, Averell.'

'He did warn you, Papa. That you were setting your sights too high.'

'Good advice. I need more of it. I could do with him here right now.'

'So could I, Papa.'

Churchill coloured and fumbled for a new cigar.

'Do you know when he will be coming back, Papa?'

'We're sending him to Moscow, Pamela, with Max Beaverbrook. To see how we can help our Bolshevist brethren and make sure they stay in the fight.'

'Not just to keep him away?'

'I admit that part of me wishes he had never come.'

'Part of me, too, Papa. Please understand that. But we don't control these things.'

'I do so wish . . .' His voice trailed away.

'Me, too, Papa,' she said, knowing what he was thinking.

'Bloody Americans!' he sighed. He closed his eyes for a moment, searching for peace, but it was futile. 'They will never join this war, Pamela. Roosevelt keeps looking over his shoulder, saying he needs more time. But time won't wait for his caution to turn to courage. Already the panzers are pointing at the door of the Kremlin, while every evening the sparks from the campfires of Nippon glow more fiercely in the east. Our enemies have no intention of holding back while the President gets his wheelchair out of the mud.'

'That's cruel.'

'These are cruel times. They show no mercy. Soon we shall be fighting not only in Europe and upon the Atlantic and in the air above our own hearths, but across great swathes of Asia, too. That is a war we cannot survive, Pamela, not on our own. And what use will it be if President Roosevelt and his beloved public opinion then decide to join the war, when we are left paralysed and choking on our own blood? No. We need him now. We need the might of his America, and we cannot wait.'

Pamela rose and went to the decanter of whisky that stood beside his bed.

'You have a knack of knowing what I want,' he said.

She poured, a good two fingers' worth, but as he reached for it she drank it herself.

'Right now, Papa, I think my need is every bit as great as yours.' She swallowed the last drops, spluttering as the harsh alcohol fought its way down her throat. 'I've never known you even to think about the possibility of defeat.'

'And no one else shall. For the others I will carry on as long as I have strength, shouting defiance and making pretence, reassuring them all that we are still masters of our own fate. Masters of our own fate!' He mocked his own words. 'That's what I told the House of Commons. But it is an illusion. Our fate has been placed in the hands of others.'

'Why do you tell me this?'

'Because I have to tell someone. And because I think you understand me, perhaps better at times than I understand myself.'

She leant across to squeeze his hand, and he kept hold of it.

'We need a miracle, Pamela. That, or the Americans. And I confess I have not spoken to God nearly as much as perhaps I should have done.' He shrugged. 'Which leaves the Americans.'

'But they don't seem to be in a mood to be swayed.'

'I shall continue to woo her, try to seduce her. I must have her. No matter how coyly she plays or how harshly she protests. She has no right to stay out of this war!'

217

'So what will you do?'

He raised her hand to his lips and kissed it gently, like a chivalrous knight, but she could see the dread in his eyes.

'Everything. Anything. Whatever it takes,' he whispered.

Sawyers stood in the sunshine that was flooding across the cobbles of the rear courtyard of Chequers, perspiring gently as he worked. His coat was hanging on the stable door, his shirtsleeves were rolled up and his unbuttoned waistcoat flapped freely across his round stomach as he worked apples into a cider press. He already had a bucket filled with the thick, sweet juice and another was well on its way. Beside him, Héloise sat on a stool, slicing away the worst parts of mould and rot that were already eating into the fruit.

'Not too much,' Sawyers warned, as her knife dug deep into the pale flesh. 'Think of 'em like French cheese. Nowt wrong wi' a bit o' character.'

It was proving a bumper harvest. Cider wasn't often called for around the Churchill table, but the demand below stairs had proved an enduring tribute to Sawyers' skills. Behind him stood a row of wooden kegs that were dark with age and reeked of fermentation. Once filled, they would be stored at the back of the stables until next summer.

'Wonder if we'll still be here then?' he muttered idly, wiping his brow before giving the press another forceful twist.

Héloise swiped idly at the flies hovering above her head.

'When is "then", Mr Sawyers?'

'When this lot's all ripe and ready. Next year.'

'You think . . . ?'

'I don't think, missy. Not me job. But he were going on about how yer got to be specially careful wi' the sheets after guests've left. You know what he's like, always having a bit

218

of a go. But we're to count 'em, he says, to mekk sure the Chiefs of Staff aren't pinching 'em.'

'He always seems to be shouting at them.'

More juice flowed into the bucket and Sawyers grunted in satisfaction. 'Wonder what Jerries drink? Hope they never get a liking fer this stuff. Be such a waste.'

'Is this better?' She held up an apple for his inspection, licking the stickiness from her fingers.

He nodded.

'But I don't understand. Why would the generals take the sheets, Mr Sawyers? Don't they have sheets of their own?'

'He says they kepp wanting to hang 'em out o' ruddy window, like. That they don't seem to want to fight. I dunno. He keeps going on about how they reckon they can't fight in Middle East and won't fight in Far East.'

'But we are not fighting in the Far East.'

'And Heaven help us if we ever do, so he says.' His face was glowing red in the sun. 'Come on, lass, bring some more o' them apples over here. Let's be getting done wi' this.'

'I shall count the sheets very carefully,' she said, tumbling more apples into the press.

'Oh, I don't suppose he were being serious, like.' He stuck his finger into the flowing juice in order to taste it. 'But you never know wi' him.'

Even Sawyers hadn't known if the old man was being serious. 'Make sure she knows about the sheets,' he had instructed. He didn't explain why. Sawyers wondered if perhaps the whispers were right, that the old man was losing it.

'Anyways,' Sawyers concluded, 'let's be finished. We got gooseberry bushes to pluck after this.'

*   *   *

219

The first week of September. The anniversary of the day the war began. And a week of gathering storms.

Two years earlier, Neville Chamberlain had informed the country in a thin, tremulous voice that they were at war with Germany. He had also told them of his certainty that right would prevail. Yet now German radio announced to the world that their troops were within fifteen miles of Leningrad, pissing into Stalin's cooking pots.

The following evening Churchill attended a dinner at the Dorchester. It was being given in honour of his youngest daughter, Mary, who was about to join the Auxiliary Territorial Service, but inevitably he would be the star, and as soon as he stepped into the crowded foyer, the hotel guests turned to him and began to offer cries of welcome.

'Look,' the excited doorman cried, 'the old dears love you.'

'Some of the younger dears, too, I trust,' he said, offering the doorman a mischievous wink.

His progress through the hotel was accompanied by applause at every step. Men bowed in greeting, women reached out to touch him as though he were a medieval cardinal carrying holy relics. It lifted his spirits to be surrounded by so many people yet not to have a critic in sight.

The dining room was filled to capacity, as it had been almost every night of the war. So much had happened in the past two years, yet so little in here had changed – except for the absence of Italian waiters, most of whom had been interned. The world outside may have fallen into darkness, but life at the Dorchester went on, with diners competing in their determination to ensure that no oyster remained unshucked and no cork undisturbed. The chandeliers shone, the music was gay, his daughter looked radiant and, for the moment, the world outside was forgotten.

But only for a few steps more. It was a night when no one would leave him alone.

The maitre d' guided him towards his table but it was a slow progress; as they saw him, the diners rose, forcing him to shake hands on all sides and exchange a few words.

Then, in front of him, was Leslie Hore-Belisha – a man of such misguided ambition that he could carp even while the synagogues burned.

'Good evening, Winston.' Hore-Belisha smiled courteously, extending his hand.

'Leslie.'

'Pleasure to see you here – although I'm also looking forward to your presence in the House when Parliament returns. We miss you there.'

Insufferable bastard. What he missed was the chance to mock in public. 'Wars are not won on the floor of the House, Leslie, but on the field of battle.'

'And in the air.' Hore-Belisha drew closer, lowered his voice. 'Yet I understand that the raid last week on Rotterdam was something of a disaster.'

Damn his eyes! Seventeen Blenheims had flown on the mission, seven hadn't made it back. How dare he dance on the unmarked graves of brave young men?

'What does that make it – almost a thousand bombers lost this year already?' Hore-Belisha continued, shaking his head. 'It's all very well charging like the Light Brigade every once in a while, but not on a daily basis. We can't go on like that.'

Churchill's good humour had gone. Could he not even spend time with his daughter without being bludgeoned by idiots? 'If the armchair aviators that I find lurking in every corner showed half as much valour as our pilots,' he said stiffly, 'the situation might be very different.'

221

'The valour of our aircrews is not in question. The competence of their commanders is. I seem to remember you saying much the same thing a few years ago when you were an armchair aviator.'

Churchill had neither time nor temper for this. He turned to move on. 'I am flattered that you should wish to follow in my footsteps, Leslie, but don't let ambition spoil your dinner.'

'You never run away from Hitler, Winston,' his colleague called after him. 'So why do you run away from the House?'

Why? Because he had a bloody war to run. Because he couldn't win that war if he was forced to reveal every card in his hand. And because – because, in his heart, he was no longer certain he could win the war at all, and it might show. So in recent months he had seen them little and told them less, and many had begun to resent it. They wouldn't follow Hore-Belisha through the voting lobbies against Churchill, but neither did they shun him any more.

The barbs in his back stuck firm throughout the meal and soured every mouthful. The pleasure he showed in the celebration was little more than pretence and by ten thirty he was back at Downing Street, seeking solace with his boxes of secrets. Yet as the car drew up he saw a figure pacing up and down outside. It was the unmistakable outline of Maisky, the diminutive Soviet Ambassador.

'Forgive me, Prime Minister,' Maisky began, waylaying the Prime Minister, 'but it is a message of the highest importance.'

They stood in the moonlight, puffing cigar smoke at each other from beneath the brims of their hats. Maisky was short and swarthy, but personable and exceptionally hard-working, which perhaps had as much to do with his dull and awesomely ugly wife as with the ever-present prospect of being summoned home and purged. Churchill respected and might even have grown to like him, if he hadn't been a Bolshevik.

'I have been instructed to inform you from the highest levels of my Government' – in other words, this came straight from Uncle Joe himself – 'that the rapid deterioration of the situation within the Soviet Union has given rise to a new environment.'

Churchill sniffed. That meant new demands. He'd already sent tanks and Hurricanes to the Soviets and had promised more – weapons that the British desperately needed themselves. Yet Churchill had insisted, even in the face of outright opposition from the Chiefs of Staff. He needed Russia in this war and almost any material price was worth paying. There had been a moral price to pay, too. Only a week earlier British forces had shot their way into neutral Iran, invading the country in order to grab a supply corridor that stretched five hundred miles from the Gulf to the borders of Russia. Churchill needed it as a lifeline that might keep Stalin going, and so he'd kicked his way in before the Germans got there first. It was an act of shameless aggression that made a mockery of the high-minded principles of the Atlantic Charter, so wasn't that enough? What more could any reasonable man expect? Yet Stalin, as Churchill had once suggested to Beaverbrook, was a man who would bite through his own mother's nipple. Reason had nothing to do with it. Now he wanted more.

'Our country faces mortal menace,' Maisky went on.

'As does ours. Your Excellency, forgive me but it's late, and we've known each other long enough. Tell me directly, what is it you want?'

'Four hundred planes –'

'We've already promised you.'

'A month.'

'What?'

'And five hundred tanks. Every month for the next year.'

'Impossible! We don't have that number ourselves.'

'Prime Minister, the reason for the growing disaster in my country is very simple. Hitler has been able to invade the Soviet Union solely because he has no other opposition on the mainland of Europe. He can throw everything at us because he has come to the conclusion that the British are content to sit at home. There is no danger from the west, so he attacks us in the east.'

Churchill snorted with impatience, sending cigar smoke swirling high into the night sky. 'May I remind you, Mr Maisky, that no one, not any nation on this globe, has risked more than the British to fight that bloody man.'

'Then it is vital that he is reminded of that.'

'I strive ceaselessly . . .'

'I make no personal criticism, I assure you.'

'And Britain is doing her best.'

'I'm afraid it does not seem that way in my country.'

'What?'

'I have been given a specific instruction, Prime Minister, to pass on to you a message from the highest levels of my Government. The message is simply this. You must establish a second front in Europe by the end of the year. To draw Hitler's men away from the east.' Maisky paused while the enormity of the demand had time to settle in. 'Otherwise, I fear that the Soviet Union may be placed in a position where it is unable to continue with the armed struggle, and will have to look to other means to pursue its interests.'

It was as though Churchill's had been physically assaulted. His whole frame began to shake. He gripped the railings that ran along the front of Number Ten as he struggled to keep his incredulity and growing outrage from bursting forth. 'You mean . . .' He seemed barely able to spit the words out. 'You mean you'd do another deal with Hitler? Sign another one of your wretched pacts?'

Maisky refused to respond to the accusation. It wasn't the job of a diplomat to tell the full truth when the doubts stirred by a half-truth could be so much more effective. Anyway, he didn't know the truth himself, he only knew what he had been told to say.

'We are at a turning point in history,' he replied. 'But consider. If the Soviet Union does not survive, then neither will you.'

'How dare you?' the Englishman shouted. 'How dare you have the gall to stand on my doorstep with the rubble of our defiance lying all about us and lecture me, Winston bloody Churchill, about the fight against Hitler?'

'More calm, please, my dear Mr Churchill,' Maisky said, surprised by the vehemence.

But Churchill was not to be appeased. 'Two years ago you signed a pact with Hitler. It allowed him to hurl himself upon Poland and start this war. You began to supply him with every sort of raw material. Thousands of my people have died beneath bombs that you had helped him manufacture. And only three months ago we had no idea whether you might not even come into this war on the German side.'

Maisky was trying to interrupt but Churchill would have none of it.

'No! You will listen to this. Throughout that time, and without a breath of help from you, this country has stood alone and defiant. We have starved, we have suffered, we have sacrificed almost everything we have – except our unflinching belief in victory. So damn your diplomatic dances, Maisky. The British need no lectures from you about how to fight for our lives!'

Maisky was taken aback by the unexpected brutality of

Churchill's tone, but the Soviet diplomat was nothing if not a survivor. He hadn't made it through the purges that had left thousands of his colleagues in gulags or graveyards by losing his nerve in the face of a little shouting.

'I can tell that you are much affected, Mr Churchill,' he said in a tone that was far more conciliatory. 'And it is also very late. Perhaps it would be sensible to put what has been said to one side and return to this subject at a more appropriate time. But I fear my masters are impatient for a response. Is there anything that I may tell them by way of a preliminary reply?'

'Tell them to go down on their knees and pray for winter!'

Churchill turned his back on the Russian, anxious that he had already said too much and might yet say more. He slammed the great door of Number Ten behind him with unusual vehemence, but he couldn't shut out the pain that dragged along behind him. Maisky was a duplicitous bastard whose demands were outrageous, but the Bolshevik echoed a central truth that had been screaming at Churchill through every waking moment and pursued him into his dreams.

Alone, Britain hadn't a hope.

That night he didn't call for his usual retinue of advisers. He'd had enough rows for one evening. He took his whisky and his boxes to bed and allowed Sawyers to undress him in silence. The valet sensed the mood, poured in a little less soda than usual, and departed as soon as the final cigar of the night was alight.

Churchill was exhausted. He seemed to be losing his powers. Once, and not so long ago, his words had found an energy that carried his ideas around the world, but now it seemed that no one wanted to listen – not the Americans, not his new Russian allies, not even circumcised little pricks like Hore-Belisha. He'd always known that leadership was a friendless place, yet it seemed as if he alone was able to see the terrors that lay ahead, while others closed their eyes and hid from them like children afraid of the dark.

Churchill was hovering between wakefulness and sleep, immersed in that state where conscious thought is pushed aside by half-formed dreams and images, and anxieties swirl through the mind. His anxieties were built on a predictable tangle of fears of war, of defeat, of ill-formed loyalties and unhappy alliances, and no matter how much he shouted at them they refused to return to the dark corners from where they had come. Yet, as he lay there in the early hours, from this unruly combination of dark concerns emerged something fresh and very different. Suddenly he was awake, sitting bolt upright, snatching at his eyeshades. When he switched on the light he discovered it was twenty to three. He reached for the phone.

'See if Lord Beaverbrook is still in the land of the living,' he instructed the duty clerk. 'If he's not, return him to it.'

It took only a couple of minutes to make the connection.

'Winston?' the gruff Canadian voice growled, heavy with sleep. 'What the hell's up? You still on Placentia time or something?'

'Max, before you fly off to see Joe Stalin, I want you to go and have a talk with our German guest, Herr Hess.'

'What the hell for?'

'Oh, to see whether he has anything new to tell us.'

'Like what?'

'We won't know unless someone goes and talks with him, will we?'

'Christ, Winston, this is a strange bloody game to play in the middle of the night.'

'When I appointed you, Max, you said you would never rest. I took you at your word.'

'First goddamned time.'

'It would please me if you were able to help in this matter.'

'You want me to take him roses or something?'

'No, Max. Just take yourself. Goodnight.'

But where Max Beaverbrook went, gossip was sure to follow. Max insisted on it. Soon speculation and exaggeration about the meeting would be halfway around London, and it would take only a few days more before it reached Berlin.

The essence of leadership, Churchill had always found, wasn't in coping with success but in the ability to hop around the pitfalls of failure. To KBO. He was surrounded by a chaos of uncertainty, and if he couldn't find his way out of it in a hurry, he could at least share it a little, with Adolf Hitler.

Churchill put down the phone. He had just thrown a little raw meat to the dogs of confusion that lurked around every campfire. It made him feel very much better. Within moments, he was sound asleep.

ELEVEN

The destroyer USS *Greer* was an ugly scourer of the seas that had been built during the last war and brought out of retirement at the start of the new one. Her role escorting convoys and running nautical errands was scarcely a glamorous one, but it should have been safe enough. After all, it wasn't as if the United States was at war.

On 4 September 1941 she was carrying passengers and mail to Iceland. She had reached a point south-east of Greenland when she was signalled by a British bomber that a German submarine had crash-dived some ten miles ahead. The *Greer* went to investigate and soon picked up the trail of the U-boat on her sound equipment. The British bomber stayed in the vicinity for about an hour until, running short of fuel, she made one final pass and dropped four depth charges at the submarine, the U-652. Then the bomber returned to its base.

The American ship continued to track the German U-boat for another two hours. In the belief that the *Greer* had dropped the depth charges and was pursuing her with the intent of dropping more, the U-652 fired a torpedo. It missed by a hundred yards, but in retaliation the *Greer* dropped eight of her own depth charges. A second torpedo was fired, and another eleven depth charges were thrown at the German boat. By the time the engagement was finally discontinued, the USS *Greer* had been in contact with the German for the best part of four hours.

It was a somewhat academic confrontation, for there had been no hits and no casualties on either side. Yet it was what Churchill had been praying for, what his life depended upon and what he had been willing to trade his soul for.

The Germans had attacked the United States Navy.

Amidst the sounding of alarums and the beating of many drums, President Roosevelt recalled Congress. He also announced he would make a major pronouncement about the German attack. The world held its breath.

Churchill, of course, did not. He was ecstatic. 'At last! It means war. By God, if I'd known that was all it would take, I'd have torpedoed the bloody ship myself!' he declared. Roosevelt had told him that everything would be done to force an incident. Now the Germans had tumbled into the net.

It was also reported that the first snows had begun to fall in Russia. It wouldn't bring the German advance grinding to a halt, not yet; in fact, as Churchill told everyone within earshot, if the campaign was anything like that of Napoleon's, the freezing conditions would at first help the Germans. 'The *Herrenvolk* have found themselves getting bogged down in the muds and sloughs of autumn. Yet as the soil of Mother Russia begins to freeze, so the invader will find firmer footing, for a while. But then – then!' he roared. 'They will wake one grey and miserable morn to find they have thrust themselves firmly into the jaws of merciless winter!'

But for all his confidence, the castle of dreams that Churchill had constructed proved to be built of straw. He sat listening to the presidential broadcast in Downing Street; Sawyers had set up a radio on the Cabinet table and brought in a tray of refreshments, but as he prepared to leave Churchill motioned him to remain. 'We do not walk out on the President when he is about to declare the depths of his devotion.' He smiled in anticipation.

Roosevelt made his broadcast from the basement of the White House. He was wearing a black armband for the occasion – his mother had died a few days beforehand. His words were blunt.

The attack on the USS *Greer* was, the President said, 'piracy, legally and morally'. He said the German submarine had fired first. With no trace of ambivalence, he declared that the Nazis planned to create 'a permanent world system based on force, terror and murder.' This would be resisted, 'no matter what it takes, no matter what it costs.'

'When you see a rattlesnake poised to strike,' the President continued, adopting the fireside manner for which he was so renowned, 'you do not wait until he has struck before you crush him. These Nazi submarines and raiders are the rattlesnakes of the Atlantic. They are a menace to the free pathways of the high seas. They are a challenge to our sovereignty.'

In Roosevelt's eyes, the Germans had been not only indicted but already convicted. The palm of Churchill's hand smacked down upon the Cabinet table in approval.

'The time for active defence is now,' the President continued.

Churchill sniffed. *Active defence?* Somehow the words seemed to imply an ambiguity, a softening in the President's tone and intensity. He was introducing shade where before he had been painting only in black and white.

He declared that US forces would shoot first upon any

German rattlesnake found in American defensive waters. They would not wait to be bitten. They would defend not only American ships but all friendly ships in these waters. And those waters, he decreed, would be stretched to cover three-quarters of the Atlantic.

Fine words. A clear commitment. But he did not declare war. Indeed, he insisted that there would be no war: 'There will be no shooting unless Germany continues to seek it.'

After the President had finished speaking, Sawyers switched off the radio. Churchill remained still in his chair.

'Do we break out a bottle to celebrate, like?' the servant enquired.

'To celebrate what, precisely?'

'Active defence.'

'I think not.'

'Better than nowt, I suppose.'

Churchill's jowls had sunk. He looked intently at the brown tablecloth. It was some time before he replied. 'Sawyers, my son informs me that there is a house of ill-repute in Cairo – one of many such establishments, I believe – where the proprietor has daubed upon his wall the message: "Give us the tools and we will finish the job". You may remember the phrase.'

''Deed I do.'

'It sums up perhaps what a large part of the world thinks of me. History has cast me in the role of the common tart. I smile at de Gaulle. I am nice to any number of Arabs. I am even forced to embrace the bloody Russians. I am reduced to plying my trade on every street corner. But the President is of altogether finer quality. He is like a beautiful woman who knows she is desired, who is warm, suggestive, promises to lead you to paradise, even hitches her skirts halfway up her leg in anticipation . . .' – Churchill ground out his cigar

232

with considerable violence – 'then leaves you to finish the job by yourself. The President is halfway to war, and three-quarters of the way across the Atlantic, but no further. It may all be, as you so charmingly put it, "better than nowt", but at this moment I feel a rather desperate sense of disappointment.'

'Can't you twist his arm a bit?'

'You cannot woo with a whip, Sawyers,' Churchill replied quietly. 'So we shall continue to protest our love to the President and hope that next time his skirts will be hitched a little higher, until, before he realizes it, he has reached the point beyond which all further protestations of virtue are useless.'

At around this time, when the focus of so much of the world centred on events in the Atlantic, the Prime Minister of Japan sought an audience with His Most Imperial Majesty, Hirohito. When he had first become Prime Minister four years earlier, Prince Fumimaro Konoye had been counted as a moderate, but experience had dealt with him harshly. His mood was sombre as he led his frock-coated cabinet and military commanders into the council chamber of the Kokyo imperial palace.

While their god-king sat and everyone else stood, Konoye outlined his plans. The bullying and blockading of the Western powers had cast long shadows across their land, he argued, and their dreams were in danger of falling about them like the leaves of an angry autumn. To do nothing would be to submit to both personal dishonour and imperial disaster. So he proposed to the Emperor that Japan should launch a simultaneous attack against all the Western colonial powers – America, Britain and the Dutch – 'to expel the influence of these three countries from east Asia, to establish a sphere of self-defence and self-preservation of the Japanese Empire, and to build a new order in greater east Asia.'

But in the obtuse and formalized manners that govern such audiences, it became clear that the occupant of the Chrysanthemum Throne might not be content. His tone implied anxiety; his ministers could not promise immediate victory in such an enterprise. He would therefore understand his ministers if in their wisdom they thought it necessary to seek more time in pursuing a diplomatic solution by initiating talks with the Americans. He mentioned only the Americans. The British, it seemed, were of far less interest to the imperial mind, the Dutch of no interest at all.

Confused by the unexpected chill in the mists that clung to the imperial mountaintop, the ministers withdrew, promising that nothing would be done to pursue their plans for at least another month.

In London, Churchill could know nothing of this directly, but he did not need to. He saw the signs, even though he didn't immediately comprehend the significance of them all; the increase in Japanese military signal activity; their renewed diplomatic activity in Washington; their ominous silence in London, where Shigemitsu, their ambassador, had long since been recalled and not replaced.

Churchill was an old campaigner, with the scars of one who had fought in many wars and the instincts of a survivor. As the sun of summer cooled and another long winter beckoned, Churchill could hear the sounds of infamy on the march from halfway round the world.

Harriman walked with hunched shoulders down the steps that led from the rear of Downing Street towards the park.

He was dressed in a raincoat even though the night was neither cold nor damp. He was worn out. He had only just stepped off the plane at Heston when he'd been summoned to The Presence; he hadn't even had a chance to wash. He was sore from the buffeting of the flight, his eyes ached from the weeks of close work, yet Churchill demanded still more. Everyone, it seemed, demanded more of him right now.

He was also bruised from the time he'd spent with his wife. Both of them realized they had wanted to be elsewhere. She had new interests, he was sure of it, just as he had grown distracted by Pamela, but they hadn't spoken about any of it. There were still the formalities of marriage to observe, and they were both formal people.

As he reached the bottom of the steps at the back of Downing Street, he stumbled. After six weeks in the bright lights of Washington and New York, he'd fallen out of the practice of walking almost blind in the blackout, and there had been so much of Winston's bloody brandy.

Suddenly he was aware of someone nearby, trying to catch up with him. A woman, judging by the rustle and the click of her heels.

'You all right, love?' a raucous voice enquired. 'Fancy a good time, do yer?'

He groaned. He wasn't in the frame of mind to enjoy being hassled, particularly by a Piccadilly warrior. He put his head down, strode forward, but she was plucking at his sleeve, slipping her arm through his.

'You don't know how lucky you are, Mr Averell Harriman. One smile at any other woman on your first evening back and I'd have left much of your anatomy dangling from the hands of Big Ben.'

'Pamela!'

235

And they were locked together in the darkness, panting out their greetings.

'I was expecting you . . . back at the Dorchester.'

'Couldn't wait.'

'Wonderful surprise.'

'Missed, missed, missed you!'

Then they were silent for a long time, holding each other, listening to the sounds of the night in the park. Owls, coots, the whisper of drying leaves. When at last they parted, they began walking towards the lake.

'You must be tired,' she said.

'Better now I'm with you.'

'Even so.' She could sense a weariness that had burrowed through to his bones. 'How was it back home?'

He wasn't sure if she meant his homeland or his wife. He chose the diplomatic path.

'Chaotic. Confused. Washington crawling with quiet men who are determined on war and appeasers who would die to prevent it. The President sitting in the middle, bearing the imprint of the last opinion poll.'

'You sound bitter.'

'Not really. More frustrated. Roosevelt's heart's in the right place, but I guess in a wheelchair you learn to take things cautiously.'

An autumn moon shimmered off the lake. Ducks chattered to each other. One of the park's pelicans, ghost-like in the distance, stretched its wings.

'Washington's floating on a lake of poison right now. Lies, rumours, distortions. Everything we do gets twisted. The Germans are behind it, must be. There's an organized campaign – German money – to undercut everyone who gets involved in the war.'

'You, too?'

'Right in the damned middle.' He sighed, sounding old. 'They've been peddling stories that I'm spending huge amounts of the Lend-Lease money on champagne and luxury hotels.'

'That's so unfair.'

'And off the mark. Who the hell have I bought champagne for? Apart from you, and that was with my own money.'

'I suspect I'm not the safest alibi for you to offer, either,' she whispered, clinging to his arm.

'So then they tweak the story, and claim it's the British officials who are spending the Lend-Lease money on high living. Oh, it makes great headlines. It's one bunch of cynical bastards we have back home.' His tiredness was causing him to lose his normal restraint. 'Right now I feel as if I've spent the last month with every rat in the business taking free shots at me. Like St Sebastian. You know – the one who died with all those arrows sticking out of him?'

'Now, would that be the Sebastian who was a member of the Imperial Roman guard? The one who was persecuted for his faith?' she enquired sweetly, mocking him gently, but he was too tired to notice.

'I guess so.'

'But he didn't die from the arrows.'

'Truly?'

'No, he was nursed back to health – by a woman. You men can be so useless on your own.' She held him tight, trying to squeeze some warmth back into him. 'Book of Saints. Read under the covers on cold winter nights in Dorset. Sebastian didn't die until later, when the Emperor had him beaten to death.'

'Sorry. I guess at times I underestimate you.'

His guard *was* down; it was as close as he had ever come to a compliment. It would have to do.

He sighed. 'You know, Pam, if I were a cowboy, I'd be on my horse and riding into the sunset right now. Damn them all!'

She snuggled into his armpit as they walked slowly beneath the trees.

'I used to ride a lot when I was a young girl in Dorset,' she said, trying to lead him away from his cares.

'Yeah?' he muttered, not listening.

'Near our home there's a huge giant that's been cut into the chalk. A mystical place called Cerne Abbas. Our giant is very famous, more than two thousand years old. He has a huge club and . . .' She laughed gently.

'And what?'

'A huge phallus.'

'How huge?' he asked, stopping to face her, inevitably intrigued.

'When I was ten, it was almost three times my length when I lay down beside it.'

'Did you, now?'

'And on May Day it points directly to where the sun rises.'

'Oh, it's an astronomical instrument, then.'

They were holding each other tightly once more. Harriman had his back against a tree. She could tell from the pressure of her body on him, and his on her, that he had begun to put aside both the war and his weariness.

'You've been away a very long time, my love.'

'Seems like for ever.'

Her fingers had begun to edge their way down his shirt-front and behind his belt.

'Pamela . . .' His voice was torn between desire and discretion. 'What if someone . . .'

'It's dark. And you can always plead diplomatic immunity.'

'But you're the Prime Minister's daughter-in-law, for Heaven's sake.'

'And who would believe that,' she whispered, as her hand began searching deep within his trousers.

More American ships were attacked that September. A freighter, the *Steel Seafarer*, was sunk by a German plane in the Red Sea the day after the *Greer* had been attacked, and a week later the *Arkansan* was damaged. No one was killed in these attacks, but then the merchantman *Montana* was torpedoed and sunk in the North Atlantic, and twenty-six of its crew drowned. She was flying the flag of Panama, a US protectorate, rather than the Stars and Stripes itself. A few days later the *Pink Star*, laden with food and heading for Iceland, was torpedoed, leaving thirteen dead, and a week after that the oil tanker *I. C. White* en route to South Africa was lost along with three of its crew. But, like the *Montana*, they were both flying the Panamanian flag, and they were merchantmen. It seemed to make a difference. Still the United States would not go to war.

There was too much confusion. Too many Americans who wanted Communist Russia to lose. Too many who thought Britain couldn't win. Too many with burning memories of the last war, when American sons had died to save Europe – and what a waste of sons that had been. And too many who believed Roosevelt when he had promised again and again and again that their sons were not going to be sent to die in another foreign war.

The clash between the *Greer* and the U-boat had been a game of no hits, no strikes, no runs, while the tangles with the other boats were no more than the inevitable fallout from someone else's war.

And that's the way the majority of Americans wanted it to stay. Someone else's war.

'The leaves are turning, Winston. Time for birds like me to fly.'

Churchill cast an eye at the beeches. 'They will be magnificent while they last, Max.'

It was still stiflingly hot for the time of year. There had been croquet on the lawn for Clementine and other members of the family, followed by afternoon tea served with much laughter at the antics of Mary's new dog, with everything accompanied by the scraping tones of the gramophone, but the old man hadn't been part of it. He had sought the shelter of the woods, and Beaverbrook, his old friend, had dragged behind him.

'Sarah seems out of sorts,' the Canadian said.

'Locked herself away in her room. Says she has a headache.' They both knew that wasn't true. 'She's leaving the comedian. Wants a divorce.'

'I know.'

'Why can't . . . ?' Churchill trailed off, knowing the futility of his protest.

'Is it Gil Winant?'

'No!' Churchill said, but too quickly. Beaverbrook would know, Max always knew! 'I don't think so,' Churchill continued, knowing absolute denial was futile. 'I think she is simply desperately unhappy. I feel so wretched for her.'

'Not your fault.'

'Oh, but somehow I always feel it is.'

And, in a way, it was. He had set an Olympian example for his daughters that no other man could match. It had gone a long way to ruining his son, too, but there was little point in telling him so. Deep down, he already knew it.

They walked in silence for a while, Churchill striking forward with the gold-topped cane that had been given to him as a wedding present by the late King Edward. He was wearing one of his romper suits, a rich, vivid purple that clashed dramatically with the wood around them, and a broad-brimmed soft hat to keep the sun from his eyes.

'You've upset the War Office, Max.'

'Good.'

'Yes, you're probably right.'

'You've made me Minister for Supply. So, dammit, I want to supply,' he growled. 'But most of those guys don't know their bollocks from their backsides. Keep complaining that we haven't sent them the right colour tent pegs or haven't recycled their envelopes, or some such bloody nonsense.'

'But did you really have to write to the War Secretary offering to supply string for his bows and arrows?'

'Hell, I even said I'd send him flints from my own back-yard at Cherkley in case he wanted to get his flintlocks ready. What's the problem? Did I use the wrong form or some-thing?'

He was going to get nowhere with Max on this one. Beaverbrook was irascible, irrepressible, irreverent, and at the moment irreplaceable. And he knew it. Supplies to the factories, supplies to the army, supplies from America, supplies to Russia, they all came under his remit and he used it to push his way ruthlessly around Whitehall. 'I'm just your delivery boy, Winston,' he had joked when appointed. 'My bike is always at your service.' Which is why Churchill had told him to get on it and go to Moscow.

'Keep them in the war, Max,' he had said. 'Give them what-ever it takes. Help them. But don't bleed us dry in the process.'

Yet Beaverbrook, as always, had followed his own

instructions. In preparation for his trip he had tried to bully the Chiefs of Staff into giving up all sorts of vital supplies so that he could promise them to Stalin; it had led to endless rows, with Churchill stuck in the middle.

Typically, as soon as the Chiefs turned hostile, Beaverbrook raised the stakes. He proposed an immediate raid on the mainland of France, using tanks, in the knowledge that it was what Churchill and the Russians also wanted, and in the certainty that the Chiefs would object yet again. And he would go on raising issues, wearing the bastards down, argument by argument; they couldn't carry on objecting to everything. Easier to give in to Max right at the start, everyone knew that.

'I need more, Winston,' Beaverbrook barked gruffly, bustling along beside Churchill.

'That's what Maisky said. I told him to bugger off.'

'You can't send me to Moscow empty-handed.'

'And neither can I strip the entire British Army naked in order to satisfy your enthusiasm for Comrade Stalin.'

'You wanna help him or not?'

'Of course I do but . . . There are limits, Max.' Churchill knew it was a wasted argument; Max Beaverbrook had no understanding of limits. They were a lot alike. That was why they had been friends for so long, and why Churchill could never fully trust him.

'For Pete's sake, Winston, if you're determined to send me to Moscow with nothing, then I will have nothing to give 'em. Dammit, doesn't seem much point my going. Send Eden instead. He can talk them into stupefaction; maybe they'll never notice he's brought bugger all but words.'

'No, Max.'

'I tell you honestly, Winston, maybe I've been around too long. I'm not getting any younger. My eyes are going, my bloody asthma cripples me. Perhaps it's time I found something a little less adventurous to do.'

God, not that again. Another of Max's temperamental threats to resign. One day he would go too far.

'Like what, Max?' Churchill asked wearily, playing along. 'What do you have in mind?'

'Ambassador to Washington. You know Edward Halifax is about as useless as yesterday's newspaper. He's not one of us. But I know everyone there. It'd be a great way to wrap up my career. So let's make it Washington. Not Moscow. I'm getting too old to be sent sledging through a Russian winter.'

Perhaps he meant it. But Churchill doubted it. Max was, after all, five years younger than him. He still had ambition. That was why, along with his new job at Supply, he'd insisted on moving into Downing Street. At Number Twelve, just two doors down. He was camping on the doorstep.

Churchill knew that events were slipping out of his control – even here, at home. Everyone getting a touch too uppity. Not just those plodders in Parliament like Hore-Belisha but also the fornicators in Fleet Street. Always carping, finding fault. The *Daily Mail* reshuffled his Cabinet for him almost every week, and *The Times* had just had a spasm of ill temper and pronounced that he should be preparing for his successor! Max would have read it and laughed – knowing Max, he might even have written it.

They trudged on through the woods until they came to a glade. Sunlight dappled across the clearing. In the middle had once stood a huge, overpowering tree, but now it had been reduced to nothing but a rotting, moss-covered stump. Churchill poked the tip of his cane into the bowels of the stump; it splintered and fell apart at their feet.

'As all great things eventually do,' he whispered. Beaverbrook ignored it.

'So, do I get the job?'

'What?' Churchill said, startled, dragged back from his thoughts.

'Ambassador. Do I get to be Ambassador?'

It was a game. Beaverbrook didn't want it, but he wanted to be offered it. He was like a boy in a sweet shop, damn him. But what did it matter? In a few weeks the whole world might have turned on its head. Hitler might have him shot.

'Yes, if you want, Max. After Moscow. Do the job there and the post in Washington might make a lot of sense.'

Beaverbrook nodded in silent contentment.

'So you go to Moscow, Max. Pay the Soviets whatever they need to continue the fight, like the bloody-handed mercenaries they are, because their fight is our fight, too. I hate what Russia represents, its system of malevolence and murder, and I detest its leader above all. But I need him. So we must pass a sponge across the past and promise them treasures and arms in abundance. Stalin will be duly ungrateful for what he is about to receive, even while our own sailors die in large numbers trying to deliver it.'

He started slashing at a huge fern with his cane.

'And when he complains about a second front, remind him that there might even now be a second front, in his own backyard, if Japan hadn't been left so short of raw materials by our sanctions. Tell him we shall tighten the blockade on the Japanese, screw it so tight that their babies will scream with hunger and their war machine will be starved until it is driven ever further south, towards the oilfields and rubber plantations of our own Empire. And remind him that with every step the Japanese take away from the borders of Russia, they march closer to their war with us.'

The fern lay in pieces at his feet.

'Tell him all that, Max. Give him what he wants. Just

make sure you leave us with enough to give ourselves a chance of surviving, there's a good chap.'

The maid Héloise had a weekend off. It was inconvenient, but she hadn't spent a weekend away from Chequers since her arrival, and it seemed only fair. She had a cousin who was passing through London, she told Mrs Landemare, and he might have news from home.

Soon after she arrived in the capital, she could be seen perched on a park bench by the Serpentine in Hyde Park, throwing crumbs to the ducks. A man came to sit at the opposite end of the bench, but he was not her cousin. He was the same young Japanese she had bumped into on her last trip. They appeared to ignore each other; he read a newspaper while she concentrated on the insistent ducks.

Within a few minutes she had exhausted her supply of bread. She shook out the last remnants of crumbs from the paper bag in which they had been carried, then screwed it up and placed it on the bench beside her. She stood, brushed down the front of her coat and left. A few seconds afterwards, the Japanese gentleman disappeared in the opposite direction. The paper bag was nowhere to be seen.

The temperature had dropped sharply with the setting of the sun. The clear skies that had brought warmth and pleasure during the afternoon now threatened an early frost. Chequers was always a cold house, its bricks imbued with chill and its mullioned windows and ancient doors never a good fit in their frames. Churchill put his head around the office next to the front door in which the secretaries sat, to discover them rubbing their hands for warmth.

At times he could be unutterably rude and impatient with his staff but on other occasions also innately kind, and, for the moment, the welfare of his helper-women became his greatest priority – or was it merely a quest to find distraction, something other than the war to focus on? In any event, he became determined that their comfort should be taken care of.

'You shall have fire!' he declared. He poked his head into the hallway and bellowed: 'Sawyers!'

But Sawyers was nowhere to be found. And the maid had a day off, while Mrs Landemare was sweating over dinner, so Churchill decided there was only one thing for it. He got down on his knees before the grate, screwed up large twists of paper, covered them with kindling and began hurling matches into the middle of it all. Soon smoke began curling its way up the chimney.

It was while he was leaning in triumph on one of the desks that his eye encountered a piece of paper that, in ordinary circumstances, would probably never have come to him. A civil servant would have intercepted it and decided it was not of sufficient significance or interest to engage the Prime Minister's mind. It was nothing more than a note reporting that the factories of the United States were producing a record number of cars and refrigerators.

More cars, more refrigerators. Suddenly the smile was gone, the rage was upon him. 'Do they expect to choke the damned Fuehrer on ice cream?' he roared at the hapless secretaries before storming out.

It was a mood he carried with him to the dinner table. He showed no indication of joining in the discussions of his guests. His head was down, he was slurping, picking up food in his fingers, spilling his wine in impatience, paying others no heed. They carried on without him. He seemed to have time only for Nelson the cat, who sat on his lap throughout the meal and was paid for his loyalty with a puddle of cream that Churchill poured onto the polished table top beside him.

His performance was not so exceptional, little more than the exhibitionism of age and authority covered in a generous smearing of exhaustion. His humour had been blowing as unpredictably as the winds of autumn, and they no longer knew what to expect. They were finishing off the last of the summer pudding when someone mentioned the stories that were emerging of wholesale executions in Czechoslovakia, and the new Nazi edict that all Jews should be marked by wearing the yellow Star of David on their clothes.

'You feel so helpless,' Winant ventured, 'watching this all from a distance.'

Suddenly Churchill's fists pounded on the table for attention.

'Then how long will it be, pray, before Americans stop feeling so bloody helpless, cease watching from a great distance and get stuck in?'

'Ladies,' Clementine instructed, demurely but firmly. As one, they rose and followed her off to the Long Gallery for coffee. Nelson had also deserted his post.

'Winston,' Winant eventually responded, in a tone that implied his total lack of eagerness to get involved in a shoot-out.

'Don't "Winston" me, Mr Ambassador. We've danced around this one too long. I apologize for asking a diplomat a straight question, but there it is. How long will it be?' His tone was curt, the formality suggested he had put aside their friendship in order to pursue the matter.

At the far end of the table, Winant's shoulders sagged. 'Prime Minister,' he said, reluctantly taking up the challenge as the other guests sat back in their chairs to give them a clear line of fire. 'I wish I could tell you. But what with the state of public opinion . . .'

'Yes, I understand the President likes to keep his ear to the ground.'

'He does.'

'Bloody undignified, arse in the air. Ripe for kicking.' Churchill threw back the last of his claret and reached for his glass of brandy.

'As you well know, the opposition to war amongst the public remains intense and inside the Senate is extreme. Some believe that what the President has already done is unconstitutional.'

'Reminds me of a heretic worrying about whether the knots of his bindings are comfortable while the flames are about to scorch his nuts.'

'You can't ignore public opinion, not in a democracy. And it's all very well going on about the Unites States' refusal to fight the war, but what about the British?'

'What about the British?'

Winant loosened his bow tie, feeling constricted, unhappy at the direction this was taking. 'The way many Americans see it,' he replied slowly, 'is that ever since the British Army got pushed out of Norway and France you've shown a distinct reluctance to get stuck back in. You fight the Germans at a distance – in the air, on the sea, in the Middle East. But not where it is truly going to matter, on the mainland of Europe. Even the Russians are saying so.'

'Don't quote me bloody Marx and Stalin!'

'I could quote you a dozen US Senators. You have no troops on mainland Europe, so why should we?'

'We are in this war, up to the hilt and to the death! You've walked around the streets of London, of Coventry, of Liverpool, of Portsmouth' – he was pounding the table with every name – 'of Bristol, of Birmingham, of Cardiff, of Plymouth. You have seen us crawling out of our basements and bunkers, brushing the debris from our eyes and wondering which of our loved ones survived the night. We are in this war, every man, woman and child of us. But America? Are you in, or out? Are you Spectator, Umpire or Player?'

'For my own part, Winston, you know that I would have us with you tomorrow but –'

Churchill rode roughshod over his attempt at pacification. 'The President told me to my face that he would find a pretext, some provocation that would justify you coming into this war. Your ships get attacked and sunk with devastating regularity, yet –'

'The *Greer*? Well, she was scarcely an innocent bystander, Winston. She pursued the U-boat for four hours in the middle of a hostile engagement. That's why some are saying the President's already gone too far, and most others agree that the German provocation hasn't gone far enough.'

'Provocation?' Churchill exploded. 'What more do you need? Hitler has murdered half a dozen countries for far less. You are blind, blind.' The fists came crashing down upon the table once more. 'Can you not see what he's about? "One by one": that's his plan, that is the guiding rule, and with it he's already enslaved a vast proportion of the world.'

Winant tried to respond but Churchill held up his hand.

'I warned, I warned so many times. But no one would listen. They all stood idly by while Germany rearmed. Austria was occupied. Czechoslovakia subjugated. Poland crushed. The Low Countries and the Scandinavian countries wiped from the map. France humiliated. Even this year, I pleaded with the Balkan countries to stand together and save themselves from the ruin by which they are now engulfed. But, one by one, they were undermined and overwhelmed. Never has the career of pillage and plunder been made more smooth. And now he inflicts his slaughter upon the peoples of Russia, after which it will be our turn in this country. And then what, Ambassador?' With a sweep of his arms he pushed away all the cutlery and glasses on the table in front of him, leaving nothing but chaos. A glass of old wine had toppled, spilling its dregs across the table top; he ignored it. 'When all the rest of the world has been reduced to a featureless swamp of untold suffering, that Devil's butcher will call you Americans to order. Oh, I do not doubt that you will give a good account of yourselves. You will exchange vacillating pacifism for the brightest jingoism and you will bring all your might to bear. You will promise to defend your independence to the death, and Hitler will do his best to grant you that wish. But even if you were able to withstand the onslaught, what then? What would there be left in your world apart from the piteous cries of ghosts? You will look back and beat your breasts and proclaim that you should have seen sooner, moved faster, listened more carefully, understood that lonely little Britannia was fighting for your cause and the cause of all free men. But don't you dare say you were never warned.' His finger was jabbing down the table at the American. '"One by one!" "One by one!" History will never forgive you if you allow that monster to become master of our world!'

Sawyers was at his side, making a hash of refilling his balloon of cognac, deliberately distracting him. 'Sorry, zur.'

'Bugger off, Sawyers!' the old man snapped. 'I've got business to attend to.'

The servant, having watched the performance from the wings, had wondered whether Churchill was ill or too far in alcohol, but one look at his steady and voracious eyes told him otherwise. He could not save Churchill from himself and there was no point in trying. With the briefest nod of his head, Sawyers withdrew.

'I went to meet your President wanting war, Gil. But instead I got an Atlantic Charter that talks about some far-off and fanciful peace your country would like to impose upon the world, even though you will not fight for it. So I ask you to understand my sense of overpowering disappointment, to indulge my suggestions that the position of the *Americanus Ostrichissimus* is undignified and wholly immoral, and I ask you – as a friend – to forgive anything I have said that has gone beyond the immoderation that should be permitted between us. But I tell you this, Gil.' Churchill pushed himself to his feet, staring down towards the American. 'Your country will enter this war. You will have no choice in the matter, for if you do not decide for war, then there will be others who will make that decision for you. You will not be permitted to stand aside.'

Winant's dark, angular features appeared more than usually severe. His eyes filled with puzzlement, as though he were not fully certain of the meaning of what he had just heard. 'As a friend, my dear Winston, I forgive most willingly. As a diplomat, I understand both your passion and your argument, even if I cannot travel all the way along that road with you. But I feel bound to point out what many others will rush to remind you of, if you try to push the President too far. Your own words. "Give us the tools and we will finish the job." They will hoist you with your own rhetoric, Winston.'

'Tools, tools, the tools of war!' Churchill rasped. 'Not motor cars and bloody refrigerators.' With that, he threw down his napkin and stalked from the room.

*　　*　　*

251

Sawyers helped him undress silently that night. The silk pyjamas were laid out on the bed, the eyeshades on the pillow, the whisky, cigar and matches on the table beside the bed. He helped the old man out of his dinner jacket and watched as Churchill climbed unselfconsciously into his nightclothes.

It was only after Churchill had hauled himself into bed that he spoke.

'You think I went too far.'

'You're the politician.'

'Yes, and I ventured way beyond the limits of safety. All but cut my own throat.'

The valet busied himself with tidying Churchill's clothes.

'The problem with committing political suicide, Sawyers, is that you so often live to regret it.'

TWELVE

The Empire Stadium, Wembley.

'Thought you might like to see it,' Churchill growled out of the side of his mouth. 'Our version of a Nuremberg rally.'

Winant bent to bring his ear closer, deafened by the roar of a crowd that numbered more than sixty thousand.

'They seem to love you,' Winant shouted.

Churchill gave him a mocking glance. 'The only reason they cheer is because they know I won't be making another infernal speech.' He continued to wave, raising both his arms high, his fingers extended in his two-fingered V-for-Victory salute. 'They tell me that if I get the fingers the wrong way round it means something entirely different,' he continued, 'the sort of thing that should be reserved exclusively for the Germans.'

'Which way round is that, then?'

'Buggered if I know. They seem to cheer whichever way I do it. Look!'

And to prove him right, the packed crowd continued to roar its approval, while the military band parading on the field below struck up the tune of 'For He's A Jolly Good Fellow' and the song began to roll around the concrete expanse of the national stadium as they waited for the start of the game between England and Scotland.

'My God,' he said as at last he resumed his seat in the VIP box, 'if only we could fight them here, the Germans would never stand a chance.'

Winant smiled, deeply impressed – as it was intended he should be. Churchill had little interest in the sport of football but the international at Wembley was an ideal opportunity for him to make amends for the previous weekend – 'and to have some other Englishmen apart from me shouting at you,' as he had told Winant. He also wanted to give the lie to the rumour that they were all beginning to turn against him, not just the press and Parliament, but the people, too. Not that their ovation meant anything; they would cheer just as loud if a chicken ran onto the pitch.

On the way to the ground Churchill had insisted that they stop at Buckingham Palace to watch as some of the railings were torn down. The Minister of Works himself, clad incongruously in goggles, heavy leather gauntlets and three-piece pinstripe suit, had posed in front of photographers with an oxyacetylene cutter. All around the country railings, fences, gates, saucepans, pots, prams – even entire cars and old refrigerators – were being melted down for the war effort. Widows were sending Churchill their wedding rings with painfully scrawled letters about how 'my dear husband, who fought in the last one, would have understood'. So the Palace railings had to go; it was important to show that the burden was being shared.

'They'll be melted to make a Buckingham Palace tank,' Churchill had declared as the wrought iron clattered to the ground. Another bit of nonsense. The metal was far too meagre in both quality and quantity to construct a tank, but Winant was no engineer, and Churchill was the most experienced of salesmen.

An hour later they were in the stadium in the midst of a

forest of waving caps, scarves and rattles, when a sudden hush fell across the crowd. A drum rolled. As one, they stood for the national anthem. The band struck up the music and sixty thousand voices competed to lift the refrain high. 'Send him victorious . . .' Never had Winant heard the words delivered with so much passion. The mood of the crowd was infectious and the pride that filled their hearts and swamped many an eye began to touch Winant, too. He was visibly and deeply moved. Churchill saw this, and was content. His outburst of the previous weekend had startled everyone, including those old hands used to his volcanic temper, but whatever damage it might have inflicted on his friendship with the American seemed to have been repaired.

The match proved to be a one-sided affair. Even after the depletions of war, the English side could still muster names like Stanley Matthews and Denis Compton, and they were a goal up within fifteen minutes and threatening more.

When they scored for the second time the crowd erupted yet again, most in celebration, a minority in Celtic despair. Winant was applauding but Churchill seemed not to have noticed. His mood had grown heavy.

'Winston, where are you?'

'Forgive me, Gil,' he answered morosely. 'I was just looking at the crowd. Reflecting.'

'May I be allowed to share in your reflection?'

'It is simply this. That for every man who stands here today, Hitler has killed one of their neighbours. Not soldiers, mind you, but defenceless civilians in their homes, in their streets, in their places of work and places of worship. War no longer has boundaries, it no longer respects distinctions of class, or age, or sex, or creed. It spills everywhere, and in blood. There is no front line any more, nothing but one limitless and interminable killing field.' He gazed around the vastness of the stadium. 'So many. Where will it all stop? How many more will die before it is all over?'

In front of their box, two young boys were jumping up and down, bursting with innocent joy, sounding their rattles and hugging each other in friendship.

'They ask for little more than a quiet life behind a solid oak door, yet they have become statistics. Cold-hearted numbers. That's how we wage war nowadays, with charts and graphs, where an upward arrow means hope and a downward slope is disaster. Yet every squiggle, every flicker of the line, is measured in the lives of brave men. Men such as these, Gil.' He began pointing at them, as if counting. 'A crowd as vast as this, yet it is nothing but the first fraction of the price of victory.'

Winant hailed from New England where they take pride in their restraint, but behind his dark eyes he was a deep and sensitive man who possessed neither the thickness of skin nor the hardness in his heart to resist the passions of this moment. Around him, men and boys were joined in innocent fellowship while beside him, Churchill's hand was falling as he counted, like a metronome ticking off the number of the newly dead. One by one.

'I understand the point, Winston,' the ambassador responded quietly.

Churchill looked at his guest. His task had been completed.

'Good,' he said, getting to his feet. 'Two-nil. That's enough. We know who's going to win here. Let's get back to the other game. See if we can sort out who's going to win that one.'

The Prime Minister turned to Harriman.

'So, how was our friend, Joe Stalin?'

'Bloody.'

'Stalin is a bear with voracious appetites.'

'And then some,' Beaverbrook chipped in from the other side of the dining table. 'Never seen a man put away so much alcohol at one sitting. Pepper vodka, white wine, red wine, champagne, brandy – Russian, mind you, not the French stuff. He either has an extraordinary stomach or a very short life expectancy.'

The Canadian's light tone didn't seem to sit well with Churchill, who merely grunted. Harriman and Beaverbrook had arrived back from Moscow to receive the usual peremptory summons to come straight to Chequers, where they had found the Prime Minister in a strangely restrained mood. So far he had failed to throw upon them the accolades that Beaverbrook had been expecting.

'And caviar, I suppose, Max,' Churchill enquired distractedly.

'Buckets of it. Tables piled high with everything you could want. Sweetest suckling pig I ever did taste. I tell you, if that's Communism, I'm a convert.'

'He has far more extensive tastes, Winston,' Harriman interjected, failing to pick up on Beaverbrook's enthusiasms. 'He wants planes, tanks, transport, raw materials, the lot. He's also, deep down, very scared. Insists on a second front. Says that a British Army that doesn't fight is useless.'

'Damn him.'

'He also wants you to shoot Hess.'

'What?'

'Thinks you may be doing a secret deal with him.'

'A secret deal . . . Whatever gives him that idea?'

'Says you're obviously up to something because you've been so damned silent,' Beaverbrook came in once more. 'One night – oh, it was after a bellyful of toasts – he told me that Winston Churchill had been known to keep his mouth shut only about two things – his drinking habits, and Rudolph Hess. Stalin's exact words. He doesn't understand why you haven't stood him against a wall in front of a firing squad.'

'Doesn't he, now?' Churchill muttered, sounding more fascinated than offended.

'He'd heard somehow that I'd been to see him. Kept wanting to know why.'

'What did you tell him?'

'That you were keeping him as a hostage in case the Germans captured Randolph in action.'

'Did he swallow that?'

'No. Said that from the intelligence reports he was seeing, Randolph was getting plenty of action but none of it anywhere near the front.'

Churchill grunted.

'Trouble is, Winston – I'm damned if I understand about Hess myself. When I saw him he said nothing he hadn't told us a hundred times before. Why in Hell's name did you send me?'

'Perhaps because I'd hoped you might be able to weave your magic, Max,' Churchill said, his tone liberally sprinkled with disdain.

'What's bothering you, Winston?' the press baron growled. He looked up from his plate to find himself confronted by Churchill's piercing blue eyes.

'I send you to Moscow, Max. It is a capital under siege. One of the greatest battles of all history is being fought before its gates. I have implored our own people to go without in order to assist the Soviets. We starve. We struggle. Our seamen risk their lives to bring us the basics of life. But what do I read in the newspapers about your priorities?'

Beaverbrook's brow wrinkled in confusion.

'Caviar. I pick up my morning newspapers and read that Max Beaverbrook has gone to Moscow and he buys twenty-five pounds of caviar.'

'Oh, that,' the Canadian mumbled. 'Silly story. You know what these press men are like. Hell, the stuff wasn't for me.'

'So I read. Apparently, according to the *News Chronicle*, it was intended as a gift for me.'

'Winston, you know how they work. They found out about it and started pestering. I might've mentioned I was going to bring a little of it back for you but . . .'

'They found out about it. You realized how it might look. So you saved your own arse by thrusting mine into the fire.'

'No, Winston, that's ridiculous!'

No more ridiculous than the mutterings that had been appearing in the press, pushed by Beaverbrook's most intimate friends. They'd been suggesting he should become the man in charge of all production, the Czar of the Home Front, responsible for every detail of domestic matters while the Prime Minister was left to handle foreign affairs. Beaverbrook would run the war, Churchill would fight it, so the rumours went, two old friends in harness. But it might not end there, of course. Beaverbrook, the imperialist, had now become the new friend of Russia, a man of all seasons. It made him the natural choice to replace Churchill, when that time came. And with his friends everywhere in the press, that time might never be much further than the next edition. He seemed to have forgotten all about the Ambassador's job; perhaps he had set his sights on an altogether more powerful position. Churchill's. Trouble was with Max, you could never be sure.

'Then, Max . . .' Churchill continued.

Beaverbrook found himself pierced on the other man's gaze.

'Then, Max,' Churchill repeated, 'I apologize. Most profusely.' But the eyes didn't flicker and both men understood that no apology was intended. 'You will forgive me, and understand why at times like this I might have wanted rather more from your trip to Moscow than headlines about fish eggs.'

'Dammit, it's me who should apologize.'

'No need, Max, no need. We've known each other too long for such trifles. The war is the only thing that matters, and winning is everything.'

'I'll drink to that.'

It was time to step back. They had known each other for decades, in and out of affection, and always found themselves pulled together like magnets. In old age, perhaps a little rust had settled upon their relationship. Time to wash it away. They raised their glasses.

'Anyhow,' Churchill growled, 'since we can't drop the bloody stuff on them and wipe out a few Huns, we may as well eat a bit of it.' He turned and bellowed loudly enough for his voice to blast its way through the closed door. 'Sawyers!'

Weekends at Chequers were inevitably surrounded by an element of chaos. The front door constantly swung on its hinges as guests arrived and others left, as despatch riders brought more pouches and official cars drew up laden with more boxes. Telephones rang at all hours and the radio blared with the latest glimmerings from the BBC. Churchill tried to keep track of everything that happened, but the war was taking place elsewhere, and increasingly he felt a pace or two behind.

Max Beaverbrook departed, rather earlier than expected,

claiming travel fatigue and taking the rest of the caviar with him. Pamela arrived, along with many others, and a doctor, too. Harriman was feeling off colour. He'd suffered from sinusitis on the journey back from Moscow and was clearly in need of a rest, but he refused to take to his bed.

He went in search of Churchill and found him looking deep into the flames that flickered in the hearth of the Hawtrey Room. A single sheet of paper hung limply in his hand.

'Am I interrupting, Winston?'

'If you are, it will be the only agreeable disturbance of my day.' He waved the paper. 'It seems that the Government in Tokyo is on the point of crumbling, split between those who wish to pursue the diplomatic route, and those who would prefer a bloody good war.'

'Then it may be good news.'

'I doubt it. The name of General Tojo keeps bubbling to the surface.'

'Who's he?'

'The Minister for War – and with good reason. Through and through a military man, an exponent of the theories of total war who has spent time training in Germany. A few years ago he was the Japanese Army's chief of police in China – you may remember the stories – when Japanese troops tossed around babies for bayonet practice. I suspect General Tojo is not much given to the ways of patience and diplomacy.' Churchill looked up from the flames. 'This is the moment I've feared most of all, Averell – more even than invasion. We have reached a point, a climacteric, where the Soviets may be almost out of the war, the Japanese almost in it, and America is nowhere to be seen. Invasion I can fight – and may yet have to. But over events in Russia, and Japan, and America, I am utterly powerless.'

'I am so sorry.'

'Not your fault, my dear friend. And you must know how intensely grateful my country is for everything you are doing.'

'No need, Winston. Your fight is my fight. Soon it will be America's fight, too.'

'Ah, but when?'

'I've got to return to Washington in a few days. I'll do everything I can.'

'Will you? Will you, indeed?' He began scrabbling amongst the papers in his box. 'You've been away, so I thought . . . I dictated a note for you, a brief appraisal of where I think your country and my country should be heading. Your voice, in support, might count for so much, my friend.'

As Churchill handed across an envelope, Harriman was bent double with a fit of coughing.

'Are you all right?'

'It's nothing. Just the travelling.' The fit subsided. 'I need to rest my boots in one bed for a little while.'

'Of course,' Churchill said, ignoring the slip of an exhausted tongue. 'Then I prescribe bed and whisky, in that order!'

'You never rest.'

'I have my family about me. You do not. It makes a very great difference.'

Churchill looked intently at the other man and seemed to be on the point of saying more about the subject, but instead changed his mind and slapped the arm of his chair. 'Anyway, I make sure to take my own prescription. The whisky I take to bed is purely for medicinal purposes, you understand, a preventative measure.' He smiled broadly and tapped his chest. 'As you can see, taken regularly, it works wonders!'

*   *   *

The note that Churchill had given to Harriman was brief.

From: W.S.C.

To: W.A.H.

11.10.41.

Subject: UPDATE - FAR EAST.

This note is to be destroyed by fire upon reading.

1. Pressure from Russia for second front requires Britain give priority to land forces in Europe.
2. No independent action by ourselves will deter Japan: we are too much tied up elsewhere.
3. US and Britain require alternative military presence capable of deterring Jap. intentions, or dealing decisively with any act of aggression.

ACTION:

i. Britain forthwith will send a considerable naval battle squadron (carrier, R-class battleships) to show itself in and around Singapore;

ii. US to follow with own naval task force to Far East. Together with British ships, this most powerful Allied fleet should exert paralysing effect on Japanese naval action;

iii. US-Britain to announce military alliance to come into effect in event of Jap. attack on forces of either party anywhere in world.

Churchill had made a small manuscript correction in the margin, and had initialled the note in his usual scrawl. It was a typical Churchill communication. Tightly argued, double-spaced, on a single page. Ideal for immediate digestion – although, taken out of context, not everyone might understand that it was by way of a proposal, an aspiration, rather than an agreed undertaking.

But that was Churchill's challenge, to ensure that anyone who was to catch sight of the paper, whether by accident or underhand means, would believe it to be the most solemn and binding of obligations. Churchill's task was to transform a scrap of paper into a declaration of war.

'You're tired, my darling.'

'Like a dog. A whole pack of them.'

'You're pushing yourself too hard.'

'If I don't push, who else will?' He lay back on her pillow, his eyes closed.

'Was Moscow horrid?'

'Bloodiest thing was trying to figure out which one was going to throw the biggest tantrum, Joe Stalin or Max.'

'You don't like Max?'

'Love him. Don't trust him.'

'He's always been very kind to me.'

'I'm also told he cries when he wrings the necks of pheasants.'

'Who told you that?'

'He did, of course. You should've seen him with Stalin after a few bottles together. Tears pouring into each other's laps. They sure made an interesting couple.'

'That's probably what Max says about us.'

'He suspects?'

'I believe so. With the baby staying at Cherkley, he pretty much knows where I am all the time. I think he's probably figured it out.'

He fell silent.

'That bothers you?'

'Yes, I suppose it does,' he admitted reluctantly, his mood growing bleaker by the moment. 'Makes me feel he has a hold on me. Max does so love his little games.'

'Come on, darling, don't let's worry about Max. Let's forget about them all, just for a while. Pretend for one night there's only you and me.'

He sighed. 'If only I could, but . . .'

'But what?'

'Got to go back home in a few days.'

'Again?'

'There are so many things I need to sort out, Pam.'

'What . . . sort of things?'

'The politics in Washington, the supplies for Russia.' Another sigh, deeper, more fractured. 'My wife.'

A silence. Then: 'What do you have to sort out with her?'

'We've scarcely seen each other for months.'

'I thought you lived – what's the term you used? – separate lives.'

'We're still married, Pamela. There are formalities to be observed, arrangements to be discussed. Practical things. And family things, too. We don't want gossip, and I don't want to humiliate her.' The words came without hesitation, almost as if he had practised them.

'Are you beginning to regret all this? Me?'

'No, but . . .'

Ah, so there was a 'but'.

'You still love her.'

'Do you still love Randy?'

'No.' She'd never had to answer that question before, not even to herself. She was surprised how easily it came.

'But . . .' – that word again – 'I've been married to her for a long time. Did you expect –'

'No.'

'Pam, you haven't fallen –'

'No!'

'There can't be any future between us, can there?'

Time for a tear to fall in the darkness before, once again, more softly: 'No.'

'Perhaps I should go back to my room.'

'No.' She reached for him, determined not to let him go. 'If this has to be our last night, let's not swim in sad thoughts.' She laid a kiss, gently, upon his cheek.

'I'm sorry, Pam.'

'Don't be. I'm not. Why should I be? But I've never forgotten what Papa once said: that war is the most ferocious mistress of them all.'

'He said that?'

'He also told me that no good would come of our relationship.'

A soft cry of alarm: 'He knows, too?'

'Yes.'

'How?'

'I told him.'

'Christ . . .'

'Does that bother you?'

'How can he continue to treat me as a friend?'

'Because you are his friend.'

Suddenly what had seemed to be their tightly held secret had become a public drama. Soon others would know. Harriman had persuaded himself he could control this relationship; now it was all growing much more complicated.

He needed the break back home, to recover his energy, and to think about things.

He turned. The bed creaked. And another sound.

'Did you hear anything, Averell?'

'No. What?'

'I thought . . . like a squeaking floorboard. Outside.'

'Old houses always creak.'

'You, too, I think, you poor goose. Come here.'

The last weeks of October came laden not simply with caviar, but with sorrows.

It wasn't only what had been happening in Russia, although the headlines were lurid enough with their images of German hordes gathering for a final assault on Moscow. The Soviet Government had already moved out of the capital. From the shores of the Black Sea all the way to the frosty Baltic a thousand miles north, hope was fading.

Churchill could always maintain – and did – that by this date in his invasion Napoleon was already stabling his horses in the palaces of Moscow; Hitler was behind schedule, slowed down by the mists and the rivers of blood.

Yet it wasn't so much events in Russia that captured his attention. As Churchill had feared, the Government of Prince Fumimaro Konoye in Tokyo had crumbled in disarray, eaten away by its own uncertainties. The quarrels that had ebbed and flowed behind the gates of the Imperial Palace had suddenly burst forth onto the public scene in a manner the Japanese found demeaning but weren't able to prevent. The rivalries could no longer be suppressed; the decencies were swept aside, and with them so was the prince. It was, according to the headline that dominated the main page of *The Times*, the nation's 'Greatest Crisis'.

As he devoured the pages for every glimmering of news, Churchill couldn't fail to notice that the reports from Tokyo contained many words about how the Japanese might extend the hand of compromise towards America, yet about Britain there was barely a mention. For the Japanese, Britain was irrelevant. 'No, no, you blasted heathens, not irrelevant,' he swore to himself. 'Impotent, we may be. But never irrelevant!'

Within hours, it had grown much worse. The bald, bespectacled General Tojo had taken over. His Cabinet consisted mostly of military men.

On the same day – was there never any respite? – the announcement came of another attack on a US Navy ship. The destroyer USS *Kearny* had been torpedoed while on patrol to the south-west of Iceland. She was a ship of war bearing the Stars and Stripes, and her outline, nationality, purpose were clear even through the dirtiest periscope. This wasn't a case of mistaken identity but an act of deliberate aggression – and a bloody one, too. The *Kearny* didn't sink, but she crawled into port with eleven bodies on board, victims of the Reich. The first American servicemen to die in the war.

Deliberate. Deadly. And still it made no difference. Roosevelt would not ask the Congress to declare war. It was the sort of incident that had caused the United States to declare war in 1917, but that was precisely why so many Americans now chose to ignore it.

Harriman wrote to Churchill within days of his return to Washington: 'The news on Saturday of the torpedoing of the *Kearny* did not cause even a ripple. It seemed that the public had expected – and were thoroughly prepared for – such occurrences . . . It is not at all clear what or when something will happen to kick us into it. As to opinion regarding Britain,' he continued, 'people are wondering why you don't do something offensively.'

Soon after dictating his note, Harriman fell sick, and went back to his wife.

Days later, a U-boat torpedoed the USS *Reuben James*. She wasn't so very different from the *Kearny*, another destroyer escorting a convoy in a similar part of the Atlantic. Except the *Reuben James* wasn't simply attacked, she sank, and took with her one hundred and fifteen American sailors.

And still they refused to declare war.

THIRTEEN

On the second day of the new month of November the Domei, the official Japanese news agency, issued a statement. It stated bluntly that Japan was completing her war structure in expectation of an armed clash in the Pacific. The Domei reported that the armed clash was 'inevitable', and attributed the remark to well-informed sources within the Government.

Such an outcome could only be averted, the Domei went on to say, if the United States eased the economic pressures on Japan, 'otherwise Japan will be compelled to seek her essential supplies elsewhere, whatever the consequences.'

The agency went on to emphasize that on no account was it possible for Japan to maintain her relations with America on the present basis. Things would have to change. It predicted that the Prime Minister, General Tojo, would announce in his speech to the Diet that he would impose a strict time limit to any negotiations with America. It seemed that whoever had supplied the story to the Domei clearly knew the Prime Minister's mind.

And it was also emphasized that Tojo had again been received by the Emperor. This made it clear that whatever the Prime Minister said, whatever was to happen, had already been given the imperial seal of approval.

The Domei concluded by stating that if the American

economic blockade against Japan continued, Japan would have to dare to seek supplies of materials from elsewhere. Such an action would be a vital measure of self-defence.

It outlined precisely what this 'daring-to-seek' policy would involve. It meant 'breaking through the encirclement of hostile nations.'

It meant war. But against whom? The Domei did not say.

He was alone on the roof of the Annexe, dressed in his over-coat. His shoulders were hunched and he was at the parapet, looking westward into the setting sun.

He held a sheaf of papers in his hand. They were the text of the President's latest speech.

'What more do I have to do? What in the name of all the gods do I have to do?' Churchill whispered, gripping the papers so malevolently that it seemed as if he was trying to throttle the life from of them.

'Damn the torpedoes and full speed ahead!' the President had announced to his people. Oh, the man sat in front of his fire and wrapped himself in such fine phrases – phrases that Churchill would be proud to call his own. But then he sat back in his wheelchair, and watched the flames die and the hearth grow cold.

Slowly, Churchill let the President's words slip from his fingers. They drifted lazily away in the still evening air.

He was watching them disappear when there was an inter-ruption from behind. A breathless duty clerk arrived bearing an anxious smile and a note.

'Well?' Churchill snapped.

'Report from Tokyo, sir.' The fellow beamed. He was young, new, keen, from the Foreign Office, and had welcomed the suggestion from the Downing Street private secretary that he take the note up to the rooftop himself. 'The Japs,' the clerk said enthusiastically, 'they want to negotiate.'

Instantly the note was snatched from his hand and Churchill fumbled for his reading glasses in various pockets, but they proved suddenly elusive. Irritated, he thrust the note back at him. 'Read!'

'It's a news agency report,' he began, quoting. '"Hopes of maintaining peace in the Pacific have risen with a bound with the announcement that the Japanese Government have decided to send Mr Saburo Kurusu, one of the country's most experienced diplomatists . . . to Washington. To assist the Ambassador, Admiral Nomura. In crucial talks. Seen in Japan as holding out high hopes of a positive results."' The clerk lifted his head from the paper. 'The American State Department has welcomed the move, sir.'

'You are from the Foreign Office, are you not?'

'Yes, sir.'

'You embrace diplomacy, do you not?'

'I try, sir.'

'You are taught the virtues of conciliation and compromise, are you not?'

'Most certainly, sir.'

'Do you know that in a long and diverse career I have held most of the high offices of state?'

'Absolutely, Mr Churchill!'

'Except for the Foreign Office.' Churchill paused. 'Why do you think that is?'

Suddenly the eager expression had vanished from the clerk's face. He felt as though the rooftop had melted beneath his feet and he was tumbling, a little like Alice, into a bottomless pit.

'Young man, you are an ass. This war won't be won through the virtues of compromise and conciliation, or by splitting the difference or even dividing your sister in two and offering half of her up to our enemies. It'll only encourage them to come back for the other half soon as dammit. Their appetite is insatiable. Didn't your father teach you the simplest facts of life?'

'Sir?'

'It's not by splitting the difference that we shall win this war but by hacking our enemies in two and roasting the separate bits in the flames of eternal hell. The only good news that can come out of Japan is that all their Government and military chiefs have committed ritual bloody suicide. That includes Mr . . .'

'Kurusu, sir.'

'May his blade be sharp.'

'But what if he can agree peace?' the young diplomatist persisted. 'Wouldn't that make it worthwhile?'

'The only means by which his trip can achieve peace is if his plane is shot from the skies as soon as it reaches American airspace. Then, perhaps, they might be deterred. By force, by strength, by a sign that at last America intends to hurl back any insult or aggression with a hundred times its force. Then we might have peace.'

'The Americans have welcomed . . .'

'Ah, Rip van Winkle rolls over in his bed to make room for the Wop of the Pacific!'

'Sir?'

'Now you know why they never asked me to be Foreign Secretary.'

'Yes, sir. I mean . . .'

'Bugger off, young man.'

'Th . . . thank you, sir.'

As the young man disappeared, a huge fist of starlings rose from the park and lunged into the air, wheeling and sweeping across the darkening sky as they prepared to abandon London. Churchill, alone once more, continued his vigil, a lonely helmsman, staring westward until the sun had gone down.

Every year, by invitation, the Prime Minister came to the City of London to join in the ceremonies to honour the newly appointed Lord Mayor. In normal times it was a colourful pageant, but these were not normal times and there was little colour in the affair, only remorseless shades of grey and shining, rain-licked pavements that glistened like fish skin.

He drove with Pamela through streets that were unrecognizable from a year earlier. One third of the entire City of London lay in ruins more profound than those of Pompeii. Much that had once stood was now waste, and everything that still stood was broken and smeared with soot and scorchmarks.

The crowds were sparse; there was no heart to the City any more. They had cleared up most of the wreckage caused by the bombers, but it had left many acres razed and empty. Sir Christopher Wren had built sixteen splendid churches within the Square Mile, now only six were left. The rest were nothing but heaps of charred stone. Bow Bells had been destroyed, the Tower of London hit fifteen times, so much had gone.

There were family groups amongst the onlookers; the parents managed to wave, but the children stared in curiosity, their heads hanging like waifs from a charcoal sketch by Lowry. They looked thin.

'These are my people, Pamela,' he said. 'Will they ever forgive me?'

'Papa?'

'I cannot win this war on my own.'

'You're not alone.' She took his arm, but he did not hear.

'And if I do not win the war, what has all this been for?' He stared at the devastation around him. 'A whole world betrayed.'

'Not by you.'

'The Japanese threaten, and Roosevelt turns his back. The Germans lash out, and he runs away.'

'Averell thinks he'll never ask Congress to declare war. He's afraid that if he does, they'll refuse, and the consequences then would be appalling. So better as we are.'

'A leader who runs not only from the enemy, but from his own people!' He did not try to hide his contempt.

'Averell sent me a clipping of an opinion poll. So few Americans support their getting involved in a shooting war that they'd have trouble raising a baseball team.'

'You had a letter from Averell?'

'Yes, Papa. And one from Randolph.'

'Ah, I see. Then I suspect I'm not the only one carrying their troubles this evening.'

'Randolph says he's very happy with his promotion. A full colonel.'

'And perhaps the additional pay will assist him to clear his wretched debts.' Roosevelt. Randolph. All sympathy appeared to have been squeezed from the old man's heart. There was room in his life for nothing but the winning of this war. Looking out of the window, it was not difficult to understand why.

They were drawing near to their destination. Ordinarily they would have gathered at the Guildhall, a splendid medieval structure that served as the City's Parliament and was exceeded in magnificence only by the Great Hall at Westminster. But now it had burnt to a shell. So instead they would use the Mansion House, the residence of the Lord Mayor. It was a mere newcomer on the City scene, less than two hundred years old, and it lacked the soul of the Guildhall. But at least it still had its roof.

'When the whole world insists that you are wrong, Pamela, isn't there at least the smallest chance they are right?' he asked as the car drew to a halt.

'I remember what the world said at the time of Dunkirk, Papa, when they said Britain couldn't fight on alone, that you should stop the fight and do a deal.'

'We may soon be on our own again, and this time it will be so very much worse.'

'There comes a point where the arguments have to be put aside and you reach down deep within yourself to rely on instinct.'

'What, put aside all reason, all morality – and rely on instinct?' He turned on her, troubled, wanting to test his own feelings through hers.

'I'm not sure I'm the one to lecture you about morality. All I know is that you must be true to yourself, Papa. Above all, reach down within yourself and be true to what you find.'

'And what do I do if, when I burrow down so deep, I meet the Devil halfway?'

Then he was out of the car and gone.

Many men had gathered to listen to his words in the Mansion House – not just the City men of money but twenty members of Churchill's own Government, the three Chiefs of Staff and even the Archbishop of Canterbury – God, State and Mammon, all come to judge. As Churchill rose to address them, his eye caught upon the gaping cracks that ran through the plasterwork and the naked brickwork that disfigured many of the walls. There were ragged holes and patched windows, and beneath him rows of worn faces. These people needed reassurance, yet he had so little to give.

'Alike in times of peace and war, the annual civic festival we have observed today has been, by long custom, the occasion for a speech at the Guildhall by the Prime Minister upon foreign affairs,' he began. 'This year our ancient Guildhall lies in ruins. Our foreign affairs are shrunken, and almost the whole of Europe is prostrate under the Nazi tyranny.'

This was not what they wanted to hear, but those seated in front of him today were not his main audience. They couldn't know it, but they were no more than his supporting cast. They had been brought together to give his message a little weight, but his message would have wings, too – radio technicians had erected a bank of microphones in front of him, and pressmen sat at a table to one side. His words would reach every corner of the planet.

'The condition of Europe is terrible in the last degree,' he continued. 'Hitler's firing parties are busy every day in a dozen countries. Norwegians, Belgians, Frenchmen, Dutch, Poles, Czechs, Serbs, Croats, Slovenes, Greeks' – his voice lifted up the names like the tolling of a great bell – 'and above all in scale Russians, are being butchered by thousands – and by tens of thousands – after they have surrendered, while individual and mass executions have become part of the regular German routine.'

As he spoke, a cloud of dust broke away from the cracked plaster ceiling and settled upon the dark varnish of the rostrum and the table around him. The Lord Mayor's wife pulled out a handkerchief and began to wipe it away.

'A river of blood has flowed and is flowing between the German race and the peoples of nearly all Europe. It is not

278

the hot blood of battle, where good blows are given and returned. It is the cold blood of the execution yard and the scaffold, which leaves a stain indelible for generations and for centuries.'

They were beginning to warm up, slowly, nodding their heads. His voice rose in anger at the enemy.

'Here, then, are the foundations upon which the "new order" of Europe is to be inaugurated. Here, then, is the house-warming festival of the *Herrenvolk*. Here, then, is the system of terrorism by which the Nazi criminals and their quisling accomplices seek to rule a dozen ancient, famous states of Europe, and if possible all the free nations of the world.'

His hand slapped the rostrum, more dust rose. And he promised them that never – *never* – would the future of Europe be confided to such bloodstained, accursed hands.

Now they applauded, but he cared little for it, for he was soon to come to the most critical part of his speech. He recounted to them the stories of some of their naval successes in the Mediterranean and Atlantic. Then he told them that he intended to go still further.

'Owing to the effective help we are getting from the United States, owing to the sinking of the *Bismarck*, owing to the completion of our splendid new battleships and aircraft carriers of the largest size, I am able to announce to you . . .' – his eyes lifted; they waited on his words – 'that we now feel ourselves strong enough to provide a powerful naval force of heavy ships, with the necessary auxiliary vessels, for service if needed in the Indian and Pacific Oceans.'

They cheered lustily. Britannia still ruled the waves.

'This movement of our naval forces, in conjunction with the United States Main Fleet, may give practical proof, to all who have eyes to see, that the forces of freedom and democracy have not by any means reached the limits of their power!'

More cheering. And it might have seemed to many as if the US Navy was joining in. But his words were ambiguous, deliberately so, and the British fleet was not quite what it seemed. The backbone of the force was supposed to be a carrier that would provide it with air cover. Yet the *Indomitable*, which had been marked for the job, had run aground on a Caribbean reef. Silly, these things happen, but without it the Admiralty protested that the other ships shouldn't be sent. They would be too vulnerable. The First Sea Lord made a considerable fuss about it at the Defence Committee and strongly urged delay. But Churchill had insisted. If there was to be any chance of deterring the Japanese, the ships had to go now, otherwise it would be too late. It was time to gamble.

'I must admit that, having voted for the Japanese Alliance nearly forty years ago – in 1902,' he told his audience, 'and having always done my very best to promote good relations with the island empire of Japan, and always having been a sentimental well-wisher to the Japanese and an admirer of their many gifts and qualities, I should view with keen sorrow the opening of a conflict between Japan and the English-speaking world.'

'Keen sorrow'? A strange use of terms. But his tone suggested a measure of confidence. After all, he had talked not just of Britain but of 'the English-speaking world'. What did he mean by that? He left barely a breath before he removed any measure of doubt.

'The United States' time-honoured interests in the Far East are well known.'

He paused, then paused some more, catching their eyes and compelling their attention. He needed them to know that whichever else of his words they listened to, these were the words they must heed.

'The United States are doing their utmost to find ways of

preserving peace in the Pacific. We do not know whether their efforts will be successful.' A pessimistic shake of the head, another pause. 'But should they fail, I take this occasion to say – and it is my duty to say . . .' – he looked across to where the reporters sat, their faces expectant, their pencils poised, his voice now an uplifting rumble of defiance – 'that should the United States become involved in war with Japan, the British declaration will follow – within the hour!'

The whole hall began to cheer, loudly, and pound their fists upon the tables, even the jaded men of the press. It was an automatic response, almost like a football crowd, supporting the team, no matter what the odds, because they had only one team to support. When, later, they began to think about what he had said, they would realize that they were bound for yet more agonies and suffering. As if there weren't already enough cracks in their ceilings. And when they had thought about it some more, they would begin to wonder about the Americans. Were they part of this pact? If Britain were forced to declare war, would the Americans follow?

It was the greatest question of Churchill's time. In this hour, in this place of ruins, he had begun his game that would decide the future of the world. In the note he had handed to Harriman, he had set out a course of action in three parts. A British naval force sent to the Far East. A larger American naval force to follow. And a joint declaration of war against Japan.

Churchill had begun to deliver. The question for him – and even more so for the Japanese – was how well America would play the game, too.

Words, words, words. Sometimes a man has nothing else to fight with. Throughout his years in the wilderness Churchill had laid into his own Government with little more than the breath in his body. Then, through the first terrible year of war, he seemed to have held back the bombers and the invasion barges with little more than rhetoric. When he spoke, the world had learnt to listen. And he was counting on that.

There were many who felt the full thunder of his words during these days, not just hapless Foreign Office clerks but Ministers, editors, colleagues and friends. No man could take the strain that Churchill bore without cracks appearing in his countenance. And on Armistice Day they were placed on display for all to see.

Sir Waldron Smithers was a backbench Member of Parliament, a man of dedicated appetites that centred mainly around religion and alcohol. He visited both regularly. So when he and another colleague rose in the House of Commons to ask a pointed question about the salary paid to one of Churchill's closest advisers, Lord Cherwell, implying that he might even have German origins, the Prime Minister made no attempt to hide his temper. He was bloody, he was bellicose, he made a point of treating the questions with the utmost impatience and contempt.

But the matter was not to be left there.

Later that day, Sir Waldron was sitting in a leather-encrusted corner of the Smoking Room, the place where Members of Parliament retired for refreshment and gossip. It was crowded as usual, but Sir Waldron was alone at his table.

He became aware of a shadow falling across his life. He looked up to find Churchill, shaking like an infuriated bull.

'Why in the Hell did you ask that question?' Churchill roared. 'Don't you know he's one of my oldest and greatest friends?'

The entire room fell silent. All eyes were fixed upon Smithers. His lower jaw began to drop.

282

'But Winston, I . . .'

'Don't "Winston" me. I'm the bloody Prime Minister and I'm fighting a war to save this country,' he bellowed. 'I don't get up in the morning expecting much help from people like you, but neither will I put up with idle sniping from those who know even less about running this war than they do about holding their drink.'

Smithers was transfixed. He hadn't even got to his feet, and wouldn't be able to now; his knees were gently buckling. He pushed away his brandy and ginger. 'Prime Minister, I can assure you of my total personal loyalty and . . .'

But there was little point in protesting. He had already been condemned without chance of reprieve.

'You attack Cherwell, you attack me!'

'I really don't think that anything I said –'

'That's your trouble,' Churchill shouted, driving right through him. 'Damn well didn't think about anything you said!'

The knight from the shires was still trying to splutter his innocence when Churchill turned his back and stormed out.

As *The Times* reported, 'The House got the impression that Mr Churchill is not in the mood for any gentle handling of critics of the Government.'

The dark cloud was still hanging over him on the following day when the King opened the new session of Parliament. The ceremony was traditionally followed by a debate in the House of Commons but, uniquely, on this occasion it took place on the floor of the House of Lords. The peers had taken pity on their commoner cousins and had moved out of their own chamber so that the elected politicians could meet once more within the precincts of the Parliament building. This new home was a far more splendid affair than the Commons, its leather benches the colour of imperial claret rather than insipid green and surrounded by gilt that sparkled even on the darkest of days. The place had an altogether more relaxed atmosphere – until Churchill rose to his feet.

'Mr Speaker, sir,' he opened with a gruff voice and more than a hint of impatience, 'it has been aptly remarked that Ministers, and indeed all other public men, when they make speeches at the present time, have always to bear in mind three audiences: one our own fellow countrymen, secondly, our friends abroad, and thirdly, the enemy.'

He glared around him, as if to remind them that in his view the enemy was not necessarily confined to foreign shores.

'This naturally makes the task of public speaking very difficult,' he continued, 'and I hope that those who feel that their war work lies especially in the direction of criticism will make allowances for these difficulties inherent in the situation.'

They laughed, but his own taut smile suggested Churchill found little humour in the situation. His eyes caught Hore-Belisha, and said something very rude.

'I hope they will also remember that no sensible person in wartime makes speeches because he wants to. He makes them because he has to, and to no one does this apply more than the Prime Minister.' More glares. He didn't want to be here, and he wanted them to know that.

'No, I tell you, it is impossible to please everybody. Whatever you say, some fault can be found . . . In war it is very hard to bring about successes, and very easy to make mistakes' – another profound glare – 'or to point them out when mistakes have been made.'

Some Members began to shuffle uneasily. This was neither elegant nor inspiring; what was its point?

'There was a custom in ancient China that anyone who wished to criticize the Government could have the right to criticize, *provided* . . .' – he stuck his thumbs belligerently inside his waistcoat – 'he followed that up by committing suicide. Very great respect was paid to his words, and no ulterior motive was assigned. That seems to me to have been, from many points of view, a wise custom.'

He was beating them, flaying them for what he suggested was disloyalty. And throughout his speech he continued to give them back their own weight in criticism. It was petulant, a crusty old man barking at those who had the temerity to snap at his heels. He even attacked the *Daily Herald* for some grudging comment it had made about Christmas dinners. It had probably not been intended as a personal slight but Churchill took it as such, and replied at extraordinary length.

It seemed strange that at a moment when the world was about to lose its grip on its self-control, the great man should insist on going on – and on, and on, as he did – about potatoes and sugar beet, dairy cows and meat cattle, even finding a mention for the humble chicken. It was the old man at his least gracious – and yet, though severely stretched in spirit and body, Churchill hadn't lost sight of his objective. At the very start of his speech he had set out the proposition that his words would be listened to, not simply by friends at home and abroad, but also by their enemies. That had also been the point of his speech earlier in the week at the Mansion House. Now he was going to provide something for the enemy to chew on.

'There is nothing that Hitler will dislike more than my recital of these prosaic but unassailable facts. There is nothing that he and his Nazi regime dread more than the proof that we are capable of fighting a prolonged war, and the proof of the failure of their efforts to starve us into submission.'

There was no transcending oratory in this – Hitler didn't

285

deserve the honour of fine phrases. But now Churchill came to his point.

'In the various remarks which the Deputy Fuehrer, Herr Hess, has let fall from time to time during his sojourn in our midst, nothing has been more clear than that Hitler relied upon the starvation attack even more than upon the invasion to bring us to our knees. His hopes were centred upon starvation, as his boasts have made the world aware. So far as 1941 at least is concerned, those hopes have been dashed to the ground.'

And that was it. It wasn't so much about food, but about Rudolf Hess. Almost Churchill's first words on the matter since the man had arrived six months earlier. Hitler would pick up on that, of course. Now in Berlin they would hear the words of defiance, the insistence that Britain was still resolute. Yet what they would remember more than anything else was the news that Hitler's right-hand man, Rudolf Hess, was still alive and, tantalizingly, still talking.

What he was talking about, Churchill was content to leave to Adolf Hitler's peculiarly febrile imagination.

'I feel so wretched tired, Sawyers.'

Winter. The last of the leaves were gone and an insistent east wind slid through gaps around the ill-fitting window. For once he was glad of the thick blackout curtain. The window rattled, the curtain shivered in the draught, and so did Churchill.

'I'll fetch Nelson,' the valet said.

'I'll need more than a bloody cat. Light me a fire, would you, Sawyers?' The plea seemed uncharacteristically plaintive.

'Hot toddy. That'll do the trick,' the valet suggested, tucking in a trailing blanket.

'I heard someone say that alcohol cools the body down.'

286

'Also sends you to sleep. So's you won't notice, like.'

'In Russia, the snows have begun to fall and the ice has taken its grip on the war. They say that bodies are being found – German bodies – frozen to death. Dressed in women's furs. You understand what that means?'

'Best be sticking to proper underwear, me mother would say.'

'No, you fool. It means Hitler isn't prepared. He's forgotten his history. He's not ready to meet the challenge of camping out upon the frozen steppes through the onslaught of winter.' He pulled the blanket up around his chest. 'It is a game of Russian roulette. The invader always loses. Forfeits everything. It is the disaster of Napoleon all over again.'

'Then I'd best be fetching toddy – and Nelson, too. Fer luck.'

The *Prince of Wales* was the most modern of ships. Thirty-five thousand tons of marine malice that had been commissioned less than eight months previously. She was so new that when she had sailed into action against the *Bismarck* she still had civilian fitters on board; then she had sailed for Placentia Bay with the Prime Minister and secured her place in history. Her life had been brief, but already the *Prince of Wales* was the most famous battleship afloat.

The entire world knew of her intentions – Churchill had made sure of that. Her route would take her to Freetown in west Africa and Cape Town in South Africa on her way to the Far East, with every stop accompanied by a blaze of publicity. Yet, while this greatest of British battleships was still making her way through the grinding tropical heat, on the far side of the world another naval force was being brought together in absolute secrecy.

Tankan Bay in the bleak and frozen Kurile Islands to the north of the Japanese mainland formed an excellent rendezvous. It was well away from prying eyes and at that time of year was shrouded in mists and snowstorms. Here they gathered: the aircraft carriers *Akagi* and *Kaga*, *Zuikaku*, *Hiryu* and *Soryu*, the battleships *Hiei* and *Kirishima*, plus cruisers, destroyers and tankers, thirty surface ships in all, accompanied by many submarines. Last to arrive was a sixth carrier, the *Shokaku*. She had taken such care to fool any onlookers of her intentions that she was almost late. All these ships had slipped quietly away from their stations, one by one so as not to arouse suspicions, making it seem as though they were on independent and unexceptional missions.

Now they had come together beneath the snow-capped mountains of the bay, the most powerful carrier strike force ever assembled, swallowed up by the vastness of the cold northerly sea. As winter winds blew around them, the Japanese Navy kept complete radio silence, switched their engines to winter oil and chipped away at the accumulating ice while they waited for their orders.

It happened somewhere between Manchester and Birmingham on the way south. They were travelling on Churchill's new train, which made them all feel a little like royalty. The train had been put together to enable him to travel long distances in relative safety, and consisted of several panelled coaches. There was space for a dozen staff to sleep and work, a well-appointed dining room, a kitchen, diesel generator, and a carriage set aside for the exclusive use of the Prime Minister that included a bedroom, sitting room and bathroom. There was a pattern to his trips.

288

Overnight they loitered near some convenient tunnel, just in case of an air raid, while the days were spent in broken towns, witnessing scenes that were as harrowing as any in London, and trying to reassure the inhabitants. Everywhere his presence seemed to revive them, just as their response seemed to lift him from his own sorrows. He delivered impromptu speeches through a megaphone, conducted chaotic walks through pressing crowds, his cigar clamped firmly in his jaw and his hat raised upon his stick for all to see, just as they expected. 'Never, never, never let us be downhearted,' he had told them that morning. 'And if the Luftwaffe insist on coming back for a return match, let's hope next time they get the tax office!' They were able to enjoy that. They hadn't suffered as much as the East End of London.

Clemmie had been unwell, so he had asked Pamela to accompany him. While she was on the trip she had taken the opportunity to visit Randolph's constituency at Preston – 'Just to remind you that we Churchills haven't forgotten,' she had told them.

Yet, back in the privacy of his own carriage, the old man's confidence seemed to wane and the brightness melted from his eyes. Something was disturbing him and it was digging away at his confidence.

Pamela sat in the armchair opposite him; the rest of the company, sensitive to his mood, seemed to have discovered important work that required their attention elsewhere. For some time he said nothing, gazing sadly at the fleeting scenes of England as they flashed past the window, his coffee and his papers left undisturbed, paying Pamela no attention.

Eventually he stirred. 'Averell will be back in a few days.'

'Will he?' She sounded coy.

Another mile passed before he spoke again.

'He's been away so long.'

'With his wife.' It slipped out – she hadn't intended it to – and there was no disguising the hurt.

'Who told you that?'

'He did.'

It hadn't bothered her so much at first, but as the weeks apart had dragged on it had come to be more difficult for her to deal with. She couldn't get him out of her mind, yet now the images were of him with his wife, a woman she had never seen but who somehow had managed to burn her way deep within Pamela's imagination.

'We shall have him at Chequers this weekend,' Churchill said.

'I can't.'

'Why not?'

'I'm committed elsewhere.'

'On his first weekend back?'

'Papa, it's over.'

'But . . .'

'Averell feels it's inappropriate.'

'Why?'

'Because of you.'

'Pamela, I'm so . . .'

'So sorry?'

He knew his position was absurd. Another mile passed in silence. He took refuge in his coffee; he was glad to notice that Sawyers had spiked it with rum.

'You seem so sad,' he suggested.

She shook her head defiantly.

'He still writes to you, Pamela?'

'Pen pals. Silly really, when there's such a shortage of paper.'

'Nevertheless, I wish you'd come this weekend.'

'I don't think that would be wise.'

'Pamela, I want you to come. Very much.' His words were slow, insistent.

'I can't.'

'You – must.'

'Papa?'

Silence. More coffee. Torment filled his eyes.

'Papa, have I got this right? Do you realize what you are asking me to do?' she whispered, incredulous.

'Nothing that is not within your heart to do,' he said ponderously. 'I ask nothing that you would not want. But, my dear Pamela, I cannot emphasize enough how important it might be.'

'Papa? Have I misunderstood? You want me to sleep with Averell.'

He did not – could not – respond.

'What sort of father are you?' It wasn't a taunt or a criticism, simply a question born of bewilderment.

The train was travelling through the foothills of the Pennines. Outside the countryside was bleak, bitten by frost.

'In some ways I am father to an entire country. Sometimes I must put personal feelings aside.' He couldn't look at her, his eyes clinging desperately to the images of his beloved country as they flashed by.

'Go with Averell – for you?'

'For England.'

'What sort of woman do you think I am?'

'Pamela . . .' Suddenly he seemed tired, and very old. 'I see you as a woman much like my own mother. A woman so full of love and the many joys of existence that your life will never be contained within just one channel – or through just one man. For myself, I have always walked a more conventional path, and never strayed from it. Whether Clemmie has been so sure of foot, I do not know and have preferred never to enquire. Ah, but my darling Mama . . .' He sighed, and already his eyes had softened. 'I remember the day when I had been sent home from school with a fever. My nanny, Mrs Everest, put me straight to bed and I wasn't expected to rise for several days. But children can be so fickle. In the morning I felt very much recovered, so I rose from my sickbed and came down to breakfast. Papa was away – had been away already a long time. In India. And there was another man at the breakfast table. A European called Count Charles Kinsky – I was to get to know him well. Grew to like him. Yet there they were, that first time, sharing my father's breakfast table and . . . laughing. I suddenly realized it had been a long time since I'd heard my mother laugh. I wasn't old enough to understand these things, but later, when I did, when comprehension of what I had witnessed dawned upon me and my heart flooded with all the turbulent emotions that such episodes inspire, I was always left with that sparkling, vibrant memory of my beautiful Mama and her laughter.'

Tears were tumbling onto his waistcoat.

'I loved my mother, and I loved her no less for loving others. And I grew to love her all the more for having the courage to be the woman she had to be. And you, Pamela, are so very much like my darling Mama.'

They were both in tears now.

'We Churchills are not always so very good at these family things,' he sobbed.

'No, Papa – but at least we try. And perhaps they will say we had other qualities.'

'Not unless we win. At the end of the day, everything comes down to that, Pamela. Victory.'

'But how will my sleeping with Averell . . . ?'

'I have asked for your absolute trust. So I feel I must show that my trust in you is absolute, too.' He searched around to make sure they were still alone. 'You see, there is something else, my darling Pamela. Something that I shall explain to you, which I beg you never, never to repeat to another soul.'

And, as the rain began to fall, slashing its way across the window of the train and casting mean, grey shadows across the land, he leant forward and began to tell her what no one else knew.

FOURTEEN

Harriman's B-17 dropped down through the clouds on the last leg of the journey from New York to Northolt. As the familiar green fields of the English countryside appeared outside the window, a knot of anticipation began to twist inside his stomach. He'd been away four weeks – too long. He'd grown used to the stimulus of living life on the edge in a Britain at war, and as a consequence had begun to develop a contempt for much of what he had found in Washington, where senatorial chickens ran headless through the farmyard in fear of a fox that hadn't left its lair. His time at home in New York hadn't helped. He had required a surgical operation, an abscess in his gut, and his wife had nursed him dutifully, but they were like an elderly couple sitting on the stoop of their house with nothing much to say to each other. He knew there was another man in her life, while she understood that he wanted desperately to be back in England rather than in her bed. There was no animosity or ill language, just a hollowness that, for Harriman, could only be filled by returning to the war. At home he slept on pillows of Egyptian cotton and goose down, yet it left him aching for the experience of shaking bomb dust from his hair and feeling the indescribable joy of knowing he had survived one more attempt to kill him.

295

While he was in New York he had yearned to be back amongst this slow, stubborn race they called Britons. The last day spent with his wife had been his fiftieth birthday; there was no celebration.

Now, from the aircraft window, he could see England, its patchwork fields, red-tiled roofs, smoking chimneys, hangars, aircraft, men, and as they dropped lower he could even pick out the colours of their uniforms. Then the wheels touched, bounced, and touched again. He was back. And the knot in his stomach began to unwind.

An official car was chasing the aircraft as it slowed down, pulling alongside as the Boeing finally came to rest. He stepped a little wearily down the rickety ladder from the plane, one hand clamped on his hat, the other clutching his briefcase, and was glad to see an army driver waiting for him, holding open the rear door.

He ducked his head to climb into the back and was startled to hear the voice that greeted him.

'Hello, Mr Harriman.'

'Pamela? But . . .'

'I suspect you feel like a rest, but it's off to Chequers for you. The Prime Minister insists. And as you already know, we Churchills are an insistent family.'

The men had dined together, just the two of them, in privacy and with so much passion that Harriman soon found himself in some disarray. The old man had never seemed more pleased to see him, more eager to interrogate, and never more ardent about everything he said. Harriman felt as if he were being pounded by human artillery. The pressure was relieved only by Sawyers, who seemed more than ever assiduous, never allowing the American's glass to empty.

296

'The talks – with Kurusu. How are they treating him?' Churchill demanded, slurping at his glass in impatience.

'Cautiously.'

'But will they concede. Will they compromise?'

'Some want to, Winston. Others are more determined.'

'They must not give an inch or show him any sign of weakness.' He waved his knife like a bayonet. 'Kick him out! Otherwise Japan will pick us off one by one. Us for a starter and you for the main course.'

'They feel they have to listen, Winston.'

'But they must not! To listen is to delay, and to delay is to fall into their trap. Every day that passes, Japan moves closer to war.'

'There are those in Washington who argue we must grasp at even the smallest glimmering of peace.'

'And by so doing they invite the most catastrophic consequences and uncompromising war. They will be betrayed, those peacemongers, by their own good intentions. Even Christ came to the point when he was forced to kick the moneylenders out of the temple. Force – the only language Tojo and his thieves will understand!'

'The Senate disagrees.'

'Men who have never been so proud as to allow rank failure to ruin them!' Churchill exploded. 'American ships are being blown out of the water and yet still they haggle about the flimsiest detail.' He had a chicken bone in his fingers and was flicking morsels of food across the tablecloth. He was also spilling his wine; Sawyers rescued the bottle and refilled his glass, Harriman's too.

'But there are those who want to fight, Winston. Who realize we shall have to.'

'And the President – what of Mr Roosevelt? He talked the other day about liberty and freedom and democracy, and how those great gifts are retained only by those who are willing to fight for them. Fine, fine words.'

'Which come with big problems. Not just in the Senate, but with strikes. Coal. Steel. The labour unions have him by the balls. The President calls for more effort, they call for more pay.'

'Some say this war is being decided before the gates of Moscow, but I disagree. It will be decided in Washington. And in places like Poughkeepsie and Pittsburgh.'

'In their present mood, they may choose not to fight.'

'Men don't always get a choice.'

'Meaning?'

'The Russians didn't choose to fight the Nazis, Averell, any more than I choose to fight the Japanese. But I may have to, nonetheless. It's the way of war.'

'Most people in Washington think it unlikely that the Japs will attack an American target. More likely to be you.'

'And if they do, if they do – will America declare war, within the hour?'

'If it were left to the President alone, I think yes. But Poughkeepsie and Pittsburgh?' Harriman shrugged.

And so it went on throughout the meal, as if through willpower alone Churchill intended to drag America from its slough of indifference. Sawyers danced deftly around him, retrieving lost food, repairing dismembered desserts, making sure most of the wine remained in their glasses. Harriman became a little confused – there seemed to be so many glasses in front of him – it was as though he were back in the Kremlin. And, a little like Stalin, the man who was now sitting opposite him was full of vices and seemed so keen to parade them all. Yet over the months Harriman had also come to understand Churchill's more complex virtues, his strength of vision, his relentlessness, his courage, his ability to love his country more profoundly than any man Harriman had ever met. As the dinner progressed the American grew increasingly puddle-headed – the long plane journey, or perhaps Sawyers had got him a little drunk. Yet he was so very glad to be part of this moment with the older man.

'Winston,' he said, when at last he could sneak a word into the tirade that Churchill had continued over cigars and brandy, 'I want you to know that I am very glad to be here.'

'And no man is more welcome in my home, Averell. Come!' the old man said, throwing his soiled napkin to the floor. 'Let us remind ourselves of how real wars are fought. We shall spend an hour in the arms of Lady Emma!'

The wretched film, yet again. Harriman consoled himself with the thought that, in the darkness, he could sleep while Churchill wept. But Pamela was waiting for them in the Long Gallery, sitting at the other end of the sofa, reminding Harriman of things other than the war that were somehow still unresolved. He was all the more grateful for the large balloon of brandy that Sawyers placed on the table beside him. Then the lights dimmed, the film flickered, and Harriman found himself cast into another world, one he recognized only vaguely, for he began to see things in the film he had never seen before.

Nelson, fighting to keep his troops from starvation – as Churchill had done. Impatient for the arrival of every new hour and every fresh wind. Denouncing those who would grasp at a compromise peace with the enemy. Bemoaning the fact that 'our allies have forgotten we are fighting for their cause'. A man who had become the embodiment of everything England wanted.

And Emma, a woman of extraordinary beauty and ambition who demanded more for herself than the role of dull and dutiful wife. 'Married women are bestowing their favours

299

so cheaply nowadays,' Nelson's son, Josiah, declared in a bar-room outburst against her, but there was nothing cheap about Emma. She was passionate, determined, calculating yet headstrong, running through the night to throw herself into the arms of her departing lover even as her wedding ring glinted in the moonlight.

'You'll come back, won't you?' she had cried.

'I wonder if I shall,' Nelson had replied. 'I feel I should not. You are married and I am married, and the magic and the music of the ballroom stand out very clearly in the dawn. Your life is here; my life is there. We must obey our creeds and codes. I know I must not come back. And I know nothing in this world will keep me away.'

And, glittering in the corner of Harriman's eye from her place at the end of the sofa, sat Pamela. Somehow he felt they were all part of this film, all three of them, and their relationship was playing a role in this war every bit as vital and as personal as that being acted out between Emma and Nelson. Yet he wasn't sure of the script. And he wanted very much to be back in Pamela's bed.

When the film had finally clattered to its end, he turned to his host.

'Useful weapon, a blind eye,' he said, stumbling over the words, knowing now that he was more than a little drunk.

'I wish I had a blind eye, my dear Averell,' the old man replied, wiping his eyes with a huge handkerchief. 'At times I fear I see things all too clearly.'

'Does truth always catch up with a man?'

'What is truth? History is littered with victors and villains, but the difference is rarely more than a matter of who won and who lost. Victory has a thousand followers, while treachery is always left to stand alone. Yet what is treachery, other than failure? If Nelson had lost at Trafalgar, he would have been tried and condemned and we should all spit on his memory. As they will spit on me, Averell, if I fail.'

'So I drink to your victory,' Harriman offered, raising his glass.

'Then to victory! And damn its cost! For without victory, there will be nothing left of any value. So Nelson broke the rules, he put his telescope to his blind eye and he disobeyed, at times he deceived. But he never lost hope, and he never, never, never gave in. If that was good enough for him, it'll do for me.'

He hoisted himself to his feet. 'I feel a little tired. I must take myself off for a bath and then bed. I bid you both goodnight.'

Without another word, he disappeared from the room. They could hear him plodding up the stairs, humming the tune of 'Danny Boy'.

'Sawyers, pretend for a moment you are a common crook,' Churchill suggested as he scrubbed away in his bath.

'Very well, zur,' the valet called from the bedroom.

'You have two neighbours. You wish to take unfair advantage of both. Indeed, you wish to beat them both to a pulp.'

'What would I want to do that fer?'

'Because you are a villain, you fool!' The outburst caused Churchill to lose the soap, and there was a moment of cursing while he retrieved it.

'Your neighbours are an old man and his young son. The son is tall, very powerful, more than a match for you in strength and speed. He represents a profound danger. On the other hand, the old man is not. You know that almost whatever the circumstance, if you had to deal with the old man on his own, you would be able to overpower him.'

'How old would the old man be, then? About your age? Or even older?'

'Sawyers, you are a pedant!'

'If you say so, zur.'

'Dammit. Assume he's about my age, man. If you prefer it, *exactly* my age. Will that satisfy you? Now listen!'

'I'm doing me best. But someone kepps shouting. Mekks it difficult, like.'

An impatient snort erupted from within the bathroom. 'Listen! You have one opportunity to mount an attack, and in surprise. Either on the man alone, or the son, or both together. After the initial attack, you will know that whoever is left standing will be warned and therefore wary. You may attack from behind, is that clear?'

A silence. 'Will I be attacking him wi' a hammer or an iron bar, like? Or what?'

'Does it make a difference?'

'Not sure. Never beaten anyone to a pulp before.'

'Sawyers – pray – bear with me. Just a little while longer.' Churchill began once more, his voice rising in cadence, his hand beating like an oar upon the soapy water to mark every fresh thought. 'You have – a hammer. You are going to attack – from behind. And in surprise. Just once, before you have to engage the wrath of whomsoever has survived the initial onslaught. Is that clear?'

The servant was standing at the door, holding a huge white towel, looking dubious.

'Now tell me, Sawyers. Who do you attack first?'

'The big 'un, of course.'

'And why?'

'I can deal with the old man later. Best be getting the big bastard first, like. It's obvious.'

Churchill rose from his bath. The water cascaded around their feet. 'Sawyers, you are brilliant.'

'Why, thank you, zur.'

'If you are right, you may have just changed the course of history. And let loose the dogs of war.'

She was beautiful, she was young – far too young for a man of fifty – and they were both married to other people. Futile. So he had told her it was over, but he hadn't meant it. Pamela made him feel alive, and when a man didn't know how soon he was to die amidst the madness of this war, life meant everything.

He had followed Churchill up the stairs and for some time he paced his room, befuddled by the flight and the alcohol, wondering what he might say. He tried to gauge her mood. She had been very quiet, but she'd had little chance beside the torrents that had flowed from Winston during the evening. She had shown no signs of resentment, yet perhaps she was simply being no more than polite, in the English way.

He paced back and forth, retracing the arguments in his mind until nothing made a lot of sense any more. In the end it came down to one very simple thought. What did he have to lose?

A faint light shone from beneath her door. He knocked very lightly. There was no reply. Gently, he pulled at the handle and stepped forward. He had the intention of saying something trite about his fiftieth birthday.

But there was no point. She was standing beside the bed, washed in the light of a reading lamp, the shadows accentuating her shape and her nakedness. To Harriman, she had never looked more compelling. It was an image, a snapshot, that was to wrap itself around his memory and cling to him for the rest of his life.

'Why is it,' she whispered, 'that you Americans are so late for simply everything?'

*　　*　　*

Late – but optimistic. An American trait.

There were still many optimists in America, in spite of the news. Large numbers of Japanese troops were reported heading south towards Indo-China from Shanghai, but since the only target they could attack was British, not American, it seemed not to matter so very much. And although it became clear that something was up with the Japanese Navy, many US analysts greeted it with a shrug of the shoulders. What could the Japs do? They wouldn't dare. If the Nips were headed anywhere, it was probably south, towards Singapore. The British again.

The United States of America had nothing to fear. The annual Army-Navy football game was about to be played and the commemorative programme had a dramatic photograph of the USS *Arizona* forging its way through a huge swell. 'It is significant,' the programme suggested, 'that despite the claims of air enthusiasts, no battleship has yet been sunk by bombs.' So there was no great cause for concern. Anyway, the *Arizona* was safely tucked up in port, halfway across the Pacific, in Pearl Harbor.

Inevitably, this came as little comfort to the British. Intelligence reports began to arrive suggesting that all Japanese merchantmen were returning to home waters at a pace that would bring them back by the first week of December. A most sensible precaution, if you were about to start a war.

Intelligence also picked up a strange pattern to Japanese naval radio traffic, with mentions of the refuelling of a task force. But what task force? It added to the pressure. And, with every day that passed, the army of Nippon ignored the threat of the economic sanctions and poured south into Indo-China.

Confronted by so many signs, Churchill found little

reassurance in a Foreign Office analysis that concluded the Japanese would give way so long as the Americans stood resolute and firm. 'The broad experience of the Foreign Office in giving way to any show of resolution may not be relevant to this situation,' he scribbled in the margin in red ink.

The United States had a Foreign Office, too. It was known as the State Department. It ran on similar principles, driven by a need to embrace the arts of diplomacy and the belief that war represented failure on their part. So, when the Japanese envoy Kurusu arrived in Washington, they talked, and they talked. And when that produced nothing, they talked some more. After all, no one else seemed to have any better suggestion.

26 November 1941. Tankan Bay.

The order came through. Proceed.

The departure had its problems. The *Akagi*, the flagship of the task force, fouled her propeller on a cable and divers had to be sent down to clear it. But soon they were under way through the freezing mists of the bay. Almost no one on board knew where they were headed or what their mission might be, but at last it had begun and they were happy. For a military man, unlike a diplomat, anything is better than sitting around waiting.

While others pursued their plans and plotted their schemes, the most important man of all, President Franklin D. Roosevelt, remained an enigma. He was for war, and he was against it; he was ready to wage war without the Congress, yet he couldn't move a spent cartridge case without their approval. The mists that floated off the Potomac and settled upon the American capital provided an ideal cover for those who, in truth, weren't sure of their way.

Other American politicians were less difficult to pin down. The US Congressmen who crowded into the Cabinet Room in Downing Street were courteous, but clear. They didn't want their country 'getting dragged into no foreign shooting war', as one put it.

'You are from the South, sir?'

'Virginia, Mr Churchill.'

'Then you will know that there are times when, no matter with what reluctance, a state must fight for what it holds to be right.'

'Home and hearth, Mr Churchill. I'll fight for that any time. But our boys camped out in Europe twenty years ago. Many of 'em didn't make it back. Don't seem to have made a deal of difference.'

The American politicians were on a fact-finding tour, but the facts they had found didn't appear to have left them much impressed. They had seen all too much of the shabby clothes and shuffling queues, the thin faces of the children, the wasteland that had once been a city. It was not what they wanted for their own.

'We respect your ardour, Mr Churchill, but we also have to listen to Mr Gallup. He tells us that not one in five of the folks back home want to get involved in this war.'

'No one *wants* war, gentlemen,' the Prime Minister said from his chair in front of the fireplace, 'but America is the greatest power on earth. That condition brings with it jealous enemies – many of them. They will not let you rest. I believe they will force you into this war, and sooner rather than later.'

'We believe other outcomes are possible, sir. Consider this – as we must. Russia may collapse. Then in the spring you might get invaded, while most of your boys are away fighting in the Middle East. I hate to think of it, but this time next year, instead of more war as you predict, there might be no war at all. It might all be over. And we're not about to buy a ticket for a show just as the last dancer's on her way out the door.'

'This act, gentlemen, is far from finished.'

'You suggesting invasion isn't possible?'

'I am not.'

'So what happens if the Germans arrive here and you folks get overrun?'

The question propelled Churchill to his feet. His chin was forward, his eyes burned with the passion of a tormented bull and the words emerged like the rumble of distant thunder. 'Then, sir, as we lie choking in our own blood, with dying hands we shall pass the torch to you.'

There was an embarrassed silence. Then the Congressmen filed out with barely another word.

The northern Pacific was relentless. Huge seas, unremitting gales, impenetrable fog. Yet the task force made four hundred miles a day. They attempted to sail in precise formation with the carriers in two parallel lines of three, the tankers trailing behind, the cruisers and battleships guarding the flanks, but during the hours of darkness the tankers would stray, and in the morning the destroyers were forced to round them up again like sheep dogs.

Refuelling in such conditions was a nightmare. Hoses would become unbuckled and lash violently across the decks. Several sailors were swept overboard. The sea showed no mercy.

The fleet was running on high-grade fuel to reduce smoke and sparks, rubbish was stored on board rather than being thrown into the seas, everything was done that could be done to erase all sign of their passing. Radio silence was absolute; transmitters were disabled to make sure of it.

Beneath the decks the task force carried more than four hundred aircraft; bombers, fighters, spotters, torpedo planes. They were constantly checked, their oil changed, their engines warmed, their pilots given exercises to keep them alert.

Inevitably, those on board speculated about their destination. With so many tankers around, they were clearly set to cover a long distance – as far as Singapore, the Philippines, Indonesia, perhaps. But why the carriers, why the planes? Now that the Japanese had air bases at Saigon, they already had aircraft within striking distance of all of these targets. Anyway, the task force was steaming east, not south.

Héloise had fallen in love with her bicycle. No longer did she pester for time off in London; she seemed content to wrap herself in the local countryside around Chequers, cycling to the village of Ellesborough or covering the several miles to the towns of Wendover and Great Missenden, often through inclement weather and sometimes even at night. Mrs Landemare smiled. It seemed simple enough. Héloise had found a boyfriend.

Yet Héloise had other distractions. She no longer met with the Japanese gentleman – there was no chance of an inconspicuous meeting with any Oriental so far away from London at an unsettled time like this – but he had a friend who worked in the Spanish Embassy and was young enough to pass as her lover, if need be. On some of her cycling trips, Héloise would call him from a public telephone at a prescribed time, and a day or so later she would meet with him. She quickly discovered that the number she was calling was also a public telephone. She had been given another number, but was told that was strictly for emergencies.

Yet most of the time Héloise simply cycled, so that people would grow accustomed to her coming and her going. She wanted no one to raise an eyebrow or to ask intrusive questions whenever she decided to get on her cycle and pedal away. She wanted cover. Just in case of an emergency.

29 November 1941. No more room for doubt. The Japanese were up to something. But no one knew what.

The British Chiefs of Staff met to discuss the growing pile of intelligence reports. They considered all the options they could think of – that the Japanese were preparing to strike against Thailand and Singapore, perhaps the Philippines or even the frozen wastes of Russia. Almost every possibility was put before them, but they couldn't reach a conclusion. They were clear on only two points. That *something* was about to happen. And, in the words of their unanimous report, that 'we should avoid taking any action which would involve us in a war with Japan unless we were certain that America would join us.'

In other words, run away as far and as fast as possible. Britain was too weak to resist on her own, but that had been the case for months, and the Japanese knew it. Ever since the capture of the *Automedon*.

The report of the Chiefs of Staff went directly to Churchill. When he had read it, he let forth a great sigh, as though his last breath were leaving his body. Then he reached for his whisky.

'Bugger it,' he muttered to the shadows around him, 'I'm just too old to run.'

*   *   *

Sawyers drew back the curtains, then settled the tray on his bed.

'What's this?' Churchill growled, not looking up from his papers.

'Champagne. Smoked salmon. Scrambled egg. More champagne if yer want it. By way of marking the occasion. Happy birthday.'

'There is little enough rejoicing to be squeezed out of the day at my age, Sawyers.'

Churchill was sixty-seven years old. And he felt it. He'd had no rest, his sleep overflowed with nightmares – or, in truth, one repeated nightmare. In his dream he was waiting, helpless, bound hand and foot beside a road. Roosevelt was walking by – *walking* by – on the other side. Churchill tried to call out, but as loudly as he hollered and screamed there was no sound. Roosevelt disappeared without even a backward glance.

Churchill found a dread in waiting for America to decide whether the British Empire should live or die. He had come to the point where he feared falling asleep almost as much as he did waking, yet whether in his dreams or in daylight, the result was the same. Roosevelt passed on by.

That morning, Churchill had drafted a telegram to the President asking outright for a declaration of war. He couldn't command, so instead he had crawled. 'I realize your constitutional difficulties, but it would be tragic . . . I beg you to consider whether, at some moment you choose right . . . Forgive me, my dear friend, for presuming to press such a course . . .' The words of supplication had made him feel physically sick; he was in no mood for Mrs Landemare's salmon and egg.

Sawyers poured him a glass of champagne. 'A birthday wish,' he suggested. 'You're allowed on yer birthday.'

'What could I possibly wish for?'

'No war. I would. And for Japs to drop down hole.'

'It's too late for that. We will have war. Perhaps even today.'

'It's Sunday,' Sawyers protested.

'They always attack on a Sunday. Our Christian day of rest, when they can take us unawares. Oh, dear God,' he sighed, falling back upon his pillow, clutching another note from his box. It was from the War Office. An analysis in the most emphatic and insistent terms.

'The effect of war with Japan on our main war effort,' it said, 'might be so severe as to prejudice our chances of beating Germany. Our policy must therefore be – and is – avoidance of war with Japan.'

'But the policy's no bloody good! It won't bloody well work!' Suddenly Churchill was shouting, so violently that Sawyers removed the tray for safekeeping.

'Mrs Landemare won't like that, you not eating her breakfast, like,' Sawyers warned, trying to drag his master's attention away from his sorrows. 'She and the girl have been up all hours mekking sure yer get a proper dinner, too. A cake and all.'

'Tell her to –' Churchill began angrily, then restrained himself. He examined the note once more. Suddenly he was more composed. 'Give me back my tray. What the hell do you think you're doing with it, man? And pay attention. This is what you will tell Mrs Landemare . . .'

'How is he this morning?' the cook asked, bent over a bowl. Sawyers handed the empty tray to Héloise and sat down beside the long preparation table that dominated the centre of the kitchen.

311

'Odd, cook. Being honest, I'd say very odd.'

'Having another of his turns, I'll be bound. Miserable at getting so very old.'

'Nowt like that. Asked me to thank you fer yer scrambled egg, like, said it's better'n Lord Beaver's caviar. Then started talking about Mr Hess.'

'What's so odd about that?' the cook enquired, wiping her brow. 'My egg's better than any Russian muck. And that old Hess was about the only decent present he's had this year.'

'No, cook, it's *Mr* Hess now. *Mr* Hess this, *Mr* Hess that. All of a sudden it's like they're old friends,' Sawyers said, nibbling on an edge of toast. 'He were even asking me if I'd like to serve breakfast to him one day. Like he might even come to Chequers. As a guest.'

'You're not pulling my leg, are you, Mr Sawyers?'

'Not even a little, cook. He says that a new year demands new friends – and *Mr* Hess might be a man who's wi' us rather than agin us.'

'What do he mean by that, then?'

'Haven't faintest idea. War breeds strange bedfellows.'

'Too right, in this house.' Mrs Landemare giggled.

'But he were back to his normal self by time he'd finished breakfast. Shouting and hollering as usual, he were.' He wiped the crumbs of toast from his mouth. 'Any chance of another slice, cook?'

''Course.'

He stretched in contentment, his task completed. 'And can yer do that washing-up a little quieter, girl,' he said, turning to Héloise at the sink. 'Racket's proper doing me head in.'

Tojo didn't celebrate Churchill's birthday. Instead, he seethed. He raged. He accused Britain and America of trying to 'exploit the one billion people of East Asia to satisfy their greed.' He insisted that Japan would go forward no matter what, even over the corpses of fallen Japanese comrades. He said they must 'purge East Asia with a vengeance of the practices of Great Britain and the United States.' These were not off-the-cuff remarks, but words supplied by the Japanese Government's official translator.

The following day, Monday, the first day of December, the Japanese Government ordered their diplomatic missions in every part of the world to destroy their code books. Yet another sign they were expecting war.

But they did not break off negotiations in Washington.

Still the diplomats talked.

As the hours passed, Churchill became like a man possessed, a great sea beating upon the rocks, roaring, impatient, implacable. His demand for news was remorseless, particularly from the Admiralty and the code-breakers at Bletchley Park. It had become clear from the pattern of naval signals emanating from Tokyo that a Japanese fleet of considerable size was somewhere on the seas and had been under way for several days, but in spite of his rage, no one could tell him where.

Shortly before midnight, he asked his private secretary to contact the Admiralty for the latest news. The Duty Captain explained that there was none, and promised to ring back as soon as he had any information.

An hour later Churchill demanded the Admiralty be contacted again. The Duty Captain, full of sleep and injury, insisted that no event of any consequence had taken place anywhere in the world and tartly reminded Churchill's secretary of his earlier promise to contact him whenever it did.

At two-thirty in the morning, yet another call was made.

313

Roused from a deep and necessary sleep, the Duty Captain let fly with language that would have done justice to a quarterdeck under direct enemy fire. A torrent of abuse tumbled down the line and when the old man, pacing back and forth, heard the noise, he assumed great events had at last taken place. He grabbed the phone. His reward was a remorseless outpouring of insults.

'Captain,' he said in his most distinctive growl when at last the officer paused for breath, 'you have summed up my sentiments entirely. And if you fight as violently as you profane, then we shall prevail and I shall forget we have spoken. Goodnight.'

Tuesday, the second day of December. Tokyo sent the signal.

'Climb Mount Niitaka 1208.'

The signal was sent in its top-level JN-25 naval code. It was to become one of the most notorious orders ever given in military history. Tokyo had made up its mind. The point of no return had been reached.

It was also the day that the *Prince of Wales* arrived in Singapore, accompanied by the ageing battleship *Repulse* and several support ships. They steamed in single line into the naval base, watched by thousands of English, Chinese and Malays who had gathered on the rooftops and who greeted them with fanfare and overwhelming expressions of relief. They believed that the arrival of the fleet would force the Japanese to put their sabres back into their scabbards.

But already it was too late.

Codes are constructed, and codes are broken. The British were particularly good at breaking codes. They'd decrypted many of the Japanese naval and diplomatic ciphers, including JN-25, yet even with such an advantage it still didn't reveal all. However, it gave a shape to things, like a man using his sense of touch in the dark.

Churchill received the latest intelligence as he was eating lunch in the makeshift dining room that had been constructed in the basement of Downing Street as protection from the bombing. He was eating on his own – an exceptional occurrence – and was lost deep within his thoughts. He was like a relative waiting for a child to die. His head was down, he was uncommunicative, monosyllabic, his eyes twitching with every movement at the door, braced for terrible news. He was pushing a lamb chop distractedly around his plate when the telephone rang. It was the duty officer in the naval section hut at Bletchley Park. Immediately Churchill's eyes grew alert. The two men pushed buttons so that the conversation was scrambled.

'A JN-25 transmission from Tokyo, Prime Minister. It reads: "Climb Mount Niitaka 1208".'

'What's it mean?'

'In all honesty, we don't know. Yet at least.'

'Guesses?'

'Niitaka is the highest mountain in their empire. A puzzle as to why they should instruct the navy to climb a mountain – but it can't be taken literally, of course.'

'An attack code.'

'Possibly.'

'If not, what else?'

'We don't know.'

'It's your job to know!'

'It's only just arrived, sir. We've had no time –'

'I can give you anything you want, man, anything – except time!'

'I'm sorry, Prime Minister.'

Even through the echo of the scrambling device, Churchill could hear the strain in the other man's voice. He knew that at Bletchley they were working to their limit, laying his 'golden eggs'. It might be lunchtime in Downing Street, but he guessed the other man had probably worked through the previous night, probably many previous nights, and had little idea what time of day it was. Churchill had the highest regard for the code-breakers and analysts at Bletchley. He had visited them only recently and seen one of them being physically sick with the tension. Yet still he had to push.

'No need for apology. Only information. What do the numbers mean?'

'1208? Probably the date. The eighth of December.'

'But if it's an attack code, why are they giving so much prior notice?'

'Well . . . I'm guessing now . . . something has to happen before it can be implemented, some preparation made – if it *is* an attack code. Perhaps we'll get more of the jigsaw in a while.'

'You will –'

'Of course, sir.'

'Any time. Day or night. Don't hesitate for a second.'

When he sat down again, the lamb chop lay glutinous and ignored. He didn't flinch or twitch as Sawyers removed it, nor when it was replaced by a slice of Mrs L's apple pie, which was also left to grow cold with neglect. When he did eventually rise to his feet, it was slowly, as though he were weighed down with concerns.

'Bring it to the study,' he mumbled at Sawyers.

'What, the apple pie?'

'No, dammit, the . . .' – he waved around, his mind else-where – 'whatever it is I'm drinking.' And disappeared like a sleepwalker.

Yet when Sawyers found him in the first-floor study, he was once again transformed. The lethargy had gone, and in its place was a dervish who danced around the central table as he pored over the pages of several atlases.

'I can't locate it, Sawyers. Where the hell is it?'

'Where's what?' the valet asked, setting down the glass.

'Mount Bloody Nittacky or whatever it's called. Gimme . . .' – he wagged a finger in the direction of the bookcase – 'the encyclopedia.'

And soon it was found. 'It's not in Japan at all. It's in Formosa. One of the bits they grabbed in 1895.' He began reading out loud. 'Jade Mountain. Also known as Mount Morrison. Hah! Y'see, man, we got there, too!'

'Never had much of a head fer heights meself,' Sawyers muttered.

'But that's it.' Churchill thumped the table in excitement. 'To climb great heights is a noble feat. The message implies courage, dedication, pride, achievement. The conquest of extraordinary heights. That must be it, don't you see? Conquest. It's the attack order!'

'Mebbe.'

Churchill had become a man possessed, bursting with impatience as he raced through the collection of books. He grabbed atlas, then encyclopedia and gazetteer, whipping the pages back and forth in his haste. Sawyers removed the glass – a fine claret – to a safe distance.

'But one thing I cannot understand, Sawyers. Why – *why* – decide now about an attack on the eighth of the month, dammit? Six days hence.' He stood over the books, searching for the elusive answer. 'It's not to give them time for preparation – they have had that, they know what they're doing. We should never underestimate those monkeys. So – they must need the time – not to prepare – but – to arrive.

Wherever it is they're going. That's it! They're already under way! But where?'

He rummaged furiously across more pages, but found no inspiration.

'How long does Bletchley think they've been at sea? Six days? A week? So they're halfway to wherever it is they're going. At – what? – three hundred miles a day? Perhaps a little more? But probably not on a direct course.' Churchill had served as First Lord of the Admiralty during the early part of this war and through much of the last; he knew his dreadnoughts and destroyers. 'Let's say a radius of around three thousand miles.'

He fiddled with the atlas, sticking his thumb on Mount Niitaka and drawing a circle with his index finger. It cut through Australia. 'That doesn't bloody work.' He replaced his thumb over the mainland of Japan, experimenting. 'Of course, three thousand miles exactly! Singapore! Or the Philippines. But . . .' He stood like a pathologist over a corpse, dissecting the parts, trying to see how it all fitted together. 'That would take the Japanese task force across some of the busiest sea lanes in the world, yet no one's seen a thing.' He shook his head and drew another circle. His finger dropped off the page. 'It's the projection, don't you see, Sawyers. The map's centred on Europe, with Japan at its far edge. That's no good. We've got to look at things through Japanese eyes. They see themselves as the centre of the world, the heart of civilization, not its distant edge.'

He cast around the room for a moment, trying to think of any book or gazetteer that might give him the answer, until he saw an antique globe that stood in the corner. It had often been a favourite toy. He would sometimes give it a whirl, glorying in how much of the globe was coloured red, but that held no interest for him now. His thumb was on Japan

318

once more, drawing a wide arc. Through Singapore, Burma, China, the frozen wastes of Siberia, the Aleutian Islands . . .

'Oh, my God.'

With just a little flexing, the three thousand miles stretched all the way to Hawaii.

'Pearl Harbor,' he gasped.

The simplicity of it all swept away his doubt. With a finger and thumb he had discovered what the intelligence agencies of the entire world had failed to see.

'Sawyers, I believe they intend to attack Pearl Harbor.'

The servant chewed on his lip. 'What'll we do about it, then?'

Churchill stared out of the window. Through the bare trees of the park he could see the outline of Buckingham Palace. Fluttering from its flagpole was the Royal Standard, the flag of Britain's islands and her Empire. How could he permit it to be lost?

When he spoke, his words came wearily, as though they had travelled an immense distance.

'If we alert the Americans, they will denounce the Japanese. Then the attack will never happen. The Japanese will turn back their fleet, say it was a training exercise, that it was never their intention . . .' Churchill was standing so close to the window that his breath began to form a mist upon the pane. He wiped it clear with a cuff.

'Their fleet would disperse, but the mass of their soldiery would continue to pour into Indo-China. They will attack Singapore. The volcano will spew forth. Then Britain will be at war with Japan as well as with Germany. A war we cannot hope to win. While America talks and America fiddles, we shall be left alone with the wolf at our throat. And that would be the end.'

'You sure, zur?'

'It's not a mathematical equation, Sawyers, but even if it were no more than a strong possibility . . .'

'So – what'll we do?' Sawyers repeated.

'If I fail to tell the Americans, I shall be rightly condemned. But if I do tell them, I may be condemning not only myself but every Briton in the Empire. That would be a desecration of the whole of our history,' he whispered. 'How could I do that? How can I decide? But we have until the eighth. Time to think, Sawyers, time to reflect. To pray for God's guidance.'

And in an instant the hesitation was gone. Churchill turned from the window and grabbed his servant by the arms.

'We must say nothing! To anyone! Never breathe a word of this, even under torture, Sawyers. Not another soul must know. Do you understand?'

The servant looked at the master, eye to eye, closer now than they had ever been.

'You must be with me on this, Sawyers.' Churchill's voice carried the passion of a man with his foot upon the gallows.

'No need worrying about me, zur. I've not much idea what yer been talking about, to be honest wi' yer. Anyways, I'm just a stupid valet. Only good for pressing trousers, so yer keep telling me. And, if I remember right, none too good at that.'

FIFTEEN

The men of the task force had been mustered. Now they knew.

Maps were unrolled, plaster relief models of the harbour produced, identification exercises carried out with the silhouettes of US ships. There were other targets, too – airfields, barracks, Marine bases to be located and destroyed. The military complex at Pearl Harbor was huge.

Sake was poured and the Emperor saluted with great cries. There was much rejoicing.

But alongside it all there was also great tension for, even at this late stage, if they were sighted, they were under orders to abort and return home.

It might still have been stopped.

They went on talking in Washington. But there had been a change in the atmosphere of negotiations. The Americans demanded to know why the Japanese kept moving more troops into Indo-China, and the Japanese kept promising a detailed reply, yet none came.

But they continued to stir up optimism. Admiral Nomura, the Japanese Ambassador in Washington, told the press that 'the Americans talked and we listened'. The Japanese wanted 'to avoid war if possible, for war would not settle anything. It is a question of war or peace, but war would not help and there is no reason why we should not settle these issues by diplomacy.'

Tokyo was reported as still being hopeful, and kept promising a reply to the American demands within days. The Japanese even insisted that Prime Minister Tojo's remarks about 'purging' British and American influence from Asia had been mistranslated, even though the words had come from the pen of their own official. But, in spite of all this, a gloom settled across the proceedings. 'Japan's reply to the United States has not yet been made,' *The Times* reported, 'and it is still a question whether it is not already taking the form of military action rather than words.' The paper speculated about possible targets. The list included Thailand, Hong Kong, Malaya, the Philippines, the Dutch East Indies, even Australia or New Zealand.

But no one mentioned Pearl Harbor.

On Friday, which was the fifth, the Japanese gave their formal reply to the State Department. There was enough wool in it to cover a flock of sheep. It was accompanied by a suggestion that a more detailed reply might come soon, with just a little more time, but no more talks were scheduled. The waiting game so beloved of the diplomats was almost done.

In London, it seemed that not a thing was going right. On Saturday, the sixth day of December, reports from Russia told of the Germans still falling in fury upon Moscow, while in North Africa it became clear that the latest British offensive against Rommel was being ground into the sand.

And Max Beaverbrook had declared that he was going to resign. He said he was tired of fools getting in the way of his work and was exhausted by his asthma. Was it a ploy, another game, the start of a plot to replace Churchill himself? Or did he really mean it? Max would do anything for a headline.

The uncertainty took a terrible toll on Churchill. It came to a head at the meeting of the Chiefs of Staff over which Churchill himself presided, with Eden also in attendance. He was about to depart for Moscow – in the wake of Churchill and Beaverbrook – and was insistent on taking some gift with him. How about three hundred tanks? Or three hundred aircraft? Or both? The Chiefs of Staff were as desperate to bring the figure down as Eden was to push it up – after all, he argued, hadn't Beaverbrook taken much more when he'd been to see Stalin? It was like some childish spat, boy scouts arguing over badges. And where was bloody Max? Plotting? Or truly suffering?

As the time moved towards midnight, Churchill could stand the bickering no longer.

'We're going round in circles,' he said, banging the table in exasperation. 'Let's conclude. Ten squadrons, Anthony. Offer him ten squadrons – but only after the Libyan offensive is done with.' He closed the file in front of him to indicate the discussion was at an end.

Yet the Chief of the Air Staff had other ideas. These were his aircraft, after all. And in the last war he had been a despatch rider during the retreat from Mons, so he knew a thing or two about being shot at by his own side.

'Prime Minister, I've no objection in principle. Wish to help the Foreign Secretary, of course – and Comrade Stalin. But I think the numbers of craft involved and the timing are a little too definite. I must recommend we leave ourselves a bit of elbow room on this one. After all, we haven't yet been able to establish that the Russians can even fly these machines.'

It was an entirely valid point, but set against the imminence

323

of the end of the world, a dispute about ten squadrons seemed somehow desperately trivial. Suddenly Churchill could take it no longer. He hurled his papers across the table and accused them of deliberately obstructing his intentions. He said they were supposed to be men of ideas and initiatives but all they brought with them were their objections. And he swore most profoundly.

'You can't make up your bloody minds, so I'm going to make them up for you!'

He proceeded to gather the papers that he had hurled around the table, stuffing them back into his file and pretending to study them. All the while his chest heaved, his fists remained clenched, and for some considerable time his eyes were closed. He said not a word. He was pursuing private dragons, and wherever his mind was, it was not in this room.

Abruptly he slammed the covers of his file together and stalked out of the room.

For a few moments, these most powerful of men remained silent, stunned at what they had witnessed.

'That was very sad,' one of them said quietly.

'Pathetic, really.'

'Entirely unnecessary.'

'Such a pity.'

'God knows where we'd be without him'

'But God knows where we shall go with him . . .'

He didn't know where he should go, or what he should do. He had as yet done nothing, but doing nothing was the most momentous decision of all.

He invited the Americans for the weekend at Chequers – whatever happened he knew it must involve them – but

Winant had official duties elsewhere and couldn't make it until Sunday. He was summoned, nonetheless. Harriman came, bringing along his daughter, Kathleen, who had come to spend time with her father. It was her birthday, so Churchill instructed Sawyers to arrange a cake with candles for dinner on Saturday evening, yet when the lights were dimmed and it was brought in it caused surprise. It quickly became clear that Churchill, distracted, had grown confused. Her birthday wasn't until the following day. Anyway, no one seemed to be much in the mood for celebration. The tension was affecting them all.

When Sawyers put him to bed that evening, it was, at first, in complete silence. They had a routine, long established, which meant there was little need for words. It was only after Churchill had climbed into bed that he spoke.

'I must decide tomorrow. It is the last chance.'

'What will yer do?'

'I'm going to sleep on it.'

'No yer won't. You've not slept fer days.'

He sighed. 'What do you think I should do?'

'Not fer me to say.'

'No one else can say, Sawyers. No one else knows.'

The valet bent to pick up the socks from the floor, trying to ignore the question.

'I feel very lonely, Sawyers. I don't think I can do this alone. I think I shall have to speak out.'

Sawyers straightened. 'Speak out? So who'd believe you?' he said belligerently. 'They'd only say yer gorrit all wrong again.'

'What?'

'Well, like yer did when you tried to save old King from abdicating.'

'You're right there, I suppose. He wasn't worth it.'

325

Churchill's career had been crowded with many moments when his judgement had proved disastrous, but Sawyers decided this was scarcely the time to recall them all.

'And what'd yer tell 'em anyhow?' the valet continued. 'That yer worked it all out on yer fingers?' He shook his head. 'That's how yer do the household accounts.'

'And I'm not so very good at that, am I?'

'Below stairs, we have a rule, like. No one gets into trouble fer what they see and don't say. Eyes open, mouth shut, that's the way it works best. Particularly in a household like this 'un.'

'Above stairs it's different. Usually quite the reverse.'

'I'm not in the business o' giving a Prime Minister advice. Not me job. Fold yer clothes, serve yer food, sweep up after yer, like, but you're the one what gets paid for running this war. Not me. I'm a servant. Nowt wrong wi' that. Proud to be so. Not got much to me name, but I do know that if Hitler were to get here I'd end up wi' nowt. Wouldn't be a servant, wouldn't even be a slave. They'd put me up against a wall wi' you in front of a firing squad, more than likely. And what wi' the size o' you and me after Mrs Landemare's cooking, not much chance of 'em missing, I suppose.' He folded Churchill's trousers immaculately and placed them on a hanger. 'Whatever you decide is best, Mr Churchill. That'll be right wi' me. Have no doubts.'

'Thank you, Sawyers.'

'Goodness. Feel like I've been mekking a speech. That's your job.' He hesitated. ''Cept sometimes . . .'

'Go on. Please.'

'Well, all I know is that yer mekk some right fine speeches, so yer do, but seems to me that some of yer best moments were when yer were kepping yer mouth shut. Like over Lord Halifax.'

326

'Ah.'

It seemed so long ago when Neville Chamberlain, on the point of resignation, had summoned Churchill to the Cabinet Room and asked him to endorse Halifax as his successor. Churchill had gazed out of the window and said nothing. The moment – and Lord Halifax – had passed.

'You make a powerful argument for saying nothing.'

'Not giving advice. Just saying, like.'

'And I thank you for it.'

'I'm not the one to be telling what yer should do,' the other man continued to grumble. 'Particularly about something that's already clean slipped me mind.'

For the first time in days, Churchill smiled.

Sawyers had begun vigorously brushing the lapels of Churchill's jacket. 'You don't half make a mess wi' yer dinner at times.'

'Does it matter? That is not what history will remember me for, Sawyers. It may well mark me down as its greatest scoundrel.'

'That'll depend.'

'On what?'

'Who writes it. Yer always talking about going back to Chartwell after it's all over to write history o' the war.'

'But if I am to write it, I must win it first. Is that what you're saying?'

'I'm not saying nowt. But if that's what yer want, that'll be fine by me, too.'

Sunday. The seventh day of the month. Winant was late for lunch, delayed by the demands of diplomacy. It seemed not to matter; food was little more than distraction to the earnest ambassador, particularly at times such as these. He had phoned ahead and apologized, insisting that the others begin their lunch without him, yet when his car drew up on the gravel before the front door of Chequers, he was surprised to see Churchill striding up and down, pulling impatiently at his cigar. A cold December wind was blowing, but he wore no overcoat.

'Winston, my profound apologies . . .'

'War,' the Prime Minister barked, pacing relentlessly and neglecting the usual pleasantries of welcome. 'D'you think there will be war?'

Winant was still only half out of the car. He straightened slowly, his clothes more than usually crumpled after his journey. 'Yes,' he replied simply, brushing his forelock from his eyes.

Churchill suddenly stopped his pacing and turned on him with startling vehemence.

'If they declare war on you, Gil, we shall declare war on them within the hour. Within the minute!' He was agitated, stabbing at the ambassador with his cigar.

'Yes, Prime Minister, I understand. You've made that very clear and in public.'

'So what I very much need to know is this. If they declare war on us, will you declare war on them? Will you join the dance?'

It seemed a strange performance to Winant. Churchill already had the answer, he knew what the ambassador must say.

'Has something happened, Winston?' the American asked, perturbed.

'No. I just need to know. Need to hear it. We will back you. Will you back us?'

Winant's tone grew formal. 'You know I can't answer that, Prime Minister. Under our Constitution, only the Congress has the right to declare war.'

328

Churchill had been standing before him with his fists clenched as though ready to fight, but as he listened to Winant's words his shoulders fell and the energy seemed to drain from his body. 'I was hoping – just hoping – you might have had fresh instructions,' he said softly.

'My hands are tied. As are the President's.'

Churchill's jaw was set. 'I had allowed myself to hope, Gil. It would have made things so much easier.'

'There is nothing I can say.'

'Nothing you can say, eh?' Churchill said, slowly echoing the other man's words and shaking his head in sorrow.

Winant was perplexed. The old man appeared crestfallen, yet their exchange couldn't possibly have come as a surprise. He felt there was some part of the conversation he was missing.

Churchill took one last pull at his cigar before hurling it into the bleak flowerbed. He had smoked less than an inch. His eyes were rimmed with tears, his voice so choking with emotion that the words emerged only with difficulty.

'You are my friend, Gil. And we are late, you know. Come in and get washed so the two of us can go into lunch. We can at least do that together, can't we?'

They dined together, too, with Harriman, Kathleen and Pamela, yet Churchill found no pleasure in it. He sat morose, his face grim, making no attempt to join in the conversation. He had withdrawn deep within himself.

Sawyers came in with a small portable wireless set that he placed on the table. The old man liked to listen when the news was read at nine o'clock. It was the most comprehensive news broadcast of the day and he rarely missed it, yet tonight he seemed to have lost all interest. He sat with his

329

head in his hands, saying nothing. It was almost a belated half-thought when he reached out and flipped the lid of the wireless set to bring up the voice of Alvar Liddell, the newsreader. The headlines were already being read – reports about fighting on the Russian front and depressing news about a tank battle in Libya. The others picked up their conversation to avoid dwelling too long on gloom.

It was only at the end that a fragment about the Pacific was mentioned. Something about the Hawaiian Islands, but it was lost in the banter. Then it was more news about Tobruk.

And still he sat, head in hands.

'Yer not listening tonight, then?' Sawyers enquired, gruffly, in a voice that seemed unnaturally tight.

Only slowly did the old man's head begin to rise.

'Didn't it say something about Pearl Harbor?' Harriman murmured.

'No, no, I thought it said Pearl River,' someone else chimed in.

Already Liddell was announcing that the weekly Brains Trust programme would begin immediately after the news.

Churchill suddenly sat bolt upright, alert, as though trying to catch an echo of the missed item that might still be lingering in the room.

'Did he say something about an attack?'

Even as Churchill spoke, the newsreader began to read out a fuller report in clipped, unemotional tones.

'The news has just been given that Japanese aircraft have raided Pearl Harbor, the American naval base in Hawaii . . .'

Churchill was snatching for the volume knob.

'. . . The announcement of the attack was made in a brief statement by President Roosevelt. Naval and military targets on the principal Hawaiian island of Oahu have also been attacked. No further details are yet available.'

330

Churchill appeared bewildered. 'Did we hear him right?'

'That's what he said,' Sawyers replied, almost belligerently. 'Those Jap monkeys have gone and bombed America.'

From the end of the table, Winant looked on, taking in a fragment of history that would live with him for the rest of his life. Armageddon. Yet for a moment of such extraordinary drama there was something out of place. It seemed strange that a servant should be breaking so impetuously into their conversation, and still stranger that he was smiling.

'But ... Today? I thought ... The timing ...' Churchill mumbled in confusion, struggling to fix his mind upon what he had heard. Then the pieces seemed to fall into place. He thumped the dining table and sprang to his feet. 'We shall fight! We shall declare war upon Japan!'

Winant's face was creased with concern. 'Shouldn't we get confirmation or something? After all, it's only the BBC. We can't go to war on the word of the BBC.'

'Then,' Churchill said, smiling even more broadly than the valet, 'we shall telephone the President. He will know.'

Before dawn, the Japanese fleet had arrived at a point less than three hundred miles north of Pearl Harbor. The carriers swung into the wind; it was a heavy sea, unsettled, but it would have to do. The first wave of aircraft took off while it was still dark – torpedo planes, high-level bombers, dive bombers, fighters – accompanied by the roars and frantic waves of those left behind.

Once the flight decks had been cleared, a second wave of planes was ferried up from the hangar decks. Dawn was breaking as they set off south towards Hawaii.

Just before eight in the morning, Hawaiian time, and almost unopposed, the Japanese planes hurled themselves upon Pearl

Harbor. They found the ships waiting in line on what was called Battleship Row while, almost unbelievably, they discovered the Americans had huddled all their planes together in the middle of the airfields to guard against sabotage. At first there was some confusion amongst the Japanese as to whether the torpedo planes or bombers should attack first, but it made little difference. The devastation was immense.

The attack lasted for almost two hours. Within minutes of its start, the battleship *Arizona*, which eight days previously had so proudly adorned the programme for the Army-Navy football game, exploded in an earth-shaking ball of flame. More than a thousand of its crew were killed instantly. The battleship *Oklahoma* capsized soon after. Sixteen other ships were sunk or seriously damaged. The morning had started with nine American battleships in the Pacific; by its end only two remained operational.

Nearly two hundred American aircraft were destroyed.

The human toll could only be reckoned after the flames had died and the smoke had cleared. 2,403 Americans were dead.

Pearl Harbor would be officially declared the worst military and naval disaster in American history.

The President, of course, did not yet know all this. Confusion reigned, the details would come later, but for the moment it was enough that they had been attacked. 'We're all in the same boat now,' he told Churchill, somewhat clumsily. 'I'm going to ask Congress tomorrow for a declaration of war against Japan.'

Against Japan ...

'And we shall follow your declaration within the hour, as we promised,' Churchill replied, standing over a phone in the study.

'Have they attacked British territory, too?'

'I do not know. I expect they shall. But it doesn't matter. America is our dearest friend, your enemy is our enemy. That is enough.'

The fingers of war had reached across the widest oceans in the world.

'We must meet again. I shall come to you,' Churchill said.

'Of course. It'll be hell here in Washington for a while, and you'll be up to your eyes, too, but . . .' Roosevelt was about to suggest a date in the New Year. Churchill was having none of it.

'Have no care for me. Nothing is more important than that the world sees us together, united. I shall be there within the week.'

Roosevelt was about to object, it was too soon, he could do without Churchill trying to run his war for him, but there were so many other battles to fight that there seemed little point in opening yet another front.

'Be seeing you, Winston.'

'Indeed, my dear friend,' Churchill replied. He stared at the receiver, then replaced it on its cradle as gently as a priest putting aside the chalice after Communion.

The world had changed. All was bustle. The study filled with secretaries, Americans, guests. He embraced Winant, Harriman, welcomed them to the war. Another telephone was ringing. News that the Japanese were attacking Malaya, too. And a map, unrolled on the desk, of Pearl Harbor and Hawaii. Churchill bent low to examine it, then jerked in surprise. He swore. No one seemed surprised. 'There will be work for many hands this night,' he announced. 'No one shall rest.' Then he swept from the room.

Outside in the hall, he found his valet.

'So they attacked the big bugger, then,' Sawyers said.

'They did indeed.'

'Wrong day, though. Said you'd get it wrong, didn't I?'

'I am a fool, Sawyers, but a most fortunate fool. I had quite forgotten that the International Date Line slices through the Pacific between Pearl Harbor and Japan. It's so easy to miss – runs along the very edge of most European maps.'

'So what?'

'In Tokyo, it is already Monday. December the eighth. Twelve-oh-eight.'

'All fingers and thumbs, you can be, at times, zur.'

Churchill smiled, took the other man's hand and grasped it as if he were thanking his oldest friend for a most profound tribute.

'But our work is only half finished. We've dealt with those thugs who are clambering in the back window, but there are still those kicking down our front door. We may yet be left to fight the Nazis on our own.'

'Can't persuade 'em to drop a few bombs on New York, I don't suppose.'

'Perhaps that won't be necessary, Sawyers. I want you to organize refreshment and sandwiches for everyone – it will be a long evening. I am to make another trip to America to see the President. I shall leave almost immediately. Make sure all the staff are informed.' His voice dropped; he drew closer. 'And I shall need the girl. Send her up to my room with a tray of tea and sandwiches in . . .' – he examined his pocket watch – 'thirty minutes. Be precise about that. You will tell her that I am working on my plans for the trip and she is to take care she makes no sound to disturb me. Is that clear?'

''Cept for one thing, zur.'

'What is that?'

'What do yer want in yer sandwiches?'

*   *   *

334

She knocked lightly upon the door, but there was no answer. From within came the sound of his deep, rasping voice. Very quietly, as she had been instructed, she entered the bedroom.

He was in the bathroom, dictating. The door was open, a tap was running, and in a fragment of mirror she saw a flash of nakedness. He often dictated while he was in the bath, to a male secretary who would perch on the lavatory in considerable steamy discomfort while the old man splashed around, composing his thoughts. She placed the tray on the table, checked it one last time, and was about to leave when the tap was turned off and she could hear his voice very clearly. What she heard made her freeze to the spot.

'We must coordinate our timing – with great care, Mr President,' Churchill was saying in the stilted manner of a man impatient for a scribe to catch up with him, 'but in my view it is essential – that you announce your declaration of war upon Germany – before Christmas. We do not wish – no, change that – we should not permit – the comforts of the festive season – to dull wits that have been honed so sharp by the dastardly attack upon Pearl Harbor.'

The flow was interrupted by renewed splashing of water and what sounded like a muttered search for soap.

'I will be there at your side – to display the united front that exists between our two nations – which will make its mark not only upon the enemy – but also upon any doubters that may remain within your own country. I intend also – as we discussed this evening on the telephone – to bring with me the message from Hess – wait! Make that *Herr* Hess. Bloody man deserves a little respect – in which he will call on his countrymen to accept the un-wisdom of continuing with a war – that sets Germany against four-fifths of all mankind. At the same time as we reveal his message I shall ensure that the Deputy Fuehrer – appears before the

335

representatives of the media – at some suitable location in London – to affirm his message. New paragraph. My dear friend – the news will be certain to stun every soul in Germany – and may yet contrive to sweep Hitler from power – have you got all that?'

With that, Churchill hauled himself from the water. He was quite alone. There was no scribe. As he stood dripping beside the bath, he listened very carefully. He thought he heard the soft clicking of the latch at the bedroom door.

Harriman and Winant were standing bleary-eyed on the doorstep of Chequers, wrapped in overcoats, saying goodbye to Churchill in the light of a grey, misty dawn.

'It feels good to be waging war together at last,' the ambassador said, gripping the other man's hand. 'I'm a man who no longer has to keep saying no.'

'I intend to be insatiable in my demands.'

'You always are.'

Then Harriman was shaking Churchill's hand. 'We're in it together now, Winston.'

'I fear not, Averell. Not yet.'

'Roosevelt has recalled Congress. There's no doubt left. They'll declare war.'

'On Germany?'

'Ah.'

'And once you declare war in the Pacific, can you give me your word that your Lend-Lease supplies and military aid will continue to flow to Britain at their present strengths?'

'No,' Harriman replied glumly. 'I can't guarantee that.'

'Then all that has happened, my friends, is that Britain is now condemned to fighting in Asia as well as upon all the other battlefronts, and with less to fight with. I do not wish to appear ungrateful, but I must be impatient. We may yet be ruined – unless America joins with us everywhere. That is why I must visit the President without delay.'

'You know he thinks it's too soon,' Winant said.

'While I fear it may already be too late.'

'If there is anything we can do to help . . .'

'My two musketeers, you have already done so much. But I promise to ask for more.'

Churchill opened the door of the car for the ambassador. Harriman lingered for a final shake of the hand.

'I will do my best, Winston, with the supplies.'

'You have already done so much, Averell. More than you could ever realize.'

He waved as the car swung down the long drive from Chequers. Just before it disappeared into the heavy mist, Churchill noticed it swerve slightly to avoid a bicycle that was being ridden, with great determination, by Héloise.

Roosevelt did as he had promised. He appeared in front of a joint session of Congress, declared the attack on Pearl Harbor to be 'a date which will live in infamy', and asked for a declaration of war on Japan. It was voted in less than an hour.

It took only slightly longer than an hour for the Japanese to sink both the *Prince of Wales* and the *Repulse*. The ships had set to sea the day after the attack on Pearl Harbor, expecting to meet and destroy a Japanese invasion force and hoping that air cover could be provided from land bases in northern Malaya. But the airfields had already been overrun. In the vastness of the ocean it was entirely possible that the British fleet would escape detection, but on the tenth a flight of

Japanese aircraft all but stumbled over the ships. After that, it was only a matter of time.

The Japanese attacked with bombs and torpedoes. The British ships manoeuvred desperately, but without air cover they soon sustained many terrible hits. The *Repulse* capsized and sank first, the *Prince of Wales* shortly thereafter. The deck upon which the President and Prime Minister had sat and prayed, and also many of the men who had prayed with them, were now at the bottom of the sea. Another thousand lives lost.

Churchill had gambled with the lives of these British sailors. It was what leaders were required to do in war. And he had lost. The British Navy's effective presence in the Indian and Pacific oceans had been wiped out even as the US presence lay crippled. Within four days, Japan had achieved mastery of all the seas in Asia.

It was a huge personal tragedy for Churchill. He had known the men on board the *Prince of Wales*, they had been his sailing companions, some were his friends. Against the advice of his admirals, he had sent them to their deaths. He said to his staff that never had he received such a direct shock.

Yet hand in hand with the loss of these two ships, Churchill had also found victory. Japan was at war with America, prompted in part by the awesome prospect of a great Allied fleet of which these two ships would have been part. Perhaps his gamble hadn't failed, after all.

And there was other news to help bring light to the dark watches of that night. The Russians had taken advantage of the winter conditions and had launched counter-attacks along the entire Eastern Front. German reconnaissance troops had reached a point only twelve miles from the Kremlin, the panzers only a few miles behind, but they were now being pushed back. The temperature had dropped to minus thirty-two degrees Fahrenheit. It was to be a desperately cold Christmas for Hitler's men.

The next day was to bring events that were still more momentous.

Hitler spoke at the Reichstag in Berlin. Ever since the attack on Pearl Harbor there had been furious speculation around the world as to what he might say. The speech had been postponed more than once and repeatedly rethought and redrafted by the Fuehrer himself, so when he finally arrived during the afternoon in the Reichstag building, it was clear he would have something new to announce.

It proved to be an eighty-eight-minute oratorical bombardment of the sort the world remembered from the days of the rallies at Nuremberg – the flags, the symbols, the theatrical arm gestures, the rising cadences, the broad Austrian accent, the rerouting of history along his own extraordinary ideological channels. He attacked all of his opponents, but above all he attacked Roosevelt. Germany had never had any designs on America, the Fuehrer thundered, not in all its history, so why did their President so viciously oppose the German people? It was simple. He was mentally unsound. And surrounded by Jews.

The length of the attack on Roosevelt was so great that it was well past the hour before Hitler came to his main point of his speech. Yet as the world waited, listening on their radios, his words were lost, drowned out as his audience of deputies rose to its feet and cheered wildly.

But some already knew. About two hours earlier, the German Chargé d'Affaires in Washington had walked into the US State Department to present them with a note. It accused the United States of flagrant violations of its neutrality, of provocations, of systematic attacks, of open acts of aggression on a scale so widespread that in effect America had created a virtual state of war.

As a result, the note declared, Germany considered herself to be at war with the United States.

In London, it was Winant who heard first. Even as Hitler was getting to his feet, he received a cable from Washington.

War.

He was on the point of telephoning Downing Street when he was overcome by a sudden impulse to tell Churchill in person. It was an extraordinary moment of history and he wanted to share its excitement and awe with one of the greatest men alive. He wanted to see the other man's face, wanted to have that memory with him for the rest of his life. He called for his car.

He arrived at Downing Street a few minutes later in a state of considerable anticipation. He dashed across the threshold and was almost running down the long corridor that led to the Cabinet Room. He could contain himself no longer: he burst in, without formality or knocking.

He found Churchill alone, signing letters.

'Winston – it's war!' he cried, still clutching the doorknob. 'Hitler's declared war on the United States.'

The words seem to take a long time before they connected with Churchill. The old man's chest heaved once, then he carefully screwed the cap back on his pen and closed his blotter. When he spoke, his tone was almost dull. 'Even Hitler couldn't put up with your Government's dilly-dallying, Gil. Instead of waiting for you to move he decided to jump himself.'

Winant was taken aback. He had expected more. He had brought with him such a priceless gift, and he'd expected some show of enthusiasm if not gratitude. It was almost as if the old man knew . . .

'You seem remarkably untouched by it all.'

'Far from it, Gil. I am so overwhelmed with emotion that I feel my heart will burst.'

Yet the old man seemed so remarkably unsurprised. As the adrenalin and excitement drained from his body, Winant was beginning to realize that there were many things about this new situation that he didn't understand.

'Why, Winston? Why did Hitler declare war? Britain, the Soviet Union, now the United States – the three greatest opponents on earth. He didn't need to do it. So why?'

'Because of Japan, perhaps? They've been signing pacts and treaties declaring their undying devotion to each other.'

'No,' Winant responded. 'He didn't declare war on the United States simply because of some treaty. They are meaningless to him, nothing more than empty boxes to put in the shop window. He didn't go to war because of a scrap of paper.'

'But he had a speech to make. What else was he to say?'

'You surely don't think he declared war simply to fill a speech.'

'He is an orator, Gil, consider that. He is driven by a desire to move people – not like me, with mere phrases, but with raw, animal passion and grand gestures.'

'Even so, you don't make war simply to fill a few headlines.'

'Several centuries ago, Shakespeare wrote about rulers who seek to busy giddy minds with foreign quarrels.'

'I reckon waging war on America counts as a bit more than just some foreign quarrel, Winston.'

'Remember, Gil, he is a man almost eaten up by his vanity. He must have suspected that war with America would come eventually, so why wait and allow you the moral authority of declaring it? Better to grab the moment for himself than give you the chance to prick his pride.'

'Then why this moment? There was no sign that we were about to declare war on him. Not just before Christmas.'

'You must understand that man's overwhelming need to fill the moment. The winter is upon him and the news from the Russian front begins to turn against him. He's too proud, too conceited to send his people off for Christmas with nothing to feed upon but Japanese fish soup.'

'You make it sound as if you know him.'

'Oh, I believe I do. We British have been at war with him for more than two years, his guns lie twenty miles from our shore, his aircraft fill our skies. Of course I have studied him. It pays to know your enemies, as well as your friends.'

Yet Winant continued to be troubled. He paced around the long Cabinet table, his tall back stooped, his untidy hair falling into his eyes. He had always seen this room as a source of power and splendour, yet for the first time he began to see how shabby it had become. There was blast-tape on the windows and the curtains were full of grey dust. Outside the skies were low, heavy with winter rain, and the buildings all around still bore the scars of their battering from the bombs. Churchill spoke of the enemy's pride but the British, too, had their pride, yet in the last couple of years they had taken a terrible kicking. And Winant still bore the marks of Churchill's own boot, which had been applied to him only a few weeks earlier at Chequers when the old man had raged about America's ineptitude and immorality. The ambassador was beginning to remember other things, too. It caused unruly thoughts to run across his mind.

'Winston, will you allow me to impose upon our friendship?'

'Always.'

'Did you suspect? Did you know?'

'About what, pray?'

'That Hitler was about to declare war? Even that the Japanese would hit Pearl Harbor?'

'Why on earth do you ask such questions?'

'It's because . . .' Winant began to beat his hands in frustration. 'Tojo and Hitler between them have handed you everything you wanted, everything you desired, everything you were committed to achieving. Bully for Britain – but, hell, the United States didn't want this, and I doubt whether in their hearts even Japan and Germany wanted this. They'd have been more than happy setting about poor little England all on its own. And yet . . .'

'What are you suggesting?'

'I'm not sure, but . . .' He stretched past his doubts to grab at something solid. 'If you could have, I think you would have guided this.'

Churchill paused for some while before replying. He studied Winant, who was bent double and in such earnestness that he seemed in physical pain.

'How could that possibly be?' the Englishman replied softly.

'Through intelligence, perhaps, or manipulation, all the murky ways of war in which I guess you have more personal experience than any man in the world. You know, the other day when news came through about Pearl you seemed shocked – not so much that it had happened, but more about its timing. It was almost as if you were waiting for it.'

'Gil, why are you persisting with such extraordinary conjectures?'

'Partly because every question I've asked you've deflected with another question. And because I remember what you said at Chequers that night. You said that we would enter

343

the war, and that we would have no choice in the matter.'

Silently Churchill chastised himself. It had been a rage too far.

'And you told me, Winston – I remember your words precisely; they made such a deep impression – that if we did not decide for war, we would not be permitted to stand aside. You said that others would make the decision for us.' He paused. 'So did you?'

'As a diplomat, Gil, you should know better,' Churchill said dismissively.

'Then let me ask as an American,' Winant said more heatedly. 'We lost two thousand men at Pearl. I believe that gives me the right. So did you know?'

'Two thousand men?' Churchill washed the words round his mouth like wine. He seemed to find in it some deep distaste, for his expression grew stern and his voice filled with anger. 'Two thousand men?' His hand slapped down upon the Cabinet table. 'Britain lost as many when the *Hood* was sunk, the Germans as many when the *Bismarck* disappeared, and the French as many when we blew their fleet to pieces at Mers-el-Kébir. Why, we lost nearly a thousand yesterday alone on the *Prince of Wales* and the *Repulse*. What makes your men of any greater value than those who have gone before? This is your war as much as it is ours, it is a battle for the survival of democracy and human decency. If you have come to it late, then it is a cause for a little shame as well as great sorrow. But not recrimination.' Churchill's lips were quivering with emotion. 'Look out through those windows, Gil. You see a city brought to the point of ruination by the forces of terror – a terror that Americans have for so long refused to recognize. In one single night, and for so many nights, we have lost as many as you have in the entire course of this long war. Not military men like those at Pearl Harbor but innocent civilians, mere women and children, babes in arms who bore not a trace of guilt for this conflict yet who still lie out there undiscovered beneath the rubble. So if the deaths of two thousand men at Pearl Harbor gives you the right as an American to question my actions, then how much greater is my right to question yours?'

'That is still not an answer, Winston,' the ambassador responded doggedly.

'Gil, believe me, I do not intend to decry your dead, but freedom has a fearful appetite and over the centuries she has required terrible sacrifice. Your men did not die in vain. America is now part of the greatest moral crusade since the night Beelzebub was cast out of Heaven, and while I weep for their loss, I welcome your dead into the place of honour that is reserved for heroes.'

Winant's dark eyes continued to stare at him steadily from across the table. His persistence was beginning to make Churchill feel greatly discomfited.

'Pray, don't pursue this illusion of yours, Gil. What would you have me say? It was a blessing that Japan attacked the United States. It is an undisputed triumph that Hitler has turned upon you and thus brought America wholeheartedly into the war. I tell you in all sincerity that greater good fortune has rarely fallen upon the British Empire, and history will record this as the moment in which we were saved. But how could I have done anything to manipulate or manufacture such events? Turning on America would be like . . .' – he reached for a comparison – 'like turning on my own son.'

That was a mistake. Winant would know about Pamela and Harriman – Sarah would have told him. There wasn't much point in resting his case on morality.

'Gil, you search for the truth, but sometimes in times of war there is a greater need *not* to know. A need to turn a

345

blind eye. Not simply for military commanders and political leaders, but for diplomats, too. Why, even for husbands and wives . . .'

'Oh, Winston –'

'And for fathers.'

Winant fell silent.

'Sometimes, Gil, we have to turn a blind eye in order to see through the chaos that surrounds us. Vision isn't about seeing everything, but seeing the important things, and what is right. If that is what I am charged with, I shall sleep easily. We can let history decide upon the details of who knew or did whatever it is that has been done.'

'A history written by the victors, Winston.'

'Then let us be content that, as from this day, it will be written in English.'

The bath water was exactly the right temperature.

'Have you ever been to the United States before, Sawyers?' the old man asked, sliding in.

'No, zur. Closest I got was that last time. Newfoundland.'

'You'll be spending Christmas there now.'

Everyone from the President to his own Foreign Secretary had tried to persuade him to delay his trip, but he was insistent. So much to do, so many allies.

'I shall miss Mrs Landemare's turkey, like. She'll miss cooking it fer us, too.'

'Yes. It means that Chequers won't be quite so busy for a while. I think it would be a good time to make a few new arrangements.'

'Arrangements?'

'The maid.'

Sawyers fell silent.

'Time for her to move on, I think, Sawyers.'

The Prime Minister disappeared beneath the water. When he surfaced, the valet was still hovering awkwardly at the end of the bath.

'I know she's been silly, like,' Sawyers said, 'but she's young and I don't like to think of her . . .'

'Not to worry. We can't have members of the Prime Minister's staff being stood up against a wall and shot,' the old man said quietly. 'Wouldn't look good. Give rise to too many awkward questions. About who knew what.'

'So . . . ?'

'Back home. That's where she belongs. Where she can do no harm.'

He'd already given instructions to Menzies. It gave him no pleasure. Back home Héloise would be treated with suspicion, both by her own countrymen and the Germans. She was a collaborator and a woman who had fed Britain's enemies with grotesquely false information – the enduring silence of Hess would confirm that. At best, she might be allowed to disappear back into the folds of France, at worst . . .

One more young life, amongst so many thousands.

'Let Mrs Landemare know about the new arrangements, will you, Sawyers.'

The servant sighed, and went off in search of a fresh towel.

Harriman had telephoned. He had only an hour to spare, and suggested dinner, but she had asked instead for a walk around the Serpentine. The moon was full and they had walked slowly, listening to the rustle of winter branches and the cry of sleepy ducks, trying to forget about other things. Down at the water's edge there was no sign of the war; it was as close as they could get to how things had once been, but as she held his arm she realized she never wanted to go back. War had happened, it had changed everything. It was time to move on.

'Come out of your cave, Averell.'

'What cave?'

'The one you crawl off to when . . .' When he had something bad to say.

She bit her lip, trying to control the tremble that was creeping up on her.

'I know, Averell.'

Silence.

'You have to go again. Back to America.'

'I'm sorry.'

'You're not, not really. You love your job. It's important – no, not just important, it's much more than that. It's the starting point for everything else that happens.'

'So are you.'

'Thank you.'

'But . . .'

'Yes, I know. You have to go. And you don't know when you will be coming back. Fact is, Averell, you don't know if you will ever be coming back.' She struggled with this. She had never cried when he left before, but every time it seemed to get a little more difficult.

'Sorry, Pam. I wanted to tell you myself. How do you know?'

'Papa told me. He apologizes to you for that, but he said that he was responsible for your going so he thought he should be the one to tell me.'

'It's become so much more complicated. The war will be fought in every corner of the globe now – not just here but everywhere you look.'

'He said that from now on the decisions would be made

in Washington and Moscow, that he had to share control of the war, and that I had to share you.'

'He said that?'

'And a lot more.'

'He seems to know so much, and to see so much.'

'Not bad for a blind man.'

'What?'

'Nothing. Just something he said.'

Somewhere across the park an owl called; their time was almost up.

'Oh, I shall miss you,' she whispered, squeezing his arm tight.

'But?'

'No "buts", Averell. I shall miss you.'

'When this is all over . . .'

'First things first, eh? Let's finish the job. Then we'll see.'

EPILOGUE

So why did Pearl Harbor happen – or why was it allowed to happen? After all, many of the Japanese codes were broken, an attack was expected. A 1946 Joint Congressional Investigating Committee described Pearl Harbor as 'the greatest military and naval disaster in our nation's history.' So whose fault was it?

For decades the hunt went on to identify appropriate scapegoats, and it still continues today. Explanations range from simple chaos to sublime conspiracy. Roosevelt knew, some believe, and withheld the knowledge in order to force a reluctant America into the war. No, others claim, it was Churchill who knew, and who deceived.

Far too much of the argument for conspiracy depends on assuming not only that the statesmen knew everything but understood everything and had no blind eyes. Surely what is far more interesting in trying to understand that extraordinary character of Winston Churchill is not simply what he did but what he might have done. If he had known beforehand, would he have allowed the attack on Pearl Harbor to go ahead?

Churchill was a man of overwhelming and at times self-consuming emotion, yet he was also capable of setting aside emotion to reveal the foundations of fact that lay beneath. The facts of Pearl Harbor are these.

The loss in lives was, by comparison to other wartime disasters, minor. Placed in the scales alongside so many other calamities of war, the numbers were neither unique nor even exceptional.

Of the eight American battleships that were hit, three returned to service within three weeks, and three more within three years. All the vessels that were hit were elderly. The American aircraft carriers that were to prove the crucial weapon in the battle for supremacy in the Pacific had left port several days beforehand and escaped entirely unscathed.

Pearl Harbor may have been a day of infamy, but it was not in historical terms a tragedy. Indeed, from some perspectives, it was more of a deliverance from the doubts and jaded arguments that had blinded the United States for so long. As Roosevelt told both Churchill and Stalin at the Yalta Conference in 1945, without Pearl Harbor it would have been very difficult to get the American people to agree to go to war.

So far as Churchill was concerned, Pearl Harbor was everything.

'No American will think it wrong of me if I proclaim that to have the United States at our side was to me the greatest joy,' he wrote afterwards. 'We had won the war. England would live; Britain would live; the Commonwealth of Nations and the Empire would live. How long the war would last or in what fashion it would end no man could tell, nor did I at this moment care. Once again in our long island history we should emerge, however mauled or mutilated, safe and victorious. We should not be wiped out. Our history would not come to an end . . . Being saturated and satiated with emotion and sensation, I went to bed and slept the sleep of the saved and thankful.'

So let us return to the question: if Churchill had known, would he have allowed the attack on Pearl Harbor to proceed?

Would he have exchanged two thousand American lives for survival and victory? Would he have turned a blind eye?

Yes, he would. It would have been what was required of him as a statesman. England expects.

That was why he was also able to deal with the extraordinary conflict between his role as a war leader and his role as a father. Churchill was not a careless father, far from it; he struggled all his life to build around him the family that he as a child had never enjoyed. Yet for a time he was also, in a very real sense, the father of the entire free world. That he was able to deal with this personal conflict of loyalties was not a measure of his callousness but of his greatness.

The story of his family and the other characters in this book did not, of course, finish with 1941. Averell Harriman continued to play a leading role in the Allied cause, and in 1943 was sent to Moscow as the US Ambassador. After the war he returned to his marriage and to the United States to take up several hugely important roles. He became governor of New York and even ran for President.

Meanwhile, Pamela led a life of considerable notoriety with many other men that became the subject of several books, yet she never forgot about Harriman. They had become war-tossed lovers in the mould of Admiral Nelson and his beloved Emma, and their trans-Atlantic passion had been still more far-reaching. It had helped ignite a world war.

And, thirty years after they met in wartime London, Averell and Pamela were married. They spent fifteen years as man and wife before Averell died only a few years short of his one-hundredth birthday.

Even that failed to slow down Pamela. President Clinton appointed her US Ambassador to France in 1993. She died in Paris four years later, one of the most controversial yet acclaimed women in the world.

The story of the relationship between Sarah Churchill and Gil Winant had no soft and happy ending. Winant had been a fine public servant and a superb ambassador to London, but he was an intense and often lonely figure, and when President Truman succeeded Roosevelt, he was shunted aside. He wanted to fill the gap left in his life through his relationship with Sarah, but she was not willing. In 1947, spurned by Sarah and by his former colleagues in Washington, this talented but tormented man retired to his bedroom, put a pistol to his head and killed himself.

Randolph's life continued to be tempestuous. He returned from the war to discover Pamela's infidelities and their divorce came shortly thereafter. What he seemed to have had far more difficulty in dealing with was his parents' refusal to turn their back on Pamela. It caused intense rows; more than once Randolph was thrown out of the family home. His life thereafter was dominated by anger and alcohol, interspersed with some very fine writing.

Max Beaverbrook did eventually resign – two months after Pearl Harbor, and although he later returned to the Government he was never the same force again. It was Eden who became Prime Minister, in succession to Churchill in 1955, but only after he had left his wife and married Clarissa, Churchill's niece.

And Sawyers – what became of Frank Sawyers? The historical record is sparse, yet it attests to a man of character, humour and discretion. He was undoubtedly one of the great English manservants and was an immense support to Churchill. Yet he left Churchill's household in 1947 of his own accord and his trail runs dry. Whatever he did, wherever he went, let us hope he found fulfilment. He was one of those many, many unsung heroes who helped Churchill finish the job.

ACKNOWLEDGEMENTS

It's usually at this point that I spend a few lines emphasizing that this series of books should be read as fiction and not as history. And I happily do so again. However, even the very best of histories can provide only a fragment of any story, and although the life of Winston Churchill has been trawled as assiduously as any man's, there is so much of importance that historians cannot know. I'm thinking here not simply of those quiet events in his life that inevitably went unrecorded but even more of the emotions, the inspirations, the ambitions – those 'inner' events – that drive us all. In many circumstances they may prove to be decisive, but we can only guess at their nature. Such guesswork isn't fruitless; indeed, it can illuminate what we know and make it more intelligible, and can open our eyes to possibilities that we hadn't previously considered. Even if we then come to reject those possibilities, we do so on the basis of having got to know our man just a little better.

Churchill was a most complex man. He was always restless, never settled, driven by many 'inner' events. While I have tried to be faithful to the record of events in 1941, I hope the reader will forgive the inevitable dramatic flexibilities I have used to turn them into a novel. And if at any point I have failed to capture the 'inner' events accurately, that is my fault and not the responsibility of the many kind people and Churchill enthusiasts who have tried to help me as I worked on *Churchill's Hour*.

Among them, as always, are the Churchill Centre and Societies whose excellent organization has done so much to promote the understanding of Churchill's achievements. The Centre's website – www.winstonchurchill.org – is a mine of both information and inspiration, as is their journal, *Finest Hour*, so admirably edited by Richard Langworth. I suspect that some of the members may disagree with the manner in which I have portrayed him – how could Winston have been less than totally honest with the United States? – but that is part of the challenge and delight in dealing with a man with as many facets as Churchill. He always enjoyed a bloody good argument, and it seems only right that he should continue to provoke others.

I would also like to thank Terry Charman and his colleagues in the archives of the Imperial War Museum. They seem to have the answer to almost any factual question that is put to them, and they provide the answers in a manner and at a speed that would have impressed even the impatient old man himself.

There have been some close personal friends who have, as always, been magnificent – Andy Mackay for his ability to guide me through the dance of the Latin pluperfect subjunctive; Roger Katz, who is perhaps the finest bookseller in the world and who helped provide the initial inspiration for this series; Quintin Jardine, who is a magnificent crime writer and whose common sense kept me on the Churchillian course; and Eddie Bell, who has always been there to guide my hand, my head and my heart along the sometimes tangled pathways of authorship.

The words seem ridiculously inadequate, but I also want

to express my love to Rachel, who was wonderful enough to allow our wedding date to be squeezed in between the first and final drafts of *Churchill's Hour*. Thank you, Mrs Dobbs.

Finally, I want to express my best wishes to Lady Soames, Churchill's daughter, and Mr Winston Churchill, the son of Randolph and Pamela, who find their way into the pages of this book. I have trespassed into their private lives, and done so without seeking their permission. I decided at the start of this enterprise that it would be wrong to ask them for their help; if I hadn't agreed with their conclusions, it might have caused much greater offence than not asking them at all. Yet the problem for those who want to write about their father and grandfather is that it is impossible to do so in a rounded manner without taking into account the private life of the Churchill family – and during 1941 that private life was, at times, tempestuous. He was a father as well as a statesman; the roles did not always sit comfortably with each other. It took a great man to deal with the conflicts that arose, and I hope Lady Soames and the current Winston Churchill will forgive any indelicacies or inaccuracies that might have crept into this book as a result of my trying to portray those elusive 'inner' events.

As the old man said himself: 'One of the most misleading factors in history is the practice of historians to build a story exclusively out of the records which have come down to them.' Well, I've taken Winston at his word. I like to think he wouldn't have minded.

MICHAEL DOBBS
Hanging Langford, July 2004.